HANS CHRISTIAN ANDER

*For Chris
with all my love*

Hans Christian Andersen and Music

The Nightingale Revealed

ANNA HARWELL CELENZA
Michigan State University, USA

Routledge
Taylor & Francis Group

LONDON AND NEW YORK

First published 2005 by Ashgate Publishing

Published 2017 by Routledge
2 Park Square, Milton Park, Abingdon, Oxfordshire OX14 4RN
711 Third Avenue, New York, NY 10017, USA

First issued in paperback 2017

Routledge is an imprint of the Taylor & Francis Group, an informa business

British Library Cataloguing in Publication Data
Celenza, Anna Harwell
    Hans Christian Andersen and music : the nightingale revealed
    1.Andersen, H. C. (Hans Christian), 1805-1875 – Knowledge – Music 2. Music – 19th century – History and criticism
    I.Title
    839.8'136

Library of Congress Cataloging-in-Publication Data
Celenza, Anna Harwell
  Hans Christian Andersen and music : the nightingale revealed / Anna Harwell Celenza.
    p. cm.
  Includes bibliographical references and index.
  ISBN 0-7546-0140-4 (alk. paper)
  1. Andersen, H. C. (Hans Christian), 1805-1875 – Knowledge – Music. 2. Authors, Danish – 19th century – Biography. 3. Music in literature. I. Title.

PT8119.H32 2004
839.8'136–dc22

                                                                                            2004013256

ISBN 13: 978-1-138-27425-9 (pbk)
ISBN 13: 978-0-7546-0140-1 (hbk)

Contents

Acknowledgements

The long process of writing a book can be both an exhilarating and daunting experience. Periods of enlightenment brought on by interaction with other scholars and the discovery of new sources often alternate with solitary periods of writing marked by looming deadlines. Such was the case with this book. Yet thanks to the encouragement and assistance offered by numerous friends and colleagues, the periods of enlightenment greatly outweighed the occasional darker moments.

To thank every individual who contributed an insight, criticism, or reference would be impossible. However, several were indispensable to the writing of this book. Rachel Lynch and Heidi May, my editors at Ashgate, made this book possible, not least by finding two anonymous readers who offered insightful critiques that proved incredibly helpful during the final stage of revision. Drafts of the entire book were also read by Johan de Mylius, Aubrey Garlington, and Phyllis Weliver; thanks to their meticulous care and vast knowledge in their respective fields, many inaccuracies and oversimplifications were corrected. The ones that remain are obviously my own. I also thank the colleagues who read early drafts of various chapters: Kathryn Lowerre, Alan Gosman, and Gordon Sly at Michigan State University and R. Larry Todd at Duke University. Special thanks also goes to the graduate students in my spring 2002 'Music and Literature' course for their enthusiasm and curiosity in this project, and to my copy editors, Rebecca Meador Bennett and Kristen Thorner, as well as the Editorial Manager at Ashgate, Ann Newell, for their keen eyes and attention to detail.

I am grateful to many libraries and museums for allowing me access to their collections, most notably The Royal Library and The National Museum at Fredriksborg in Copenhagen, Denmark; The Andersen House and The Andersen Center in Odense, Denmark; and the Stiftung Weimarer Klassik in Weimar, Germany. Grateful acknowledgement also goes to the University of California Press and the American Liszt Society, respectively, for permission to revise material that previously appeared in the periodicals *Nineteenth-Century Music* and the *Journal of the American Liszt Society*.

Finally, the person to whom I owe my deepest and most heart-felt gratitude is my husband, Christopher S. Celenza. For many years now he has been my best friend and most trusted colleague. He read countless drafts of each chapter and stood by me at every stage of the writing process, offering the perfect mixture of support, encouragement, and constructive criticism I needed to complete this book. My husband has been everything that authors say on these occasions and more. I dedicate this book to him with the warmest love and affection.

List of Figures and Tables

I long for music like a man sick with fever longs for a drop of water.
Hans Christian Andersen

Introduction

Hans Christian Andersen, or H.C. Andersen as he was called by readers in Denmark, was undoubtedly the most prominent Danish author of the nineteenth century. Although Andersen is now known primarily for his fairy tales, during his lifetime he was equally famous for his novels, travelogues, poetry, and stage works, and it was through these genres that he most often reflected on the world around him. Unfortunately, few of today's readers know this side of Andersen. Although his fairy tales have stood the test of time (who does not know *The Ugly Duckling* and *The Emperor's New Clothes*, stories that, in addition to being entertaining, have come to symbolize the relative nature of beauty and the power of public opinion), they represent only a small portion of his prodigious output, an output that has been largely ignored over the last half century.

Another contributing factor to Andersen's present-day reception is the proliferation of such movies as *Hans Christian Andersen* (1952, with Danny Kaye) and Walt Disney's many adaptations of Andersen's tales, the most recent being *The Little Mermaid* (1989) and a scene in *Fantasia 2000*.[1] These films have cultivated the general impression that Andersen was little more than a quaint story teller. No doubt in reaction to this depiction, a number of scholars have recently published studies that present a darker, more troubled image of him. By offering new readings of Andersen's fairy tales and presenting psycho-analytical studies of his life, they have created an image that reverts Andersen to the status of the character in one of his best-known tales, an 'ugly duckling.'[2] As a reviewer at *The New York Times* recently wrote, the Andersen portrayed in Jackie Wullschlager's biography, *Hans Christian Andersen: The Life of a Storyteller*, is a 'histrionic, effeminate, uneducated gawk working the most painful emotions into great literature.'[3] I must admit that my image of Andersen is quite different. As I have worked on this project over the last three years, I have grown quite fond of Andersen, often empathizing with his attempts to define his artistic voice and discover his place in the culture surrounding him.[4] Andersen has received much criticism over the years, both from his contemporaries and from modern scholars. Yet there is something that keeps his works alive, a certain compassion that I found also permeates his views of music and culture.

Andersen's possible homosexual leaning has become a much-debated topic in recent years, and it should be noted that the points of argument closely resemble those surrounding discussions of Franz Schubert. Andersen's fictional works, like Schubert's Lieder, have been mined for evidence of emotional instability and repressed homosexual yearning, and his letters to male friends and colleagues have been read from a specifically twenty-first-century point of view.[5] Thus, recent research on Andersen has tended to be influenced by 'identity politics' – finding in Andersen answers to questions that are particularly appealing to present-day audiences.   That being said, this book will not focus on Andersen's sexual orientation, although it does indeed represent a specific perspective.   As a musicologist, I have looked to Andersen's writings in search of a better understanding of nineteenth-century music culture.   I am interested in Andersen the musician and audience member, Andersen the critic and aesthetician; and these are the elements of his life and work upon which I have directed my gaze. There is much about Andersen that is not yet common knowledge, and this book attempts to explore a single aspect of that void – his interest in and relationship to the music culture he saw changing around him.

But why look to Andersen for information about music? What makes his writings better sources than the works of many other nineteenth-century authors? To begin, Andersen had a musical background.   As a teenager he enjoyed a brief career as an opera singer and dancer at the Royal Theater in Copenhagen, and in later years he went on to produce a large number of singspiel and opera libretti for the Danish and German stage. Additionally, Andersen was an avid music devotee, attending performances around the world. He made thirty major European tours during his seventy years, and on each of these trips he regularly attended opera and concert performances, recording his impressions in a series of travel diaries.[6]   In short, Andersen was a well-informed listener, and his reflections on the music of his age serve as valuable sources for the study of music reception in the nineteenth century.

Recent Andersen research has given us a fuller view of Andersen's personality and private concerns, but it is still necessary to broaden our vision of his creative output in order to better understand the aesthetic concerns underlying much of his writing and the reception of his works by like-minded contemporaries. We know much about Andersen's fairy tales and his complex personality, but what about his many novels and travelogues, his interactions with patrons, performers, and composers? What can these things tell us about his creative interests and aesthetic concerns? How did Andersen's early career as a musician influence his view of music culture later in life? In what ways did the many descriptions and discussions of music in his literary works reflect and/or affect the views of his readers? Questions such as these are what drive the discussions in this book, and in the final chapters they inevitably lead to descriptions of how, toward the end of the nineteenth century, Andersen and his contemporaries envisioned the intersection of music's future and its monumental past.

In an effort to explain the evolution of Andersen's musical tastes and thus offer a fresh perspective on music culture in the nineteenth century, this book presents new interpretations of some of his lesser-known fairy tales and offers a more complete discussion of many of his larger works – i.e. his novels, travelogues, essays, and opera libretti. These lesser-known works are not literary masterpieces the equivalent of Andersen's most famous, universal fairy tales. Indeed, as the discussions of these lesser-known works reveal, they are not universal and timeless, but rather securely tied to the era in which they were written. This 'time-bound' quality is what I found most intriguing, and it is what makes these works invaluable sources for the study of nineteenth-century music.

Until recently, critical reconstruction of how nineteenth-century music was understood, performed, and heard was dismissed as either speculative or irrelevant. Such an attitude was often no doubt due, at least in part, to the phenomenon that nineteenth-century taste appears increasingly at odds with present-day sensibilities. This disconnect becomes all the more obvious when one begins to read excerpts from Andersen's novels, travelogues, and opera libretti. Designed to reflect the specific tastes and interests of nineteenth-century adults, Andersen's larger works appealed to thousands of contemporary readers (including Heinrich Heine, Felix Mendelssohn, and Clara and Robert Schumann) but became less popular when literary tastes changed and the cultural references in the works became less applicable to later generations. As Leon Botstein has noted, the structure of meaning in nineteenth-century musical discourse (i.e. the character and significance of gesture and expressed sentiment displayed within specific rituals of music) can no longer be assumed to be continuous with our own.[7] Today's audiences have lost touch with the acoustic environment in which nineteenth-century music functioned. Also missing is the connection of musical life to the patterns of social and cultural meaning that dominated the period. New methodologies for construing nineteenth-century perceptions of music have only recently been developed, and to a certain extent, I hope the present study of Hans Christian Andersen and music will expand such methodologies.[8] By observing Andersen's reaction to the musical world around him and exploring the manner in which he explained his reactions in his fictional works and autobiographies, I hope to present a reflective, historical consideration of how general audiences might have heard music in the nineteenth century and the nature of their perceptions.

There are numerous sources of information about Andersen, not only of a general biographical nature but also in connection with his travels abroad and his insights into being a writer and musician. Andersen left behind several autobiographies, a series of extensive diaries, almanacs, and a vast amount of letters and scrapbooks. Taken together these sources contain many detailed narratives that offer almost a daily account of what he saw and did, his public and private thoughts about music, literature, and the world around him.

Andersen's first attempt at an autobiography was completed in 1832 when he was twenty-seven years old. Called *Levnedsbogen* (The Book of My Life), it was intended for publication in case Andersen died prematurely. For many years this manuscript was thought to be lost. It was discovered in the Royal Library by the literary scholar Hans Brix and first published in 1926.[9] In 1847 Andersen completed a second autobiography, *Das Märchen meines Lebens ohne Dichtung*, which was published in connection with a German edition of his collected works;[10] that same year an English edition, *The True Story of My Life*,[11] was published in London and the United States. It should be noted that the Danish edition of this autobiography, *Mit eget Eventyr uden Digtning*, did not appear until 1942 – sixty-seven years after Andersen's death! But Andersen did publish a separate Danish autobiography during his lifetime. In 1855 he expanded his German autobiography from 1847 and published it as *Mit Livs Eventyr*.[12] An American edition of this 1855 account with additional chapters covering the years 1855–67 was published in New York in 1871 as *The Story of My Life*.[13]

Of these three basic sets of autobiographies, the first is the most reliable, and therefore it is used almost exclusively when dealing with Andersen's early years as a performer and writer. The second and third autobiographies were written much later, and although their presentations of Andersen's earlier years are less reliable, they nonetheless present a view of what he thought his contemporaries would like to read and thus give us greater insight into the cultural climate of the time.

In an effort to balance the 'public' opinions presented in Andersen's autobiographies with a more accurate view of his private opinions, the contents of his diaries, correspondence, almanacs, and scrapbooks are often quoted in the chapters of this book. Andersen's diaries give us a more intimate and straightforward view of his life and career. Never intended for publication, they present a matter-of-fact record of what he encountered rather than the poetic renderings of such events found in the autobiographies. As Andersen himself noted in a diary entry dated 9 May 1870: 'If anyone ever reads this diary he will find empty, commonplace remarks – I do not take great care in describing accurately on this paper what has really touched something inside me and moved me.'[14] Instead, the diaries served as a mnemonic tool that Andersen used to keep track of his experiences. Brief records of his thoughts, moods, and reactions to almost every element of daily life fill the pages with details of nineteenth-century social conditions and cultural life found in few other places.

Andersen began keeping a diary on 16 September 1825 and continued until the final days of his life in 1875. Unfortunately, some sections of the diaries no longer exist. The diaries from 1827 until 1831 are lost, and from 1831 until 1861 Andersen usually only wrote in a diary during his travels abroad – their purpose being to serve as a wealth of ideas and recollections for his many fictional works and articles.[15] In this respect, all three of his youthful novels and all of his travelogues were indebted to his diaries. The same is also true, of course, for his autobiographies. Andersen's diaries, along with the many letters he wrote to friends and colleagues, clearly reveal his hectic social life, constant attendance at theatrical performances, recitals, and concerts; his friendships with internationally-known writers and musicians; and his visits with patrons across Europe. They also reveal his many doubts and anxieties, and so in contrast to his carefully composed autobiographies of 1847 and later, the diaries provide what seems to be an inexhaustible source of primary evidence that gives us insight into how he experienced the world.

For the times when Andersen's diary entries are missing, his almanacs serve as an excellent supplement. Beginning in 1833 Andersen kept track of his daily activities in these small books. Although the brief annotations do not make for engaging reading, they do provide information concerning his daily life in Denmark, the evolution of his works, and his social habits.[16]

Finally, Andersen's novels, travelogues, essays, and fairy tales offer insight into his view on music and culture, as they were often written as personal, artistic commentaries on real-life events and circumstances. As he explained in a letter written in 1842, 'I seize an idea for older people – and then I tell it to the young ones, remembering all the while that father and mother are listening and must also have something to think about.'[17] In his fragmentary comments on his fairy tales that were included in the collected editions of 1862–63 and 1870–74, Andersen emphasized the reality behind his imaginative treatment. He often used his tales as a means of voicing opinions he dared not state directly. As a character named Dame Fairytale explained in a story called 'The Little Green Ones:' 'One ought to call everything by its right name; and if one does not dare do it in everyday life, at least one should do it in a fairy tale!'[18]

Given the immense amount of research sources available in Danish alone, the writing of this book has required the creation of many translations. Except when noted otherwise, the translations in this book are all my own – either because no other English translation exists, or because those that are available were unsuitable for the job at hand. Many of Andersen's Victorian translators censored his works – most especially his novels – and had no compunction about editing them according to their own tastes and interests. The fairy tales, however, are a different story. There are many fine translations of these works, most notably those by the Andersen scholar and translator Erik Haugaard. But even these at times are in need of revision. As Haugaard stated in a public lecture in 1973, 'A translation of any work that has been translated before implies dissatisfaction with the existing version…. But this is not always a criticism, for the meanings of words do change.'[19] Thus in an effort to express Andersen's writings with as much clarity as possible, particularly his thoughts concerning music and aesthetics, I have sometimes felt the need to update translations that were otherwise quite readable and reliable. That being said, since my intent to present the content of Andersen's words took precedence over trying to capture the craftsmanship of his writing, I did not attempt to recreate the rhythmical or rhyming characteristics found in some of his texts. When presenting translations of Andersen's poetry, I have included the original Danish along with my literal translation.

In general, this book is organized along the lines of a chronological narrative with the hope that as the reader progresses from one chapter to the next, he or she will get a sense of how Andersen's musical tastes and opinions changed over the course of his lifetime. Chapter 1 discusses Andersen's early years as a singer, dancer, and librettist at the Royal Theater in Copenhagen; while Chapter 2 reveals how Andersen's earliest European tours engendered in him a fascination with the virtuosity of Italian opera. In Chapter 3 we discover how in the 1840s this interest in virtuosity was transferred from vocal music to instrumental music, particularly as it was captured in performances by Ole Bull, Thalberg, and Liszt. A detailed discussion of Andersen's professional relationship with Liszt and his patron, Grand Duke Carl Alexander of Weimar, is presented in Chapter 4. This is followed by an investigation of Andersen's reactions to the rise of Danish Nationalism in Chapter 5 and his musings about the future of music and literature in Chapter 6.

Over the course of his life, Andersen embraced and then later rejected performers such as Maria Malibran, Franz Liszt, and Ole Bull, and his interest in opera and instrumental music underwent a series of dramatic transformations. In his final years, Andersen promoted figures as disparate as Wagner and Mendelssohn, while strongly objecting to Brahms. Although such changes in taste might be interpreted as indiscriminate by modern-day readers only familiar with Andersen's fairy tales and personality quirks, this study hopes to show that such shifts in opinion were not contradictory, but rather quite logical given the social and cultural climate of the age. The subtitle to this book – 'The Nightingale Revealed' – refers to Andersen's artistic self image, a self image which is perhaps best described as a composite of the real-life and fictional musical figures he praised and emulated in his literary works throughout his career.

In an effort to make some of Andersen's lesser-known music-inspired works more familiar to non-Danish readers, translations of a few of these have been inserted as 'interludes' between the various chapters. Although I know my translations can never capture the 'true' Andersen reflected in the original Danish, I hope these interludes will nonetheless give my subject the opportunity to speak in his own voice.

Chapter 1

The Nightingale

Hans Christian Andersen's entrée into Europe's professional music culture began like many of his fictional works did – with a journey. On 4 September 1819, the fourteen-year-old Andersen departed on a two-day trip to Copenhagen after bribing the driver of a mailcoach with three rixdollars to let him ride as a stowaway. Convinced of his talent as a singer and dancer, he was not daunted by the twenty-mile stretch of Baltic Sea that separated him from his destiny, and with just ten rixdollars left in his pocket and a letter of introduction addressed to the Royal Theater's prima ballerina, he was on his way to a life in the theater.

Andersen had already proven himself in the provincial theater life of Odense. As a child, he had enjoyed listening to folk tunes performed by his father and uncle, and he quickly gained a reputation as one of the city's finest young singers.

> My beautiful voice drew the attention of other people towards me. My habit on summer evenings was to sit in my parents' tiny garden, which ran down to the river.... Councilor Falbe's garden was next to that of my parents, and nearby was old St. Knud's Church. While the church bells rang in the evening I sat there, lost in curious reverie, watching the mill wheel and singing my improvised songs. The guests in Mr. Falbe's garden often used to listen. (The lady of the house was the famous Miss Beck, who played Ida in *Hermann von Unna*.) I often sensed the presence of my audience behind the fence, and I was flattered. So I became well known; and people began to send for me, 'the little nightingale of Funen,' as they used to call me.[1]

Andersen's childhood was not an easy one. His father, Hans Andersen, was a struggling shoemaker with an elementary education and a love of fantasy. For a man of his social status, he had a broad knowledge of contemporary literature, and he spent many hours reading aloud to his son from some of his favorite books: *Arabian Nights*, the fables of Jean de Lafontaine, and the comedies of Ludvig Holberg (1684–1754). Andersen's mother, Anne Marie Andersdatter, was markedly different from her husband. Seven years his senior, she could barely read and could not write at all.[2] She took little interest in contemporary literature, yet was fascinated by folklore. Like most mothers, she had complete confidence in her son and strong hopes for his future.

Information concerning Andersen's early education is sketchy. When he returned home at age seven from the local grammar school complaining that he had been struck by a teacher, his mother quickly transferred him to a small Jewish

Fig. 1.1 H.C. Andersen. Papercut of Andersen's own silhouette with dancer.
(Copenhagen: The Royal Library)

school led by Fedder Carstens. Andersen cherished his time there, for he was warmly received by the other children and encouraged by his teacher.[3] But this school was shut down shortly after Andersen's arrival, leaving him no choice but to attend the city's Poor School. Here he was often chastised for not concentrating on his studies, and although he acquired a basic education in reading, writing, and arithmetic, he never learned proper spelling and punctuation.

Though Andersen's autobiographies idealized his family life and childhood years in Odense, the oppression of poverty must have been tremendous. His father had little success as a shoemaker, and in a futile attempt to gain financial stability, he agreed, for a fee, to take the place of a wealthy young landowner who had been drafted to fight in Denmark's war against Russia and Sweden for control of present-day Norway. Hans Andersen departed Odense in 1812 and headed south, but he got no further than Holstein when his health failed him. The promised payment for his services was withdrawn, and he soon returned home ill and spiritually defeated. He died several years later, in 1816.

After her husband's death, Andersen's mother went to work as a washerwoman, and Andersen was sent to work in a local cloth mill. There he entertained the other workers with songs and dramatic performances that soon led to trouble.

> I had at that time a remarkably beautiful and high soprano voice that I kept until age fifteen. I knew that people liked to hear me sing; and when someone at the mill asked me if I knew any songs, I immediately began to sing, and this gave great pleasure; the other boys were told to do my work. After I had sung, I told [them] that I could also perform comedies; I remembered entire scenes from Holberg and Shakespeare, and I recited them. The workers and wives kindly nodded at me, cheered, and clapped their hands. In this way I found the first days in the mill very entertaining. One day, however, when I was in my best singing vein, and everyone commented on the brilliancy of my voice, one of the workers cried out: 'That is definitely no boy, but a little maiden!' He seized hold of me. I cried and screamed. The other workers thought it very amusing, and held me fast by my arms and legs. I cried out at the top of my voice and, bashful as a girl, rushed from the building and home to my mother, who quickly promised me that I would never have to go there again.[4]

Money was still in short supply, however, and Andersen needed to contribute to the family income. A second job was found for him, this time in a local tobacco factory.

> Here my voice also made me a success; people came into the factory to hear me sing, and yet the funny thing was that I did not know a single song properly, but improvised both the text and the tune, and both were complicated and difficult. 'He ought to be on the stage,' they all said, and I began to get ideas of that kind.[5]

At first sight, Odense, with its brightly painted row houses, winding streets, and small squares, seemed a typical Danish country town. Even though it was the second-largest city in Denmark – Copenhagen being the first – and the capital of

Funen, its population never exceeded six thousand during Andersen's adolescence. The Crown Prince had a summer residence in Odense, and his occasional presence led to the addition of several cosmopolitan elements to the city, the most prominent being a theater (fig. 1.2). Built in 1795, this simple, nondescript building served as a performance space for theater troupes from Germany and a summer stage for a touring company from Copenhagen's Royal Theater; it was in this theater that Andersen saw his first theatrical performances, a German singspiel by K.F. Hensler and Ferdinand Kauer called *Das Donauweibchen* (The Little Lady of the Danube) and a German version of Holberg's comedy *Den politiske Kandestøber* (The Political Tinker).[6] Andersen was seven years old when he saw these works,[7] and as he later explained, they had a profound effect on his interest in the theater:

> From the day I saw the first play my whole soul was on fire with this art. I still recall how I could sit for days all alone before the mirror, an apron around my shoulders instead of a knight's cloak, acting out *Das Donauweibchen*, in German, though I barely knew five German words. I soon learned entire Danish plays by heart.[8]

Andersen made friends with the theater manager, Peter Junker, who let him have a theater program from each performance in exchange for help in giving them out; 'with this I seated myself in the corner and imagined an entire play, according to the name of the piece and the characters in it. This was my first conscious effort towards poetic composition.'[9]

Evidence of Andersen's growing interest in the theater is preserved in the back of an account book that his father bought when he joined the army. Since his father had little use for the journal after returning home, he apparently turned it over to his son, who promptly began using it as a sketchbook for creative ideas[10] (fig. 1.3). Andersen recorded his first entry in 1813, a short poem called 'Yes, I Sing,' a clear testament to his early identity as a musician.

Yes, I sing and use vibrato.
Yes, I can play like a musician.
I sing Ut, re, mi, fa, Sol.
I modulate in major and minor.
I can bray like a donkey.
In the land no one can match me.
I sing bass, descant, and tenor.
Yes, a virtuoso stands before you.

Ja jeg synge gjør Tremulanter;
Ja jeg kan spille som en Musikanter;
Jeg synger Ut re mi fa Sol;
Jeg modulere i Dur og Mol;
Jeg som Æsel kan skrige;
I Egnen findes ei min Lige.
Jeg synger Bas Decan Tenor;
Ja en Virtuos til Mand du for.[11]

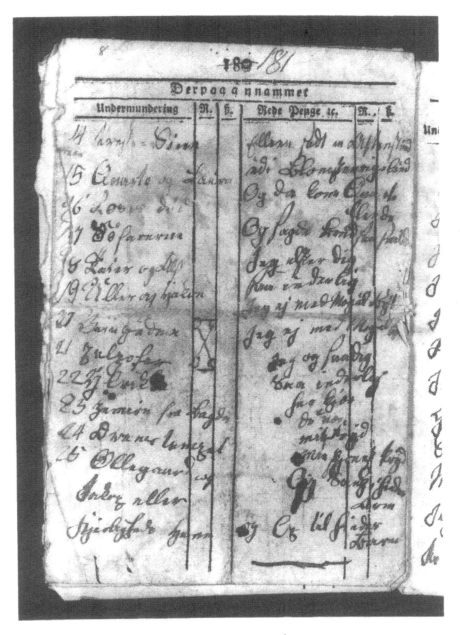

Fig. 1.2 Hans Andersen's account book with H.C. Andersen's first attempts at creative writing. (Copenhagen: The Royal Library)

Fig. 1.3 Lithograph of Odense Theater (ca. 1840).
(Odense: The Andersen House Museum)

Also preserved in this sketchbook is a list of titles for twenty-five projected dramatic works. No trace of these works now exists, but it is nonetheless interesting to see that as a youth, Andersen was already making plans for a future in the theater.

Andersen's connection to Odense's seasonal theater culture continued throughout his adolescent years. In the summer of 1818, he was even allowed to go back stage during performances and socialize with actors visiting from the Royal Theater.

> My child-like manners and my enthusiasm amused them; they spoke kindly to me, and I looked up to them as to earthly divinities. Everything that I had previously been told about my musical voice and my recitation of poetry became intelligible to me. It was the theater for which I was born; it was there that I should become a famous man, and for that reason Copenhagen was the goal of my endeavors.[12]

His enthusiasm that summer led to a walk-on part as a page in Nicolo Isouard and Charles Guillaume Etienne's opéra-comique *Cendrillon,*[13] an honor that he took seriously: 'I was always the first out there, put on the red silk costume, spoke my line, and believed that the whole audience thought only of me.'[14] After his première, Andersen's talents quickly became known among the city's elite:

> I was called to their houses, and the peculiar characteristics of my imagination excited their interest. Among others who noticed me was Colonel Høegh-Guldberg, who with his family showed me the kindest sympathy; so much so, indeed, that he introduced me to Prince Christian, afterward King Christian VIII.[15]

Andersen also came in contact with Christian Iversen, a wealthy printer who was rumored to have strong contacts with the elite of Copenhagen's theater society. Andersen was intent on moving to the capital, but he knew he would need a letter of introduction if he hoped to make it at the Royal Theater. The actors in the traveling company told him that the 'queen' of Copenhagen's theater world was Anna Margrethe Schall, the Royal Theater's prima ballerina. Convinced that only a letter to Schall would do, Andersen harangued Iversen relentlessly: '[Iversen] confessed that he was not personally acquainted with the dancer; nonetheless, he agreed to give me a letter to her.'[16]

But Andersen needed more than a letter if he hoped to move to Copenhagen. He needed money, and in 1819 he gave numerous impromptu performances in the homes of Odense's elite in an effort to raise funds. Andersen's presentations must have been quite a sight. A first-hand description of one performance, preserved in the diary of a young girl named Ottilie Christensen, gives us a sense of Andersen's frenetic impromptu style:

> Master Comedy-Player arrived at dusk ... and for two whole hours the little gentleman played parts from various comedies and tragedies. As a rule, he did well; but we were much amused whether he succeeded or not. The light-hearted parts were the best; but it was most absurd to watch him doing the part of the

sentimental lover, kneeling down or fainting, because just then his large feet did not look their very best. Well, perhaps they can improve their style in Copenhagen. Perhaps in time he will make his appearance as a great man on the stage. In the evening we had sandwiches and red fruit jelly; our actor joined us, but in hot haste so as not to lose any time parading his talent. At half-past ten the bishop's wife thanked him for coming, and he went home.[17]

Two days later, Andersen left for Copenhagen, arriving in the capital on 6 September. When he first set foot in the city, he was struck by the lively atmosphere: 'The whole city was in commotion, everybody was in the streets. But all this noise and turmoil did not surprise me – it corresponded to the commotion I had imagined must always exist in Copenhagen, the capital of my world.'[18] Unbeknownst to Andersen, the commotion that surrounded him was not typical, but, rather, the result of a violent pogrom against the city's Jews that had broken out just two days before[19] (fig. 1.4). Order had not yet been restored when Andersen arrived, and one can only imagine how the throbbing, unruly crowds invigorated the young man. All around him windows were smashed and storefronts burned. At night, the sounds of gunshots rang through the streets intermittently. 'All the people were greatly animated, like blood in the veins during a fever sickness.'[20]

Upon entering the city, Andersen's first order of business was a visit to the Royal Theater, a graceful, neo-classical building in Kongens Nytorv, a fashionable square in the center of Copenhagen (fig. 1.5). 'I walked around [the theater], looked at it from all sides, and made a heartfelt plea to God: "Let me enter in here and become a good actor."'[21] As Andersen admired the building, a crowd gathered outside the entrance in search of inexpensive tickets for that evening's performance. Hawkers were there as well, and when one approached Andersen and asked if he would like a ticket, 'I did not understand what he meant. I thought he was offering me a present and said Yes! Then he asked me where I wanted to sit, and I said that it was completely up to him.'[22] Thinking that he was being mocked, the hawker flew into a rage, calling Andersen a 'stupid dog.' Terrified, the boy made a quick escape.

The next day, Andersen put on his best clothes – a confirmation suit that was too short in the sleeves, new boots, and a hat that fell over his eyes – and made his way to Schall's residence to deliver his single letter of introduction. At first, he was denied entry into the house – the maid mistook him for a beggar, and Madame Schall claimed to have never heard of Iversen – but Andersen would not be turned away. Eventually, he was allowed to explain himself and was consequently granted permission to enter.

[Schall] looked at me … and thought I was a little crazy, for when she asked me if I had talent for the stage, I offered to perform a scene for her and chose the part of Anine in *Cendrillon* – a role that greatly impressed me, but which I had only seen two times at the theater in Odense and had never read nor actually sung. Hence I improvised both the text and music, and in order to better portray the dance scene with the tambourine ('Hvad vil Rigdom vel sige?'), I set my shoes in the corner and danced in my socks.[23]

Schall was not impressed, and her disapproval caused quite a commotion. In tears, Andersen confessed his desire to join the theater and offered to do anything, even run errands for her, if she would only assist him. 'Naturally, she could not offer me much hope. "I will speak with Bournonville [Director of the Royal Theater's Ballet School] and see if you can join the dancers," were her words as she dismissed me, and I went away weeping.'[24]

When the visit with Schall proved unsuccessful, Andersen called on Professor Knud Rahbek at Bakkehuset, a grand house in Frederiksberg where the liberal poet played host to the city's intellectuals and writers in a sort of permanent salon/house party.[25] Iversen had apparently mailed Rahbek a letter concerning Andersen several weeks before, but it had little influence. Rahbek showed no interest in the boy and recommended that he return the following day and talk with Colonel Frederik von Holstein, Lord-in-Waiting to the Queen and Director of the Royal Theater. Andersen did as he was instructed, but this visit proved even more disastrous than the encounter with Schall:

> Once he [Holstein] saw me, he assured me that there was no prospect of me joining the theater. I was too thin, had no physique, which would cause laughter on the stage. In addition, only educated young men were wanted.[26]

Confused, Andersen asked if he could at least join the theater's dance school, as Schall had suggested. The answer was a definitive 'No.' There would be no openings in the school until May, and even then his chances of being accepted were slim.

Distraught, Andersen returned to the Royal Theater and, in an effort to lift his spirits, spent his last shillings on a gallery ticket to *Paul et Virginie*, an opéra-comique by Jean-François Le Seur. As Andersen watched the performance, he could not help interpreting it as a variation on his own struggles.

> The piece moved me greatly; it seemed to me as though it was like my own life. Paul was like me, and Virginie was to him what the theater was to me. Consequently, when in the second act Paul was torn away from Virginie, I burst into violent crying. It was just like with me; one also wanted to tear me away from my beloved, the theater. Those who sat nearby became aware of my intense weeping and gave me apples and talked kindly to me. – I thought them all such nice people, knew nothing of the real world, considered them kind and excellent, and therefore naively told them all, the whole upper gallery, who I was, how I had traveled here, and how terrible it was that I could not enter into the theater....[27]

Such a reaction to a stage work would later prove typical of Andersen. Like the highly emotional Werther in Goethe's novel, Andersen viewed the world around him as a reflection of his own state of mind, a tendency that would later lead to a penchant for seeking allegorical interpretations in literature and creating

Jødefejden.

Fig. 1.4 Etching of 1819 Pogrom in Copenhagen.
(Copenhagen: The Royal Library)

Fig. 1.5 Etching of Copenhagen's Royal Theater in Kongens Nytorv (1833).
(Odense: The Andersen House Museum)

double meanings in his tales and novels. Luckily for Andersen, the librettist for *Paul et Virginie*, Alphonse du Congé Dubreuil, had changed the story's original tragic conclusion.[28] Instead of remaining separated for life, the young lovers were miraculously reunited at the end of the opera. This filled Andersen with a renewed sense of hope for his future in the theater. 'The happy ending in the piece moved me equally greatly; I was filled with courage and a lust for life. It seemed to me impossible that all would not go well for me.'[29]

Over the next ten days Andersen made several return visits to Schall and Director Holstein, but with no success. In an attempt to support himself financially, he signed on as an apprentice to a carpenter, but quickly abandoned the position when the other boys ridiculed him. At this point, Andersen had been in the capital for twelve days, yet had little to show for it. He was out of money and low on hope. 'Then a thought ran through my head: "My voice, which everyone praised in Odense, no one at the theater has heard it yet."'[30]

He remembered reading in Odense's newspapers that an Italian composer named Giuseppe Siboni had recently been appointed director of the Royal Theater's Opera Academy. Certain that his destiny now lay in his talents as a singer, he looked up Siboni's address on Viingaardstrædet and headed for the composer's home.

> It was four o'clock in the afternoon. Siboni had guests – among them was none other than the poet Baggesen and the composer Weyse. A housekeeper who could speak Danish answered the door. I told her with an open heart my story and my wish. Then she apparently told everyone inside, for they all rushed out to see me. Like some sort of curiosity, I was brought into the dining room. Baggesen took me by the hand, asked me if I weren't scared of what people called critics. [He] asked me to sing, and I gave them a pastoral love song: 'Nei ingen Pige!' (which I had learned in Odense from Miss Hammer). They applauded me merrily, and I imagined that it was in true wonder. Siboni persuaded me to say that I would come again someday soon.[31]

When Andersen was dismissed, he explained to the housekeeper that he only had seven schillings to his name. She assured him not to worry. He had made a good impression, and both Siboni and Weyse had agreed to assist him. Siboni offered Andersen free voice lessons and daily meals, and Weyse was organizing a subscription to raise money for Andersen's housing expenses. Elated by his good fortune, Andersen knew he was finally on his way to a life in the theater.

Andersen's description of his months under Siboni's tutelage gives the impression that he was perhaps seen more as a charity case than as an up-and-coming talent. His lessons with Siboni were few and far between, and he was often asked to run errands and help the cooks in the kitchen. Still, Andersen was happy with his situation, taking full advantage of the benefits it offered. In addition to a private lesson once or twice a month, he was allowed to sit in on opera rehearsals at the Royal Theater, a privilege that gave him his first taste of musical politics in Copenhagen. As Andersen himself later explained:

Siboni was an excellent singing master ..., but not so esteemed by the public as he deserved to be. Most people looked on him as a foreigner who was eating bread that might just as well have been given to a native, not realizing that among the natives there was no one as good as he. The Italian operas, which at the time had a great reputation throughout Europe and were brought upon [Denmark's] stage by Siboni, were received with hostility only because they were Italian operas and Siboni an Italian. '*Gazza ladra*' was hissed, also '*La Straniera*.'[32]

Siboni received much criticism for his attempts to bring works by Rossini and Bellini to the Danish stage.[33] Although Copenhagen audiences would eventually embrace these composers in the early 1840s, Siboni did not live to see this change in taste.

In addition to his lessons with Siboni, Andersen interacted on a regular basis with the composer C.E.F. Weyse. Indeed, it was likely Weyse who put the boy in contact with many members of Copenhagen's musical elite during his first year in the city. Andersen's life was progressing smoothly under the tutelage of both men, until tragedy struck in May 1820. One month past his fifteenth birthday, the inevitable happened. His voice changed. Suddenly, his beautiful soprano tone was gone forever, and with its sound went any hope he had of continuing his studies with Siboni.

Siboni called me in one day and told me that my appearance and my manners were quite against me, that I didn't have any education and that now that my voice had changed, it was no longer any good. He wouldn't be able to find me a position in the theater for at least three or four years, and he didn't want to have me in his home that long.[34]

Andersen was dismissed from Siboni's studio, and another young singer, Ida Wulff, soon took his place. Despite this setback, Andersen was not discouraged. In the months that he had studied with Siboni, he had managed to maneuver his way into the collective heart and consciousness of Copenhagen's theater community. He knew that there were others who would help him, and he quickly set to work winning their confidence. One of the first new patrons he sought out was the poet Frederik Høegh-Guldberg. Guldberg was the brother of Andersen's earliest patron in Odense, and he offered the boy free instruction in Danish and German and helped to organize a second subscription to cover his living expenses. This time, contributors to the fund included Weyse, the composer Friedrich Kuhlau (1786–1832), and the philologist Just Matthias Thiele, an avid collector of folk tales and stories. After learning that his second subscription had procured a total of eighty rixdollars, Andersen took it upon himself to thank each benefactor in person. Thiele described one such visit in his memoirs, giving a clear picture of how Andersen must have appeared to many of his patrons in Copenhagen:

I was sitting at my desk with my back to the door, when there was a knock on it. Saying 'Come in,' I didn't even turn my head, but as I looked up from my papers, I was surprised to see a brazen boy, with quite peculiar looks, standing by the door in a deep theatrical bow towards the floor. He had already thrown his cap off by the door, and when that lanky figure … rose, I saw … a surprising character who became even more surprising when, after taking a few steps forward and repeating his bow, he began to speak in an affected manner: 'May I have the honor to express my feelings for the theater in a poem I have written myself?'

In my astonishment, I did not even start to move before he was in the middle of the declamation, and when he ended with another reference, there followed immediately the performance of a scene from [Oehlenschläger's] *Hagbarth and Signe*, a scene in which he played all the roles. I sat dumbfounded and waited for the entr'acte that might give me an opportunity for a question and an answer, but in vain. The performance took me from one scene in a tragedy to another in a comedy; and when he finally reached the epilogue, which he moreover had written himself, he ended with several theatrical bows, grasped his cap lying like a gaping spectator by the door, and was off down the stairs.[35]

Andersen was grateful for the financial assistance given to him by his new benefactors in Copenhagen, though the most encouraging assistance he received after his dismissal by Siboni came from Carl Dahlén (1770–1851), a solo dancer at the Royal Theater. Dahlén was only a few years older than Andersen, and the two had become friends during Andersen's months in Copenhagen. Dahlén and his wife, an actress at the Royal Theater, welcomed Andersen into their home. The dancer was apparently impressed by Andersen's determination and enthusiasm for the theater. Consequently, when he was appointed interim director of the Royal Theater's Ballet School in the spring of 1820 (the permanent director, Antoine Bournonville, was on leave in Paris), he invited Andersen to audition. Indeed, it appears that Andersen's will and exuberance, as opposed to any natural talent, were what finally enabled him to secure a position at the Royal Theater.[36]

Andersen's tenure at the Ballet School began in September 1820, and shortly after its inception, he began to record his impressions of his new surroundings in what is perhaps best described as a 'theatrical diary.'[37] This diary catalogues the performances that took place at the Royal Theater during Andersen's presence there in 1820 and 1821. Although humble in nature and little more than a list of performances, the diary nonetheless marks the beginning of Andersen's lifelong role as a chronicler of European musical culture. Obsessed with his new occupation, he kept track of the Royal Theater's various performances; and in the years that followed, he returned to his diary for inspiration when writing descriptions of Copenhagen's theater life in his novels and fairy tales.[38] A close examination of the entries reveals that Andersen marked with an asterisk the performances that most impressed him. These included Kuhlau's *Røverborgen* (The Robber's Castle); [39] Weyse's *Sovedrikken* (The Sleeping Potion);[40] Johann Bartholdy's three-act opera *Dyveke*; Mozart's *Don Giovanni*; Ludvig Holberg's *Den Stundesløse* (The Restless One); and the première of Carl Maria von Weber's overture to *Der Freischütz*.[41]

Andersen also made special note of each performance in which he himself appeared. For example, on 14 September 1820 he first trod upon the stage as an extra in the one-act operetta *Les Deux Petits Savoyards* by Nicolas-Marie Dalayrac.[42]

> [Ida Wulff] told me that in the market scene, anyone, even the machinists, could appear on stage as an extra as long as they put a little makeup on their cheeks first. I did so right away and then walked out with all the others. I saw the stage lights, the prompter, and the whole darkened audience. I was in my everyday clothes.... I dared not stand up straight, for everyone would be able to see that my vest was far too short.... I was tall and thin, and I knew from experience that people might make fun of me. Still, in that moment I was completely filled with the joy that comes from appearing in front of the stage lights for the first time. My heart pounded as I stepped out. Then one of the singers, who was well known then but is completely forgotten now, took me by the hand and mockingly wished me luck on my dèbut. 'Let me present you to the Danish public!' he said as he led me to the front of the stage. I knew that he expected the audience to laugh at me. Tears came to my eyes. I pulled myself free from him and left the stage.[43]

Andersen's next stage appearance was less traumatic. On 25 January 1821 he played the role of 'a musical servant' in *Nina*, a pantomime ballet by Vincenzo Galeotti (1733–1816)[44] with music by Claus Schall. *Nina* is a typical eighteenth-century sentimental comedy about a passionate young girl who is driven mad by love,[45] and Andersen's assignment in the production was to serve as one of two musicians called to soothe Nina's madness with the beauty of song. In this capacity, Andersen again found himself at the front of the stage, but this time with far better results: 'Madame Schall danced the role of Nina, and I was pleased when she directed most of her attention toward me.'[46]

Andersen's most successful appearance on stage, however, took place several months later, when he appeared as a demon in Dahlén's four-act heroic ballet, *Armida*.[47] He took the role seriously, seeing it as a turning point in his career – the first time his name appeared in print. 'I imagined I could see a nimbus of immortality. I was continually looking at the printed paper. I carried the program of the ballet to bed with me at night, lay and stared at my name by candlelight, set the program down only to pick it up again. This was happiness!'[48] Based on Gluck's opera of the same name, the ballet featured a number of special effects that Andersen later recalled in his travelogue, *Fodreise fra Holmens Canal til Østpynten af Amager i Aarene 1828 og 1829* (A Walking Tour from Holmen Canal to the Eastern Point of Amager in the years 1828 and 1829): 'The curtain rose, and one was looking into an enormous kaleidoscope that rotated very slowly. Cliffs with waterfalls, burning cities, skies of fiery rain, and stranded ships tumbled broken among each other.'[49]

Andersen was featured in several scenes. Wearing a 'hideous mask' as one of Armida's eight demons,[50] he seized Rinaldo's sword and shield in Act 2 and drew attention to himself in the finale by 'tumbling headfirst out of a crevice' high above the stage.[51] Despite the ballet's spectacular effects and Claus Schall's music, *Armida* 'closed the following week' after only seven performances.[52] Still, Andersen's confidence in his ability to perform had grown immensely, and he quickly sought further opportunities. For example, shortly after his appearance in *Armida*, he expressed to Guldberg an interest in tackling more significant roles. In an effort to assist his student, Guldberg arranged an audition with Ferdinand Lindgren, one of Copenhagen's premiere comic actors. Lindgren agreed to take Andersen into his studio, but he was skeptical when the boy insisted on studying only serious roles. 'My God, dear boy, your looks are against you; such a lanky, thin hero would only make people laugh out loud!' he reportedly said. But Andersen was determined. Eight days after his admittance into the studio, he performed an emotionally-charged monologue from Oehlenschläger's *Correggio*, which quickly put an end to his dramatic training. Expecting accolades for his unique interpretation (Andersen apparently burst into tears during a section that was generally interpreted with shouts of joy), he instead received a blunt dismissal: 'You have heart, and a good head – but you should stop wasting your time.... You weren't made to be an actor,' declared Lindgren. Then, perhaps in an effort to soften the blow, he added: 'There are other worthy things you can do besides [acting].'[53]

Much to the surprise of Andersen, Lindgren's prediction proved true. In May, he suddenly received an invitation to join the Royal Theater's Opera Academy from its new director, Peter Caspar Krossing (1793–1838).

> The singing teacher Krossing (with the Theater's Opera Academy) heard about me. He was angry with Siboni; he knew that I had been there and that I still had a voice. That's why he wanted me in his school, why he wanted to see if he could make a singer out of me. But I had to begin by singing in the choir.[54]

In this new capacity, Andersen officially joined the personnel of the Royal Theater on 4 June 1821, and as a tenor in the chorus he appeared in a number of performances during the 1821/22 season. The fragment of his theatrical diary that survives from this period lists his roles as 'a peasant' in J.A.P. Schulz's *Høstgildet* (The Harvest Festival); 'a footman' in Oehlenschläger's tragedy, *Axel og Valborg*; 'a page' in Holberg's *Maskerade*;[55] 'a shepherd' in N.T. Bruun's translation of August von Kotzebue's tragedy *Johanna Montfaucon*;[56] 'a Brahman' in a singspiel based on Simon Mayr's heroic melodrama, *Lanassa*; and 'a warrior' in a Danish version of *Zoraïme et Zulnar*, a three-act opéra-comique written by the celebrated French composer François-Adrien Boieldieu, whose better-known work, *La Dame blanche* (1825), later had a decisive influence on nineteenth-century Danish theater. In addition to his appearances on stage, Andersen made his first attempt at writing for the theater in the winter of 1822. In less than two weeks he wrote a tragedy called *Røverne i Vissenberg* (The Robbers of Wissenberg), which was inspired by Schiller's drama *Die Räuber* (The Robbers) and based on local legend. Andersen submitted the libretto anonymously to the Royal Theater in March, and his hopes were high that it would be favorably reviewed. Six weeks later, however, the manuscript was returned with a letter from the management stating: 'They desired to receive no more pieces like this one, which betrayed, in so great a degree, such a lack of elementary learning.'[57]

As upsetting as this rejection must have been, the most crushing blow was yet to come. In May, Andersen received a letter from the directors of the Royal Theater informing him that his services were no longer needed. Formally dismissed from both the Ballet School and the Opera Academy, he was advised to attain a basic education before pursuing any further connections with the Royal Theater.

Despite these setbacks, Andersen refused to abandon his dream of a life on stage. Determined to obtain a position as a librettist, he began work on a five-act tragedy entitled *Alfsol* and sought out new supporters among Copenhagen's elite. Having recently read a biography of Shakespeare, he was struck with the thought that the bard's life 'resembled his own.' This realization influenced Andersen's decision to seek out Denmark's foremost translator of Shakespeare at the time, a naval officer named Peter Frederik Wulff (1774–1842). As Andersen explained, 'I imagined that it would please him to meet a person who resembled his favorite poet. I was also eager to know him. And so, with my *Alfsol* in pocket, I introduced myself....'[58]

Wulff's reaction to the play is not recorded, but he was obviously taken with Andersen, who became a welcome member of the Wulff home for years to come. Other figures subjected to a reading of *Alfsol* included the noted physicist and philosopher Hans Christian Ørsted (1777–1851) and the dean of Copenhagen's naval church, Holmens Kirke, Frederik Carl Gutfeld. Gutfeld was especially impressed by the play, and he agreed to submit it to the Royal Theater on Andersen's behalf. Although *Alfsol* was rejected several weeks later, the letter accompanying the returned manuscript was more encouraging than Andersen's previous rejections. This time, instead of simply criticizing him, the directors of the Royal Theater (Rahbek, Holstein, and Jonas Collin) invited him to meet with them in person. This fateful meeting took place in September 1822. According to Andersen,[59] Rahbek led the meeting; after explaining that the directors agreed Andersen's play was 'useless for the stage,' he noted that they nonetheless 'found a few golden kernels, which showed some promise.' But Andersen was 'in need of a proper education' if he ever hoped to produce 'something that would appeal to well-educated audiences.' Consequently, the board decided to assist Andersen in this endeavor. With funds supplied through a grant from Frederik VI, Andersen would attend a well-reputed grammar school in the provincial town of Slagelse, where writers such as Jens Baggesen and B.S. Ingemann had trained and the headmaster, Simon Meisling, was a recognized classic scholar and translator. Jonas Collin, the theater's new managing director and an influential court official, had agreed to secure the needed finances. He would act as Andersen's sponsor and check up on him regularly. One month later, on 26 October 1822, Andersen left his beloved Copenhagen and traveled fifty-seven miles west to Slagelse. This was the beginning of what he would later describe as the five most miserable years of his life.

Andersen's tenure in Slagelse (and later Helsingør, where he transferred with Meisling in 1826) has been described in depth by various biographers.[60] In general, Andersen's misery was caused by two factors: his distance from the theater life in Copenhagen and his dysfunctional relationship with Simon Meisling. A strict disciplinarian who had little patience for Andersen's melodramatic behavior and fantastical ideas, Meisling never welcomed his student or fully understood him. He forbade Andersen from writing fiction and poetry and constantly criticized him for his academic shortcomings. 'Every day [Meisling] told me that I would never amount to anything, that I was stupid, that I could get nowhere. The feeling that I was consequently receiving support and assistance unworthily weighed heavily on me.'[61]

Studying did not come easily to Andersen, who struggled constantly with his exams. Five years older than the other boys in his grade, he made few friends. Indeed, the only bright spots during his school years appear to have been his holidays in Copenhagen and his visits with B.S. Ingemann, a noted poet who lived nearby (and one of the few people who still encouraged Andersen's literary interests). On Sundays, Andersen was occasionally allowed to make the eight-mile walk to the village of Sorø, where Ingemann lived, to discuss literature and exchange books. Ingemann had traveled to Germany a decade before, where he forged strong bonds with romantic writers such as Friedrich Schlegel, E.T.A. Hoffmann, and Ludwig Tieck. He encouraged Andersen to read their works along with the novels of Walter Scott; Andersen's exposure to these works had a strong effect on his own ideas concerning creative writing.

In 1825, Andersen began to keep a diary. Its entries clearly reveal the tormented nature of his relationship with Meisling, which worsened with each year under his tutelage. Andersen wrote to Jonas Collin on a regular basis, begging to be taken out of school, but with no success. Indeed, it was only in the spring of 1827 that Andersen was at last allowed to leave, when a teacher named Christian Werlin wrote to Collin about Meisling's disturbing behavior.

Once in Copenhagen, Andersen began to prepare for his entrance exams at the University. Although he felt confident enough in mathematics to study the subject on his own, he knew that he needed help with Latin and Greek and sought out a private tutor. Following the recommendation of Collin, Andersen began studying with a young linguist and historian named Ludwig Christian Müller in the fall of 1827. Müller lived on Amager, a small island connected to central Copenhagen by several bridges. Andersen made the trip to his teacher's home and back twice a day by foot for nearly a year. Although the walk was long, he did not seem to mind. As he later explained, he made a pact with himself to focus on his studies on the way there, and allowed 'bright, poetic ideas' to overtake his thoughts on the way home.[62]   Andersen passed his exams in September 1828, and with this obstacle out of the way, 'bright, poetic ideas' quickly dominated his mind: 'The ideas and thoughts ... flew like a swarm of bees out into the world, and indeed into my first work, *A Walking Tour from Holmen Canal to the Eastern Point of Amager in the Years 1828 and 1829.*'[63]

Andersen wrote *A Walking Tour* in the winter of 1828, and it displays, perhaps better than any other source, the breadth of his general education and the depth of his knowledge of contemporary literature.[64] Alongside references to Nero, Cicero, Aristophanes, Marcus Aurelius, Cervantes, Shakespeare, Catherine de Medici,

Molière, Rousseau, and Hegel, *A Walking Tour* highlights works by Goethe, Schiller, Johan Ludvig Heiberg, Ingemann, Jean Paul, Lessing, and Oehlenschläger, to name a few. Chief among all figures mentioned in the book is E.T.A. Hoffmann. Andersen was fascinated by Hoffmann's life and works; so much so that in 1828 he organized a reading group with two friends called the Serapian Brotherhood, after Hoffmann's last volume of short stories. Hoffmann had belonged to a reading group of the same name in Berlin, and Andersen's imitation of it in Copenhagen was a sign of his indebtedness to the German writer's work. Even a cursory reading of *A Walking Tour* reveals that it was inspired by Hoffmann's fiction, most notably his short stories 'New Year's Eve Adventure' and 'The Devil's Elixer' and the novel *Fantasy Pieces in Callot's Manner: Pages from the Diary of a Traveling Romantic*. Excerpts from all three of these works are parodied in Andersen's *A Walking Tour*, which is perhaps best categorized as a fantasy travelogue, for it depicts a young poet's late-night walk from Copenhagen to Amager – the route Andersen had walked daily during his tutoring sessions with Müller – and describes his chance encounters with figures both real and mythical. Andersen began his book with the following lines:

> On New Year's Eve I sat all alone in my little room and looked out across the snow-covered roofs of the neighboring houses; then came the evil spirit, whom people call Satan; he encouraged my sinful thoughts about becoming a writer.[65]

This passage recalls the opening of Goethe's *Faust*, and not surprisingly Faust himself makes an appearance in the book, along with St. Peter, who offers the narrator the keys to Amager. But no figure has a more dramatic entrance than 'Long, lean Death.' He rides madly across the island at the helm of an express mailcoach, 'grinning nastily with his wide mouth in the moonlight.' Exhilarated by his skillful play with metaphors, Andersen struggled to find his own voice, to situate his proper place in Copenhagen's artistic circles. He satirized the deluge of letters in mass society and contemplated the boundaries between life and death, art and artifice.[66] As Andersen himself later explained, *A Walking Tour* was meant to be 'a peculiar, humorous book, a kind of fanciful arabesque,' but one that fully exhibited his own individual character at the time, his 'disposition to sport with everything, and to jest in tears' over his own feelings – 'a fantastic, gaily colored tapestry, a poetic improvisation.'[67]

Andersen's approach to what he described as his 'poetic improvisation' was firmly rooted in Friedrich Schlegel's ideas on creativity and the characteristic literary style found in Hoffmann's *Fantasy Pieces*. Writing about the creative process in 1798, Schlegel stated: 'It is equally fatal to have a system and not have a system. One must try to combine them.' Schlegel was referring to the creative act of writing, but he just as easily could have been talking about the performative act of musical improvisation. For the creation of an effective musical improvisation depends on both the rejection and the embracing of a formal structure – a thematically and/or harmonically constructed musical foundation.[68] Hoffman clearly recognized this correlation between the literary and musical genres when writing *Fantasy Pieces*.

Previous discussions of this novel have looked to Schlegel's aesthetic of the fragment as a primary influence. Indeed, Hoffmann presented the novel as a collection of literary fragments. But even a cursory reading of Schlegel's *Athenaeum* fragments and Hoffmann's *Fantasy Pieces* reveals stark differences. Whereas Schlegel's work is a philosophical treatise arranged as a list of numbered aphorisms, Hoffmann's piece is an entertaining narrative composed from fragments of previously-published music criticism and newly-composed tales. This difference in structure is due to the divergent views both men held in reference to the idea of the 'fragment.' Whereas Schlegel defined the fragment as a single, self-contained unit: 'A fragment should be like a little work of art, complete in itself and separated from the rest of the universe like a hedgehog,'[69] Hoffmann viewed the fragment in a more traditional manner, as a small part of something greater. He intended the various fragments in *Fantasy Pieces* to be read and interpreted as a whole. Consequently, he structured his novel along the lines of a musical improvisation, a 'fantasy,' in order to create a sense of cohesion. Like a musician, he tied the various fragments together with a thematic string; in this case the thoughts and experiences of the novel's central character – the semi-autobiographical Kapellmeister Johannes Kreisler.

References to instrumental music and opera pervade Hoffmann's *Fantasy Pieces*; structure and meaning, as well as the subject matter, have musical overtones. For example, in the first fragment, 'Ritter Gluck,' a mysterious apparition in the guise of the noted composer, Christoph Willibald von Gluck, appears and performs his most famous work for an unnamed narrator:

> Fixing me with his gloomy stare, he took out one of the books – *Armida* – and strode solemnly toward the piano.... He opened the book and – picture my astonishment – I saw the lined pages, but not a single note was written upon them. 'Now I will play the overture!' he said. 'Turn the pages at the right time!' I promised I would, and with full chord harmony, he played, beautifully, masterfully – almost true to the original – the majestic *Tempo di Marcia* that begins the overture. But Gluck's major themes were only woven in and out of the *Allegro*. My astonishment grew at all the inspired new variations he introduced. His modulations were striking without being jarring. He managed to string together so many melodious embellishments to the simple main themes that the themes themselves seemed to return over and over in new rejuvenated forms....[70]

The next section of the novel, a group of fragments labeled 'Kreisleriana,' reveals the identity of the unnamed narrator to be Kapellmeister Kreisler and gives the layout for the rest of the novel. Kreisler, an eccentric composer, has mysteriously disappeared, and what follows are 'fragments' of his writings, 'hastily penciled at convenient moments on the blank reverse side of some pieces of sheet music ... the unpretentious productions of a momentary inspiration.'[71] Parallels between writing and musical improvisation appear throughout *Fantasy Pieces*, the most obvious being a fragment entitled 'Kreisler's Musical-Poetical

Club.' Here we find Kreisler preparing to perform an improvisation on the piano for members of the Musical-Poetical Club when a character named Circumspect drops a candelabra inside the instrument and consequently breaks a number of the strings.

'I shall improvise all the same,' cried Kreisler. 'The bass is still all there, and that should be enough for me....' Kreisler began in the bass, pianissimo, with the soft pedal, the full A-major chord. While the notes rumbled, he spoke: 'What is it that rustles so wondrously, so strangely, all around me? Invisible wings float up and down – I am swimming in fragrant ether – but the fragrance gleams into flaming, mysterious, intertwined circles. Lovely spirits move their golden wings in rapturous, beautiful notes and chords.

A-Minor Chord (mezzo forte)

Ah! They bear me to the realm of eternal longing, but the way they grip me evokes a pain that lacerates my breast as it tries to escape.

E-Major Sixth Chord (ancora più forte)

Be firm, my heart! Do not break from the scorching radiance that penetrates my breast! Go, my brave spirit! Rise and soar into the element that bore you, which is your native land!

E-Major Third Chord (forte)

They offered me a glorious crown, but it was the thousands of tears I shed that sparkled and glittered in the diamonds while flames glistening in the gold consumed me. Courage and power! Trust and strength to the one who is called to rule in the Realm of Spirits!

A-Minor (arpeggiando dolce)

Why do you flee lovely maiden? Do you not like being held so tightly by invisible bonds? Don't you know how to speak and complain of the gnawing pain that lives in your heart and stirs you with sweet desire? But you will know everything when I speak to you and caress you in the spirit language that I can speak and that you understand so well!

F-Major Chord

Ha! How your heart opens with longing and love when I embrace you with melodies full of glowing enchantment, as if with loving arms. Never again will you want to recoil from me, for the secret feelings that constrict your breast are fulfilled. Like a comforting oracle, the music has spoken from my soul to yours!' ... Etc., etc.[72]

Six more chord changes with text follow the quote above, presenting the reader with a hybrid musical-poetical improvisation. Kreisler plays the series of chords indicated in the text: A major, A minor, E-major sixth chord, E major third chord, A minor, and so on, and these chords provide a preconceived structure for the musical/poetical improvisation while the text, spoken simultaneously by Kreisler, represents an on-the-spot creative invention. Here the art of improvisation is blatantly portrayed as the motivational force behind Kreisler's – and Hoffmann's – musical/poetical creativity.

It is not surprising that Hoffmann used music as a model when constructing his narrative form. A talented composer and conductor, he valued his activities as a musician far more than his abilities as a writer.[73] Andersen was drawn to this element of Hoffmann's persona, and as we have seen, he viewed himself in a similar light. When writing *A Walking Tour*, Andersen looked to Hoffmann's *Fantasy Pieces* as a model. In addition to constructing his fictional travelogue as a collection of loosely connected improvised fragments, Andersen recreated a series of improvised performances – in one instance a poet 'similar in spirit (and appearance) to Hoffmann's Kater Murr' sings an improvised duet with his alley cat aunt. Like Hoffmann, Andersen also broached the topic of musical taste in *A Walking Tour*. As the young poet wanders through the city's streets, he thinks to himself:

> It would be very interesting to make a brief visit to earth every three hundred years in order to see all the changes to stages and scenery, costumes and repertoire. One would certainly often think he recognizes the same actor, but appearing in a new piece, in new costume, and among different decorations. Many scenes would certainly resemble those from an older piece. Indeed, many a drama simply seem transparent and passé according to the interest of the hour.[74]

Having said this, the poet is suddenly transported to the year 2128, where he finds himself standing before the doors of a theater. Upon entry, he discovers that the theater is a type of museum, built 'in the form of an enormous kaleidoscope' and designed to 'show all the theater effects of the nineteenth century.' The overture consists of 'bare dissonances pillaged from various compositions,'[75] while the scenery on-stage, with its 'burning cities' and 'skies of fiery rain,' is both a reference to Hoffman's description of *Armida* in the fragment 'Ritter Gluck' and a replica of the scenery used for the ballet adaptation performed at Copenhagen's Royal Theater in 1820. Yet despite these contemporary references, a sense of disorientation permeates this fragment of Andersen's text. Although the action takes place three hundred years in the future, the poet nonetheless finds himself sitting in the theater he knew from his youth. This melding of time and place can be interpreted as a reflection of Andersen's own reaction to the state of the Royal Theater in 1828. Although he had been absent for what seemed to him an eternity, the theater that he returned to was much the same. A look at the Royal Theater's opera repertoire reveals that it had changed little over the decade of Andersen's absence.[76] Among works by Danish composers such as C.E.F. Weyse and Frederik Kuhlau, there was still a preference for singspiel, and the works of foreign composers were mostly represented in vaudevilles and ballad operas, where patchworks of arias from various works were pieced together. Among the few foreign composers whose works were presented in whole, Mozart held the most dominant position. But this was not simply the result of an aesthetically motivated preference among Danish audiences. Mozart's widow, Constanza, had moved to Copenhagen in 1810, a year after marrying her second husband, the Danish diplomat and writer Georg Nicolaus Nissen. The Nissens remained in Copenhagen until 1820 (they left shortly after Andersen's arrival), and their residency influenced the avid admiration of Mozart's music among Danish audiences.[77] The Royal Theater gave regular performances of many Mozart operas, including *Die*

Entführung aus dem Serail, La Clemenza di Tito, Die Zauberflöte, Don Giovanni, and *Le Nozze di Figaro.*

The influence of Copenhagen's musical life on *A Walking Tour* was clearly recognized by contemporary readers. Indeed, Johan Ludvig Heiberg, a noted playwright and critic who wrote a review of the book for *Maanedsskriftet for Litteratur,* described *A Walking Tour* as 'a musical fantasy' full of originality and grace. He compared Andersen to 'a young painter who, before daring to take up stronger compositions, practices with the arabesque.'[78] Heiberg's opinion was important to Andersen. By 1829, Heiberg had come to dominate Copenhagen's literary scene. He had won high praise from contemporary audiences for his popular vaudevilles and a romance called *Elverhøj* (Hill of the Elves). In addition, Heiberg's ties to the Royal Theater were close. He served as a censor for all new plays and libretti submitted to the theater and often had the last word on what was staged and what was rejected.[79] Heiberg was a powerful ally to have won, and Andersen lost no time in making the most of the situation.

Immediately after his success with *A Walking Tour,* Andersen submitted a Heiberg-inspired vaudeville called *Kjærlighed paa Nicolai Taarn* (Love on St. Nicholas Tower) to the Royal Theater.[80] The work was quickly accepted and premièred in April 1829. This was Andersen's first box office hit. Subtitled 'What does the Pit say?' the vaudeville tells the story of an elderly watchman who tries to marry off his daughter to one of his colleagues, even though she is in love with a young, handsome tailor. It was left to the audience to decide which suitor would succeed – if they applauded, she married the tailor; if they booed or hissed, she was forced to wed her father's choice. The incorporation of an improvisatory interaction between the actors and the audience was a novel idea, and it led to a nice profit for the young playwright. It also led, unsurprisingly, to the end of his academic career.

After the success of *Love on St. Nicholas Tower,* Andersen became more determined than ever to establish himself as a poet. He left the university after passing a so-called second examination in philosophy and philology in October, and brought out his first collection of poems, *Digte,* for Christmas.[81] This volume included a number of texts designed to be set to music, and in the final stanza of a poem entitled 'Aftenen: et Træsnit' (The Evening: a Woodcut) Andersen included a comic portrait of himself in the guise of a lone, Goethe-inspired minstrel:

Look, yonder on the slope, a lanky person.
With a face as pale as blessed Werther;
And with a nose as big as a cannon;
And eyes as tiny as green peas.
He sings something German with a '*woher?*'
And then stares out longingly toward the west.
Why, I wonder, does he stand there so long?
Oh my God! One cannot be expected to know everything;
Yet it is surely, if I've seen correctly,
A madman, a lover, or a poet.

Se, hist på skrænten star en lang person
med ansigtet så blegt, som salig Werther,
Og med en næse, stor som en kanon,
Og øjne bitte små, som grønne ærter.
Han synger noget tysk med et 'woher?'
Og stirrer derpå ud i vesterlide.
Hvorfor mon han vel står så længe der?
Ja Herre Gud! Man kan ej alting vide;
Dog er det sikkert, har jeg rigtigt set,
En gal, en elsker, eller en poet.[82]

Clearly Andersen now saw himself, at least ironically, as a quintessential romantic figure. He no longer considered his odd appearance as a hindrance to his career. Indeed, it was his unusual looks and idealistic convictions that linked him to the characters from German literature that he so admired. In his own mind, Andersen had finally found his artistic identity – like Werther, he was a natural poet whose genius was reflected in the world around him and revealed through his impulsive, improvisatory temperament.

In the spring of 1830 Andersen began working on another project for the stage, an opera libretto called *Ravnen eller Broderprøven* (The Raven or The Test of Brotherhood) based on Carlo Gozzi's *Il Corvo* (1761). After reading Hoffmann's *Die Serapions-Brüder* (wherein it is suggested that *Il Corvo* is as an appropriate opera subject) Andersen became convinced that Gozzi's *commedia dell'arte* play would serve as the basis for his next project. Using a Danish translation of *Il Corvo* as his guide,[83] he completed the libretto in several weeks and then gave it to a young, up-and-coming composer named J.P.E. Hartmann. Andersen hoped that Hartmann would take an interest in the work and agree to write the music. He knew that his chances of getting the libretto accepted by the Royal Theater's censors would be better if a composer were already secured for the opera. Hartmann showed a keen interest in *Ravnen* and agreed to take on the project.[84] On 28 May Andersen submitted the text to the Royal Theater for approval. Christian Molbech was the first to read the submission, and he began his report to the Theater with a general discussion of romantic opera. Although Molbech clearly did not agree with Andersen's assertion that 'romantic opera is *the only truth*' (an idea Andersen got from E.T.A Hoffmann), he nonetheless concurred that a libretto for such an opera should be one that 'gives a composer ... the richest and perhaps most sacred material....' Mozart's *Magic Flute* and *Don Giovanni*, Weber's *Der Freischütz*, 'and many other operas like them' were listed as the finest examples of 'romantic opera' since they had enjoyed 'the greatest and most universal success....' About Andersen's libretto in particular, Molbech continued with the following comments:

The author's treatment of the subject by Gozzi is both fantastical and romantic enough (actually, mostly *the former*) to give the rich material needed for such a musical drama; and I can do nothing but find the manner in which the author has used it good enough for the following recommendation: to serve as the text for an opera. The modifications he has made to Gozzi's piece, which he altogether followed rather closely, were not done without judicious consideration of the changed character the piece has received in revision. The author has not been as successful with the comic parts and characters, which are less complete and less characteristic of Gozzi. His versification is *on the whole* flowing, and in my view not inappropriate for the musical composition. However, what success the work will have depends completely on ... whether the composer has genius and art enough to make a good opera out of the author's work, which [the author] himself could only describe as ... 'a ribbon upon which the composer shall string his pearls.'[85]

Molbech continued by explaining that the Theater could go ahead and accept the libretto without the completed music, but maintained that such a decision would be risky given the composer's youth and inexperience. He suggested a compromise: Hartmann would complete the music for the first act, and then a final decision would be made concerning the quality of the opera as a whole.[86] The second censor, Ludvig Manthey, agreed to this compromise, but in general he found little worth in Andersen's submission:

In any other form *Ravnen* would be unacceptable for the stage; as an opera libretto it depends completely on the music, which cannot be judged until it is completely finished. Therefore, I recommend that we refrain from offering an opinion until both the libretto and score are submitted.[87]

Andersen turned *Ravnen* over to Hartmann and set to work immediately on another libretto – this time for a singspiel. Entitled *Bruden fra Lammermoor* (The Bride of Lammermoor), the libretto was closely based on the popular novel by Walter Scott.[88] Having learned his lesson with *Ravnen*, Andersen sought out a well-established composer, Ivar Bredal, to serve as his collaborator before he submitted the libretto to the Royal Theater, and this foresight proved beneficial. The censors' reports were encouraging. Molbech was impressed with Andersen's ability to capture the essence of Scott's novel in a work for the stage, and it surprised him that a Danish author had never attempted to dramatize his novels before. About the libretto specifically he wrote:

Although the author of the singspiel in question can be said to have borrowed each and every scene, situation, and character from the famous English novelist, it cannot be denied that in doing so he has shown that there is poetry in his songs and that he has united the most prominent moments to a hero who is undeniably more epic than dramatic, but has enough of the latter for a singspiel, where more attention is given to situations, effect, and the opportunity for the composer to express his ideas than to the plot's dramatic and artistic development.[89]

Manthey, the second censor, was still unimpressed by Andersen's attempts to write for the stage, but he apparently had nothing against the composer 'trying his luck' with the libretto.[90]

Both *Ravnen* and *Bruden fra Lammermoor* premièred at the Royal Theater in 1832.[91] *Ravnen* was performed a total of six times to mixed reviews,[92] while *Bruden fra Lammermoor* fared a bit better. Indeed, one of Andersen's early patrons, the composer C.E.F. Weyse, was particularly impressed with *Bruden fra Lammermoor*, and he commissioned Andersen to write a libretto based on another Scott novel, *Kenilworth*.[93] Andersen set to work on the commission right away, and six weeks later, on 22 June, submitted the new libretto to the Royal Theater. Unlike before, the censors took two full months to critique the work. Obviously unimpressed by the Theater's production of *Bruden fra Lammermoor*, they were cautious about the creation of yet another stage work based on a Walter Scott novel.[94] In his report to the Theater dated 28 July, the first censor, Molbech, wrote:

> This opera text leaves a very bad impression.... The manner in which the author
> has handled both this piece and *Bruden fra Lammermoor* shows that he is far from
> having the superior gifts for the difficult work of making a play out of a novel and
> consequently chooses the easier [task] of bringing a *dialogued novel* to stage. If I
> must judge according to the impression that this new Andersen product has had
> upon me while reading it – it interests me as little and bores me as much as seeing
> the performance of the previously named 'Bride.' But since [*Bruden fra
> Lammermoor*] managed to have some success in performance, and since it seems
> the public was content with all the slapdash, coarse, and immature talent thrown
> together in the singspiel, I will not hinder Mr. Andersen and Mr. Weyse in their
> attempt to give the public a similar sort of pleasure with this trash.[95]

The second censor, L. Kirstein, rejected the libretto completely: '[The work] must be returned to Mr. Andersen, and he or someone else must go through the entire text and meticulously revise and correct it before submitting it to the Theater again in a legible and proper copy (not like this rough draft here).'[96]

Andersen received a formal rejection letter on 8 September. Although the censors could find no redeemable features in Andersen's libretto, he was nonetheless given permission to resubmit the text after extensive revision. The letter concluded by stating that, despite the low quality of Andersen's text, *Festen paa Kenilworth* would eventually be produced at the Royal Theater due to the prestige and talent of the opera's composer, C.E.F. Weyse.

If Andersen was despondent about the criticism he received concerning *Festen paa Kenilworth*, it did not dissuade him from pushing on with new projects. Three days after receiving his rejection letter, he submitted another libretto – this one for a patriotic, one-act opera called *Den anden April* (The Second of April). Like his previous submissions, *Den anden April* was a dramatization of a well-known story – in this case the infamous day in 1801 when the British navy attacked Copenhagen's naval harbor. The intended composer was an amateur musician named Christian Wulff (1810–56), who, in addition to being a lieutenant in the Danish navy, was the son of Admiral Peter Frederik Wulff, one of Andersen's early patrons. Despite such prestigious military connections, the censors were obviously unimpressed by both the text and music:

This most weakly composed, terribly dialogued and horribly versified work could only be considered for production through goodwill or because of the musical composition's excellence: but since the latter is no better than the text, there can be no talk of producing this work.... That this day in Denmark's naval history, which is unforgettable in more ways than one, could be properly honored or remembered by the performance of a product so poor seems impossible; furthermore it would not be correct politically.... The work's only redeemable feature is that it is very short.[97]

The harsh criticism found in this last rejection appears to have finally had an effect on Andersen. It was not just his errors in punctuation and spelling that irritated the censors; it was his lack of creativity, his tendency to 'retell' other writers' stories and tales from the past. Andersen could no longer submit first drafts to the Theater – his relationship with the censors was too tenuous. If he hoped to salvage his status as a legitimate librettist, he would need to submit something well crafted and inventive – something similar in style to the impromptu, light-hearted work that led to his first success, *Love on St. Nicholas Tower*. Intent on regaining Molbech's favor, Andersen set to work on two new vaudevilles: *Spanierne i Odense* (The Spaniards in Odense) and *25 Aar derefter* (25 Years Later).

Andersen hoped that the two vaudevilles would be performed together, since both featured the same pair of star-crossed lovers, a Danish girl named Augusta and a Spanish soldier, Frederico. In the first work, the lovers meet during the Spanish occupation of Odense in 1808. Augusta is attracted to the exotic, young soldier, but her sense of duty and fear of becoming ostracized cause her to marry a local boy named Ludvig instead. The vaudeville ends with Frederico and the rest of the Spanish soldiers marching off into the distance. The second vaudeville takes place, as the title indicates, twenty-five years later. Augusta and Frederico meet once again, and this time the story ends on a happier note. Augusta is now a widow, and she takes joy in the fact that her daughter Louise has fallen in love with Diego, the son of a Spanish Ambassador, who at the end of the vaudeville proves to be none other than Augusta's long-lost lover, Frederico.

Andersen worked on the pair of vaudevilles for five months, and letters from the time reveal that he took the project seriously: 'Do not imagine that my new vaudeville will ridicule the dear town of my birth; no, the play is sentimental, very serious, written from the heart. I read some scenes for Heiberg recently, and they pleased him greatly because of the melancholy tone.'[98]

Unfortunately, the censors at the Royal Theater did not share Heiberg's enthusiasm. Andersen submitted the vaudevilles in March, and on 4 April Molbech gave his opinion of the pieces:

I have just learned from reading this vaudeville pair, neither of which has anything to offer in the least, that Mr. Andersen intends to scribble – or, if one wants a finer word, create – a vaudeville with the same inferior, childish, bungling, truncated goose feather that he uses to write his opera libretti. But what the creator seems to have forgotten in his blithe, fanciful dream is that one lets a lot pass in an opera libretto – because the composer has many opportunities to cast a veil of notes over the author's exposed parts (pudenda) – that one cannot let go unpunished in a vaudeville. This work is far below what I had imagined; and because this, the first original dramatic work of Mr. Andersen's that I have read, ... is so feeble, unpoetic and tasteless, so sloppy, one could say so foppish and childishly handled, I would no sooner want to recommend its production than I would want to see a single scene of it performed.[99]

Molbech continued by saying that reading the vaudevilles had nearly caused him 'to become enraged at the author,' and declared that he would not 'waste any more time' giving a detailed critique of the submission. An unnamed second censor agreed with Molbech, stating that their rejection of the vaudeville was due to the low quality of Andersen's submission, 'not the result of envy or any other sort of personal grudge.'[100]

But Andersen did not believe them. Convinced that the censors at the Royal Theater were conspiring against him, he decided to leave Copenhagen and seek his fortune in the other capitals of Europe. With the help of Edvard Collin (Jonas Collin's son and Andersen's life-long friend and advisor), he secured a travel grant from *Ad usus publicos*, an endowment set up by the king to benefit the advancement of Danish artists and scholars, and made plans for his departure. As his album book from the time reveals, Andersen's many friends and patrons visited him during his last week in Copenhagen and wished him well.

With a generous stipend and a renewed sense of artistic purpose, Andersen bid farewell to the city that he believed had so cruelly forsaken him. There was nothing more his friends and patrons in Copenhagen could do for him; he would now have to find his own way in the world. With this goal in mind, Andersen boarded a ship in Copenhagen's central harbor on 22 April 1833 and set sail for foreign shores.

Interlude 1

An Excerpt from *Shadow Pictures from a Trip in the Harz Mountains, Switzerland etc. etc. in the Summer of 1831*

by Hans Christian Andersen

Chapter XIII

... With a letter of introduction from Ørsted I visited the poet Adelbert von Chamisso. He is, as is well known, a Frenchman by birth who was an officer and since then has traveled around the world as a naturalist and is now in Berlin with a post at the Botanical Garden. I was very eager to see him, the author of *Peter Schlemils wundersame Geschichte.* I walked in and Peter Schlemil himself stood before me in the flesh, at the very least in the exact same form that is found on the copperplate of the book – a tall, thin figure with long, grey curls down to his shoulders and with an open, good-natured face. He was wearing a brown smoking jacket, and a swarm of red-headed children were playing all around him. With the innermost warmth he welcomed me, and I now had an acquaintance in the foreign city.

In the evening Weber's *Oberon* was performed at the opera house. It pleased me greatly, and although I had secured a place in the 'reserved seating,' I was one of the first to arrive. Here is surely where I should have first gotten my idea of what opera is, to see how the painting of the scenery is handled as an art in itself and what machinery can really do. After the overture, someone called 'Da Capo.' And as the curtain rose, the overture was repeated. This gave me the opportunity to study the splendid scenery and the pretty groups [of characters]. Here Oberon did not lie on a solid bed, as he does with us [in Denmark]. No, the entire airy hall was planted with lilies. He lay in one of the lily's swinging cups, and all around in the other lilies stood smiling genies. Meanwhile, the more grown-up [genies] floated around in a light, airy dance. Each piece of scenery was a true artwork, as was the layout of the entire stage. But the machinery – *mirabile dictu* – was bad, especially given the theater's resources. I call it bad because the clouds got stuck half way, and a genie had to help glide them along. Also, the otherwise beautiful ocean scenery in the second act was ruined for those seated in the middle of the parquet on the second row: although the wind appeared true to life, one could see over the flying carpet right into the uppermost loft. All of the lighting was very splendid, one saw the stars come out little by little; if only the loft had not come out as well, then it would have been blessed! The scene changes were also a bit off, and when the Persian [Abdullah] was at sea [in his ship] one could also spot one of the machinists walking over the surface of the water, this shocked me quite a bit, although I had also seen similar effects at home. I was told that generally it never goes as badly as it did this evening, and that the machinery is a true artwork – obviously tonight was just a bad night; I'll just let it slide by adding that. Such things, however, can at least still be found in Berlin's large theater, where the resources are so great. What should we say about our small theater, where such things are almost nonexistent? A Madam Walker, maiden-name Gehse, prima donna of the Royal Theater in Dresden, acted the part of Reiza. Acted? – Indeed, I dare not step forward as a critic – but with most singers one can still set a question mark after this word. She also bowed in the German manner every time there was applause, and when she was called out again at the end of the opera, she was obviously moved emotionally – and this was genuine, for it was self evident in her performance. She said a few words to us about her gratitude and that she would come again soon. Nonetheless, her singing was beautiful. Mr. Bade acted and sang Huon's part. He is a handsome man in whom I found both an actor and a singer. A *pas de deux* by Mr. and Madam Taglioni, also one by Miss St. Romain and Mr. Stullmüller received what some here at home call storming applause, and they certainly earned this success.

Concerning machinery, it went better in the Königstädtisches Theater. I was here a few nights later and saw 'ein großes romantisches Zauberspiel von Adolph Bäurle, mit neuen Decorationen und neuer Maschinerie' entitled *Lindane oder der Pantoffelmacher im Feenreich*. It was a true mishmash of nothing – a watered-down soup colored with beautiful melodies and dressed up in scenery like buns and vegetables. I believe to have almost dreamed something similar. At the very least, here there was the type of loose coherence that is usually found in a dream. Of the melodies, the most notable were a mournful duet, a spinning song, and a big singing number that was undoubtedly composed of forty different melodies from *Der Freischütz, La Muette de Portici, Don Giovanni*, etc., which Miss Vio, a fantastic figure on the stage, presented. I also saw here the two well-known comedians, Schmelka and Spitzeder, the second of whom performed 'der Pantoffelmacher,' the story of a commoner, who, on his wedding day, receives a letter stating that his cousin is dying and that he must go to him without delay. But then during the trip through the forest ... he is snapped up by a fairy who holds him so dear that, in the end, she gives him her magic wand.... The scenery and scene changes are something to see, from [Italy's] 'Tivoli' to a steam engine that sails in the air with passengers, and a whole tent scene that springs up out of a cup.

In the third theater here, the actual, so-called 'Schauspielhaus,' I got to see the old Devrient as Uncle Brand, in a comedy by the same name, after the French. With the greatest naturalness and truth he presented this character, this 'hothead' with the warm heart. His presentation, acting, and entire costume made such a living impression on me that it seemed as though I had already lived a long time with the good Mr. Brand. I can not imagine Devrient in any other role, without some of his Uncle Brand slipping in, and yet it is not by accident that he can give his characters so much variety. Schylock in Shakespeare's *Merchant of Venice* was apparently his first role.

In a large city it is thus quite convenient that there are many theaters to choose from, but when good works are being presented the same evening àt all of them, one can also come in conflict with oneself, for it is impossible to be in more than one place at a time. I truly felt this here one evening. The French Society presented three vaudeville by Scribe in the 'Schauspielhaus': 1) *La devote*, 2) *La famille Riquebourg*, and 3). *Les premieres amours*. In 'Charlottenburg': the comedy *Der Fächer* and the posse *Der Nasenstüber*. In 'Königstädtisches Theater': *Das Mädchen aus der Feenwelt* oder *Der Bauer als Millionär*, and in the opera house they were performing the famous ballet *Die neue Amazone*. In addition to this, Chamisso had invited me to go with him to the Zoo, where he wanted to introduce me to Berlin's splendid spirits. I felt like Hercules at the crossroads, and in the end followed Chamisso. At the Zoo I didn't find any wild animals, they were all tame Berliners, many warm-hearted and friendly people. Here a little festival had been set up in recognition of the poet Hölty's homecoming from Darmstadt, where he had given speeches and his wife, who is engaged at the 'Königstädtisches Theater,' had played some guest roles.

La Motte-Fouqué, Raupach, Clauren, and Streckfuss were all traveling; otherwise I would have wanted to have made their acquaintance. However, here there were still many whom I was quite happy to meet. I got a seat between Chamisso and Simrock, a young poet who had received a great deal of attention for his political poem 'Drei Tage und Drei Farben.' It got him fired from his post, but he nonetheless enjoys general admiration and waits to be appointed again. Here I also met the poet Hoffmann's friends; he knew Hitzig and was friends with Willibald Alexis (Häring), who warmly spoke about Denmark and the happy hours he experienced there with Oehlenschläger. A rare, warm feeling arises within when one hears good things about one's homeland while traveling in a foreign country, since one cannot help but feel that he is bone of its bone and flesh of its flesh. Just like each insult and every censure that seems to be allotted, it is only a small part of it. However, it happens here just as at home, where one always sets the homeland on the one side of the scale and yourself on the other.

In the evening there was entertainment, song, and fun. Here I felt that if I had owned St. Peter's glasses or von Tütz's [Hoffmann's Meister-Floh] microscopic glass, where one could see inside people and learn what they think, then Berlin would become the most interesting capital of the entire trip. Here, among a circle of 'Kaloi kai Agathoi,' we would see how an entire 'Liebes Roman' haunted one head, here a volume of attractive small poems, there politics, here polemics, there – – Indeed, there was also surely a head here that had absolutely nothing inside it.

Here there were otherwise many experiences, and all of them followed me home to Denmark, especially the deep affection for which they named their King, and to whom we drank the very first toast.

Fig. 2.1 Albert Küchler. Portrait of H.C. Andersen (1834).
          (Copenhagen: National Museum at Fredricksborg)

Chapter 2

The Improviser

I am nothing but an improviser!
Hans Christian Andersen

When Andersen set off on his tour of Europe in 1833, he believed his only hope for artistic survival was to leave Copenhagen. As he explained in a letter to Henriette Wulff: 'I have this abiding idea that only by being torn away from my immediate surroundings will I ever come to anything; if I have to stay here [in Copenhagen], I will be destroyed.'[1] Andersen's need to escape Denmark had been growing for several years. As early as December 1830 he wrote: 'I don't feel happy. I am not as I used to be; I feel I am getting older, I am beginning to recognize in life something far deeper than I ever dreamt of and feel that I shall never, never be really happy here.'[2] Two months later his mood grew even worse: 'Last year I was a gay, wandering minstrel who made fun of Werther, and now I am almost the same fool. Life has already shown me its darkest sides; how I wish it were all over. Yes, how peculiarly romantic it sounds ... I do wish that I were dead!'[3]

In an effort to rid himself of his melancholy, Andersen made a brief tour of Germany in the summer of 1831 and visited with authors such as Ludwig Tieck and Adelbert von Chamisso. His intent was to reinvigorate his imagination and strengthen his reputation as an author. Although the trip was successful and led to the publication of *Skyggebilder af en Reise til Harzen* (Shadow Pictures of a Journey to the Harz Mountains) and *Phantasier og Skizzer* (Fantasies and Sketches), works inspired by Heinrich Heine's *Die Harzreise* and *Buch der Lieder*, respectively,[4] the relief that came from Andersen's respite quickly dissipated. As criticism against Andersen's theatrical works increased at the Royal Theater, his need to escape again grew ever stronger. Andersen's European tour of 1833–34 marked his first extended visit outside the borders of his homeland. Passing through Germany first and then France and Switzerland, his ultimate goal was to visit Italy – the cradle of civilization and, more importantly, the birthplace of opera.[5]

When Andersen left Copenhagen, he was only marginally known outside Denmark; but that did not stop him from calling on established individuals whom he hoped might aid him in his pursuit of a career as a librettist. Although many descriptions of Andersen's first extended trip abroad have been printed over the years, none have focused on the fact that the personalities he sought out on his way to Italy were all strongly connected to the theater – either as composers, librettists, and/or critics. On his journey across Germany, Andersen's first order of business was to pass through Kassel and call on the composer Ludwig Spohr:

> At 7:00 I went out to visit Spohr, the composer of *Jessonda, Faust, Zemire and Astor*, etc.... Spohr had a little room on the first floor that looked out on the harbor and city. There he sat at a table and composed music. At first he gave me a cold and serious look, but his face soon brightened.[6]

By the time of Andersen's visit in April 1833, Spohr had already firmly established his reputation as a composer and conductor. The triumphant production of *Jessonda* in 1823 had done much to confirm his position as one of Germany's leading composers, and his reputation had been further strengthened by the production of his oratorio *Die letzten Dinge* at the Lower Rhine Festival of 1826.[7] Spohr was famous throughout Europe by the early 1830s, and his attentions in Kassel were primarily centered on the production of new operas.[8] Andersen's diary entry of 30 April reveals that the majority of their visit was spent discussing German and Danish opera: '[Spohr] believed [Kuhlau's] *Røverborgen* was completely German. He promised to take a look at Hartmann's *Ravnen* and asked me whether there were finales in the piece.'[9] Spohr studied Hartmann's music closely and voiced an interest in producing the opera in Kassel.[10] Taking the composer's interest in his work as a cue, Andersen continued their conversation by describing the wealth of music in Copenhagen: 'I told him about [the composers] Bredal and Berggreen, and he said that Denmark was the only country that could have a repertoire of original music.'[11] They talked about literary works that would serve well as models for opera, plays by the Danish authors Baggesen, Oehlenschläger, and especially 'Kruse, whom [Spohr] had lived with in Naples.' They 'read aloud [Kruse's] tragedy *Enken*' and discussed Spohr's opera *Zemire and Astor*.[12] Spohr was eager to have the work premiered in Copenhagen, and Andersen regretted having to relate to the composer that none of his operas had ever been performed in Denmark.[13] But Spohr apparently did not take offense at the news; he treated Andersen as an equal and expressed an interest in working with him in the future. 'At the end of the visit, he wrote a canon in my album,[14] asked me to give his greetings to Weyse and the Danish musicians ... shook my hand warmly, and showed me the way through the garden.'[15]

From Kassel Andersen continued to Frankfurt, where he sought out the tenor Friedrich Schmertzer and the composer Aloys Schmitt (1788–1866). Schmitt's opera *Valeria* had recently enjoyed a successful run in Mannheim, and Andersen was eager to make contact with the rising star. On 4 May Andersen and Schmertzer visited Schmitt, an encounter later recorded in Andersen's diary:

> We walked across Rossmarkt, known from Hoffmann's *Meister Floh*, and through the gate to Aloys Schmitt, who was especially hospitable and ended up requesting me to write the text for an opera for him; he wanted something from a young, fiery spirit. In my album he wrote an excerpt from his *Valeria*.[16]

Schmitt was already familiar with Andersen's work before their encounter – he had read the German translation of some of Andersen's poems that Adelbert von Chamisso had published in 1832 and was impressed by the poet's romantic, sentimental style. But Andersen was wary about entering into a new opera project too quickly. As he explained in a letter home several days later: 'I excused myself due to my lack of fluency in the German language. But [Schmitt] said he would wait, that he would even be happy with just a rough outline that someone else could supplement.'[17] Still, Andersen never accepted the commission – he was eager to move on to Paris. In addition, he was already hard at work on a new dramatic project:

> The idea for a literary work occupied my thoughts more and more, and as it became clearer to me I began to hope that I might win over my enemies with it. It was an old, Danish folk ballad about *Agnete and the Merman*. ... I was free in my lyrical and dramatic adaptation of the ballad. Indeed, I dare say it all grew out of my heart, and every memory of [Denmark's] beech forests and the open sea came together in it.[18]

The story of Agnete and the Merman exists in many versions. In its earliest ballad form (ca. eighteenth century), Agnete is portrayed as a selfish, rebellious girl who deserts her family to live with the Merman and bear his children, only to callously abandon him as well at the end of the story. Contrary to this simple, ego-centric characterization, the Agnete of most nineteenth-century versions, including Andersen's, displays loving feelings of familial loyalty. She is torn between her loyalty to God (being a faithful wife) and her love for the Merman.[19]

Andersen's work on the drama progressed quickly. On 28 May he wrote to Edvard Collin from Paris:

> I have been very industrious; I have already written the first scenes of 'Agnete,' and I am pleased with them. I won't send anything home until I have a large section completed that is more worthy than anything else I have written until now. At the very least I will force my enemies into silence.[20]

Andersen remained in Paris for just over three months, and as he explained in his autobiography, 'I saw, or rather I spoke, with few celebrities in Paris.' This being said, it is interesting to note that the people Andersen did seek out during his visit were all associated with the theater in one way or another. 'One of those to whom I was introduced by a letter from the Danish ballet-master, Bournonville, was the vaudeville-poet, Paul Duport. His drama *The Quaker and the Dancer* has been performed at our theater and was very well executed. The old man was much pleased to hear this information and received me very kindly.'[21]

Andersen's next encounter was with the composer Cherubini. Apparently Weyse supplied Andersen with the needed letter of introduction; he also asked Andersen to deliver a copy of his 'Ambrosian Hymn of Praise' to Cherubini. 'Cherubini was old, but looked quite genial. He didn't know Weyse, but asked about Professor Schall.'[22] Andersen was no doubt excited by his encounter with the composer. As he later explained, 'At this very time the attention of the Parisian public was attracted to him. He had just composed a new grand opera, *Ali-Baba* or *The Forty Thieves*.'[23] *Ali-Baba* was the most ambitious score Cherubini had ever produced. Encompassing more than one thousand manuscript pages, the opera told the story of a father who gave away his daughter in unwanted marriage purely to satisfy his own greed. Cherubini paid close attention to the instrumentation of *Ali-Baba* in an effort to give the entire work a 'fairy tale' atmosphere and make the characters more dramatic. But the ensembles were not as effectively engaging as the choruses in the political and religious plots of Auber's *La muette de Portici* (1828), Rossini's *Guillaume Tell* (1829), and Meyerbeer's *Robert le Diable* (1831),[24] models of grand opera with which *Ali-Baba* was unfavorably compared. Despite a lavish production at the Paris Opéra with Habeneck conducting, a production that Andersen possibly saw, *Ali-Baba* folded after eleven performances.

In addition to the work of Cherubini, Andersen sought out performances of operas by other composers active in Paris. On 15 May he attended a performance of Auber's *Gustavus III*, which fueled an instant interest in the city's finest singers.[25] Andersen was particularly taken with the talents of Madame Damoreau and Adolph Nourrit. 'Nourrit was then in his full vigor, and was the favorite of the Parisians.'[26] But it was the grandeur of the theater's interior and scenery that remained in Andersen's memory when he recorded his visit to the Paris Opéra in his diary:

> Paris is the place! Berlin, Hamburg, and Copenhagen, all of them are nothing....
> This evening I was at the grand opera house, ... a gigantic building painted white
> and red with gilding. Between the loges, arabesques and sphinxes hover over one
> another ... I counted thirty chandeliers and twenty candelabras.... The music and
> acting were similar to that at home, but the sets! Indeed, now for the first time, I
> have an idea of how these things can be! They were performing *Gustavus III*.
> The costumes were relatively accurate, and the first interior, like a re-creation of
> the real thing. Everything regal and grand. In the second act you were looking out
> a window – ships in the harbor, a clear, bright day, as in nature. But in the third
> act! Oh, if only everybody could have been here to see it! The setting was the
> environs of Stockholm – the moon was mirrored in the water; light shone from
> windows in Stockholm; clouds drifted lightly through the air, where you could see
> up into God's great, blue heaven.[27]

Andersen's letters home reveal that a new world had opened up to him in Paris. The French theater was unlike anything he had ever experienced in Denmark and Germany. His encounter with Parisian opera overwhelmed his senses and caused him to look at his previous experiences in Copenhagen from a different point of view. Compared to the opera house in Paris, wrote Andersen (perhaps reflecting his own insecurities), the Royal Theater in Denmark was nothing but 'a spiritually well-endowed individual who is shabbily dressed and doesn't know how to behave himself.'[28] Andersen now realized, perhaps for the first time, just how provincial and unsophisticated his early experiences in Denmark had been in comparison to the theater world of France. He even came to understand how he must have appeared to his critics and colleagues during his early years in the theater. As Andersen's perspective on European theater traditions broadened, he shunned the shabbiness of Copenhagen's theater, and in doing so, quickly embraced a newfound self identity as an international traveler and connoisseur.

In addition to his interactions with French librettists and composers, Andersen made the acquaintance of several poets in Paris, most notably Heinrich Heine and Victor Hugo. As Andersen explained in a letter to Christian Voigt dated 26 June 1833, his first encounter with Heine was quite by accident:

> I had just been introduced to the 'Europe littéraire,' a kind of 'Athenæum' for Paris's beautiful spirits; I had decided *not* to seek out Heine, but the Creator willed that he was to be the first that I encountered here. He approached me in a rather friendly manner, talked very honorably about our literature and said, in a loud voice that all could hear, that Oehlenschläger was Europe's greatest poet. I was asked to give an overview of our literature, especially [the work of] Oehlenschläger, as well as the younger poets. This [overview] is now being translated into French and published; but you should not tell that to anyone who will talk of it again. – Heine visited me, or more correctly the doorman. I don't have his card. I will not, however, submit to him; I believe that one should be extremely careful of him.[29]

Such a mistrustful reaction from Andersen seems odd given his previous enthusiasm for Heine. What led to such suspicion? More than likely, it was the general reception Heine was receiving from critics across Europe at the time. When Andersen came in contact with Heine in 1833, the German poet had already earned a somewhat dubious reputation as a journalist. As a correspondent for the *Allgemeine Zeitung* in Augsburg, he painted a lively portrait of the Parisian music scene in the 1830s. Witty, brilliant, and sometimes malicious, his writings on music were among the first to focus on social issues, as he documented the important shift in cultural dominance from the private salon to the large audiences of the public concert hall.[30] This shift in literary genres, from poetry to journalism, was not always warmly received. As early as 1830, German critics began to comment on how Heine's move to Paris had led to a change in personality and poetic attitude. For example, in a review of *Reisebilder III*, Moritz Veit wrote that Heine's poetic brilliance was being fatally damaged by the influence of 'conventional society:'

> Swept into the midst of the enticing bustle of cosmopolitan corruption and excessive delicacy, Heine has poisoned the innocence of his heart; without being able to destroy it totally and without definitively choosing one side or the other, he alternates between both: at one point, sorrows at the pain of a lost paradise in an elegiac sigh, or in a long-forgotten fairy tale, breaks through the bitter pain of the present; at the next, he anesthetizes this pain through bitter mockery which turns against that which he loves most, against himself or against the object of his yearning.[31]

No doubt it was this malicious side of Heine, and his reportedly quixotic temperament, that Andersen wished to avoid. As Andersen tried to sever his contact with Heine during his final weeks in Paris, he aggressively sought out the acquaintance of Victor Hugo (1802–85):

> The first French book I tried to read in Paris was Victor Hugo's novel *Notre-Dame de Paris*. I used to visit the cathedral daily and look upon the scenes depicted in that poetic work. I was captivated by those stirring pictures and dramatic characters, and what could I do better than go and see the poet who lived in a corner house in the Place Royale?[32]

In a letter to Henriette Wulff dated 23 August, Andersen described the encounter:

> I was told that he wasn't home, but I said, 'I am leaving tomorrow!' and then I was received. He resembled the portrait you have, only he is thinner and looks younger.... We sat down together, talked about Danish literature, but he did not even know Oehlenschläger. I believe I could be fond of him as a person; there was something about him I really did like.[33]

Greater insight into the visit can be found in Andersen's diary, where he reports that Hugo 'received me in his nightgown, underwear, and elegant slippers.'[34] Andersen no doubt wanted to impress upon Hugo the idea that the two had a great deal in common when it came to their pursuits in literature and the world of opera. In general, literary historians have presented Hugo as being rather hostile toward music, but this is something of a misconception. It is true that Hugo generally opposed the production of musical works based on his plays, but he nonetheless revered music quite highly, especially what he referred to as 'retrospective music.' Almost uniquely among contemporary writers, Hugo praised the concerts put on by Fétis in the early 1830s, where the music of Palestrina, Monteverdi, and Pergolesi was revived and presented to the public.[35] Hugo introduced Andersen to the idea of music's historical essence, its ability to reflect the social and cultural norms of its age. For Hugo, music served as a mirror of society – a reflection of popular taste and concerns. Hugo praised the operas of Mozart and, more often, Gluck, betraying a preference for strong links between an opera's text and its music. He was especially wary of operas where the libretto was altered by the composer or given secondary importance to the music, so much so that he brought lawsuits against productions of *Lucrezia Borgia* and *Rigoletto* simply to defend his copyright. According to Hugo, Weber's *Der Freischütz* and *Euryanthe* were some of the finest musical works ever written. Above all he admired Beethoven, whom he hailed as 'the greatest thinker' in all music, and whom he always placed among the great geniuses of humanity.

Andersen was eager to establish a professional contact with Hugo, and it appears he asked the poet for a letter of recommendation. When this was not possible, Andersen settled for the next best thing. 'Taking leave of him, I asked him for his name on a sheet of paper. He complied with my wishes, and wrote his name close up to the edge of the paper.'[36] Apparently, Hugo suspected that

Andersen might later try to forge a false accolade above his name.

In September, Andersen traveled to Le Locle, Switzerland, where he completed the final section of *Agnete and the Merman* and then sent it on to Edvard Collin with the following letter:

> Herein I send you my Agnete completely finished; so far no eye has seen it but my own.... Be kind to the good child, who was born between the mountains but is Danish at heart.... If only Agnete may now receive air and sunshine.... Be a father for my Agnete.... Dear friend, how my heart pounds as I now pack Agnete off! What if it is not the work that I hope and wish it to be? Now it seems I haven't said at all what I wanted, and yet I know nothing better.... Oh, let me soon hear something from you, something about Agnete.[37]

With *Agnete and the Merman* complete and out of his hands, Andersen was ready to move on to his long-awaited goal, Italy. It is clear from Andersen's diary that he expected much from the land south of the Alps. Many Danes, most notably the artist Bertel Thorvaldsen, had already immigrated to Italy and found great fame and fortune there. In Andersen's mind, the Alps became the threshold to destiny. As he crossed the Italian border on 19 September he wrote in his diary: 'It is with a sickening feeling that I leave this side of the Alps – I almost said Europe. Well, in the name of God, now begins my journey out into the world. May the Lord let it go for me as best as it can!'[38]

Andersen's diary clearly reveals the impact his travels through Italy had on his artistic sensibility. In the 1830s, Italy was unlike any other place in Europe. Music surrounded one constantly, and Andersen kept a detailed record of each and every encounter with it, from hearing the castrati in St. Peter's Basilica in Rome to the gondoliers in Venice and the gypsy musicians in Genoa and Florence. On 20 September Andersen arrived in Milan, where he was struck by the profusion of music that surrounded him and the grandeur of the opera theater La Scala. The next day, he wrote:

> This evening I went to the Teatro alla Scala, where *I due Sergenti*, a melodrama by Luigi Ricci, was performed; it was about two men who are condemned to die. One is pardoned, and they throw the dice to see which one it will be. – The recitatives were only accompanied by a cello; they were so boring that I wasn't surprised when the Italians talked to one another during the performance. Next came *Giuditta Regina di Francia*, a beautiful ballet without any real plot. The manner in which they performed it was quite unusual, each movement was exaggerated; they looked like marionettes. Everything was strongly accentuated; the old king in silver with a gold crown looked like the king of diamonds [from a set of cards] and had a true Pierrot face; he looked so funny in his confusion. – The theater itself has six floors of boxes with curtains of blue silk and a huge chandelier. The muses are painted on the ceiling. – The royal box is right in the middle with a chandelier. Entrance cost around two francs.[39]

Ten days later, in Genoa, Andersen gave another lengthy description of a visit to the opera:

I went to the opera at eight o'clock. All the houses along the way were palaces, with each one I believed I had reached the theater. In one house a man was singing down in the cellar and a woman's voice answered from the top floor; there was such an eternal harmony therein that people gathered around and listened. The theater wasn't as large as La Scala, but still very large – six floors, white and gold. Over the curtain was a transparent clock that showed the hour and minutes. – They performed *L'elisir d'amore*, but with new Italian music; between acts there was a ballet: *Il flauto magico.*[40]

A look at Andersen's diary reveals that every week was punctuated by several visits to the theater. Captivated by the elaborate scenery and virtuosic vocal displays, Andersen soon became a man obsessed. As he wrote in his diary on 25 January 1834: 'I long for music like a man sick with fever longs for a drop of water.'[41] He was addicted to Italian opera, and he sought it out in any form available, be it in grand theaters like La Scala or lowly puppet theaters. After each performance, he returned to his quarters and recorded an informal review in his diary.

1 October: Comic opera is a good buy here in Italy – In Genoa there is a second theater, Teatro Diurno.[42]

9 October, Florence: We went to the opera, a beautifully lighted building. Five floors. They performed *Ciara di Rosenberg*, music by Ricci, and a ballet *L'Orfanea di Velberg*. In the opera there was a brute of a knight with bowed legs, in the ballet an elderly, well-built dancer.... All the works of art, all the great things I saw have taught me that I knew nothing, could do nothing! If only what I know and understand *now* could have begun at age seventeen; there is so much to learn and so little time![43]

10 October: In the evening we were in Teatro Soletico and saw *Donna Caritea, Regina di Spagna* with music by Mercadente. – [The theater] was a dirty little crate with three cramped floors. Entrance cost one-half *poul* (10 shilling Dansk). The female lover wasn't so bad but perhaps a little old. Both she and her lover had bare hands. The whole thing was mediocre; one could become melancholy over it.[44]

21 October, Rome: Was in the theater; it was large and filthy. Bad sets, *Due case in una casa* and an opera, *Orlando furioso al Isola* [Donizetti's *Il furioso all'isola di S. Domingo*] – I left after seeing one act of each part.[45]

30 October: Was in the theater and saw a comedy and Bellini's opera *La Sonambula*, which seems to be a parody on our beautiful ballet. The choristers looked like milkmaids from Fyn, and one was blind, one had a harelip and a third was missing a nose. La sonambula herself was pretty. Bad sets.[46]

5 November: In the evening went to the puppet theater. It only cost three *bajok* and we received a whole comedy; a superb Casander and marvelous dancers. It lasted only an hour; the attendance was very good.[47]

29 December: Went this evening to Teatro Alibert, the largest in Rome and where the carnival masquerade is held. There are five balconies, and like the French Opéra, it was packed, but received a miserable performance of *Il Barbiere di Siviglia*. The voices sounded like they were wrapped up in wool. Miserable acting, or more accurately, no [acting] at all. A terrible Count, who looked like a dressed-up shoemaker's boy; when he played the drunken soldier, he seemed to

really be in his element. Figaro was a cheeky, flippant youth. Bazile was almost dressed like a Jesuit except for the Pierrot-face.... The audience clapped for everything. There was also a ballet, acrobats; in all nine acts and all of it for only one *poul* (one Danish mark). At 9:30 there were still five acts to go when I left.[48]

In Naples Andersen heard the voices of Italy's best singers, and he was especially moved by the artistry of Maria Malibran (1808–36). Andersen first heard Malibran sing on 23 February 1834 in a performance of Bellini's *Norma*. On 11 March he heard her again, this time in Rossini's *Il Barbiere di Siviglia*. In his diary, Andersen recorded his impressions of the singer: 'Malibran was a pretty Rosina.... Her voice was like a swan that first beats its wings against the high ethereal currents and then dips down into the deep sea and splits the hollow surf.'[49]

Andersen was fascinated by the universality of music in Italy, and as he traveled from one city to the next, the wealth and variety of Italian musical forms fueled his creative ideas: 'If France is the land of reason, then Italy is the land of imagination (Germany and Denmark, of the heart).'[50]

Andersen's first three months in Italy were perhaps some of the happiest of his life. But on 16 December, dark clouds passed over his sunny disposition. A letter from Jonas Collin arrived. Andersen's mother had died – and to make matters worse, Heiberg had enclosed a scathing review of Andersen's last two attempts at writing for the theater. Andersen was crushed; that night he wrote in his diary:

> There was a letter from Collin Senior; it reported my mother's death. My first reaction was: Thanks be to God! Now there is an end to her sufferings that I haven't been able to comfort. But even so, I cannot get used to the thought that I am so utterly alone without a single person who must love me because of the bond of blood. I also received some critical commentary from Heiberg about my two singspiels – I am nothing but an improviser![51]

But Andersen did not succumb to Heiberg's criticism; the art of improvisation was the core of his creative identity. From his earliest days in Copenhagen through his first success with the theater, he had depended on his active imagination and the use of the unexpected to gain the attention of patrons and audiences. At heart, Andersen truly was an improviser, and he refused to abandon the one quality that he believed most clearly defined his artistic genius. Heiberg's criticisms would not deter Andersen's pursuit of his own poetic voice. On the contrary, the condemnation that Andersen's work was nothing more than an 'improvisation' served as the motivational force behind what would prove to be his first full-fledged novel, *Improvisatoren* (The Improvisatore).

Andersen began work on *The Improvisatore* on 27 December, and within days turned Heiberg's criticism into the defining characteristic of the novel's protagonist, a young singer named Antonio, whose beautiful voice and gift for improvisation serve as a commentary on the role of the creative artist in society.[52] Inspiration for the story did not only come from the criticism Andersen had received from Denmark. His exposure to Italian culture, specifically theater and

Fig. 2.2 H.C. Andersen. Drawing of Thorvaldsen's house in Via Sistina in Rome. (Odense: The Andersen House)

literature, had an effect on his writing. Many of the musical encounters Andersen had recorded in his diary came to life again as descriptive episodes in the novel. Although many of these depictions were relatively accurate, a few were not. Occasionally, Andersen created fictional genres and experiences in an effort to promote his own ideas about creativity and musical genius. The most notable example involves the character Antonio and his talent and reception as an improvisatore. In creating the artistic identity of Antonio, Andersen blended two distinct artistic traditions of Italian culture: the poetic tradition of the improvisatore and the musical tradition of Italy's finest opera theaters.

In Andersen's novel, Antonio is a gifted improvisatore who uses his skills as a poet and singer to astonish listeners in Teatro San Carlo. After the audience suggests a variety of historical topics and literary themes, Antonio blends the various ideas together, much like a rhapsode would, into an operatic, one-man performance.

Contrary to the musical performances described in Andersen's novel, the dramatic presentations associated with the Italian improvisatore tradition were strictly literary in nature; they were never sung. Designed to show off the performer's memory, imagination, and formal education, the performances often took place in the literary academies that flourished throughout Italy during the seventeenth and eighteenth centuries. By the time Andersen was traveling through Italy in the 1830s, the art of the improvisatore was on the decline. Performances were rare, and the art form was slowly giving way to the more formalized practice of simply reciting pre-composed poems and speeches.

Andersen's diary reveals that he was on the lookout for an improvisatore when he entered Italy. While passing through the village of Nepi, he wrote: 'In the evening we heard a frightful squall from the street; I thought that it was an improvisatore, but it was a monk who was standing up on a stool in front of a wine shop. [He] had erected a cross beside himself and was preaching; at the end he shouted Viva Sancta Maria and all the people shouted Viva.'[53] Shortly after this experience, Andersen traveled to Rome, where he was finally exposed to the real thing.

Thanks to his connection with the Bertel Thorvaldsen, a famous Danish sculptor who had been living in Rome for many years, Andersen received tickets to two improvisatore performances. Unfortunately, he missed the first performance scheduled for 5 December when he could not find the meeting place of the Arcadian Academy. But he had better luck three days later:

> This evening, with Thorvaldsen's ticket, I went with Berg and Hertz to the Adademia Tibernia, a lovely locale with busts of Homer and other Italian poets, between each one there were flowers and a candle. Guards at the doors; three cardinals with their red hats and socks sat in the front. Just in front of them, on a platform, sat fifteen poets, among them many abbots and two senators. Each recited his poem; most of them half sung it with the most dramatic gestures. The audience applauded enthusiastically; [the poets] applauded reciprocally as well, but quite tastefully. It seemed that one did not highly appreciate the other; you could tell by the various sideway glances and the whispering. The one who was

supposed to recite did not listen to the one before him at all, but instead memorized his own work; nonetheless he clapped. It sounded as if it were a base subject that was sung with pindarsk escape. One had written a poem about Holophernes. Three were in Latin. Hertz went up to the busts and then said to me: 'I can't find yours.'[54]

Andersen's diary reveals that he clearly cherished each day he spent in Italy, and his experiences there reinvigorated his creative output. Although the thought of returning home was painful to Andersen, by the spring of 1834 his travel grant had begun to run low, and it became clear that he had no choice but to return to Denmark. Andersen left Italy in April, carrying little more than his diary and the first few chapters of *The Improvisatore*. His letters home reveal the melancholy mood induced by his travels north: 'I greatly fear going to Copenhagen. Northward, northward, there, where my dear ones live in snow and fog, awaits the iron ring to be fastened to my foot. Yes, yes. Denmark is a poor country! Italy's cornucopia is filled with fruit and flowers, while we have only grass and a sloe-hedge.' Having heard that a band of robbers had been sighted on the road between Rome and Florence, Andersen fantasized: 'Perhaps they will stab me to death. Then I shall die in Italy, and not return home, where much sorrow, much mischief ... are awaiting me.'[55]

Andersen's time in Italy had enabled him to view himself, no doubt for the first time, as an international writer and connoisseur; and during a month-long stopover in Munich he poured this new self-realization into the pages of *The Improvisatore*. A longing for the south shaped the work as he sketched prose-pictures of Italian life and culture and read numerous books about Italy: Goethe's *Italienische Reise* (Italian Journey 1786–87), Heine's *Reisebilder* (Travel Pictures, 1826–31), de Staël's *Corinne*, Rumohr's *Drey Reisen nach Italien* (Three Trips to Italy), and A.W. Kephalides' *Reise durch Italien und Sicilien* (Journey through Italy and Sicily).[56] In a letter to Henriette Wulff he wrote:

I have read many books about Italy – how empty they all are. Heine's little leap down to Lucca he might just as well have written in Hamburg; there is no sign of the Italian landscape in it. *Corinne* [by Madame de Staël, 1807] is a boring guide full of novel talk and criticism. Goethe alone gives something true, but it is so fragmentary. Is it impossible to express this superb impression?[57]

In creating his own image of Italy, Andersen planned to surpass what had come before. He hoped to give a clear image of the country he loved so dearly, but to do so through the eyes of an artist – the character Antonio, who by this point had become a thinly veiled portrait of Andersen himself.

In the past, scholars have described *The Improvisatore* as a travel novel, and although such a description is valid, it does not fully explain the work's literary purpose or Andersen's inspiration for writing it. Friedrich Schlegel was the first to contend that a work of criticism was in itself a work of art,[58] and Andersen clearly embraced this idea during the writing of his first novel. Andersen never met Schlegel, but he was familiar with the philosopher's ideas concerning Romanticism and was eager to attach aesthetic beliefs to the characters in his novel. While in Munich, Andersen sought out one of Schlegel's colleagues, the philosopher Friedrich Wilhelm Schelling: 'I went [to Schelling's house] and found a friendly man, who spoke with me a long time about Italy and then invited me to come into his family circle.'[59] This interaction with Schelling greatly influenced Andersen's approach to the writing of *The Improvisatore*. By placing music aesthetics and criticism at the core of his novel, Andersen presented readers with a commentary on the role of the artistic genius in society. His novel defended the dying art of improvisation and claimed that creativity and ingenious invention could serve as the foundation of any art form. The years of rejection Andersen had suffered in Copenhagen fueled his belief that a new aesthetic, similar to that found in German literature and Italian opera, needed to find its way into Denmark. Consequently, his exaltation of the critical process was essential to his rejection of earlier standards; to his invention of a new, romantic sensibility. In many ways, Andersen's placing of the critical act at the center of *The Improvisatore* was not so much an act of judgment against his critics as it was an act of personal understanding. *The Improvisatore* was Andersen's first substantial work of music criticism, and as such it served as a personal statement about what Andersen believed was his own artistic worth.

As Andersen approached Denmark, his resolve strengthened: he would no longer accept the petty criticisms offered by friends and critics. 'I won't stand for it!' he wrote. 'Now I will, and must, break old habits, otherwise these will persist for the rest of my life.'[60] But a sense of insecurity still reared its ugly head on occasion: 'The poet is dead, killed in Italy! If there is anything left of him when he returns to Scandinavia, I am sure they will finish him off. I know my people!'[61]

Andersen arrived in Copenhagen on 3 August 1834 and was heartened to find a warm reception awaiting him. 'I haven't been in such a good mood as I am now for a long time,' he wrote. 'I realize where I stand [and] see more clearly than before the value of those around me; and if a patronizing preacher appears, one of the sort who was so keen to educate me, then first I hear him out to see if it is some nonsense, and if I find that it is, then I rebuff him.... No one is going to treat me like a boy any longer.'[62]

With this new resolve, Andersen completed *The Improvisatore* and sent it off to his publisher, Carl Reitzel, on 28 March 1835. It appeared one month later in Copenhagen bookstores and proved an instant success. Andersen was thrilled. In a letter to Henriette Wulff he wrote:

> *The Improvisatore*, my novel, has now appeared in Danish. Never until now has a work of mine gripped the masses so intensely ... many people here who did not care about me are now devoted to me. Ingemann says that it marks the transition from youth to manhood in my writing .... Everyone is so kind, so nice to me; many even say that they had not anticipated anything like that from me. I am on the crest of a wave.[63]

Indeed, even Andersen's friend and fellow poet, Carl Bagger, noted that although Andersen had previously been considered a worn-out talent, *The Improvisatore* proved that he was 'not exhausted.' On the contrary, Andersen had 'swung himself into a position altogether unknown to him before.' He now 'shined in a most brilliant way.'[64]

Readers and critics alike recognized the message Andersen was sending them through the character of Antonio. Consequently only one reviewer was bold enough to criticize the work, shrewdly pointing out that Andersen's bestowal of musical talent on an improvisatore was erroneous, and that Madame de Staël's depiction of a non-musical improvisatrice in the novel *Corinne* was more authentic.[65] But this criticism had little influence on the reception of *The Improvisatore*. In general, Andersen's Danish readers were little interested in cultural accuracy. It was not the character of Antonio that enthralled them, but, rather, the musical calisthenics and amorous exploits of a secondary character in the novel, a prima donna named Annunziata. As Andersen himself once explained, he based the character of Annunziata on his impressions of Maria Malibran.[66] Through his descriptions of the prima donna's virtuosic performances, Andersen exposed Danish audiences to the music of many Italian opera composers for the first time. For example, one of Andersen's descriptions of Annunziata featured her performance in the opera buffa *La prova d'un opera seria* (1805) by Francesco Gvecco:

> Cheers and flowers greeted Annunziata when she walked on stage. She seemed full of joy, and although some called her mood mere acting, I could see that it was genuine. When her voice finally sounded, it was like a thousand silver bells that alternated in sweet harmonies, filling every heart with gladness. She sang of the joy that one could see in her eyes! The duet between Annunziata and [the tenor], in which the singers exchange parts, so that she sings the man's part and he the woman's, was a triumph for the virtuosity of both singers. But the audience was especially entranced by Annunziata's leap from the deepest contralto to the highest soprano.[67]

Through Andersen's descriptions of Annunziata, Danish readers experienced vicariously the virtuosic vocal displays of Italy's superstars and the grandeur of theaters like La Scala and San Carlo. An interest in Italian opera quickly became rooted in Denmark, and Andersen took advantage of the situation by publishing his first official piece of music criticism, an article entitled 'Music, Song, and the Theatrical Arts in Italy,' in the popular arts journal *Søndagsblad*.[68] In this article Andersen discussed the strengths and weaknesses of Italian opera, commenting on everything from dramatic plot and delivery to staging, orchestration, and recitative styles. He gave descriptions of Italy's theaters, from the fashionable La Scala in Milan to the folk theaters of Livorno and Naples. The works of Rossini, Donizetti, and Bellini were discussed in some detail, and attention was also given to the behavior of Italian audiences. Andersen concluded that the strange behavior of Italian audiences was no doubt due to what he considered some of the less favorable characteristics of Italian opera: i.e. *recitativo semplice* and the overuse of *da capo* arias:

> The recitatives at La Scala were accompanied by only a few string instruments. I found this style of recitative quite unusual and very boring. The Italians themselves simply ignored the recitatives, choosing instead to chatter away among themselves. Only when a chorus or a big aria began was there silence. After an opera had been presented a half-dozen times, most of the audience members knew the melodies. So they often sang along with the soloists in very loud voices.[69]

In addition to describing opera in Italy, Andersen explained why interest in Italian opera had so far been negligible in Denmark:

> Italian music appears to have had little success in Denmark. It has many opponents; but the reason for this mostly lies in the fact that we have only one theater, whose personnel is often stretched to the limits of human capacity. The actors who appear one night in tragedies are expected the following night to appear in comedies, vaudeville, and operas, and they are expected to sing German, French, and Italian music, even though the character of each of these national styles is quite different. [In Denmark] the beautiful recitatives of foreign operas are replaced by dialogue, and this damages the music's fluidity. Everything in opera should be music, that way the singing remains natural and the opera is a unified whole. – A second reason why so many in Denmark fight strongly against the light, mellifluous Italian melodies is because we have so many musical dilettantes, the majority of whom also compose. It is easier for them to put together harmonies than it is to create melodies. Consequently they support the belief that the more artificial a composition is, the better it is, despite the fact that it does not appeal to those of us who are not educated in the mysteries of the general bass. And it is no surprise that many follow their lead, since more than half the general public always follows the opinions of authorities and the media.[70]

Andersen's strong critique of Danish composers and their tendency to avoid recitative was no doubt due to his own interactions with C.E.F. Weyse at the time in connection with the opera *Festival at Kenilworth*. As mentioned in chapter 1, Andersen wrote a draft of the libretto for *Festival at Kenilworth* in 1832, but it was rejected. One month before Andersen departed on his European tour in 1833, he submitted a revised libretto to the censors at the Royal Theater. This version was accepted by the censors, but apparently still did not suit the tastes of Weyse, the opera's composer. During Andersen's European tour, Weyse took it upon himself to make substantial alterations to the libretto. When *Festival at Kenilworth* was finally premièred on 6 January 1836, Andersen renounced the libretto, claiming that Weyse had ruined it with his alterations. Indeed, a study of the various manuscripts of *Festival at Kenilworth* reveals that Weyse converted Andersen's opera libretto into a singspiel by replacing recitative text with blank verse and adding a happy ending. 'All the additions and changes that Weyse demanded are exactly those that do not work,' wrote Andersen in a letter dated 8 January: 'With this work I was nothing more than a submissive servant.'[71]

Despite Andersen's disgust with the changes made to his libretto, he was obviously pleased with the work's positive reception by critics. *Festival at Kenilworth* was performed seven times in 1836, and although the opening was followed by stormy debate in newspapers, the production was generally praised and Weyse's music was hailed 'a masterpiece.'[72] In fact, the singspiel quickly came to serve as something of a symbol for Musikforeningen (The Music Society), a new music organization that was being organized in the capital. Founded on 5 March 1836, Weyse's sixty-second birthday, the Music Society's primary goal was to 'support the dissemination of superior Danish compositions ... and to secure recognition for Danish composers by seeking the performance and publication of their works.' *Festival at Kenilworth* was performed at the society's founding ceremony as a representation of these goals being met. Andersen was present at the performance, and he is listed in the Music Society's charter as one of its founding members – an honor extended to few poets at the time.

With the success of *The Improvisatore* and the positive reception of his articles on Italian opera, Andersen finally earned the respect of Copenhagen's music community. His peers no longer looked upon him as a struggling performer – he was much too worldly for that. Instead they bestowed upon him a far more worthy title – that of music connoisseur and critic. Perhaps it was this new identity that led to Andersen's interaction during the late 1830s and early 1840s with an informal artistic society commonly known as the Copenhagen Davidsbund.[73]

Membership in the Copenhagen Davidsbund fluctuated from year to year, but from 1835 on its nucleus remained constant: Niels W. Gade, Fritz Schram, and the brothers Carl and Edvard Helsted – musicians at the Royal Chapel, and Frederick Høedt and Michael Wiehe – actors at the Royal Theater. More peripheral members included Peter Schram and Christian Ferslew – both notable singers; Vilhelm Holm and C.N. Lundgren – musicians at the Royal Chapel; and Ferdinand Hoppe – a dancer at the Royal Theater. The actors Nicolai Peter Nielsen and his wife Anna Nielsen were also associated with the group.

The artistic interests of the Copenhagen Davidsbund were all-encompassing. Filled with an ideal ambition, they believed that the full development of talent required a musically-trained ear, a well-trained eye, an educated mind, a regulated imagination, and pure emotions.[74] The group's activities were numerous: they visited art galleries, took walks in the countryside, critiqued each other's music and poetry, and spent many hours reading and discussing literary masterpieces and contemporary philosophy. Schumann's music journal, *Neue Zeitschrift für Musik*, was read religiously and functioned as a springboard for the group's numerous discussions concerning criticism and aesthetics.[75] Rebelling against the conservative tastes of an older generation, the Copenhagen Davidsbund took as their motto Schumann's 1835 declaration in *Neue Zeitschrift für Musik*: 'Our aim ... is simply this ... to oppose the recent past as an inartistic period ... and to prepare for and facilitate the advent of a fresh, poetic future.'[76]

To the young members of the group, Andersen, and to a certain extent the Nielsen couple, represented what the new generation could accomplish. Undaunted by hostile critics and negative reviews, Andersen had remained true to his artistic beliefs, reached beyond the confines of Denmark for inspiration, and consequently captured his much sought-after public acclaim at home. With his novels, libretti, and music criticism, Andersen had proven that the act of creating – be it music, art, or literature – was not part of an 'enlightened' program geared toward the socialization and modification of behavior; rather, it was a liberating activity capable of shaking one free from society's over-rationalized rules and expectations. Andersen had shown that the creation of an artistic work served as a de-centering experience that enabled the artist to transcend, or at least escape, the frustrating attitudes of mundane society.

Given the honored position Andersen came to hold in the eyes of Denmark's younger generation of artists, it is no surprise that in 1841 several singers from the Royal Theater asked Andersen to collaborate with them on a new concert series they were organizing. The leading actors/singers under contract at the Royal Theater were allowed to put on private concerts in the theater when no dramatic works were scheduled. However, no more than two solo singers could be featured on a single concert, a requirement that often led to musical evenings that were little more than hodge-podges of opera arias suited to a single voice type, with little or no dramatic interest. In an effort to make these concerts more appealing, and thus draw a larger audience, the soloists organizing these concerts employed Andersen to write short 'narrative frames' around the arias, transforming the concerts into a series of brief, musical dramas.

The first of these musical dramas was for a concert presented by Catherine Elisabeth Simonsen (1816–49). Inspired by Andersen's novel *The Improvisatore* and his article on contemporary Italian opera, Simonsen wanted to introduce Danish audiences to the aria 'Perche non ho del vento' from Donizetti's *Lucia di Lammermoor*. But she needed a dramatic framework that would also allow for highlights from Kuhlau's *Røverborgen* (The Robber Fortress) and Auber's *Fra Diavolo* – standards of the Royal Theater's repertoire. Andersen supplied her with *Sangerinden* (The Singer), a one-act musical about a prima donna named Maria who wins her freedom from a band of lecherous highwaymen by singing highlights from her performances at Teatro San Carlo.[77] The drama's protagonist was no doubt modeled on the famous prima donna of Naples' Teatro San Carlo, Maria Malibran. Thus, it is tempting to view Andersen's choice of characters and location in this musical drama as an attempt to make a comparison between Denmark's rising star, Catherine Simonsen, and the acclaimed Italian singer.

Reviews in a contemporary music magazine, *Figaro*, reveal that *The Singer* was a huge success when it premièred on 7 November, and Andersen noted repeat performances on 28 and 30 November. The success of *The Singer* led to the commissioning of a second concert piece from Andersen – a three-act musical tableau entitled *Vandring gjennem Opera-Galleriet* (Wandering through the Opera Gallery). As the narrator explains in the opening of the piece, this work presents scenes from a number of operas that had proven to be popular among Danish audiences over the years:

We see a picture gallery, but here every picture is a musical composition, its colors are melodies. Come let us wander together down the deep, long hall, from that which once delighted our grandfathers to that which we saw as children and the pictures we now hold dear. The pictures of music, they all hang here! From Gluck down to Hartmann, here is every painting. However, with this single visit we will have to skip many works, often even a masterpiece, painted in blazing tones. Only a few examples of what has pleased each age can be pointed out here today. And like the tones of music, these works also will pass away. For even the music of the future will eventually become an old melody.[78]

Table 2.1 shows the operas represented in *Wandering through the Opera Gallery*. A study of the narrator's text suggests that the various operas listed here must have been well known to Copenhagen audiences, for the introduction to each scene is often presented in the form of a riddle. The narrator does not always tell the audience right away which opera excerpt is to be presented. Instead he offers them a series of hints, allowing them to guess which opera might appear next. Here Andersen was purposefully reconfirming the audience's confidence in their cultural knowledge. By defining his work as an historical 'exhibition' of Denmark's opera history and by using a presentation method that allowed audiences to identify the various operatic scenes before they were actually performed, he was making a subtle statement about the cultural worth of Denmark's opera tradition – that it had a recognizable history – while simultaneously building up the audience's self-perception of their cultural worth and musical knowledge. It is unlikely that Andersen would have used this method of presentation if the works presented would not have been easily identifiable. A good example of Andersen's 'riddle technique' is displayed in the introduction to the final aria in part one of the concert program:

Sometimes his music sounds beautifully idyllic, sometimes patriarchal and grand, so good that even Cimarosa could have written it; then a great storm of tones sounds, how well it has been portrayed. He is the Raphael of music, and Germany gave him to Europe. He knew passion, and with his musical scepter he was even able to command the voices of spirits to rise up from the grave. He gave birth to melodies, and he created characters that show his mastery, even in his most minor works. Across all lands and oceans, from harbor to harbor, around the world his name blooms like a wreath of flowers. His name? I will not tell you; it lives in his work. As music's Raphael he is forever young and strong![79]

The curtain rises, and the final scene from Mozart's *Don Giovanni* is performed.

It is interesting to note that the final opera represented in Andersen's production is his own *The Raven*, set to music by J.P.E. Hartmann. Here Andersen was clearly setting up the young composer and himself as the voice of Denmark's modern theater:

Table 2.1

Operas Represented in Hans Christian Andersen's
***Wandering through the Opera Gallery* (1841)**

Part I:

C.W. Gluck	*Iphigenie en Aulide*	Overture
A. Grétry	*Les deux avares*	Act II, scenes 3 & 4
J.G. Naumann	*Cora*	Act II, scene 1
J.E. Hartmann	*Balders Død*	Aria: 'Et Egern som leger'
J.A.P. Schultz	*Peters Bryllup*	John Baadsman's congratulation song
F.L.Æ. Kunzen	*Viinhøsten*	Act I, scene 3
W.A. Mozart	*Don Giovanni*	Final Act, final scene

Part II:

C.N. Schall	*Lagertha*	Overture
E. Du Puy	*Ungdom og Galskab*	Unspecified aria
F. Paer	*Agnese*	Act I, scenes 3 & 4
A. Boieldieu	*Les deux nuits*	Act II, Servant's main aria
C.E.F. Weyse	*Ludlams Hule*	Act III, final scene
F. Kuhlau	*Hugo og Adelheid*	Act I, duet and final scene
G. Rossini	*Il Barbiere di Siviglia*	Act I, Figaro's first aria
C.M. Weber	*Oberon*	Act III, scenes 1 & 2

Part III:

L. Zinck	*Alferne*	Overture
V. Bellini	*Norma*	Act I, 'Casta diva'
H.A. Marschner	*Hans Heiling*	Act III, final scene
F. Halévy	*La juive*	Act II, Rachel's aria and closing duet
D. Auber	*Le maçon*	Act II, scene 6
J.P.E. Hartmann	*Ravnen*	Act III, scene 2
(Libretto by Hans Christian Andersen)		

Fig. 2.3 Lithograph of Jenny Lind, the 'Swedish Nightingale,' preserved in
Andersen's scrapbook. (Copenhagen: The Royal Library)

We have reached the gallery's end, and on the final wall are seen young Danish names, with strong traits one and all. Frøhlich's tones swell around Denmark's Valdemar, and Rung, your ballad is pure Danish we can tell. A large collection of paintings decorates this wall. Here the Sylph floats easily through God's natural hall. Ravenswood visits his bride from Lammermoor. We see many pieces; each projects its own gloss of sound. Yet, we can only choose one flower from this crown. And he is called grandson by one whose name is tied fast to the ballad of 'King Christian' who 'stood by the high mast.' He is the younger Hartmann, whose tone poetry, I believe, each heart will recognize in this painting.[80]

When considered together, Andersen's two concert works, *The Singer* and *Wandering through the Opera Gallery*, present a summary of opera appreciation in Copenhagen in the early 1840s. As in the 1820s, works by Danish composers still dominated the stage, and Mozart maintained his position as the most cherished of foreign composers. Nonetheless, winds of change could be felt. By the late 1830s, opera had replaced singspiel and vaudeville as the preferred genre at the Royal Theater, and a growing interest in the works of Italian and French composers, i.e. Rossini, Donizetti, Paer, and Halévy, was emerging. German composers, such as Marschner, Zinck, and Weber were also gaining a strong foothold in the Royal Theater's repertoire, along with a new generation of local talent, as represented by J.P.E. Hartmann and Andersen himself. Andersen no doubt believed that his published works had influenced this shift in repertoire to a certain extent, and he appears to have enjoyed his role as an arbiter of taste. But as he soon discovered, the musical taste of Copenhagen audiences was capricious at best, and at times contrary to what Andersen believed it should be. Consequently, Andersen began to approach his discussions of music somewhat differently in the 1840s. Instead of merely commenting on the contemporary state of opera in Denmark in his fictional works, he took up the pen of a critic and regularly reprimanded his countrymen for their philistine approach toward music.

Andersen's shift of perspective with regard to music and public taste appears to have begun in 1843, when the Swedish singer Jenny Lind made her début at the Royal Theater in Meyerbeer's *Robert le Diable* (fig. 2.3). As Andersen himself explained, the production was 'an overwhelming success. [Jenny Lind's] début began a new epoch in our opera's history. Her performance and personality revealed to me true art in its entirety; I had seen one of its vestal virgins.'[81]

Andersen noted that Lind was different from the singers he had praised so ardently in the past: 'She is not as great a singer as Malibran, but she is nonetheless comparable to her and even greater as an actress.'[82] Andersen did not praise Lind for her beauty or virtuosic prowess; instead he praised her for her ability to charm an audience and suspend reality. Lind's performances were not simply vocal displays, but, rather, dramatic presentations incorporating the skills of a persuasive actor. Her singing and acting brought the storyline of an opera to life, and in doing so showed off the creative genius of both the composer and the librettist.

Lind was generally well received by audiences in Copenhagen, but there were some who criticized her performances. For the two years prior to Lind's Copenhagen première, an Italian opera troupe had made several extended stays in the capital, enchanting audiences with lavish costumes and virtuosic vocal displays.[83] Lind's critics compared her to these Italian singers and ridiculed her lack of flair; she did not behave like the typical Italian prima donna. She did not wear extravagant costumes and glittering jewels,[84] and she rarely ornamented her arias in performances. Lind represented what was considered a more 'natural' style of singing. A pureness of tone, as opposed to virtuosic display, was seen as her primary musical gift.

As many familiar with Andersen's biography know, he fell in love with Lind during her visit in 1843, and consequently wrote several fairy tales inspired by her actions on and off stage. 'Engelen' (The Angel) was inspired by Lind's visit with an ailing Copenhagen man, and 'Nattergalen' (The Nightingale) was written as a reaction to the comparisons made between Lind's 'natural' style and the ornamented vocal displays of Italian singers.

When Andersen wrote 'The Nightingale' in 1843, his goal was not simply to amuse children, but to address an adult audience as well. 'The Nightingale' was published later that year in a collection called *New Fairy Tales* – all of his previous collections had been called *Fairy Tales for Children*. This collection was a watershed in Andersen's career for two reasons: First, it contained Andersen's earliest autobiographical tales (i.e. 'The Ugly Duckling' and 'The Lovers'). Second, it was the earliest collection designed with an adult audience in mind. Andersen himself explained this in a letter to the poet B.S. Ingemann on 20 November 1843: 'When I seize an idea for adults – I tell it to the young ones, remembering all the time that father and mother are listening and must have something to think about.'[85]

In reference to 'The Nightingale' specifically, it appears that Andersen used this tale to reprimand Copenhagen audiences for their tastes in opera. The setting for the fairy tale was inspired by the real-life fairy tale world of Copenhagen's Tivoli Gardens, which had just been opened to the public and featured a lavish display of exotic, life-size pagodas and other Chinese-inspired architectural features.

The story begins in the court of a great Chinese emperor who is astonished to discover that a special bird with a beautiful voice – the nightingale – resides in his kingdom. Eager to hear the creature sing, the emperor sends one of his knights to find it. The knight searches the entire court 'each room and hallway,' but with no success. He asks everyone he encounters if they know of this bird, but no one has ever heard of the nightingale. Finally, he comes across a young scullery maid in the kitchen who replies, 'I know it well! My God, can it ever sing!' She leads the knight, and half the emperor's court, into the countryside in search of the bird. The knight and his followers obviously have no sense of true music. Much to the scullery maid's amusement, they mistake the mooing of a cow, then the croaking of a frog, for the beautiful voice of the nightingale. Eventually, the young girl introduces them to the nightingale, and the bird is invited to court.[86]

That evening, the nightingale gives a special performance for the emperor. The entire court is in attendance, dressed in their finest clothes. The song of the nightingale is so beautiful, it brings tears to the emperor's eyes, and despite her drab appearance, she soon becomes the talk of the court. She is placed in a cage and prohibited from leaving the emperor's palace. As the days pass, her life at court grows oppressive and full of sorrow.

One day, a large package arrives from the emperor of Japan. It is a mechanical nightingale, sculpted out of gold and lavishly decorated with diamonds, rubies, and sapphires. As soon as the mechanical bird is wound up, it begins singing an ornate melody and moving its golden tail up and down. Around its neck is hung a piece of ribbon which reads: 'The emperor of Japan's nightingale is poor compared to that of the emperor of China.' But no one at court believes this message; the mechanical nightingale is so beautiful in appearance.

Eventually, the two nightingales are asked to sing a duet, 'but this didn't work out very well, for the real nightingale sang in her own manner, while the artificial bird worked off a cylinder.' When asked to give his judgment of the performance, the music master voices a preference for the mechanical bird, saying: 'Its singing style is especially well measured and completely in accordance with my teachings.' Consequently, the court becomes instantly enchanted with the mechanical nightingale, and the living nightingale, now completely forgotten, escapes to the forest.

Upon hearing of the real nightingale's departure, everyone at court declares her to be 'a very ungrateful bird.' But no matter, they continue, 'we still have the best bird here.' The music master agrees. He praises the mechanical bird to the highest degree, and even writes a treatise in twenty-five volumes asserting that the ornamented song of the mechanical nightingale is superior to the natural song of the living bird. Everyone at court claims to have read and understood this piece of music criticism, even if they have not, for they fear being called stupid or tasteless.

A year passes, and like all mechanical toys, the artificial nightingale eventually breaks. Now the bird can only be played once a year, and even then the performance sounds as if it is putting a strain on the bird's machinery. Consequently, the music master gives a short lecture on the present state of the bird's music, claiming that it is 'just as good as it was before.' Everyone agrees.

Five years pass, and the emperor grows ill. A great sorrow spreads over the court. Everyone expects their ruler will soon die. Indeed, Death comes through an open window one night and visits the Emperor.

> He took the Emperor's crown and scepter, and sat upon his chest. The Emperor looked up, and between the folds of his bed curtains he saw an assortment of strange heads – some frightful, others mild. These were the personifications of his good and bad deeds. 'Do you remember this?' each of them asked, one after the other.... The Emperor began to sweat.... 'Music, Music!'... He shouted, 'I do not want to hear what they say.'... He cried out to the mechanical nightingale, 'Music! Music! Sing to me, sing!'... But the bird just sat there silently. Death stared down at the emperor with cold, hollow eyes. Everything was silent, horribly silent.
>
> Then, all of a sudden, the sound of sweet music was heard coming through an open window. It was the living nightingale.[87]

Death becomes so enchanted by her song that he returns the emperor's crown and scepter and then turns to mist and floats away. The pure, natural voice of the nightingale proves more powerful than Death, and the emperor's life is saved.

Like most of Andersen's stories, the tale of the nightingale has been interpreted in a variety of ways by numerous reputable scholars. That being said, perhaps the most intriguing explanation of the tale's inherent symbolism revolves around the musical tastes of Andersen's contemporaries. According to this interpretation, each character in the tale has a clear parallel in contemporary culture. The living nightingale was meant to represent Jenny Lind, and readers in Copenhagen no doubt would have been able to recognize this. When Lind visited Copenhagen in 1843, she was already well known for her 'natural' singing voice, and within a few months after the publication of Andersen's tale, she became known across Europe as 'The Swedish Nightingale.'

In a similar vein, the artificial nightingale, with its extravagant appearance and virtuosic song, can be viewed as a representation of Italian prima donnas of the period, perhaps even the singers that visited Copenhagen in 1841. Competition between national styles is highlighted in the tale by the ribbon around the mechanical bird's neck that proclaims its 'Japanese' beauty to be no match for the beauty of the emperor's 'Chinese' nightingale. In addition, Andersen's description of the emperor was likely meant to represent Denmark's King Christian VIII. Like Andersen, Christian VIII was a great admirer of Lind's talents, and after her performances at the Royal Theater in 1843, he invited her to extend her stay in Copenhagen and present a private concert at court. Lind gratefully complied, and according to Andersen's almanac, this concert took place on 16 September.[88]

The music master embodies the stereotypical scholar/connoisseur, who is so enamored of his own rhetorical talents that he completely ignores the subject that he is supposed to be studying, i.e. music. One cannot help but wonder if in this character Andersen was criticizing himself, to a certain extent, for his ardent acclaim of Italian opera in the mid-1830s. Finally, the knight and his followers represent Lind's critics in Copenhagen. Unable to distinguish the croak of a frog from the song of a nightingale, they blindly follow the opinions of the music master and praise the mechanical twittering of a flashy, ornate toy.

With his story of the nightingale, Andersen asked readers to contemplate the essence of true music. By depicting the life-saving role of the living nightingale's song, he attempted to show how the 'natural' singing style of Lind presented a spiritual depth unattainable through virtuosic display. According to Andersen, true genius was not always clothed in dazzling costume or displayed through elaborate vocal ornamentation; it often came in rather presupposing packages. To discover ideal beauty, audiences had to seek out pure, natural talent, and not simply follow the lead of popular opinion that was too often guided by the intellectual babblings of inartistic critics.[89] Musical taste was a personal, subjective quality that each listener must attempt to discover on his or her own.

It is likely that Andersen had these ideas in mind when he contacted his friend from the Copenhagen Davidsbund, Niels W. Gade, and asked him to collaborate on a revised version of *Agnete and the Merman* that he was preparing for the stage.

Labeled a 'dramatic poem in two acts,' this project was an abridged version of the original and featured a series of songs and melodramas composed and orchestrated by Gade (table 2:2). It is not known when Andersen and Gade first began working together on the project, but a letter from Andersen reveals that it was well under way by the summer of 1842:

Bregentved – 17 July 1842

Dear Friend!
    Since I haven't seen a single word about our maiden 'Agnete' in the newspapers, [I assume] she will not be in service this summer, the French Count[90] has taken her place. Still, it seems best to me that we attend to our maiden, and that is why I am writing you this short epistle.
    Will you get the clean-written manuscript from Mr. Holst[91] and send it – along with a couple of words saying that you have composed the music and will now complete an overture to the piece – to the board of directors? In all probability we will receive an answer from the censor at the beginning of the season, and then 'Agnete' can be presented in September or October. You might also bring it to conference advisor Collin and talk with him about what the music involves. I will then write about the piece....[92]

Agnete and the Merman displays many characteristics associated with the singspiel tradition. Dialogue and/or melodrama link the various musical numbers, and motifs are used as a means of identifying various characters. On the whole, the songs in *Agnete and the Merman* utilize the strophic forms commonly found in the early nineteenth-century Danish ballad tradition.[93] Often characterized by syncopated triplet rhythms, symmetrical phrasing, and a limited vocal range, the melodies appear to be inspired by traditional folk models.[94]

In composing the music for *Agnete and the Merman*, Gade relied to some extent upon Weber's *Der Freischütz*. It is tempting to imagine that Andersen might have had some influence in this decision, since he was quite taken with the work when he first saw it performed in its entirety during his trip through Germany in 1831.[95]

Gade borrowed Weber's technique of key symbolism when writing the music to *Agnete and the Merman*, associating C major with the powers of good ('Barn Jesus, Brudgom faur og fiin') and D major with the robust, natural world ('Trara! Trara! Trara!'). He continued by presenting the characters of Agnete and the Merman with the keys of F and A-flat major, respectively. Only Hemming, Agnete's abandoned fiancé, is represented by minor keys ('Der voxed' et Træ' in D minor, 'Agnete var elsket' in A minor). Reinforcing this tonal structure is a carefully constructed pattern of instrumentation. Like Weber, Gade devised distinct tone-colors to represent the principal characters. Agnete is the only character given the honor of a full orchestra, while Hemming is represented by the oboe and strings, and his antithesis, the Merman, is accompanied by the winds and harp. Melodrama is reserved for the story's immortal character, the Merman. Like Samiel in *Der Freischütz*, the Merman never sings – representing the

Table 2.2

Musical numbers composed by Gade for Andersen's Dramatic Poem
Agnete and the Merman

Act I

1. Hemming's Song – 'Der voxed' et Træ.'
2. Choir of Mermaids – 'Jeg veed et Slot.'
   Merman and Agnete – Melodrama (seduction scene).

Act II

3a. Agnete's Lullabye – 'Sol deroppe ganger under Lide.'
3b. Choir of Huntsmen – 'Trara! Trara! Trara!'
4. Hemming – 'Agnete var elsket.'
5. Choir of Huntsmen – continuation of no. 3b.
6a. Repetition of no. 4, but without orchestral introduction and coda.
6b. Choir in Church – 'Barn Jesus, Brudgom faur og fiin.'
7a. The Fisherboy's Ballad – 'Lærken synger sin Morgensang.'
7b. Choir in Church – continuation of no. 6b.
8. Merman and Agnete – Melodrama (Agnete's death).

personification of sin and temptation, he uses passion and wealth to tempt Agnete and eventually persuades her to 'forsake her Savior.'

Andersen's letter to Gade reveals that he was hoping for a première at the Royal Theater in September or October 1842, but *Agnete and the Merman* was not performed until 20 April 1843. Although both librettist and composer spent many months working on the singspiel, the production itself was short-lived, closing after only two performances.[96] According to a review written by J.L. Heiberg, *Agnete and the Merman* failed for various reasons:

> It is understandable why the story has not grown better, but actually worse, with this abridged stage version of the poem which has been transported from the bookstore to the stage. Yet with this it must be remembered what has been noted publicly before, namely that the author did not decide to present the work on stage himself, but instead solicited an actor who was already swamped with summer performances. Certainly it would have been better if his [the actor's] willingness to do a favor had not induced him to sacrifice himself, and if the composer, Mr. Gade, had not wasted his characteristic, emotion-filled music on a work which, it was easy to predict, could not bear it.[97]

Edvard Collin expressed a similar opinion in a letter dated 23 April 1843. Like Heiberg, he found little worth in Andersen's libretto:

It is always my fate to write to you about the works of yours that bring you no comfort. This is also the case now with Agnete; ... I had a premonition about its outcome – a strange chill and state of boredom enveloped the entire [production]. ... The adaptation [from the book was] mediocre – in the conclusion, even terribly bad ... I waited to hear laughter from the passive mob at every moment. The music was delightful, and left nothing to be desired.[98]

After the failure of *Agnete and the Merman*, Andersen discarded the project once again and relinquished all hopes of publishing it as a singspiel. 'Agnete is abandoned forever,' he wrote in a letter to Edvard Collin. Despairing over his inability to maintain continuous acceptance of his dramatic works from critics in Copenhagen, and frustrated by the fact that, once again, one of his carefully crafted libretti had been upstaged by a composer's music, Andersen swore that he would never again write for the theater. Fortunately, this was a vow that he would eventually break – but it nonetheless marked a turning point in his relationship with the world of music. As the following chapter reveals, Andersen's growing frustration with Copenhagen's opera scene fueled an intense interest in instrumental music and virtuosity that peaked in the 1840s.

Interlude 2

Wandering through the Opera Gallery

by Hans Christian Andersen

Declamatory frame for a series of scenes of older and newer composers'
works on the Danish stage.

Music by: Gluck, Grétry, Naumann, Hartmann the elder, Schultz, Kunzen,
Mozart, Schall, Du Puy, Paer, Boieldieu, Weyse, Kuhlau, Rossini, Weber,
Zinck, Bellini, Marschner, Halévy, Auber, and J.P.E. Hartmann.

Arranged to Mr. Cettis's and Mr. Sahlertz's Evening performance at the
Royal Theater on 19 December 1841.

At the Royal Theater there was still, in 1841, the provision for theater and opera
personnel that on their Evening Performances only two persons at a time and choir
could appear in costume. The public, tired of the usual thing, longed for something
new, at the very least something that held together better than the indifferent
selection of music and declamatory pieces. The work here was thus an attempt to
bring at least an example of this idea into the Evening Performance; it was
performed, revised, and again performed with great acclaim.

ACT ONE
The stage is made as short as possible; a large curtain, which can be pulled to
one side, conceals the backstage.

Overture to Gluck's *Iphigenie en Aulide*

Cicerone:
We see a picture gallery, but here every picture
Is a musical composition, its colors are melodies.
Come let us wander together down the hall deep and long,
From what once delighted our grandfathers
To what we saw as children and what we now hold dear today.
The pictures of music, they all hang here!
From Gluck to Hartmann, here is every painting.
However, with this single visit we will have to skip many works,
Often even a masterpiece, painted in blazing tones.

Only a few examples can be pointed out of what has spoken to
Each generation and consequently has passed on – like the tones themselves!
Soon the ballad of today will become an old melody.
We are met at the entrance by Gluck's tones, his *Iphigenia*.
It is lonely here in the hall; come, let us wander further!
We pass by [the galleries of] Sarti, Salieri, Monsigny,
And most certainly, I realize it is a sin that we don't go in,
But if we see everything that's beautiful, then we'll never come out.
Remember that art is eternal, but life is short.
Here Grétry's melodies are mounted. See, there is
His *Richard Cœur de Lion, Zemire*, and especially
Les deux avares, which we will for its vivacity
Look at on our tour. The story we know!
It takes place in Smyrna, a Turkish priest is dead.
His body and riches lie in the pyramid's chamber.
Tonight the two old ones will break into it
And plunder the grave's chamber and all its treasure;
The maiden's lover has hidden in the well, watch out!
The curtain is pulled aside and we see the picture.

(He steps back, the innermost part of the stage opens. The scenery is there, as in each of the following scenes, completely arranged as it was in the opera itself, from which the scenery was borrowed.)

Les deux avares (Music by Grétry)
Act Two, third and fourth scenes. (The entire dialogue, which contains two duets and a chorus.)

> The two misers: Knapskjær and Bærhed
> Choir of Janissary

(A street in Smyrna, on the right a Turkish grave, on the left a well.)

(During the Janissary's final chorus the curtain conceals the stage again, and the Cicerone steps forward.)

> Cicerone:
> It has disappeared, the lively picture, the last tone is dead.
> Gaveaux and Benda make magic, but we must proceed forward;
> A tone picture has been called up by one of greater rank.
> The opera's sweet *Eurydice* sank into the embrace of her Orpheus,
> And in the middle of fidelity's kiss they called forth Naumann's name;
> A painting of tones he has given us in *Cora*.
> Come, let us float over the great world harbor
> To Quito where the priestess has broken her given oath,

And her great offence is her lover.
Imprisoned she sighs into the night; Alonzo leaves
And complains loudly as flames burn in the mountain's crater.
Soon the prison's walls crumble, and Cora is set free.
A glimpse of these tones now roars passed us.

(The backstage opens.)

Cora (Music by Naumann)
Act Two, first scene.

Alonzo, a young Spaniard

(The area around the priestess's home. Alonzo's aria 'You live, Cora!' At the end
of the aria, the backstage is concealed.)

Cicerone (steps forward):
The lyre touches hearts with the plucking of its strings,
Danish tones are born around him, [who stands] by the high mast,
Sounding from the fishing village and over the Danish fields;
It was the elder Hartmann, who sang this for the Danes;
It sounded where the nets hang spread out on Sjælland's coast,
It sounded from Norway's fields and from the breast of the Danes;
And the old, Norse gods descend from where the elf stood,
It rings out Nanna's love; it rings out Balder's death.
Well, let us view the field where Hother wanders forward.
See for yourself: We are in Norway, the home of the old gods. (He steps aside)
(The curtain opens.)

Baldurs Død (Music by Hartmann the Elder.)

Hother

(Hother, dressed like a Norse peasant with hunting bow in hand, comes down from
the fields and unbuckles his weapon; he steps forward into the foreground and
sings the aria: 'A squirrel that plays;' after this is over, the curtain closes.)

Cicerone:
The storm blows around the field; in the valley there is peace.
The song spoke idyllically; it was about love,
And Vedel's 'Serenade' for the ear sounds luscious,
With Peter and with Lise we share sorrow and need;
Then Schultz pushed into Denmark, his penance and flower and corn
Radiated Danish tones that sound like Oberon's horn,
The ring and call, we follow the music

And go to *Peter's Wedding.* At this very moment
The Boatswain sings a ballad, which has always been deeply touching.
The hearts of real Danes [are moved] each time they hear this Danish song.
(Curtain opens.)

Peters Bryllup (Music by Schultz)

> Peter
> John, a boatswain
> Choir of sailors

(After John the boatswain has sung his congratulation song with the choir, the curtain closes and the Cicerone again steps forward.)

Cicerone:
That was a life of tones; the Danish summer's fragrance
Can give birth to such songs in the sharp air of the North.
Is the songbird that is not born here to be silenced?
No, lusciously and freely he sings among our trees.
On the mountain grapes are collected, come let us enter there.
Come to Kunzen's wine harvest! There stands an old friend,
Our Barthel Schoolmaster, the comical figure.
But he could not wait; he has already had his portion
(Curtain opens.)

Viinhøsten (Music by Kunzen)
Act One, scene three (where Barthel comes down from the mountain, and the beginning of the following number that closes with the chorus: 'Float along in an easy dance.')

> Barthel, Schoolmaster and pedagogue
> Claus, a peasant boy

(During the chorus the curtain closes.)

Cicerone:
Sometimes his music sounds beautifully idyllic,
Sometimes patriarchal and grand,
So good that even Cimarosa could have written it;
Then a great storm of tones sounds, how well it has been portrayed.
He is the Raphael of music, and Germany gave him to Europe.
He knew passion, and with his musical scepter he was even able to command
The voices of spirits to rise up from the grave.
He gave birth to melodies, and he created characters
That reveal his mastery, even in his most minor works!

Across all lands and oceans, from harbor to harbor,
Around the world his name blooms like a wreath of flowers.
His name? I will not tell you; it lives in his work.
As music's Raphael, he is forever young and strong!
(Curtain opens.)

Don Giovanni (Music by Mozart)

Don Giovanni
Commandant's Ghost

Final Act, final scene (A hall in the home of Don Giovanni, lightning and thunder: Don Giovanni walks in with the commandant's ghost; as soon as Don Giovanni falls to the ground dead at the end of the scene the curtain closes and the curtain at the very front of the stage descends. End of Act One)

ACT TWO

Overture to Schall's *Lagertha*

Cicerone:
An army of pantomime spirits drifts across the stage,
And the tones, like swans, lead this boat.
Everything floats, all is sounding! – They drift by a village.
News, like an echo, rings out to us in Schall's tone poetry
But dear, old memories are often enclosed in sadness.
Let's move on to the next piece, it has a jovial sense.
Du Puy painted this one; he gave us this work,
And like a hedge full of blossoms, it blooms upon his grave.
He owned the heart of youth, he owned youth's lust,
He sang with a soulful heart about youth and about folly.
(Steps to the side. The curtain opens.)

Ungdom og Galskab (Music by Du Puy)
(Large aria)

Grøndahl the painter.
Wilhelmine, his ward.

(At the end of the aria the curtain closes, Cicerone steps forward.)

Cicerone:
The lively French tones were Danish, each and every one.
In Denmark the province's rose branch also thrives;

In the French valley stand fields, as in the north,
Also there, thin spruces grow out of the cliffs' side.
Thus France often sends us a deep, serious song,
That speaks to our hearts; here we shall stop in our gallery.
The curtain moves aside, – who, indeed, is the master here?
The name Paer is called out! – It is France's Paer.*
(Curtain opens.)

Agnese (Music by Paer)
Act One, third and fourth scenes; a rural area with fields, daybreak.

Count Uberto
Agnese, his daughter

(At the end of the duet, the curtain closes.)

Cicerone:
Names sound out from France, we bow before them:
See d'Alayrac and Isouard, Mehul! They stream forward!
The elder Cherubini, and he, with whom we often
Wander in the forest of tones, which stretches out so wide.
From Bagdad, remember 'Le calife,' to the Avenel palace;
In the forest we have met 'Le petit chaperon rouge' at twilight,
And over there we have attended 'La fête du village voisin.'
'Le nouveau seigneur de village' we have surely met.
Oh, Boieldieu! How each and every branch rings out here in the forest.
Oh, if instead of 'Deux nuits' you sang one thousand and one.

Le deux nuits (Music by Boieldieu)
The servant's large number in Act Two

(At the end of the song, the curtain closes.)

Cicerone:
Hush! The organ's tones blow like a storm in the North,
Listen: 'bubble, bubble the stream' – it rises up out of the earth.
How pleasant: a pretty maiden. Open up your window!
Now it rings in the valley and now on the mountaintop!
Yonder sounds 'Ludlam's Cave,' here 'Kenilworth' holds his head high!
No, Weyse's name will never die away here in Denmark!
(Steps aside.)
(Curtain opens.)

---

* Paer was actually born in Parma, but his best compositions were born in France and are so
characteristically French that they can only be classified as such. [H.C. Andersen's note]

Ludlams Hule (Music by Weyse)
The end of Act Three, where Clara walks into the Knights' hall and sings:
'Here sat the old ancestors.'

Clara
Mother Ludlam, a ghost

(When Mother Ludlam disappears at the end of the melodrama and Clara falls to
the ground, the curtain closes.)

Cicerone:
We hear hunting horns deep in the forest's green cover.
See the torch flames at the castle, a robber's song is heard,
And the dwarf Barka rocks through the cave's darkness,
As the moon observes the dance that takes place in the land of the elves.
The old melodies from the cave reach us.
Like Romanticism's songs we saw you,
Our beloved, lost Kuhlau! Denmark has few like you!
Which picture shall we choose? Preferably one in a humouros mood.
Even in the simplest work, one can see his mastery.
(Curtain opens.)

Hugo og Adelheid (Music by Kuhlau)
Duet, scene, and finale from Act One.

First Thief
Second Thief
Choir of horsemen and tradesmen

Cicerone:
In the North, bronze rings out, and every melody is deep.
We hear the waterfall roar and the storm strong and free!
From the South a mild breeze of tones billows forward,
Even the North is charmed by it, but its true home
Is under the high pines in the glow of twilight,
Where tambourines accompany the parrots' light dance.
Yes, southern breezes breathe in the sound of these tones.
Rossini's kingdom reaches up to the birch tree's home.

Il Barbiere di Seville (Music by Rossini)
Figaro's first aria in Act One

Figaro
(At the end of the song the curtain closes and Cicerone walks forward again.)

Cicerone:

In the hunting lodge Agathe sews her bridal gown,
While over in the Wolf Glen the hunt progresses.
It thunders from shots as though under the horse's hoof.
An echo sounds in the song: 'In the forest, in the green forest!'
And 'Preciosa' stands alone in the moonlight
She treads upon the wild forest blossoms with her fine feet;
The heart trembles romantically; love's beginning
Is born in the world's swarm of tones.
Titania commands fairies from sea and forest and corn
To bring her favorite, the horn of Oberon.
'The one from whose lips the sound roars out over the world,
His name will ring mightily, like the name of a god.
Yet even he is destined to die.' We heard [the horn] sound;
For Carl Maria Weber it rang – and he was dead.
(Curtain opens.)

Oberon (Music by Weber)

Fatime
Scherasmin

(Act Three, first and second scenes, with dialogue, aria and duet; at the end the curtain closes again as does the curtain at the front of the stage.)

Zinck's Overture to *Alferne*

Cicerone:

The tones that just sounded reminded us of the fairies.
Here, like a friendly house-fairy, the old one has his gallery,
Make sure that each picture gets the proper amount of pretty light,
His name we dare not forget, he wrote it out [for us] in tones.
Away! – The fairy crowd calls us thither, where the oranges grow,
Where mild winds blow, and the sky is large,
Where the almond tree blooms, while laws are lost,
Where art works live, while kings become dust.
Where the ruins of the marble hall points to the willow of time;
Nature always smiles, but with a wistful grin.
The green stands have darkened, and the song makes us melancholy.
It is as though the heart suffers, although the cheek blushes red.
Italy, you glory! You guard the memory's grave,
And place tulips and roses around your tragic marker.
What are you, and what were you? – Your cheek, indeed, grows pale,
You hum to us Bellini's song until the point of utter exhaustion!
A smile plays across your lips, I know what you want to say –;

Behind the grieving cypresses, the evening sun is going down!
(Curtain opens.)

Norma (Music by Bellini)
The scene in Act One with the aria 'Casta diva.'
(After the aria is finished the curtain closes.)

Cicerone:
When Germany's Weber died, Marschner received his lyre,
And throughout the land rushed a strong but sweet music.
The fairy tale told to us in the evening hours
About the palace next to Etna, about the one who was a vampire,
About the mountain's king Hans Heiling and the falconer's bride.
The saga of tones was almost erased from memory.
We hand Marschner the wreath, and the best place to hang his wreath
Is where he plays the hearty peasant dance.
(Curtain opens.)

Hans Heiling (Music of Marschner)
Act Three, seventh scene.

Stephen, a peasant
Ertrud, Mother of Hans Heiling's bride

(During the ballad about the fox the curtain closes.)

Cicerone:
From Babel's weeping willow, where Israel's harps hang,
While thoughts in Zion sounded around the people's need,
Joseph gave the lamentation that sounded when the temple fell,
And what the chronicler has not advocated to us since then!
The chosen people of Jehova who still exist today,
Though spread out over the world for a thousand years,
Yes, these people – their history is the world's poetry –
Yet it is not fully portrayed in a single painting!
Nonetheless, the master can paint a draft, using enterprising hands,
So that we can view with melancholy and terror a specific time and people.
And Halévy's *La Juive* is such a painting. –
We are with Eleazar, dinner is over –
The holy Passover meal. The lamp's light burns weakly.
With fearful longing, Rachel whispers: 'He's coming here!'
(Curtain opens.)

La Juive (Music by Halévy)
Scenes from Act Two (Rachel's aria: 'He's coming here!' and the following duet between her and Leopold.)

  Rachel
  Duke Leopold

(At the end of the duet: 'I am going out into the world,' the curtain closes.)

  Cicerone:
  Listen to the lively, light tones; each heart can understand them;
  It is as though both heart and feet must dance,
  As though the entire boulevard rises up in song and sound;
  Here small pagodas sound, and there is a robber's song,
  One meets *Le Dieu et la Bayadère* in this gallery,
  Fenella and Angela, every type of people of every rank!
  It is music's Scribe: Auber. When he wants it,
  People, indeed even trees and streets, must dance right away to his playing.
  (Curtain opens.)

Le maçon (Music by Auber)
(The duet in Act Two, sixth scene: 'Swift and Strong.')

  Roger, a mason
  Baptiste, a locksmith

(Curtain closes.)

  Cicerone:
  We have reached the gallery's end, and on the final wall
  Are seen young Danish names, with strong traits one and all.
  Frøhlich's tones around Denmark's Valdemar swell,
  And Rung, your ballad is pure Danish we can tell.
  A large collection of paintings decorates this wall,
  Here the Sylph floats easily through God's natural hall,
  Ravenswood visits his bride from Lammermoor.
  We see many pieces; each projects its own gloss of sound.
  However, we can only choose one flower from this crown,
  And he is called grandson by one whose name is tied fast
  To the ballad of 'King Christian' who 'stood by the high mast;'
  He is the younger Hartmann, whose tone poetry,
  I believe, each heart will recognize in this painting.

The Raven (Music by J.P.E. Hartmann)

(Act Three, second scene, where Jennaro works his way through the floor and fights with the vampires in order to save his brother's life.)

    Millo, Prince of Frattombrosa
    Jennaro, his brother
    Choir of vampires and guards

(When Jennaro must be led to his death the curtain closes.)

Epilogue

    Cicerone:
    In the past, an evening's entertainment was nothing more than a single actor,
    Appearing in his own clothes and singing God only knows about whom;
    Afterwards there were recitations, then a little music followed.
    But now our age wants more than what such old practices offer.
    One demands some unity and something a little fun.
    Therefore we strained our brains; we searched for an idea,
    And constructed a frame, as good as one can get,
    And thousands of hidden considerations did not make it easy!
    Every picture wants to live! But the frame can only endure a short time.
    I know that once the curtain falls, the frame will simply be thrown away!

Fig. 3.1 C.A. Jensen. Portrait of H.C. Andersen (1836).
          (Odense: The Andersen House Museum)

Chapter 3

The Virtuoso

*The Orpheus of our age has let his tones swell through the world
metropolis of machinery, ... his fingers are nothing but railroads and
steam engines, his genius even mightier in drawing together the
intellectual spirits of the universe than all the railways on earth.*

Hans Christian Andersen

Andersen wrote these words about Franz Liszt in 1842, and they clearly reflect his growing interest in instrumental music – an interest that appears to have been fueled by two additional trips across Europe in 1840 and 1844.

As we saw in the last chapter, by 1842 Andersen's interest in vocal music had shifted from a fascination with the virtuosic style of Italian opera to the more 'natural,' unornamented style found in Jenny Lind's performances and German romantic operas such as Weber's *Der Freischütz.* Yet even though Andersen came to accept – and indeed promote – the aesthetic of the pure and natural voice when it came to discussion of opera, he never fully sacrificed his own artistic identity, which continued to be centered on the creative act of improvisation. Andersen continued to equate poetic genius with an active imagination and virtuosic display. Consequently, his fascination with the art of improvisation did not disappear when his taste in opera changed in the early 1840s. Instead, it shifted to the realm of instrumental music, where the inclusion of a musical instrument was already artificial in itself, and where virtuosi such as Liszt and Thalberg were being hailed as the stars of a new era.

Andersen's shift of interest, from the vocal virtuoso in the 1830s to the instrumental virtuoso in the 1840s, was a gradual process that left its mark on a number of his mature works. As seen in his novels, music criticism, and diaries, Andersen's growing interest in instrumental music was not so much a conscious choice as it was a reaction to the cultural changes taking place around him. Since his youth, Andersen had struggled to make a place for himself in society, and part of fitting in was being aware of changes in fashion. An avid traveler, letter writer, and reader of foreign periodicals, Andersen kept himself informed about cultural events across Europe and closely followed the careers of countless performers and composers. For this reason, it is possible to regard Andersen as a barometer of musical taste, an enthusiastic audience member who kept his finger on the pulse of popular opinion among the general public.

Andersen's reaction to the changing musical tastes of his peers is clearly shown in the literary works that grew out of his European tours of 1840 and 1844.

Consequently, they will serve as the primary sources for this chapter. Andersen's increasing exposure to virtuosic instrumentalists such as Liszt and Thalberg and German composers such as Mendelssohn and Schumann influenced his ideas about the artist's role in society and the paradigms of musical genius. Public opinion also had an effect on his perceptions of musical culture. During his travels abroad, Andersen was exposed to a wide range of audiences, and the changes he perceived in their actions and expectations led to subtle shifts in the way he described the world around him. His use of musical metaphors changed, as did the interests of the characters in his fictional works. Describing such shifts in musical taste, however, is unproductive without the benefit of specific examples. Thus I return to the narrative of Andersen's relationship to music shortly before where I left off in chapter 2.

*

After the successful reception of *The Improvisatore* in 1835, Andersen's self image as a writer changed. More confident in his talents as a novelist and no longer troubled by financial worries, he rented a set of rooms overlooking the bustling streets of Copenhagen's Nyhavn and began making plans for the future. In a letter to Henriette Wulff he wrote:

> I may have four or six more years when I can still write well, and I must use them. I am quite comfortable at home, the fire is crackling, and that's when my muse visits me; she tells me strange tales, shows me odd characters from everyday life – aristocrats as well as commoners – and says, 'See those people, you know them; draw them, and they will live!' This is asking a great deal, I know, but that is what she says.[1]

Some of the aristocrats and commoners Andersen was referring to appeared as characters in his next two novels, *O.T.* and *Kun en Spillemand* (Only a Fiddler). Written in 1836 and 1837 respectively, these books played an important role in Andersen's struggle to attain a more respectable social status. Torn between two conflicting identities, the poverty-stricken boy from provincial Odense and the successful novelist residing in Copenhagen, Andersen used his writing as a means of coming to terms with Denmark's social structure and his tenuous place therein. With *O.T.* and *Only a Fiddler* Andersen attempted to influence his readers' points of view, to instill in Denmark's bourgeois community an appreciation for the difficulties faced by those unlucky artists who, like himself, were born into poverty but aspired to greatness.

O.T. is the story of Otto Thostrup, an underprivileged boy born in Odense Tugthus (Odense Jail) and tattooed at birth with the initials O.T. Although Otto works hard and eventually secures a position for himself in high society, the stigma of his origin, like the tattoo emblazoned across his skin, stays with him forever. Society never lets Otto forget his unfortunate past, and every success is tainted with the realization that he will never be a true member of Denmark's respected elite. Andersen was trying to send a message with *O.T.* As he explained in a letter to Henriette Hanck, the novel was not written to amuse; rather, it was meant to serve as a reflection of contemporary Danish society:

> It is a description of our own time from 1829 to 1835 and is set in Denmark only. I think the fact that the writer describes what he knows, the environment where he lives, will be valuable and will give the work a particular interest. In future years, people will have a true picture of our time, and if I have been successful in giving that, well, then the book will gain interest with age.[2]

Andersen looked at the writing of *O.T.* as a project of high cultural importance. Although he was pleased with the success *The Improvisatore* had brought him, he knew that still more could be done with his novels. As the philosopher F.C. Sibbern wrote to him on 12 September 1835, *The Improvisatore* showed that Andersen's talent was great, but in the future he might consider writing a novel with a more historical or philosophical approach:

> I read your *Improvisatore* in one sitting: 'It is good; it is very good!' [I said] as I read the first twenty-four pages. The next day I came to the end – I didn't want to do anything but read. You must know what that means – that one has felt himself filled. And the thing that filled me was happiness over the book and you. We knew you were, as the Germans say, 'eine gute Seele;' but I am happy to know that now I also know that you are a well-grounded soul.... There will come a time – or perhaps it has already come? – when you will set out, will live in another great region – that of history. It gladdens me to think about what you will bring home to us [from there]. Then, even later, there will come a time when you will be dragged out into another large kingdom and will live in it – that of philosophy. Also, I hope you will then bring us reflected images witnessing that the muse has been with you.[3]

Andersen responded to these ideas with the novel *O.T.* Influenced by Schelling's view of the fine arts as a reflection of society, he tried to come to terms with his place in the world through the creative act of writing. As he explained in his preface to *O.T.*:

> Our tale is no figment of the imagination, but a picture of the reality in which we live, blood of our blood and flesh of our flesh. We are going to see our own days, to meet people of our own time. Still, it is not only the everyday life, not only a lingering look at the mosses of the surface. We shall contemplate the whole tree, from the roots to the scented foliage – but the tree of reality cannot sprout up with the same rapid growth as the one of imagination....[4]

This last comment reveals much about Andersen's narrative technique. To make *O.T.* an effective metaphor for contemporary Denmark, Andersen invented a story that was both tied to reality and ornamented by fantasy. He used his imagination and his own personal aspirations as a means of breathing life into the character of Otto Thostrup, but with little effect. Offering a vision of society painfully familiar to most Danish readers, the novel's mix of fantasy and reality was viewed as jarring and unconvincing. The world of *O.T.* offered no escape. Set in the dreary cold of Denmark, it was devoid of the foreign landscapes and colorful characters that populated *The Improvisatore*. There were no artists, no musicians blessed with genius, and in comparison to Andersen's first novel, *O.T.* was dull and depressing. Critics found little to praise in the book, and readers were utterly unmoved by its message. Angry and distraught by his failure to reach an audience, Andersen bemoaned his fate in a letter to Henriette Hanck:

> I want to become the best novelist of Denmark! To have the few souls around me in my nook [of the world] recognize that I am a true poet. If I were French or English, the world would be speaking my name; but now I am getting dropped and my songs along with me. No one listens to them in poor distant Denmark.[5]

Andersen was depressed, but not deterred. Intent on getting his message across to readers and reviving his reputation abroad, he began writing what would become his first large-scale, international success, *Only a Fiddler*.

In *Only a Fiddler* Andersen returned to the successful formula of his first novel, a self-portrait via the life of a musical character, but retained the new social criticism of his second novel, emphasizing that those born into poverty have little chance of escaping their past while those born into privilege rarely deserve it. Christian, the protagonist of the novel's first half and Andersen's alter ego, represents the ideal romantic genius. Although most scholars describe Christian as little more than a violin-playing version of Antonio from *The Improvisatore*, there are stark differences between the two characters that reveal much about the changes taking place in Andersen's aesthetic point of view. To begin, Christian is not a singer, but a violinist. Free from the confines of a signifying verbal text, his music appeals to the subjective soul, not the rational mind. In addition, although the reader follows Antonio through his musical education in *The Improvisatore*, one never witnesses Christian rehearsing a piece or struggling to master a particularly difficult phrase. He is simply born with the ability to play beautiful, heart-rending music. Finally, whereas Antonio's mature style is seen as a parallel to the dazzling performances of Italy's finest opera singers, Christian's style shows no trace of empty virtuosity. He is portrayed as a sensitive performer who, in contrast to his grandfather, a demonic violinist modeled after Paganini, prefers clear and natural melodies to musical calisthenics. His goal is not to astonish listeners, but to touch their souls with beautifully improvised melodies.

Christian is shy, unassuming, and naive, and his poverty impedes him from making the most of his talent. Believing that genius alone will open the doors of opportunity, he takes a job as a deck boy and sails to Copenhagen, where he observes both the good and bad – though mostly the latter – sides of Danish society. Disenchanted with the capital, Christian moves to Odense, where he eventually receives proper instruction in music; yet life does not improve. Destined to remain forever in the social class of his birth, he never becomes more than a poor village fiddler. At the end of the novel, he dies of starvation, alone and unappreciated.

What does this depiction of Christian tell us about Andersen's aesthetics? To begin, his conception of society's obligation to nurture the arts was clearly explained. Adhering to a concept presented by Schelling in his *Vorlesungen über die Philosophie der Kunst* (1802–3),[6] Andersen used the character of Christian to show that true art requires the right social conditions to flourish and thus cannot be expected to help actually create these conditions. Although an artwork begins with the conscious intention of the artist, it must be the result of more than conscious reflection and technique if it is to achieve aesthetic status. A work of art, be it a novel or a musical composition, is not art simply because it shares the same determinable attributes as some other object. Rather, it is a work of art because it reveals the world in a way only art can: it unifies conscious production (skill and/or craft) with unconscious production (genius). But what is genius? Andersen appears to have dramatically changed his concept of this characteristic as well. In *Only a Fiddler* genius as displayed in the character of Christian is a divine gift, a reflection of an absolute ideal. Those familiar with composer biographies of the early nineteenth century will no doubt notice many parallels between Andersen's depiction of Christian and contemporaneous characterizations of figures such as Mozart and Beethoven: the effortless musical talent, the domineering violinist father (in Christian's case, grandfather), the struggle for public acceptance, the lonely and tragic death (fig. 3.2). Christian's genius is accentuated by the presentation of its antithesis, mere virtuosic skill, in the character of the demonic grandfather, whose portrayal says much about how effectively the press could promulgate the image of a virtuoso like Paganini. When Andersen wrote *Only a Fiddler* he had never actually seen, or for that matter heard, an instrumentalist of Paganini's stature. Andersen's conception of such a musician was the result of second-hand descriptions, the majority of which came from the pages of foreign newspapers and periodicals.[7]

But Christian is not the only protagonist in *Only a Fiddler*. The second half of the novel revolves around the story of Naomi, a wealthy Jewish girl with whom Christian becomes acquainted in his youth. Naomi is the opposite of Christian in every way; brave, confident, independent, and wild, she lives life to the fullest, never fearful of failure or public opinion. She never pays much attention to Christian, but instead becomes the mistress of a handsome riding master with whom she travels across Europe. This union ends in tragedy, however; for the riding master is unfaithful and brutally cruel. Filled with despair, Naomi runs away and after numerous vicissitudes finds herself trapped at the end of the novel in a loveless marriage with a dissolute French marquis.

Naomi is not a musical character, but, rather, a stereotype of the wealthy, uncultured elite that so often sat in the audience. Although Andersen's description of Naomi and the events in her life engenders a sense of compassion in the reader, it is nonetheless one of the earliest negative depictions of a Jewish figure in Andersen's work, and as such it is often overlooked. But as Andersen himself admitted when discussing the motivation behind her character: 'The opposition that had stirred in me against injustice, folly, and the stupidity and hardness of the public, found vent in the character of Naomi...'[8] Obstinate to the end, she is

Fig. 3.2　H.C. Andersen.　Drawing of Beethoven's grave dated 30 June 1834.
(Odense: The Andersen House Museum)

forever trapped as a member of the heartless elite, acting out the comedy of a superficial life. But why make her Jewish? Andersen never commented on this aspect of her character. Perhaps he was trying to tap into the already well-defined attitudes and prejudices of his readers. As we saw in chapter 1, anti-Semitism was not foreign to Danish shores during the first half of the nineteenth century. Although the last pogrom in Copenhagen took place in 1819, discrimination against Jews, even those who had converted to Christianity, lingered on for many decades. Jews in Denmark could own businesses and attend the opera, but they would never fully escape the stigma of being a cultural 'other.' Perhaps Andersen found it convenient to make the character of Naomi a stereotype of the uncultured elite – a Jew whose social status was nothing more than a superficial façade. Such an interpretation is supported in the final pages of Andersen's book. As a family of peasants carries Christian's coffin to its final resting place, Naomi encounters the musician for the final time:

> The lid was closed, and the peasants carried the simple coffin out of the house.... The road to the graveyard was narrow. A grand, luxurious carriage pulled by four horses rushed towards them. It was the guests at the manor house; it was the French marquis and his bride Naomi.
> The peasants stepped down into the ditch with the coffin in order to make it easier for the nobility to move forward. They bowed their heads, and the well-dressed lady, Naomi, stuck her head out and greeted them with her prideful glance and charming smile. It was a poor man they buried. Only a fiddler![9]

In his autobiography, Andersen described *Only a Fiddler* as 'a spiritual blossom sprung out of the terrible struggle that went on in me between my poetic nature and my hard surroundings.'[10] Compared to *O.T.*, it is a rambling, improvisatory novel, and Andersen apparently intended it that way. In a letter to Ingemann written in February 1837, while Andersen was still hard at work on the novel, he described a newfound approach to writing that, for lack of a better word, is perhaps best described as an improvised narrative:

> In *O.T.*, I had a prefixed plan before I wrote a single word; this time, however, I am letting the good Lord look after everything. I have two definite characters whose lives I will describe; but how they end – well, I must confess – I do not know myself as yet, even though the second half is approaching a conclusion. This time I am not writing a word without it being given to me, almost forced upon me.[11]

The final result of such an approach was readily noticeable to contemporary readers. For example, one of Andersen's most faithful friends in Copenhagen, an elderly woman named Signe Læssøe, had this to say after reading the book:

> There is much beauty in Andersen's latest novel, but I cannot understand how it all should fit together. At first it seems that he considered Christian to be the hero, but then Naomi replaces him – Can this be done? I don't believe a tribunal would accept this as correct, although there are many beautiful details in it.[12]

Læssøe was correct in her prediction that some critics might not approve of Andersen's approach.   In 1838, almost a year after the appearance of *Only a Fiddler*, a twenty-five-year-old Søren Kierkegaard published a book-length review of Andersen's text entitled *From the Papers of One still living, published against his will: About Andersen as a novelist with continual reference to his latest work, 'Only a Fiddler.'* Of course, the review was not actually released against Kierkegaard's will; it was his literary début, his first published monograph. The title was purposely evasive; it allowed him to distance himself from its biting commentary. Approximately forty pages in length, the review was written in a complicated, discursive prose reminiscent of Kierkegaard's strongest influence at the time, Hegel. Indeed, the text was so dense that shortly after its publication a rumor began to circulate that the only two who had actually read it were Andersen and Kierkegaard himself.[13] Kierkegaard's argument was thorough. After extensive philosophical considerations, he discussed the redeemable qualities of other Danish authors, concluding that each of them had either a central philosophy (a basic outlook on life that was expressed through a positive depiction of art and beauty) or a melancholy poetic feeling that infused their works with a sense of the sublime. Andersen was found to have neither of these traits. Lacking the essential qualifications of a novelist (i.e. a well-defined personality, deep emotions, and a 'serious embrace of reality'), he was described as having nothing to write about but himself. Andersen was unable to separate his own identity from the poetic work, a condition that consequently made him incapable of writing an unprejudiced, edifying novel.[14]

Kierkegaard's interpretation of Andersen's novel reveals much about the era's varying views regarding musical genius and society's obligation toward artists. About the character of Christian specifically, Kierkegaard claimed that Andersen had given no evidence of his musical genius. Christian had no outlook on life, no philosophy of his own, and, for that matter, no personality. If Christian were a true genius, Kierkegaard maintained, there would have been more evidence of his training and struggle toward perfection, his desire to achieve. He would have had the strength and will to break through life's difficulties. The character Andersen had created was nothing more than 'a sniveler about whom it is maintained that he's a genius' – a fool whose only driving force was his own vanity.

Such condemnation was difficult for Andersen to take, and it no doubt would have led to an extended period of depression had it not been countered with an enthusiastic reception by Denmark's general public and unparalleled acclaim abroad. Andersen's thousands of readers clearly sympathized with Christian and the depictions of social inequality his character represented, and composers such as Felix Mendelssohn and Robert Schumann praised the novel publicly. Indeed, in one instance, the novel's message actually engendered a change in behavior toward musicians of humble birth. In the mid-1840s, Andersen was told that, upon reading his novel *Only a Fiddler*, a wealthy woman in Leipzig promised that if she ever came upon an underprivileged boy with musical talent, she would do everything in her power to make sure that he did not come to the same end as poor Christian. When Friedrich Wieck, Clara Schumann's father, heard this, he visited her home with not one, but two young boys of remarkable talent, and reminded the woman of her promise. The woman reportedly kept her word and, welcoming both boys into her home, proceeded to pay for their training at the conservatory.[15]

Only a Fiddler was soon translated into numerous languages – German, English, Dutch, French, and Russian – and as Ingemann explained in a letter to Andersen, Kierkegaard's view of the work was of little importance:

> Let the critics say what they want! Our aesthetic criticism is like an ostrich. It gapes as if it were about to swallow up the swan of poetry, which from the moment it flew out of its egg, had already surpassed it completely.... Devotion to poetry and a feeling for it is not a rare phenomenon, but very few are good judges of it.[16]

With this letter, Ingemann encouraged Andersen to take a stand against speculative philosophy and the hordes of vain and self-indulgent critics. Andersen was grateful for this encouragement and supportive of Ingemann's ideas. Nonetheless, he could not help but think that Kierkegaard was right in some way; that something was missing in his depiction of Christian's genius.[17] In a letter to Henriette Hanck, Andersen expressed his misgivings about his writing and set forth a new set of aspirations:

> I am looking for a literature suitable for my time and instructive for my spirit. An ideal picture is emerging vaguely in my mind, but its outlines are so shapeless that I cannot render it distinct myself. It seems to me that every great poet has added a link, but no more than that, to this huge assembly. Our age has not yet found its poet. But when will he appear, and where? He has to describe nature as Washington Irving does, to comprehend the age as Walter Scott could, sing like Byron, and yet originate in our own age like Heine. Oh! I wonder where this messiah of poetry will be born.... I was born to be a poet, I feel, and I am aware that everything comes into my life as poetry, and still I want more![18]

This quotation implies another subtle shift in Andersen's aesthetics, specifically his view on the nature of art. Literature, like music, followed an evolutionary path that was reflected in each age by an artistic 'messiah.' Each generation added a small element to the ideal artistic whole, and Andersen was in search of a way to tap into this process. He sought inspiration in the world around him, which spawned a search for real-life parallels to the characters in his books. As his diary entries and correspondence from the late 1830s suggest, Andersen slowly began to take an interest in virtuoso instrumentalists, and the first to capture his attention was the Norwegian violinist, Ole Bull.

Bull visited Copenhagen in the autumn of 1838 as part of a European concert tour. Known throughout Europe as a violinist equal to Paganini, he gave his first concert on 4 November – a performance Andersen documented in a letter to Henriette Hanck:

> I have just come from Ole Bull's concert. I went there with the belief that I
> wouldn't like it. I knew well enough that I was expected to hear something
> masterful in his style, but I was half convinced that I was going to hear only an
> enhanced version of [Frederik Carl] Lemming's juggling act on the violin. It was
> a packed house, despite the fact that the [ticket] prices were doubled.
>
> [Bull] began with an 'Allegro maestoso' that was a thing of technical
> perfection – there was a storm of applause, but I was left cold. Then his violin
> began to cry just like a child. It was a broken heart that sobbed. Now tears came
> to my eyes. I was his admirer and will always remain so. [19]

As the opening of this letter reveals, Andersen was obviously skeptical at first
about the aesthetic worth of Bull's music. His attitude changed, however, as the
concert progressed. With each piece, Bull's genius grew ever more apparent in
Andersen's mind. Indeed, as Andersen's letter continues, we see that he went so
far as to compare the virtuoso to his heroes in contemporary literature and
sculpture:

> We also got a 'Capriccio fantastico.' I cannot give you a clearer idea of it than to
> say that I believed Heine's writing fluttered around me in melody, his rending
> picture world with its deep emotion and its caustic irony. Just as no one, not even
> Thorvaldsen, reproduces for us a beauty like the Medici Venus, hardly a violin
> player is found who can show it on the strings: But this is how Bull plays![20]

Bull's performance inspired a kaleidoscopic fantasy of visual images in Andersen's
mind.

> At times small snakes of fire hissed from the violin. The bow danced so merrily I
> believed I was at a peasant wedding, and Satan stood behind the bridegroom and
> laughed while the bride cried bloody tears. Oh, what Bull must have suffered in
> this world, felt time and again, before being able to fill the heart right out to the
> fingertips in such a way. Every time he stepped forward, he was applauded, and
> after the entire performance [he was] called forward again....[21]

In the end, Andersen came to see Bull's virtuosic performance as the physical and
emotional sacrifice of a creative genius, an arduous poetic outpouring inspired by
real-life struggles and emotions:

> One tells so many fantastical tales about Bull's life. Now I am almost beginning
> to believe them. The violin explained, and I seemed to hear, how lonely and
> grieving he stood in Bologna before the world knew him. How poorly he had it,
> when only the violin and the four naked walls knew what stirred inside him.
> Listening to him, I believed I saw him before he had earned his immortal
> reputation – [I saw him] rush into the Seine and fight with death. At the concert's
> close, after the curtain fell, Bull fainted and today lies sick.[22]

Bull's concert served as a transformative experience for Andersen. Perhaps for the
first time, he now looked to purely instrumental music as a medium to both the

performer's and listener's subjective imagination. In Ole Bull, Andersen had found a new source of inspiration.

Andersen first met Bull on 21 November 1838. Three days later he dined with the virtuoso and his wife and was again impressed by the musician's dynamic personality and dramatic performance style. He wrote to Henriette Hanck:

> Now a new [letter] that is practically completely about Bull, my lovable Ole Bull, who approached me in such a nice way, who played so that I cried, and – oh, you should not believe the newspapers! No, the Copenhageners tore him down; many talk against him, deny even his genius, but nonetheless storm the theater. It is something new for them; it is the genius himself who plays. [The laws of] counterpoint and God know that his subject is not quite what one would describe as 'learned;' Consequently, objections are raised. Yet I have fought to the right and left [for him] and did it before I spoke a word with him. Now I love him. He is what a true genius should be. Hear him! Hear him!...[23]

In this description, we see that Andersen's definition of musical genius was beginning to change. Here Bull's genius is defined as a mix of virtuosity and dramatic invention, free from the confines of learned counterpoint. Indeed, if we compare the above description of genius to that presented in *Only a Fiddler*, we find that Andersen has come to envision Bull, the musician who represents 'what a true genius should be,' as a cross between the character of Christian and that of the demonic grandfather.

As we learn from the second half of Andersen's letter, he and Bull soon became close friends who shared a mutual respect for each other's talents:

> You must hear how we met. He approached me in the street, 'Aren't you Andersen?' – 'And you are Ole Bull; so we know each other!' He complained that we did not meet each other in Rome, for we certainly would have become friends there. I said that we could become that still. He talked about *The Improvisatore*, which he had thought about when he walked on [stage] in San Carlo. As soon as we parted, I went to Reitzel [the publisher], took a nicely bound copy of *Fiddler* and wrote in it: 'A calling card to the tone poet Bull from Andersen' and delivered it to his doorman. Today he invited me to attend the rehearsal, asked me home to lunch, where he was so friendly. [He told] me many touching, indeed appalling incidents of his life and has now sent me a ticket for the first balcony along with Oehlenschläger and Thorvaldsen. I am flattered! But I already loved and admired him before we ever met. Hear him! Hear him![24]

Andersen was frustrated by what he viewed as Denmark's indifference toward Bull's talents. Although foreign audiences recognized and praised Bull's genius, the apathetic response of Danish listeners drove Bull to the brink of ill health:

> Tonight Bull gave his final concert. When I first arrived, I heard that he was lying in bed and that Dr. Jacobsen had forbid him to play. There was great unrest. Finally he came. He *must* play! All the educated, non-geniuses are against him. There was an extraordinarily Danish half-heartedness to the crowd. He stepped

forward precariously, looking like a corpse. The lively eyes that the day before had smiled upon me were glazed over. His knees faltered. Oh, I suffered with him! – He nonetheless played so beautifully, indeed, as though it was his swan song. He will not live long. The third number he was supposed to give he had to change; it was too long for him. At the end we got his *Polacca guerriera*, one of his best pieces. Oh, it was as if the violin cried! And with that, the Danish ice melted; everyone cheered! One called him forth again, but the more discreet part hissed at this unjustly. I went behind stage. He lay half-unconscious, was deathly pale. He put his ice-cold hand in mine, and I saw again the friendly, loyal smile. I went home, wrote him a letter that the world would certainly smile at if it read it now. Today he is somewhat better. If he can travel then he will leave Wednesday and be in Odense on Thursday or Friday. At present, there are a few beastly people who say: 'No one knows if those who were hissing were directing it at Bull, or at those who kept trying to get the sick man to come out again so that they could get more music for their money.'[25]

Andersen's contempt for Denmark's ill-treatment of Bull is clear, and in the following months he took it upon himself to promote Bull's talents. He praised the violinist in numerous letters to friends and in January 1839 published an article entitled 'An episode in Ole Bull's Life' in the popular art magazine, *Portefeuillen*.[26]

Exciting concert events, however, were sparse in Copenhagen. The Swedish-Finnish singer Johanna von Schoultz came to the capital in July 1839 and the pianists Wilhelm and Amalia Rieffel the following October.[27] But no one inspired Andersen's poetic sensibility as Bull had. Increasingly restless, Andersen began to make travel plans again. Intent on making it all the way to Asia this time, he left Copenhagen on 31 October 1840 and was gone for nine months. In that time he visited the major capitals of Europe, toured Athens and Constantinople, and sailed back on the Danube through Wallachia, Bulgaria, and Serbia. Andersen's descriptions of the people and places he encountered are fascinating, though too numerous to elaborate upon here. In his diaries he recorded volumes of inspiration for future projects, drawing pictures when words were inadequate. Music played a special role in his conception of the journey, and it shaped his account of the trip, *A Poet's Bazaar*, published in 1842. To fully understand the impact that instrumental music had on Andersen's changing image of the world, it is useful to focus our attention, if only briefly, on a few of his most important encounters.

*

Six days after Andersen left Copenhagen, he attended a concert performed by one of the most famous virtuosi of his generation, Franz Liszt. This concert took place in Hamburg at the Stadt London Hotel. Andersen's reactions are recorded in his diary:

Dinner with our ambassador at Count Holck's, where we were served oysters and champagne. They presented me with a ticket to Liszt's concert, and I went with the ladies through a back door of the Stadt London into a magnificent hall, which had been packed with people for an hour already. There lay a Jewish girl, fat and bedizened, on a sofa – she looked like a walrus with a fan. The ladies were particularly enthusiastic. The merchants from Hamburg seemed to be hearing the clink of gold pieces in the music – that's why they were sitting with smiles spread across their lips. I was seeing Liszt face to face! How great men resemble mountains – they look best at a distance, when there is still an atmosphere about them. He looked like he had been to the Orthopedic Institute to be straightened out. There was something so spider like, so demonic about him! And as he sat there at the piano, pale and with his face full of passion, he seemed to me like a devil trying to play his soul free! Every tone flowed from his heart and soul – he looked to me to be on the rack. He was Klein Zaches.[28] While he was playing, his face came alive. It was as if his divine soul was emerging from the demonic. The music sounded like sprinkling drops of water. The ladies' eyes sparkled. At the end of the concert bouquets were tossed up to him on stage (The washroom attendant at the hotel had brought most of them. He asked people to throw them. If something like this had been done ... in Copenhagen, what an outcry there would have been about it all being prearranged – for we Copenhageners are good at seeing things in the worst light!).[29]

In this description, we find Andersen making literary associations that are quite different from the descriptions he wrote of Bull's playing. Indeed, one gets the sense from reading Andersen's description of Liszt's concert that he was already thinking of the experience as fodder for a new literary project. Andersen's account of the concert is more about the audience and the performer's stage presence than the actual music or listening experience. We get no sense of what music was played, but the makeup of the listening audience, eager to be in the presence of fame but uninterested in evaluating the performer's musical worth, is described with cutting cynicism. Even a stereotypical Jewish girl is there – a figure full of self-confidence who is more interested in being seen than actually listening to the concert. Andersen's personal response to Liszt's performance is clear. Generally unmoved by the pianist's music, he focuses on the performer's appearance and obvious popularity. Andersen is no fool. He realizes that much of the audience's fervor has been carefully stoked by the artist's management, and his description of the claquers at the end of the concert confirm the descriptions of such figures later made so popular in Hector Berlioz's short story collection, *Evenings with the Orchestra.*

Although Andersen was generally unimpressed with Liszt's music, he was intrigued by the performer's larger-than-life stage presence and virtuosity. In the months that followed, as Andersen made his way through the capitals of Europe, he continued to think about Liszt's performance, and whenever possible, sought out virtuoso performers as a means of comparison.

On 21 November 1840 Andersen heard Sigismund Thalberg play a concert in Munich's Odeon Theater. In his diary he wrote: 'Thalberg plays with an amazing technique; he has great calmness, doesn't seem driven. He is not as original as Liszt, but neither of them have fully captured my emotions. Thalberg appeals to reason, Liszt to the imagination.'[30] Andersen elaborated upon this idea in a letter to the Collin family dated 28 January 1841: 'The first [Liszt] pleases me the most.

He is genial and unique. The second [Thalberg] is perhaps more clever, more correct, but he leaves me cold.'[31] Five months later, Andersen met Thalberg again, at the palace of Prince Dietrichstein in Vienna. On this occasion, Andersen got to know the performer personally; and as his interest in Thalberg the person warmed, so did his appreciation of Thalberg the musician:

> We are in the suburbs, in the midst of an English park. There is a small palace, where Prince Dietrichstein lives. We walk through a series of beautiful rooms, and the sound of a piano meets our ears.... The tones we hear come from the hands of one of the piano's masters. It is not Liszt. He and the one we hear are equally great and equally different. Liszt astonishes, we are carried away by the whirling bacchanals. Here, however, we stand at the top of a mountain in nature's clear sunshine, filled with a sense of power and refreshed with peace and grace. We feel happy in the holy church of nature, where hymns mingle with the song of dancing shepherds. Who is the mighty ruler of this piano? Look at him – he is young, handsome, noble and kind! Do you not recognize the portrait? I must write the name under it – Sigismund Thalberg.[32]

In Vienna, Andersen also heard the music of Johann Strauss:[33]

> We are in the Volksgarten. Gentlemen and ladies stroll under the green leaves in lively conversation. The waiters fly in all directions fetching ices. The tones of a great orchestra spread through the garden. In the midst of the musicians stands a young man with a dark complexion. His large, brown eyes glance around in a restless manner. His head, arms, and whole body move. It is as if he were the heart of the great musical body, and as we know, the blood flows through the heart. Here the blood is the tones; these tones were born in him. He is the heart, and all of Europe hears its musical beatings. Its own pulse beats stronger when it hears them.[34]

In Leipzig, Andersen went out of his way to introduce himself to Felix Mendelssohn. His reason for doing so is revealed in a letter to Henriette Hanck dated 5 September 1839:

> The Drewsens have returned home [from Germany], where they met many friends of Andersen's muse. They were especially happy over their meeting with Mendelssohn-Bartholdy. When he heard that they were Danish, he asked them right away if they knew the author of *Only a Fiddler*. He praised me highly ... Drewsen even had to show him my autograph and one of my shirts that he happened to have with him.[35]

Mendelssohn sent a greeting to Andersen via the Drewsens, adding that Andersen should look him up if he ever traveled through Leipzig. One year later, on 10 November 1840, Andersen took the musician up on his offer.

> I was only [in Leipzig] for a day, so I sought out Mendelssohn right away. He was in rehearsal at the Gewandhaus. I didn't give my name; I just said that a traveler very much wanted to greet him. He came, but I could see right away that

he was irritated about being disturbed. 'I have very little time and can't speak here with strangers!' he said. 'But you yourself invited me!' I answered. '[You once said that] I shouldn't travel through your city without introducing myself.'

'Andersen!' he then cried. 'It is you!' His whole face beamed as he gave me a hug and dragged me into the hall. I was to hear his rehearsal of Beethoven's Symphony No. 7.[36]

Mendelssohn then asked Andersen to join him for dinner, but the poet declined, promising to visit again on his return trip to Leipzig. That night, 'a letter arrived from Mendelssohn.... He had composed a little composition that was included on the second page'[37] – a short Canone a 2 (fig. 3.3). In letters to Henriette Hanck and Henriette Wulff, Andersen embellished the nature of his gift from Mendelssohn.[38] Instead of describing it as the short counterpoint exercise it actually was, he called the work a 'song without words,' an example of the genre invented by Mendelssohn as an expression of music's inner, poetic meaning. Thus we come across another example of Andersen's attempt to reshape the details of his musical experiences abroad into a unified, aesthetic idea. Mendelssohn's composition did not fit with the image of genius Andersen had been developing in his mind since his encounters with Bull. An example of learned counterpoint, the Canone a 2 represented a genre of pure skill, not genius. Andersen's transformation of the piece into a 'song without words' reflected his interest in evoking an aesthetic that he had come to associate exclusively with instrumental music. In Andersen's mind, Mendelssohn's 'song without words' served as a better genre for the dissemination of music's subjective meaning, its inherent artistic content.

As promised, Andersen visited Mendelssohn again during his return trip in July 1841, an event he later described in a letter to the Collin family: 'My stay in Leipzig was an unforgettable experience thanks to the famous Mendelssohn-Bartholdy's great friendship for me. I spent four days practically with him alone. He arranged a concert for me in his home.'[39] Andersen spent 'many happy hours with the delightfully genial Mendelssohn' and became especially fascinated with the musician's skills as a virtuosic performer: 'I heard him play again and again. His expressive eyes seemed to look into my soul. Few people have been stamped with the inner flame more than Mendelssohn.' But it was Mendelssohn's improvisatory skills on the organ that most impressed Andersen: 'In the Thomaskirche, where Bach once played the organ, Mendelssohn performed for me some Bach compositions and one of his own. There was a flood of notes.'[40] 'Mountain and valley, heaven and earth roared out its hymn from the organ pipes.'[41] Andersen was so taken with the performance that he composed a small poem for Mendelssohn as a gesture of gratitude:

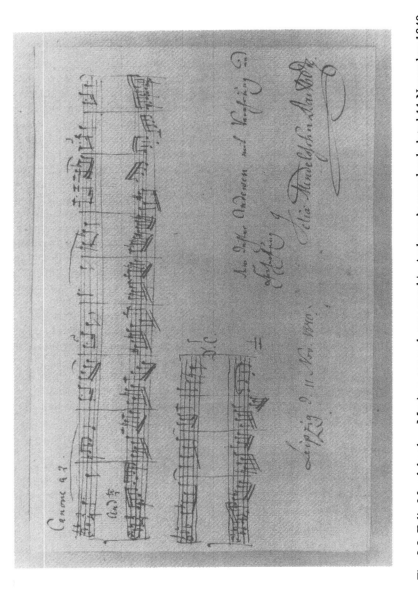

Fig. 3.3 Felix Mendelssohn. Music autograph preserved in Andersen's scrapbook dated 11 November 1840. (Copenhagen: The Royal Library)

Throughout the church organ tones proclaim:
A child is born, and Felix is his name,
Yes 'Felix' is the heavenly angels' song
To him the scepter of music does belong.

Mens gennem kirken orglets toner runged',
Et barn blev døbt og Felix blev det kaldt,
Ja 'Felix' havde Herrens engle sunget,
Thi tonekunstens scepter ham tilfaldt.[42]

*

As Andersen traveled across Europe, he could not help but notice how musical improvisation was enjoying a meteoric rise in popularity due to the proliferation of it in cities holding public concert series. Of course, the art of improvisation was nothing new; since the early eighteenth century it had been a necessary component of any musical training, amateur or professional. But in the mid-nineteenth century, the art of improvisation took on a new identity as virtuosic showmanship became an integral part of public musical performances. Musicians such as Liszt and Thalberg raised the art of improvisation to a new height, and their success appealed to writers of all sorts – most especially Andersen and his old acquaintance Heinrich Heine.

Until recently, literary scholars have tended to focus on parallels between the poetry of Heine and Andersen – but as I hope to show, an equally strong link can be found between their approaches to music criticism. As Andersen's interest in virtuosic instrumental music grew, he sought out descriptions of such performances in foreign periodicals and newspapers, in particular the works of Heine. Since his arrival in Paris in 1831, Heine had developed a new style of journalistic writing that was greatly influenced by the creative process behind musical improvisation. Andersen took a strong interest in this approach and consequently began to envision some of his own journalistic works as having parallels to musical improvisation.[43]

But what exactly was Heine writing about? What were the parameters of the musical improvisations that listeners such as Andersen witnessed? In general, these performances fell into one of two categories: free improvisations that combined fragments of one or more pre-composed melodies – these works were generally given titles such as fantasy, capriccio, or impromptu; and improvised embellishments within a larger, pre-composed work – such as an improvised cadenza within a concerto. The first type of improvisation, the fantasy, was discussed in chapter 1 in connection with the writings of Hoffmann and his influence on Andersen. The second type of improvisation, the cadenza, is the topic of present discussion, for it served as a narrative model for Heine's music criticism and later influenced Andersen's efforts within the same genre.

For nineteenth-century writers interested in creating what is now referred to as a 'performative' literary style, musical improvisation offered an alluring aesthetic model. Audiences reveled in the ostensibly spontaneous creativity of improvisation – the musician's ability to combine fragments into a virtuosic whole, to expand and comment upon a preconceived idea. Romantic writers were also attracted to the element of risk involved in improvisation – the need to make artistic decisions on the spur of the moment, to be able to move into seemingly unexplored territory with the knowledge that some form of thematic and/or structural closure would eventually be required. The musical art of improvisation was believed to be a by-product of an ancient literary practice, the performances of the rhapsode. And as we discovered in chapter 2, vestiges of the rhapsode's art could still be heard in the nineteenth century in the aristocratic academies of Italy, where improvisatori performed recitations based on classical literature and themes suggested by the audience. The art of the improvisatore and that of the musical improviser, however, were not completely parallel. In addition to using obviously different modes of presentation, verbal recitation versus musical performance, improvisatori and musicians adhered to different aesthetic goals in their attempts to appeal to noticeably different audiences. Although both the improvisatore and the musician strove to balance a preconceived structure with what appeared to be spontaneous digressions, the improvisatore used intellectual virtuosity to attract an elite audience, while a musician like Liszt relied on technical virtuosity to entertain a mass audience. The improvisatore performed privately for aristocrats; the musician performed publicly for a paying audience. Although Andersen was clearly thinking of the art of the improvisatore when he wrote his first novel in 1835, it was the virtuoso instrumentalist who served as a model for the demonic grandfather in *Only a Fiddler*, and in later years, under the influence of Heine, offered a narrative model for Andersen's essays of music criticism.

Turning to the work of Heine, specifically his journalistic writings published between 1834 and 1840 in the four-volume collection *Der Salon*, one clearly detects in his narrative structure the influence of musical improvisation. This was not the fragmented fantasy emulated in the work of Hoffmann, but the improvised cadenza as performed by virtuosi such as Liszt, Chopin, and Thalberg. In his journalistic essays, Heine embellished what was supposed to be objective music criticism with literary improvisations, much as a pianist might embellish a concerto movement with a virtuosic cadenza.

In the early nineteenth century, a musician performing a concerto was allowed to digress from the printed music at various times and play one or more improvised cadenzas. (This practice is rare today; few performers compose their own cadenzas, instead they choose to perform cadenzas written by the composer or famous nineteenth-century virtuosi.) Although the composer of a nineteenth-century concerto dictated the location of each cadenza, he often had little or no control over the cadenza's length and musical content. In other words, the performer was expected to adhere to the notes and musical indications written by the composer while playing the concerto proper with the orchestra but was allowed to temporarily usurp the composer's role as 'creator' and perform a virtuosic improvisation when playing the solo cadenza. This hybrid quality distinguished the nineteenth-century concerto as an ingenious genre. Designed to show off the talents of both the composer and performer, it was strictly a public work, created for performance in large concert halls in front of audiences with varying levels of musical aptitude.

Heine was fully aware of the concerto's hybrid construction when he began writing music criticism in the 1830s, and he was generally drawn to virtuosi such as Paganini, Liszt, and Chopin, who were able to appeal to audiences not only with their virtuosity, but also with their charismatic stage presence and improvisatory skill. As a critic, Heine found music to be the most difficult art form to explain with words. Believing that nothing could describe the content of music but music itself (an idea that Eduard Hanslick would later promote), Heine once described a vehement debate over Rossini and Meyerbeer as the best example of music criticism he had ever heard:

> As soon as the one gave the highest merit to the Italian, the other opposed him, but not with dry words – rather, he trilled out some of the especially beautiful melodies from *Robert le Diable*. The first one knew no sharper repartee than to send back eagerly some excerpts of *The Barber of Seville*.... Instead of a noisy exchange of speeches that say nothing, they gave us the most delightful table music, and in the end I had to admit that one should dispute about music either not at all, or in this realistic way.[44]

Heine never went so far as to 'sing' his thoughts about music, but he did write much of his criticism in a narrative style clearly influenced by musical improvisation. Heine did not adhere to Schlegel's aesthetic of the fragment as Hoffmann did, but his many descriptions of contemporary instrumentalists reveal that he was captivated by their virtuosic displays. An amateur musician himself, Heine understood the structure of the nineteenth-century concerto, and he used this structure as a narrative model when writing some of his music reviews. One clear example of this performative approach is shown in a review he wrote of a Chopin concert. The review begins as a narrative description of a specific performance, but as Heine lists the various attributes that constitute Chopin's technical skills as a performer, the literal event being described (Chopin's concert) is put on hold and an embellishment concerning the idea of music and the pianist's genius begins:

> Yes, we must attribute genius to Chopin in the full sense of the word: he is not merely a virtuoso, he is also a poet; he brings to our intuition the poetry that lives in his soul; he is a tone poet, and nothing equals the pleasure he creates for us when he sits at the piano and improvises. Then he is neither Pole, nor Frenchman, nor German – then he betrays a much higher origin and we recognize that he hails from the land of Mozart, Raphael, Goethe: his true fatherland is the dream-realm of poetry.[45]

With this passage Heine ceases describing the details of a particular performance. He deviates from the objective, referential narrative in order to begin a subjective, literary 'improvisation.' Like a pianist in the midst of a concerto, he temporarily abandons the score and performs what might best be described as a 'metonymical cadenza.' Taking a brief departure from reality, he stops the narrative flow and spins out meaning through the use of variation, presenting the reader with his personal interpretation of the subject at hand. Heine usurps Chopin's role as performer, and briefly becomes the virtuoso himself.

Andersen clearly embraced this performative literary style when he began writing essays about real-life musical performances in the early 1840s. His earliest use of a 'metonymical cadenza' appears in an essay on Liszt that was published in 1842 as part of *A Poet's Bazaar* (see interlude 3). After describing the atmosphere in the concert hall, Andersen begins a detailed description of Liszt's performance, commenting on his demonic appearance and comparing his fingers to 'railroads and steam engines.' He then breaks into what can only be described as a Heinesque metonymical cadenza:

> We often hear the expression 'a flood of tones' without defining it, and it is indeed a 'flood' which streams forth from Liszt's piano. The instrument appears to have been transformed into a full orchestra.... The young Hegelians ... behold in this flood of tones the surging progress of science towards the shore of perfection. The poet finds in it his whole heart's poetry, the ornate costumes for his most daring characters. The traveler, as I can tell you myself, receives tonal images of what he has seen or shall see. I heard his music as an overture to my travels: I heard how my own heart beat and bled at my departure from home. I heard the waves' farewell – waves that I was not to hear again until I saw the cliffs of Terracina. It sounded like organ tones from Germany's old cathedrals. The avalanche rolled down from the Alpine mountains, and Italy danced in her carnival dress waving her wand while in her heart she thought of Caesar, Horace, and Raphael! Vesuvius and Aetna were on fire, and the last trumpet sounded from the mountains of Greece where the old gods are dead. Tones I knew not, tones I have no words for, suggested the Orient, the land of imagination, the poet's other fatherland.[46]

Published in 1842, this description of Liszt's 1840 concert in Hamburg differs dramatically from the description Andersen originally recorded in his diary. Whereas the earlier account labeled Liszt as something of a charlatan, the final, published essay hailed him as the 'Orpheus' of a new age. Why the change in perspective? The answer is found in Andersen's interaction with the pianist during the two intervening years.

*

As Andersen traveled across Europe, he continually heard accounts of Liszt's genius. Back in Copenhagen, he had the opportunity to witness the pianist's talents once again. Liszt came to Copenhagen as part of a European tour in 1841, and on 24 July Andersen attended one of his concerts. In the following days he spent a great deal of time with the virtuoso (fig. 3.4), as he explained in a letter to Henriette Hanck written 22 August:

Fig. 3.4 Franz Liszt. Music autograph preserved in Andersen's scrapbook dated 28 July 1841. (Copenhagen: The Royal Library)

When I returned [to Copenhagen] Liszt gave his final concert. I was there, and the day after we ate together at [J.P.E.] Hartmann's home. The next day, Liszt threw a big dinner party, to which only Prume, Orla Lehmann, [Bernhard] Courländer, and I were invited. Liszt appears to consider me a friend. Here and in Germany there is talk about the similarity between our personalities…. When you can, you should hear him. It is something remarkable.[47]

As Andersen got to know Liszt personally, the skepticism he once showed toward the virtuoso's public persona was replaced by a sympathetic appreciation for his personality and musical style. Andersen's disparate descriptions of Liszt document a change in his aesthetic point of view. After seeing Liszt perform in 1840, Andersen's exposure to and appreciation for virtuosic instrumental music and charismatic performers grew exponentially. When he finally began writing his formal account of the performance in *A Poet's Bazaar* in 1842, his description of Liszt's talents differed dramatically from his original impression.

Looking at the whole of *A Poet's Bazaar*, we notice that Andersen used the image of Liszt as a framework for the description of his entire two-year trip. Andersen presented Liszt's concert as the first step of his travels into the unknown, the portal to a world both fascinated with innovation and technology and haunted by the ghosts of history. In *A Poet's Bazaar*, Andersen's description of Liszt's concert serves as a springboard for his newest aesthetic theory. As the noted Andersen scholar Johan de Mylius explains: The concert is used as an introduction to the foreign countries Andersen was about to experience. 'It is an artistic prelude to modern Europe,' and Liszt is portrayed 'as an image of the painful symbiosis between the yearning, romantic soul and the modern development of technology – a combination of art and science.'[48]

Andersen also used the image of Liszt as part of his book's conclusion. In the final chapter, Andersen describes hearing Liszt in Hamburg once again:

It is morning! Enveloped in cold, raw mist, the towers of Hamburg rise before us! We are in the North! The Elbe rolls its milky waves against our ugly steamer. We land. We drive through the dark, narrow streets! Here there is music, a great musical festival. Tonight everything will sparkle with light – across the Alster and along the green avenues. Liszt is here. I shall hear him again in the same salon as when I departed – hear again his 'Valse Infernale!' Shall I not think that the whole flight of my travels was nothing but a dream during Liszt's swelling fantasies?'[49]

But this last encounter is completely fictional. Andersen never heard Liszt give a concert in Hamburg on his way home. In fact, he was in Lübeck when Liszt's 1842 concert in Hamburg was taking place. So why create such a story? What purpose did it serve for Andersen to describe the final days of his journey in this manner? Considering the evolution of Andersen's growing appreciation for instrumental virtuosi, the answer is obvious. Andersen saw Liszt as a symbol of a new era. The ideal artist, Liszt utilized all of the characteristics that Andersen had come to see as important. Liszt was the Orpheus of a new age, a glimpse of what the future held. As such he served as the perfect interlocutor to Andersen's new vision of the world. Mylius explains:

> *A Poet's Bazaar* is a modern, picturesque ... book that unfolds images of both a classical and an extremely contemporary Europe woven into one tapestry. In this Europe, which has its roots in the past but is developing into the future with its railways, for instance, the technical romanticism of Liszt is placed as a confession to art as the Orphic force capable of releasing the soul from its shackles. Andersen uses Liszt to rough-cast a philosophy of art, an aesthetic which matches the new reality and saves a place for poetry in it. It is an aesthetic that also forms the basis of Andersen's style: a technically brilliant art as the answer to the question of what is to become of the soul of the new world.[50]

Hans Christian Andersen, like Hoffmann and Heine before him, looked to instrumental music for literary inspiration. The most subjective of all the arts, music represented the ideal Romantic medium; as such, it served as a threshold to a new realm of poetic expression.

*

Before bringing this chapter to a close, I would like to discuss briefly a few more musicians with whom Andersen came in contact during the early 1840s. Liszt was not the only noted virtuoso to travel to Copenhagen in 1842. Clara Schumann visited the city that spring, and according to Andersen's almanac, their first encounter took place on 22 March. Andersen attended all of Clara Schumann's concerts, and the two socialized on a regular basis (fig. 3.5). Although Andersen's descriptions of her visit indicate that she was generally kind to him and impressed by his work, her letters home give insight into her true impressions. After her initial meeting with Andersen, Clara wrote home to Robert:

> Andersen is as ugly as can be, but nevertheless looks very interesting; the way he moves, fools around, and makes faces probably makes him seem uglier than he really is. It takes a while to get used to him; he is awkward and clumsy, but on the whole a man of intelligence; I'm sure the better you get to know him, the more you like him.[51]

In a letter written by Robert on 24 March (two days before he received Clara's first letter from Copenhagen), his admiration for Andersen was already clearly expressed. Robert had discovered Andersen's poems on his own several years earlier, in translations by Chamisso, and had recently begun setting four of them to music: 'Märzveilchen,' 'Muttertraum,' 'Der Soldat,' and 'Der Spielmann.' Curious about Clara's impression of the author, he wrote:

> Did you meet Andersen? I'm reading something of his just because you're now in Copenhagen. He is an exquisite poetic talent, so naive, so intelligent, so childish. I'd like to dedicate to him the songs of his that I've composed – ask him if you're on good enough terms with him.[52]

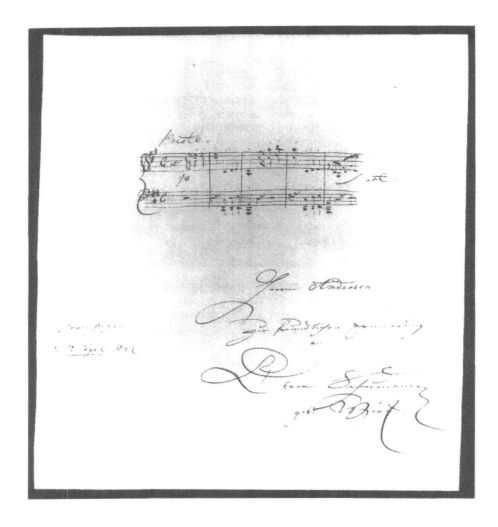

Fig. 3.5 Clara Wieck Schumann. Music autograph preserved in Andersen's
scrapbook dated 10 April 1842. (Copenhagen: The Royal Library)

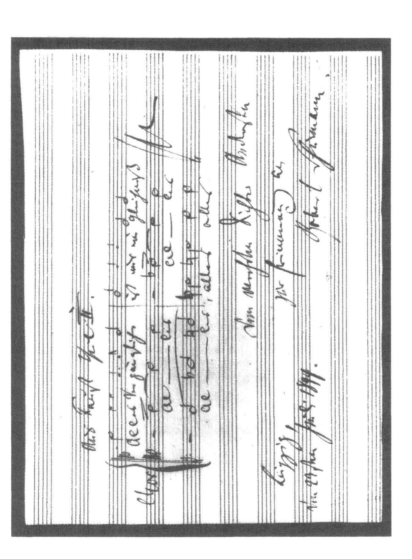

Fig. 3.6 Robert Schumann. Music autograph preserved in Andersen's scrapbook dated 23 July 1844. (Copenhagen: The Royal Library)

On 31 March Clara responded:

> I'll tell Andersen about the dedication – there is no need to ask him as he will feel honored. He recently presented me with a novel he wrote, *The Improvisatore*, which pleased me very much.... By the way, Andersen is like the prophet in his own country – they don't consider him to be a famous author here, perhaps because of his personality; many people are put off by him, so they don't go to the trouble of reading anything by him. I feel bad about that.[53]

Andersen's almanac confirms that Clara told him about Robert's songs on 31 March, and according to Clara: 'he was so overjoyed he was almost speechless and mumbled something about it being "a great honor."'[54] Andersen wrote to Robert shortly thereafter, enthusiastically accepting the thoughtful offer. He had become quite enamored of Clara during her stay in Copenhagen, and he already knew Robert through his many music articles in the *Neue Zeitschrift für Musik*.[55] Several months passed, however, before Andersen received a response. On 11 October 1842, Robert wrote to Andersen:

> Honorable Sir,
>   What must you think of me, since I have taken so long to respond to your kind letter, which pleased me very much. But – I did not want to appear before you with completely empty hands, although I know quite well that actually I am only giving back what I first received from you. Warmly accept my music to your poems. At first glance, they might appear to you as something peculiar. So it was with me when I first read your poems! But as I gradually got accustomed to them, my music also took on a stranger and stranger character. Thus the guilt lies solely on you. Andersenesque poems like 'blühe liebes Veilchen' must be composed differently.
>   In 'Der Spielman' I fear there is a mistake, in that Chamisso's translation does not fully correspond to your original verse.[56] I have marked the place on page 16. A Danish musician, perhaps Mr. Hartmann, would find it an easy task to bring the situation in order. Perhaps you could ask Mr. Hartmann about it, and I will let the correction be appended afterward.
>   My wife has told me so much about you, and I have received such a detailed description that I believe I would recognize you right away if I were ever to set eyes upon you. I also knew you already from your poetry, *The Improvisatore*, *Picturebook without Pictures*, and your exquisite Fiddler, the most exquisite that I … have found in the new German literature. I also now have a complete translation of your short stories. There one certainly finds many pearls for the musician. May the skies stretch out and kindly link all your friends and admirers, and may I be allowed to count myself among them.
>   Your admirer,
>   Robert Schumann
>   P.S. My wife sends you her friendly greetings.[57]

During another extended tour across Europe in 1844, Andersen finally got the opportunity to meet Robert Schumann in person, an encounter he recorded in his diary on 22 July:

Around seven o'clock I went to Schumann's [home] and then walked with him out to the city gate. Later, Frau Frege arrived. She sang lovely versions of 'Märzveilchen,' 'Der Soldat,' and especially 'Der Spielmann.' Clara Schumann accompanied her, and it was hard to judge which of the three [songs] deserved the most praise. We dined sumptuously that evening, drank Rhine wine and champagne.[58]

The next day, Andersen met briefly with the Schumanns again before continuing on his travels. This time he received an autograph from Robert, an excerpt from a choral work he had just begun entitled *Szenen aus Goethes Faust* (fig. 3.6). [59]

During his visit with the Schumanns, Andersen described the plot of a fairy tale opera he was working on called *Lykkens Blomst* (The Flower of Happiness). Although the Danish composer Henrik Rung was scheduled to write the music for the opera, these plans did not deter Schumann from wanting to set the text himself. In a letter dated 25 July 1844 he suggested the idea to Andersen:

My Dear Man,
    Your 'Glücksblume' haunts me; it would make a great Zauberoper and I would set all of my strength to doing it well. Could you please share the subject with me once again in a short summary, and would you and the Danish composer allow the material to be worked on by a German poet? Couldn't I get an answer from you while you're still in Berlin? Happy travels and think of me and my wife.
    Your supportive admirer,
    Robert Schumann[60]

Andersen promised to send the requested material, but it appears that he never did. Schumann soon fell ill and was incapacitated for several months. After his recovery, in April 1845, he asked his Danish friend, Niels W. Gade,[61] to deliver a letter to Andersen during a trip back home to Copenhagen:

Through Gade I send you this greeting; if only I could travel with him myself to the North, but the shackles still hold me here. In the time since we last saw each other, my worthy friend, things have gone badly for me. A dreadful nervous ailment would not leave me alone, and I am still not fully healed. With the nearing of spring I feel somewhat stronger, and I hope that my strength will increase still more.
    Work was something that I generally could not and was not allowed to do, but I thought often about our 'Glücksblume.' You sent such a friendly response from Berlin, promising to send me the sketches – may I remind you of that? Has it perhaps already been published? Otherwise, how are you doing? Do you have new tales, new stories? ... Can we hope that you will soon greet us again in Germany? A gathering like the one that evening, when you were with us – poet, singer, pianist, and composer together – will it soon occur again?... If yes, then every evening will be unforgettable for us ... May I hope for an answer from you, perhaps also for the 'Glücksblume?' Write to us here in Dresden! If there is anything else I can do for you here in Germany then make me your secretary; with pleasure I will do it. [62]

But Andersen never sent the text, and he never saw Schumann again. Schumann's health remained precarious until his death in 1856, and Andersen appears to have never been fully enthusiastic about working with him on a large-scale project. His respect for the composer, however, was revealed several years later when he paid tribute to Schumann through one of the protagonists in his fifth novel, *De to Baronesser* (The Two Baronesses). In this work, a young pianist of humble origins known only as 'the Gentleman' briefly wins the heart of a young girl named Clara, with a 'haunting' and 'demonically-whirling' performance made up of literature and music: 'On the previous evening the Gentleman had recited scenes from Goethe's *Faust*, and before and after each scene he had painted the atmosphere [for it] with music; he had turned the scenes into "artworks."'[63] On this occasion he performs a similar work constructed from a series of folk ballads. Clara is clearly moved by the performance, and music binds the hearts of these two pianists:

> Clara stepped up to the piano and laid her hands on it: two beautiful eyes looked into his, and there was music in her words. The Gentleman blushed deeply but did not cast down his eyes. Music was his world, it still whirled around him. With a single word from Clara, light, dancing melodies rang out [from the piano].[64]

The next day the Gentleman's career as a pianist comes to an end when, like Schumann, he injures his hand:

> 'O God, my hand!' he sighed. 'It is broken! Oh, the pain is insufferable!... The sick man lay in a fever.... Many thoughts passed feverishly through his mind: 'My hand is useless! Music is over! Oh, my God, how unfortunate I am! What does the future hold for me now?'[65]

But like Schumann, the Gentleman in Andersen's novel nonetheless manages to continue a career in music. He finds that he has talent for writing both music and words and, taking 'music' as his 'bride,' he becomes a successful composer who writes large compositions inspired by great literary works such as Goethe's *Faust*.

When Andersen departed on his 1844 tour of Europe, one of his primary goals was to strengthen ties with Europe's finest patrons and practitioners of art. In addition to calling on the Schumanns, he revisited some of his closest musical friends: Mendelssohn, Thalberg, Liszt, Bull, Carl Maria von Weber, Heine, etc., and sought out patrons and publishers to promote his work.

To Andersen, the German-speaking lands nurtured the careers of his generation's greatest artistic talents. Andersen wanted to tap into this resource, to become one of the immortal poets of his age. But he knew that he would have to establish an artistic home outside of Denmark to do so. He needed to find a foreign patron and community that would support him spiritually and promote his genius. As we shall see in the following chapter, Andersen believed he had found such a haven in 1844 during his first trip to Weimar. Home to literature's immortal heroes, Goethe, Schiller, and Herder, and music's modern Orpheus, Liszt, Weimar stood as a monument to both the past and the future of art. Simply stated, it offered a cultural climate that Andersen found irresistible.

Interlude 3

'Liszt' from *A Poet's Bazaar**

by Hans Christian Andersen

It was in Hamburg, in the hotel Stadt London, that Liszt gave a concert. In a few minutes, the salon was quite full. I came too late, yet I got the best place, close up to the tribune where the piano stood, for they conducted me up the back stairs.

Liszt is one of the kings in the realm of tones; and as I said, I am not ashamed to acknowledge that my friends led me up the back stairs.

The salon, and even the side rooms, gleamed with lights, gold chains, and diamonds. Not far from where I stood lay a fat, dressed-up young Jewish woman on a sofa. She resembled a walrus with a fan. Wealthy Hamburg merchants stood packed together as if an important matter on the exchange were about to be discussed. There was a smile about their lips, as if they all had bought securities and railway shares and had profited immensely.

The Orpheus of mythology could set stones and trees in motion with his music. The modern Orpheus, Liszt, had electrified them already before he began to play. Fame, with her mighty aura, had opened the eyes and ears of the multitude so that everyone seemed to recognize what was about to follow. I myself felt in the beams of these many sparkling eyes and expectant beating hearts the approach of a great genius, who with daring fingers distinguishes the boundaries of his art in our age!

It is proper to hear Liszt for the first time in London, this great metropolis of machinery or in Hamburg, the European business office: time and place correspond there – and it was in Hamburg that I was to hear him. Our age is no longer that of imagination and feeling – it is the age of intellect. The technical dexterity in every art and in every trade is now a general condition of their exercise. Languages have become so perfected that it almost belongs to the age of writing themes to be able to put one's thoughts in verse, which half a century ago would have passed for the work of a true poet. In every large town we find dozens of people who perform music with such expertise, that twenty years ago they might have been considered virtuosi. All that is technical, the material as well as the spiritual, is in this our age in its highest development. Our age thereby takes flight, even among the lifeless masses.

---

* This translation is heavily based on the one found in Johan de Mylius, 'Hans Christian Andersen and the Music World,' 194–95.

Our world's geniuses – are they not simply the fashionable foam on the ferment of the scathing development of our age? But true spirits must be able to suffer a critical dissection and raise themselves high above what can be mastered; each in his intellectual sphere must not only fill it, but add something more. Like the coral polyp, they must add a growth to the tree of art or their activity is nothing.

In our age the musical world has two princes of the piano who thus fill their allotted place – they are Thalberg and Liszt. When Liszt entered, an electric shock seemed to pass through the salon. Most of the ladies rose; it was as if a ray of sunshine passed over every face, as if all eyes were greeting a dear, beloved friend! I was standing quite near the artist, a thin young man with long, dark hair hanging around his pale face. He bowed and sat down at the piano. The whole of Liszt's appearance and movement immediately reveals one of those persons we notice for their individuality alone; the Divine hand has impressed a stamp upon him, which makes him recognizable among thousands. As Liszt sat down at the piano, my first impression of his personality was derived from the appearance of strong passions in his pale face. He seemed to me a demon who was nailed fast to the instrument whence the tones were streaming forth – they came from his blood, from his thoughts. He was a demon trying to play his soul free. He was on the rack; his blood was flowing and his nerves trembling. But as he continued to play, the demonic disappeared. I saw that pale face assume a nobler and brighter expression. The divine soul shone from his eyes, from every feature. He became as beautiful as spirit and enthusiasm can make one!

His *Valse Infernale* is more than a daguerreotype of Meyerbeer's *Robert le Diable*! We do not stand from afar and contemplate this well-known picture – we gaze fixedly into its very depths and discover new whirling figures. It did not sound like the chords of a piano; no, every tone seemed like tinkling drops of water!

He who admires art in its technical perfection must respect Liszt. He who is charmed by God-given genius must respect him all the more.

The Orpheus of our age has let his tones swell through the world metropolis of machinery, and we have found and acknowledge, as a Copenhagener once said, that 'his fingers are truly railroads and steam engines;' his genius even mightier in drawing together the intellectual spirits of the universe than all the railways on earth. The Orpheus of our age made the European business office clink-clink with his tones, and at that moment at least, people believed the gospel: a golden spirit is more powerful than worldly gold.

We often hear the expression 'a flood of tones' without defining it; and it is indeed a 'flood' that streams from Liszt's piano. The instrument appears to have been transformed into a full orchestra. This is produced by ten fingers that possess an expertise that may be called fanatical when controlled by the mighty genius. It is a flood of tones, which, in its uproar, momentarily reflects every glowing sensibility. I have met politicians who from Liszt's playing have come to understand how the peaceful citizen could be so affected by the tones of the 'Marseillaise' as to seize a rifle, rush from hearth and home, and fight for an idea. I have seen peaceful Copenhageners with Danish autumn mist in their blood become political bacchants from his playing; and mathematicians have become dizzy with tonal figures and calculations of sound. The young Hegelians – the really gifted ones, and not the empty-headed who only make a spiritual grimace at the galvanic stream of philosophy – behold in this flood of tones the surging progress of science towards the shore of perfection. The poet finds in it his whole heart's poetry, the ornate costumes for his most daring characters. The traveler, as I can tell you myself, receives tonal images of what he has seen or shall see. I heard his music as an overture to my travels: I heard how my own heart beat and bled at my departure from home. I heard the waves' farewell – waves that I was not to hear again until I saw the cliffs of Terracina. It sounded like organ tones from Germany's old cathedrals. The avalanche rolled down from the Alpine mountains, and Italy danced in her carnival dress waving her wand while in her heart she thought of Caesar, Horace, and Raphael! Vesuvius and Aetna were on fire, and the last trumpet sounded from the mountains of Greece where the old gods are dead. Tones I knew not, tones I have no words for, suggested the Orient, the land of imagination, the poet's other fatherland.

When Liszt had ceased playing, flowers showered down around him. Pretty young girls, and old ladies who had once been pretty girls, each cast her bouquet, for he had cast a thousand bouquets of tones into their hearts and minds.

From Hamburg Liszt was to rush to London, where he would throw out new bouquets of tones to breathe poetry into material, everyday life. Happy man, who can thus travel all his life, always seeing people in their spiritual Sunday clothes! Nay, even in enthusiasm's bridal gown! Shall I meet him again? This was my last thought, and chance would have it that we were to meet on our travels, meet in a place where my reader and I least could imagine – meet, become friends, and again separate. But this belongs to the final chapters of this flight. At the time, he went on to Victoria's capital, and I to Gregory XVI's.

Fig. 4.1 August Grahl. Portrait of H.C. Andersen (1846).
(Odense: The Andersen House Museum)

Chapter 4

The Poet, the Pianist, and the Patron

Weimar under the Grand Duke Carl August was a new Athens. Let us think today of constructing a new Weimar.... Let us allow talent to function freely in its sphere.
Franz Liszt

Since my departure from Weimar, my thoughts have flown there often ... where I felt so serene and so happy.
Hans Christian Andersen

Few surprises in the history of nineteenth-century music are more dramatic than that of Franz Liszt's sudden move to Weimar in February 1848. The decision to exchange an epoch-making career as a pianist for the life of a Kapellmeister baffled many of Liszt's contemporaries and drew criticism from the press. Although few understood Liszt's motives at the time, hindsight has shown that they were well calculated. With the support of his patron, hereditary Grand Duke Carl Alexander, and the resources available in Weimar and its environs, Liszt initiated what could be seen as one of the most revolutionary events in the history of nineteenth-century music: the creation of what was soon to be called the New German School.

Over the last decade a number of scholars have sharpened our vision of Liszt's years in Weimar by publishing contemporary accounts of his activities there.[1] Yet as valuable as these accounts have proven to be, they have not fully explained the complex relationship Liszt shared with his patron and the transforming effect his presence had on Weimar's intellectual/artistic community. In this chapter, I hope to broaden our understanding of these issues by presenting another collection of contemporary sources yet to be explored – the writings of Hans Christian Andersen. My aim is simply to present this familiar Lisztian narrative from a strikingly different angle – to provide a sense of how the cultural transformation at Weimar was perceived by and affected an artist of differing sensibilities, who was eventually cast aside from the new Weimar. Indeed, Andersen's story – crucial aspects of which have been published only in the original Danish – provides us with part of a 'thicker' cultural context within which we might subsequently view Liszt and his circle.

Andersen shared a strong friendship with Carl Alexander, and over a period of approximately twenty years he visited the Grand Duke on numerous occasions.

Andersen was in attendance for many of Weimar's most important cultural events, recording his reactions in his diaries, and he corresponded with Carl Alexander on a regular basis and carefully preserved the Grand Duke's thoughts concerning the role of the artist in society, the incongruence of art and politics, and the 'music of the future.' Andersen and Carl Alexander shared an affinity for the arts. The evolution of their friendship and Andersen's contact with Weimar's artistic community reveal much about the city's cultural climate in the 1850s and its ever-expanding circle of artistic associates. Andersen was an attentive witness to the changes that Liszt's presence engendered in Weimar. In his letters, diaries, scrapbooks, memoirs, and fairy tales he preserved an intriguing narrative of Liszt's Weimar years that has never been fully told, but deserves to be heard – the story of the poet, the pianist, and the patron.

*

Andersen's contact with Weimar began in 1844. Traveling through Germany to visit friends and publishers, he accepted an invitation from Baron Carl Olivier von Beaulieu-Marconnay, Lord Chamberlain to the Grand Duke of Saxony-Weimar-Eisenach, to spend a week in Weimar. With Beaulieu as his guide, Andersen visited the homes of Goethe and Schiller, attended the theater regularly, and hobnobbed with the local aristocracy. His first meeting with Carl Alexander took place on 26 June at Ettersburg castle in Eisenach, an occasion he recorded in his diary:

> Into the salon entered the hereditary Grand Duke, a young twenty-six year old man with a good figure. I didn't know him, but I could sense right away who he was without anyone telling me. He said a few kind words to me – that he was glad to meet me!... He introduced me to his wife, a daughter of the deceased king of Holland. She said a few friendly words to me, and at the [dinner] table the Grand Duke invited me to sit next to her. They treated me very nicely. After [dining] we all went outside the castle to a folk festival.... The hereditary Grand Duke and his cavalier danced. They wanted me to dance as well, but naturally I said *No!* – Then the young Duke led me alone ... to a place in the garden where Goethe had played in the open air, and where all of Weimar's famous men had written their names [on a tree]. One side of the tree was covered with bark that had just begun to grow over. Lightning had struck it here – Jupiter must have also wanted to write his name.... The young Duke was very charming; I could easily choose him as my friend, if he weren't a prince!... We walked together for an hour and spoke confidentially. In the palace I read fairy tales aloud and was admired. Then we went out under the linden trees. Colored lamps hung from the branches, and there was dancing! Later, we ate supper. I love the young Grand Duke dearly; of all princes, he is the first that really appeals to me. I only wish that he weren't a prince, or that I were one.[2]

Andersen's warm reception by Carl Alexander was no doubt facilitated by the poet's enthusiasm for the Grand Duke's newest court appointment – the pianist Franz Liszt. Although Liszt was not physically in attendance during Andersen's first visit to Weimar in 1844, his presence in the city was definitely felt. Liszt had first visited Weimar in 1841, and in 1842 Carl Alexander had surprised the music world by appointing the virtuosic showman as Weimar's 'Kapellmeister in ausserordentlichem Dienst.' Although this appointment received much criticism in the press, the hereditary Grand Duke took pride in the decision, and he eagerly embraced those who shared his point of view.

Andersen's unbridled enthusiasm for Liszt, as presented in *A Poet's Bazaar*, ingratiated him to Carl Alexander, who was in the early stages of trying to re-establish Weimar's reputation as the 'Athens of the North.' During the reign of Carl Alexander's grandfather Carl August (1757–1828), Weimar had been the most important cultural center in Germany. Under his patronage, the city had attracted the greatest writers of the day – Goethe, Schiller, Herder, and Wieland had all lived and worked there – and the memory of their achievements was preserved in various monuments. After the death of Carl August, Weimar's splendor began to fade. The city had become impoverished, and under the rule of Carl Friedrich (Carl Alexander's father), art had been reduced to little more than an occasional luxury. It was Carl Alexander's mother Maria Pavlovna, sister of the Russian Czar, who had kept the city's flagging artistic interests alive. Inspired by her efforts, the hereditary Grand Duke Carl Alexander hoped to reawaken Weimar's glorious past.[3] His first step had been to appoint Liszt Kapellmeister in 1842, and judging from his enthusiasm over Andersen in 1844, his proposed second step was to secure a position for the writer as well. During his early days in Weimar, Andersen was hailed as a new Schiller; the local aristocracy even went so far as to tell him that he shared a physical resemblance with the poet. Andersen was wined and dined by the wealthy and feted at Ettersburg castle by the royal family. Carl Alexander praised Andersen on numerous occasions, and it soon became clear that he envisioned the poet as a bright star whose growing fame would eventually illuminate Weimar's status as an international artistic hub.

Andersen spent three days in the royal family's company during his visit in 1844. Much of this time was spent with the hereditary Grand Duke. In Andersen's description of their final encounter, recorded in his diary on 28 June, we clearly see Carl Alexander's eagerness to attach Andersen to Weimar:

> We drove to Ettersburg, where they produce a journal, and read aloud several selections. Miss Amalie Winter read a love story. The hereditary Grand Duke [read] a novella, probably written by himself.... I read 'The Princess and the Pea,' 'The Emperor's New Clothes,' and 'Little Ida's Flowers.'... The hereditary Grand Duke wanted me to remain longer in Weimar. He took my hand and held it tightly, saying that he was my friend and that he hoped that sometime in the future he could prove it. His wife asked me to return to Weimar and not to forget them. My heart was truly touched.[4]

Carl Alexander then presented Andersen with a branch from one of the linden trees at Ettersburg – a memento of his time there – and asked him to submit a story to his journal. Moved by this act of kindness, Andersen left Eisenach with a heavy heart and traveled back to Weimar with Beaulieu. The next day Andersen visited the graves of Goethe and Schiller:

> In the chapel the coffins had been moved so that Goethe and Schiller lie next to each other.... I stood between them, read aloud 'Our Father,' and asked God to let me be a poet worthy of them.... Laurel wreathes lay on their coffins. I took a leaf from each one.[5]

Andersen left Weimar two days later. As the poet later explained in his initial letter to Carl Alexander (29 August 1844), Weimar was now a second home, a friendly haven where enthusiasm for his writing and royal patronage were secure:

> Since my departure from Weimar, my thoughts have often flown there ... where I felt so serene and so happy.... The evenings I spent at Ettersburg were a beautiful chapter in the fairy tale of my life. I remember so clearly the bright, blissful look in the eyes of you and your charming wife. I remember the Folk Festival on 24 June ... the fragrant linden trees, our walk, my dear Grand Duke, through the forest to the tree where Zeus wanted to write his name with a lightning bolt next to Goethe's and Schiller's. I remember it all so clearly, and I hope that soon my muse will present me with a poem that is worthy of your Ettersburg journal. I will not forget, but I wait until I can create something worthy. When I rode out of Weimar, over the bridge and past the mill, tears came to my eyes. I was so deeply moved, it was as though I were leaving home, for that is what Weimar became for me during the few days I spent there with my dear friends. If I may tell you, my Grand Duke, you and your loving wife have become embedded in my memory, as good people [als Menschen] you have become rooted in my heart.[6]

Obviously thrilled by Andersen's letter, the hereditary Grand Duke quickly responded by echoing Andersen's description of the visit as 'a marvelous fairy tale.' He praised Andersen's talent for pictorial description and commented at length on the poet's most recent play, *Horatio*.[7] Carl Alexander hoped to produce the play in Weimar, and he was making plans for such an event with the theater director. 'If our stage could be the first in Germany to produce your play, it would make me very proud,' he wrote.[8] Six weeks later, on 5 November 1844, the hereditary Grand Duke began in earnest his campaign to attach Andersen to his court on a more permanent basis with a letter written from Wartburg castle (fig. 4.3):

> I find a special worth and great pleasure in writing to you from *here* – to you, who are touched so deeply and warmly by everything. If it is true that the atmosphere within which we think and feel has a powerful influence on our thoughts and feelings, then I know of no better place, far and wide, than this one to think of you and from which to write. If only you knew this place, you would agree with me.

Fig. 4.2 Carl Hartmann. Drawing of Andersen reading aloud at Graasten (1845).
(Copenhagen: The National Museum at Fredricksborg)

Fig. 4.3 Lithograph of Wartburg by an unknown artist (1836).
(Weimar: Stiftung Weimarer Klassik)

You should first realize that with your spirit, with your elves and fairies, you truly belong here. High in the air I sit, and over me I see only the heaven's blue. Deep, deep under my feet lie the beautiful mountains of the Thuringian lands; southward they look like huge waves that have been frozen in a green sea by the command of one of your fairies, for the arboreal hills alternate in tremendously gigantic fluctuations with the darkest, deepest abysses of the forest. Closer to me, where I now sit, toward the west, the deep valleys extend and grant a clearer view of the life and deeds of man. A pretty country road built of basalt winds down here from the hills. Further on, villages glimmer between the meadows. Over toward the north, steep cliffs arise, and above them arises the mountain. To the west, the naked rock is enclosed by a lovely valley that disappears between the immense forests; and before me, at the end of the valley, lays an ancient city with pointed towers and wonderful roofs. It appears imprisoned behind numerous gardens that in the summer cast a colorful, fragrant net over their prisoner. The city is Eisenach, and the castle from which I am corresponding with you is the Wartburg, the famous medieval castle from which poetry first descended into the German regions. Only a few steps from my room there is a huge building; three rows of endless squares on slender columns quietly decorate the outside of the courtyards. The upper row belongs to the hall where the German Minnesänger first wrote poetry and sang. The second row belongs to the hall of the old Thuringian ducal court, where its armaments now shine, and to the chapel where Luther preached. The third row of rooms is where Saint Elisabeth of Thuringia calmly administered her blessing, a blessing that lives on in Eisenach today in religious establishments. On the hall where I am living, next to my bedroom, is the room where Luther translated the Bible, and so there is a huge number of historic memories that cling to each stone of this castle.... Indeed, was not this place – which breathes such enthusiasm, which served as the cradle of German literature, its child, which then grew up in Weimar – especially made so that one could think about and write to you, my dear friend? Come and inspire yourself here with me in the summer, when the mountain will have produced the sprouting, budding spring as one of its thousand blooms.[9]

Although Andersen did not visit in the summer as requested, he did continue to send his new patron a steady stream of fairy tales and poems over the next year and eventually returned to Weimar in January 1846. This time he remained for a month and socialized with the royal family on a daily basis. Andersen's diary shows that this was a marvelous visit. Constantly praised for his poetic genius, he was made to feel like a respected member of the court. As a token of his appreciation for such kindness and hospitality, Andersen presented Carl Alexander with a new fairy tale, 'The Bell,' on 15 January, explaining that it symbolized their personal relationship and mutual artistic goals.

'The Bell' is a parable about the pursuit of ideal beauty and the harmony of nature and art. It tells the story of a young prince and a poor boy who, intrigued by the beautiful sound of a mysterious, distant bell, set off with everyone else in the village to find the source of its beauty. But the bell is elusive, and eventually everyone but the prince and the poor boy abandon their search.

'Let us go on together,' proposed the prince. But the poor boy with the wooden shoes was quite shy. He pulled at the sleeves of his tunic, which were too short, and said that he was afraid that he could not walk as fast as the prince. Besides, he thought that the bell should be searched for on the right side, where everything great and marvelous is located.[10]

'Then I suppose we will never see each other again,' says the prince, and the two go their separate ways. The poor boy 'walks into the densest part of the forest, where brambles and thorns tear his worn-out clothes and scratch his face and legs.' The prince takes an easier path, lined with beautiful trees and flowers and lighted by rays of sunshine. Ugly monkeys mock him, but he pays no attention. As the long shadows of afternoon stretch across the forest, the prince despairs that he will never find the bell, and in an effort to catch a final glimpse of the sun, he climbs a steep hill.

Just before the sun set he reached the summit. Oh, what splendor! Below him stretched the ocean, that great sea that was flinging its long waves toward the shore. The sun stood like a shining red altar where the sea and sky met. Everything melted together in glowing colors. The forest sang, and the sea sang, and his heart sang along as well. All of nature was a grand, holy church, wherein trees and clouds were pillars; flowers and grass were mosaic floors; and heaven itself was the great cupola. High above, the red color had disappeared, for the sun had set. Millions of stars were lighted; millions of little diamond lamps twinkled there. The prince spread out his arms toward the sky, the sea, and the forest – and just at that moment, from the right side of the cliff, the poor boy with the short sleeves and wooden shoes arrived. He had gotten there almost as quickly by going his own way. They ran to meet each other and stood there, hand in hand, in the midst of nature and poetry's great church. And far above, the great invisible holy bell rang out; blessed spirits floated around them in dance to a joyful hosanna.[11]

This final scene, atop a steep hill overlooking the forest and sea, is reminiscent of the view from Wartburg castle as described to Andersen by Carl Alexander. The prince in the story is clearly a representation of the hereditary Grand Duke, who as a patron continued his search for ideal beauty even when others abandoned and mocked him. The poor boy in the story is one of Andersen's many autobiographical representations – as an artist, he must follow a more difficult path than his princely patron in the pursuit of beauty. Together, the two characters find what they seek: ideal beauty rings out from on high, uniting rich and poor, patron and artist, nature and art. Carl Alexander was obviously moved by Andersen's story. His reaction to it, recorded in Andersen's diary, shows that he had fully understood its artistic implications:

I read three tales. 'The Bell' made the strongest impression. I told him that the prince in the story was a reference to him. 'Yes, I will strive for the noblest and best goals,' he said and shook my hand. We sat together at the table, and he drank a toast to me.[12]

Two days later, Carl Alexander requested a private meeting with Andersen. He had been drafting a literary work himself, called *Waldeinsamkeit* (Solitude in the Forest), and he wanted Andersen's opinion of it. He also wanted to enlist Andersen in his mission to attract other artists to Weimar. Jenny Lind was scheduled to arrive in just a few days, and he hoped that Andersen could convince her to remain there permanently.

Andersen's ardor for Lind was no secret. Her clear, unadorned vocal style inspired one of his most famous tales, 'The Nightingale,' in 1842; and he openly declared his love for her when she visited Weimar in 1846. The royal family warmly received Lind when she arrived on 22 January. Andersen's diary reveals the extent to which Carl Alexander involved him in the wooing of this possible addition to court:

> 29 January: The hereditary Grand Duke talked with me about Jenny, with whom he is completely preoccupied. He wishes her to become his wife's companion and live with them.[13]
>
> 30 January: At the hereditary Grand Duke's this evening. He had written asking me to come half an hour early to talk about Jenny. I arrived at 7:30 [and] sat on the sofa with him. He was quite emotional. [He] asked me continually to write about her, but without mentioning names, just 'our friend.' He pressed my hands in his.[14]

Jenny Lind left Weimar on 28 January without committing to return on a more permanent basis. Although Carl Alexander was confident that Andersen would eventually convince her to accept a position in Weimar, Andersen himself was doubtful. In a letter to Louise Lind (no relation) dated 2 April 1846 he wrote: 'You ask me about Jenny. I hear from her regularly; they would like to keep her in Weimar. In that case, I would like to be there too; but it won't happen.'[15]

Andersen wrote to Jenny Lind about Weimar on several occasions, but with little effect: Lind had no intention of settling in the city permanently. When she finally put an end to the topic, she counted on Andersen to explain her decision to Carl Alexander:

> Dear Andersen, if you should write to our high-born friend, tell him, if you should mention me that I shall remember those few days at Weimar as long as I live. And I only speak the truth when I say that I have never found such peace of mind and utter happiness, although I have always been kindly received everywhere. I like these high-born personages, my brother, but as you say not for the jewels and decorations they wear, but for their genuine and honest hearts and souls. I get quite carried away when I think of these people! God's peace over them and theirs![16]

Although Andersen had been unsuccessful in his attempt to attach Lind to Weimar, he was still welcome at court himself and over the next two years became a regular visitor.[17] Carl Alexander had grown quite fond of Andersen. In a letter to Liszt dated 3 December 1846 he described the poet's artistic temperament and unique sense of humor:

> Andersen, the fairy tale writer, was here longer this fall. He divides his life between Copenhagen and Weimar. I love him as a person and as a writer. Although he is no star of the highest class, his flame is pure; and that is rare in our day, when writers no longer make poetry their purpose, but rather their means. No one, almost no one, I tell you, has the conscience of a writer. One day Andersen amused me greatly when he said to me, laughing: 'Oh, in Vienna I was once invited to a literary social gathering; there I found two rooms full of poets, and all of them immortal.'[18]

When Andersen was not in Weimar, he remained in constant contact with Carl Alexander through a steady stream of correspondence, and he continued to send new publications for the hereditary Grand Duke's approval.[19] Carl Alexander remained unrelenting in his efforts to attach Andersen to Weimar permanently. 'If Goethe and Schiller could work in Weimar, then so can you,'[20] he told Andersen. 'We Germans appreciate you more than the Danes do.'[21]

*

As Carl Alexander's desire to attach well-known artists to Weimar was a common theme in his correspondence with Andersen, discussions of Liszt occasionally arose. Although Andersen and Carl Alexander praised Liszt profusely in their public comments, their private musings about the artist and his music were often less favorable. For example, Andersen's original impression of Liszt's 1840 Hamburg concert, recorded in his diary on the very same evening, differed dramatically from the description he published in *A Poet's Bazaar*. Similarly, a letter to Andersen dated 16 March 1846 reveals that Carl Alexander also had reservations about Liszt's music. In fact, one gets the sense that the hereditary Grand Duke was initially more drawn to Liszt's charismatic personality than his virtuosic music:

> Liszt is gone, which makes me sad since his conversation gives me even greater pleasure than his playing, just as one admires a naked demon much less than one wearing a well-tailored jacket, who with his outer appearance alone already impresses. Yet he appears to me as an unclothed demon when at the piano. I shudder when he leads me into the world of tones.[22]

Andersen's response to this letter expressed a similar reaction to Liszt's playing. After seeing him in a concert in Vienna he wrote on 2 April 1846: 'I recently ran into Liszt, the witty, unique genius! We were together for a few hours, and I heard him bleed on the piano.'[23]

As insightful as these descriptions might be, discussions of Liszt were not common in the early correspondence between Andersen and Carl Alexander. This was probably due to the fact that Liszt was rarely in Weimar: during his first six years as the city's Kapellmeister, he was never in residence for more than three months a year. In the spring of 1848, however, this arrangement suddenly changed. Fatigued by years of strenuous concertizing and newly entangled in an adulterous relationship with Princess Caroline Sayn-Wittgenstein, Liszt began to look to Weimar as a private haven. He was intent on gaining respect as an intellectual musician from Europe's musical elite and saw no better way to achieve this than to settle down in a stable position and focus his attention on composing rather than performing. As Liszt's intentions became clear and his involvement with Wittgenstein became more intense, rumors began to spread that he had moved to Weimar permanently. Andersen got wind of such rumors in early 1848, and his interest in the matter was clearly expressed in a letter from 13 January to Carl Alexander:

> Ernst is here in Copenhagen giving concerts. He is much loved by the ladies. Recently I met him at Princess Juliane's; we talked about you, my dear hereditary Grand Duke. Ernst thinks that Liszt was in Weimar this winter – I don't believe it.[24]

Carl Alexander responded to Andersen's query on 25 January, assuring him that Liszt had not yet been there, but that he was 'expected to arrive at any moment.' He then went on to say, 'I so look forward to seeing him. He is my spiritual champagne.'[25] As the continued exchange of letters in 1848 reveals, Liszt's permanent residency in Weimar had a growing influence on Carl Alexander. On 21 February he wrote to Andersen:

> If you were here you would enjoy Liszt's presence as much as I do.... I spoke with him yesterday about you. You fascinate him. He is surprised how, despite your travels, you can hold on to the child-like quality of your soul. That's what I love about you.[26]

Carl Alexander then launched into a discussion of divine genius and the power of music over literature:

> If one is given a special gift on Earth, then it must be the will of God. For why would one have a special gift without a special purpose? And how can this special purpose be limited to Earth, where it is often misunderstood, and still more often not even recognized? Tell me what you feel about this, for such questions fill one – one does not merely think them. The feeling begins where understanding leaves off, just as music begins where speech is exhausted.[27]

In the letters of the following years, Carl Alexander's growing affinity for Liszt's music and his interest in the composer's ideas concerning the future of Weimar became clearer. Now a permanent resident at court, Liszt was able to accomplish many of the tasks that Carl Alexander had once asked Andersen to do. For example, on 24 October 1848, Carl Alexander wrote to Andersen about Liszt's exceptional organizational skills and his ability to draw other talented figures to Weimar: 'For indeed, he brings together a strength of intelligence, a rush of ideas, a breadth of culture, an energy of the will, a uniqueness of individuality' as has 'never been seen before.'[28]

Plans were also made for an upcoming Goethe festival, an event from which Andersen was noticeably excluded. In a letter dated 17 September 1849 Carl Alexander discussed the upcoming festivities and praised his 'Friend Liszt' for his remarkable talent as a music director and genius as a composer. Apparently, the hereditary Grand Duke's previous reservations concerning Liszt's music were beginning to wane, for he says later in the same letter: 'I commissioned Liszt to write an overture on Tasso. He did it with all originality and all the strength of his intellect.'[29] And on 15 March 1851 Carl Alexander reported:

> We live here in zealous enthusiasm for science and art. I have just recently taken over the directorship of the huge art exhibition [here] and one in Jena. Liszt continues to carry out incredible things. We have more very important artists who have moved here. In this way we endeavor to make the present at the very least not unworthy of the past.[30]

As Liszt's influence in Weimar grew stronger, Andersen's contact with the city's artistic community weakened dramatically. In March 1848, civil war broke out in Denmark over the country's German-speaking provinces, Schleswig and Holstein. Fueled by liberal revolts in Germany, the provinces wanted to abandon Denmark and join what appeared to be an emerging united Germany. The Danish government responded by trying to divide politically the two provinces from each other with a new constitution. Displeased, the duchies took the law into their own hands. They formed a provisional government and called upon the German states to aid their cause. Soon Prussian troops and volunteers from other German states reinforced the Schleswig-Holstein forces. What began as a civil war quickly escalated into an international struggle. With the outbreak of the Schleswig-Holstein War, Andersen's contact with friends and colleagues in Germany grew weaker. Travel between Copenhagen and Weimar became difficult, not to mention dangerous. In addition, letters were often lost in transit or severely delayed. Andersen experienced great melancholy during this war. Separated from his friends in Weimar, he feared the consequences that war could eventually bring to his personal and professional relationships. Carl Alexander was less worried, however, and he assured Andersen on 2 August 1848 that true friendship could never be torn asunder by politics: true affection, like true art, was apolitical.[31] Battles between two nations could do nothing to weaken the spiritual bonds nurtured by art:

> True friendship is like nature; it is true like [nature], unchanged like it, untouched by the bustle of the world. It is the same with us, my friend. What does the battle of opinions have to do with our mutual way of thinking? Have we loved each other for our political opinions? No, truly not. Instead the sympathy of our souls, our minds, our imaginations is what brought us together; they united us and should, I think, through the grace of God, unite us still more. Oh promise me, my dear friend, that the current opinions and notions of these days will *never, never*

win influence over our friendship. Look up at heaven, off into the immense world above – how trivial, how contemptible the busy life down here appears. And do we want this busy life to destroy our friendship? Should we let it? Now truly, it is a fairy tale, but a fairy tale that you have *not* written, and that I find horrible. Therefore, away with politics! And leave me with the cheerful hope that we will see each other again and that you will soon come to us.[32]

Carl Alexander's belief in the apolitical nature of art and friendship would later facilitate Liszt's attempts to get Richard Wagner's music performed in Weimar. Secure in his belief that music and politics could co-exist separately, Carl Alexander allowed the performance of Wagner's operas in Weimar when no other city in Germany would sponsor music by the political exile. In fact, Wagner even visited the city secretly in 1849, an event he describes in his autobiography:

I took advantage of a few days holiday in August to make an excursion to Weimar, where I found Liszt permanently installed and ... enjoying a life of the most intimate intercourse with the Grand Duke. Even though he was unable to help me ... his reception of me on this short visit was so hearty and so exceedingly stimulating, that it left me profoundly cheered and encouraged.[33]

Carl Alexander also continued to encourage Andersen. In his letters he urged the poet to persist with his writing and assured him that all would return to normal when the war was over. In almost every letter to Andersen, Carl Alexander begged him to return to Weimar. But Andersen could not: although the admiration and encouragement he received in Weimar was important to him, he could not forsake his homeland. As Andersen himself explained on 18 August 1849 in a letter to the hereditary Grand Duke: 'My heart is completely Danish, but I still love my true friends in Germany. Let there be Peace! Peace! God let peace hover over the lands!'[34] When Andersen's prayers were finally answered and peace was declared in 1850, he summarized his feelings over Denmark's victory in a letter on 12 July:

My dear beloved Hereditary Grand Duke!
     Peace! Peace with Germany! rings through the land and through my heart. It is truly like sunshine, like a festive Sunday. There are so many who are dear to me in Germany, so many with whom I have exchanged not a single letter; if I could write to them at this moment, then my thoughts would fly far and wide from here. Still I can write only to one, and this one is you, my noble friend! May you receive through this letter all of my emotions, my complete joy!
     And so I can again think about visiting you, my neighbor, my brother on the other side of the Elbe, the land where *Goethe* sang, where *Luther* preached, where art and science have cast so many rays across the world – the land where I have gained so many good things, so many friends. Peace! Peace with Germany, and should it be recognized there that Denmark simply wanted what was its right – that makes my heart so light. May no more blood flow, and may the beginnings of peace flourish in God.[35]

Andersen's correspondence after the war reveals that he was eager to strengthen artistic bonds between Denmark and Weimar. In addition to collaborating with German composers on new opera projects[36] and recommending the production of his earlier works in Germany, he suggested plays and operas by other Danes that he thought would find favor on Weimar's stage. As he wrote to the Grand Duke on 12 July 1850:

> An opera by my countryman [Siegfried] Saloman has given pleasure, so I hear, in Weimar; that pleases me. If only one knew more Danish operas in Germany, such as Kuhlau's *Lulu*, Weyse's *The Sleeping Potion*, and Hartmann's *Little Kirsten* and *The Raven*; they would surely also give pleasure.[37]

Carl Alexander encouraged Andersen's enthusiasm and, in a letter dated 30 October 1851, relayed that his efforts to work more with Weimar's theater would no doubt be aided by the fact that his good friend Beaulieu had just been appointed theater director: 'Hurry up now and send me your 'Fliedermütterchen.'[38] Perhaps we can perform it. In the new theater director, Beaulieu, you have a friend upon whose willingness you can build.... Beaulieu controls the rudder of art.'[39]

Andersen's first trip back to Weimar after Denmark's victory in Schleswig-Holstein took place in the spring of 1852. Returning from a trip to Italy, he stayed in the city from 19 May until 10 June and visited with Carl Alexander, Beaulieu, and Liszt on a daily basis. Liszt was now permanently ensconced in Weimar, and on 25 May Andersen was given a guided tour of Altenburg, the private home that Maria Pavlovna had given to Liszt and his mistress. Andersen was no doubt impressed by the residence. As Alan Walker explains in his study of Liszt's years in Weimar, 'visitors to the house could be forgiven for assuming that they were walking through a museum.'[40] Andersen was also introduced to Liszt's renowned mistress, Princess Caroline Sayn-Wittgenstein, and her daughter Marie, and he recorded the encounter in his diary:

> 27 May: ... Lunch at Liszt's house. Princess Wittgenstein resembles him somewhat – not young, very lively, [she] received me enthusiastically ... The princess accompanied me to the table. After [lunch] I read 'The Nightingale' and 'The Ugly Duckling,' she applauded and was very taken by each amusing thought. During coffee she smoked a cigar and asked me if I didn't find it strange to see a woman do such a thing. The daughter, Princess Marie, seems to be a friendly little Mignon. Liszt and the Princess [Wittgenstein] asked me to consider their house as if it were my own. They want me to dine with them tomorrow. I asked if instead we could do it on Saturday.[41]

As Andersen reports later on, Beaulieu was irritated by the poet's desire to visit Liszt again so soon: he thought that Andersen should be socializing with the aristocracy, not spending all his time with the celebrated couple at Altenburg.[42] But apparently Andersen could not help himself. He was drawn to the lively atmosphere in Liszt's home, and much to his dismay, he no longer felt completely comfortable in the company of Weimar's aristocratic class. A growing interest in

German nationalism had begun to take hold in Weimar since the war, and Andersen often sensed increasing prejudice against Danish citizens. For instance, Andersen no longer felt safe in Beaulieu's home; in the guest room next to his was a German lieutenant whom he described on 23 May 1852 as 'very offensive:'

> During the Danish war his head was split open; today here at home he nearly fainted. He complains about the pain. He is lying in the room outside of mine. I am completely imprisoned by him, and the thought occurred to me, what if he goes crazy in the night and comes in to murder me? I can't lock my door![43]

Andersen's fears may have been exaggerated: no one actually threatened his life during his stay in Weimar. Nevertheless, he was regularly criticized for Denmark's political position by members of the aristocracy. On 2 June 1852 he even got into a public argument with an officer of the court over the matter.[44]

Andersen was also discovering that Liszt and the princess were more receptive than Weimar's aristocratic circle to the new direction his most recent tales were taking. A case in point concerns Andersen's tale 'Skyggen' (The Shadow), a frightening, existential tale about a scholar who loses his shadow and a shadow who evolves into a man without a soul. When Andersen read the tale to Liszt and the princess on 4 June, both were 'enraptured' by it.[45] But a reading for Carl Alexander four days later 'appeared not to please.'[46] Although this contrast in reception might at first seem inconsequential, a reading of the tale provides insight into the division that was beginning to form between, on the one hand, Carl Alexander's continued quest as a patron to promote art that glorified the human spirit and preserved the past and, on the other hand, Liszt's desire as an artist to explore the sometimes-hidden essence of the human psyche and create 'music of the future.' Liszt may have even recognized an element of his own artistic nature in the character of the shadow:

> I have been at the Court of Poetry.... I also got to know my inner self.... I looked where no one could see, and I saw what no one else saw.... When all is said and done, it's a mean world. I'd never want to be human, but for the fact that it's the thing to be.... I saw ... what no one was supposed to know, but what everyone was eager to know – ill of their neighbor. Had I been writing a newspaper, it would have been read! ... They were so afraid of me that they grew very fond of me. The professors made me a professor, the tailors gave me new clothes (I am quite well dressed), the mint-master minted money for me, and the women said I was so handsome! And so I became the man I am.[47]

As we learn from Andersen's diary, at three o'clock in the afternoon on Saturday, 29 May 1852, Andersen joined Princess Wittgenstein for tea after a private visit with Liszt and lunch with Carl Alexander. The gathering was quite small, comprised only of Andersen, the princess, the 'French Minister Talleyrand, a relation to the famous one,' and a Frau Schwendler and her daughter. Andersen recorded that the conversation centered on first impressions of Weimar, painting, and Andersen's tales. But clearly, the main topic on Princess Wittgenstein's mind was Liszt's artistic genius:

> The princess has bought in Holland a pretty painting by Scheffer of the three wise men, one of which is a portrait of Liszt. She explained to me that in *A Poet's Bazaar* I had placed Liszt and Thalberg together, even though the ˉlatter had borrowed everything, and that too was something important. He [Thalberg] was flawless in what he was able to appropriate, but Liszt was the genius. I had to read again: she wanted 'The Nightingale,' but I read 'Svinedrengen' (The Swineherd) and sensed that she was offended by the choice.[48]

It is no surprise that Princess Wittgenstein was insulted by Andersen's choice of story. 'The Swineherd' tells of a foolish princess who, rejecting the beautiful gifts of a prince, offers kisses to a lowly swineherd in exchange for a musical toy. When her father, the emperor, catches her in the pigsty with the swineherd, he expels them both from his kingdom. But they do not live happily ever after. The swineherd reveals that he is actually the prince in disguise, and after admonishing the princess for her foolish behavior, he abandons her forever. Given the social scandal surrounding the princess's affair with Liszt and consequent abandonment of her husband, Prince Nicholas Wittgenstein, Andersen's decision to read 'The Swineherd' that day was either a thoughtless mistake or a rather cruel joke. Those listening could not have helped but compare the fate of the fictional princess with the public derision of Princess Wittgenstein. Whatever the reason for his choice of story, Andersen most likely had not intended to offend his hostess in the manner that he so obviously did. As his diary entries reveal, he held the princess in the highest esteem and felt a sense of awe when seeing her in the presence of Liszt. From 31 May 1852:

> He and the princess seem to me like fiery spirits blazing, burning. They can warm you up instantly, but get too close and you'll burn. It is a complete picture to see these two fiery beings and know their story. Between the two of them [sits Maria] the quiet Mignon – that is how she seems to me.[49]

Apparently, Andersen was equally admired by Liszt and the princess. During a visit on 2 June 1852, the couple presented him with a special gift, 'a beautiful page written in Schiller's own hand with his name underneath.'[50] Princess Wittgenstein then requested Andersen to read 'The Nightingale' once again, and this time he indulged her. After finishing the tale she announced to all in attendance that 'Liszt was the nightingale and Thalberg was the artificial bird.' She then praised Andersen for his clever tale.[51] Andersen was no doubt put off by the princess's interpretation of the story – it had originally been written as an idealistic tribute to Jenny Lind and the glory of 'natural' music over pure virtuosity – but he was also flattered by the princess's attempt to compliment him, and refrained from correcting her.

Andersen's diary reveals that he learned a great deal about Richard Wagner during his visits with Liszt. Andersen did not know much of Wagner's music before visiting Weimar in 1852. Although he had heard a performance of the overture to *Tannhäuser* in Leipzig in 1846, he had never listened to a complete opera by the composer.[52] In an effort to interest Andersen in Wagner, Liszt gave him a copy of *Lohengrin et Thannhaüser* [sic] (1851) – his own critical study of Wagner's early operas – along with tickets to performances of both works scheduled for the following week. Andersen accepted the gifts enthusiastically. As a poet, he already held Wagner in high esteem, and he was eager to acquaint himself with his music. But as Andersen's diary entries after each performance reveal, his initial reaction to Wagner's music was less than favorable. On 29 May he wrote: 'There was a full house for *Tannhäuser*. The text, good; the performance on the whole better than expected. The music competent with regard to idea, but lacking in melody. What Carl Maria Weber or Mozart couldn't have done with it!'[53] On 5 June he recorded a similar impression of *Lohengrin*: '*Lohengrin* is well written, and the music is grand, but without melody – a barren tree without blossoms or fruit.'[54]

On 9 June, the day before Andersen departed Weimar, he visited Liszt and the princess a final time. As Andersen's description of this meeting tells us, Liszt was interested in producing some of Andersen's stage works in Weimar, and he wanted to collaborate with the poet on a set of songs:

> Went to Liszt, who was more than welcoming and friendly. He entrusted me to write to Hartmann about [our opera] *The Raven*, which he would like to produce – asked me for a couple of my poems for composition, in order to link even further our names to Weimar.[55]

En route home to Copenhagen, Andersen wrote a letter of thanks to Liszt on 14 June 1852 and enclosed a set of poems that he thought might be appropriate for Liszt's music:

> Dear admired Dr. Liszt!
> My deepest thanks for all the kindness and friendliness you extended to me during the beautiful days in Weimar. Here are my lieder. Choose the ones that please you best. I would be pleased with whatever musical baptism [*Tönen-Taufe*] they may receive.
> Yours most faithfully,
H.C. Andersen[56]

Once back in Copenhagen, however, Andersen quickly discovered that Liszt's interest in his work was not as enthusiastic as he had hoped. When Andersen tried to contact the composer about future plans for their collaboration, he apparently received no reply. In a New Year's Eve greeting written to Carl Alexander later that year, Andersen asked: 'How is he [Liszt]? I haven't heard a single word from him! The good Beaulieu has completely forgotten me as well.'[57]

Carl Alexander did not respond to Andersen's query. No doubt one reason for this was because his relations with Liszt were not at their best. Over the last year Liszt had become unhappy with his position in Weimar, most especially with his lack of power at the theater. Liszt was eager to produce more operas and concerts, and he was tiring of the dominance that poetry and spoken drama obviously had over music. After a failed performance of Wagner's *The Flying Dutchman* in February 1853, Liszt expressed his complaints in a letter to the hereditary Grand Duke:

> Because of the parsimonious treatment to which music is subjected here, I consider it impossible to continue my activity in a manner worthy of the renown that its sovereigns have bequeathed on Weimar, to say nothing of the character and reputation I aim for on my own behalf. Your Royal Highness may therefore think it natural that I henceforth abstain from regular participation in a situation that remains too far below the efforts made recently to revive the Weimar theater. ... I am not in a position to request – still less to demand. I have only to safeguard the honor of the art which, in this case, is blended with your service. The experience of the recent years has demonstrated, even in the eyes of those least able to look ahead, how legitimate were my requests. And were I ever to desist, I would be acting in the same way as those ill-considered mediocrities whose easy and convenient acceptance of the situation destroys art....[58]

In truth, there was little that Carl Alexander could do at the moment. The court's finances were strained, making productions of elaborate operas almost impossible. In addition, Carl Alexander's father, Grand Duke Carl Friedrich, had recently been ill, and this too led to instability at court. Concerned by Liszt's remarks, Carl Alexander replied on the same day:

> I have just read your letter, my dear Liszt. Accustomed to find loyalty and frankness in you, ever since I was first acquainted with you, I am delighted to have garnered fresh proof of it on this occasion. You are, I hope, just as much accustomed to finding goodwill in me, guided by sincere friendship. Therein lie the excellent conditions for collaborative work. We set ourselves to it, do we not, and we do not despair if, while we are fighting, all our desires are not realized at once in this life – which is nothing but a combat.[59]

Liszt's reaction to this letter is not known. If he had been considering abandonment of his post in Weimar in 1853, his plans were put to a halt with the death of Grand Duke Carl Friedrich in July. Liszt was out of town when the Grand Duke died, but he rushed back upon receiving the news. As Liszt later explained on 17 July 1853 in a letter to Princess Wittgenstein, Carl Alexander had welcomed him with open arms and had begun immediately to discuss plans for the future. The official inauguration of his new reign as Grand Duke would be on Goethe's birthday, 28 August – 'a significant date,' wrote Liszt, 'if they really wish to keep the meaning.' It was at this point that the Grand Duke made Liszt Weimar's arbiter of taste. 'The Word must now become Deed!' he told his Kapellmeister. [60] Liszt wasted no time in his takeover of the city's artistic activities.

During these months of transition Carl Alexander did not correspond with Andersen. He failed to answer Andersen's queries concerning Liszt and Beaulieu, and when Andersen wrote to him a second time five months later, Carl Alexander did nothing more than dash off a brief note apologizing for his silence. Andersen had not even been told about the death of Carl Friedrich; instead he had read about it in the paper. When he sent his condolences to the new Grand Duke in late July, he received another brief reply. No mention was made of plans for the future, nor was Andersen invited to the celebrations scheduled for 28 August. Only in a Christmas greeting, dated 13 December 1853, did Carl Alexander return to discussion of his plans for the future:

> I am filled up with projects and endeavors. I want to build a museum: therein will be placed the beautiful, colossal statue of Goethe that we brought from Rome and that Steinhäuser[61] finished, and a monument for my grandfather should be raised before that. I am also establishing a conservatory of music and the Goethe Foundation,[62] which like a secret treasure has already risen to the surface of its concealing waters a couple of times. Yet another duty is this: [work on] the Wartburg is developing more and more into a wonderful whole. The purpose of which is more as the bearer of memory than as a restoration.[63]

*

Andersen did not visit Weimar in 1853. During his absence the divisions in taste and social etiquette that he had already sensed between Weimar's artistic and aristocratic circles grew wider. Toward the end of the year Liszt formed the 'Society of Murls,' an informal organization made up of the many young musicians who had come to Weimar over the last few years to study with him. As Alan Walker has explained, Liszt was known as 'Padischa' (president), while his adherents were the 'Murls.' The invented name 'Murl' combined two German nouns, 'Mohr' (Moor) and 'Kerl' (fellow), and its inner meaning emerges from the familiar German saying 'Einen Mohren kann man nicht weisswaschen' (You can't whitewash a Moor). Simply put, a 'Murl' was one whom the Philistines, in this case Weimar's conservative aristocratic class, could not whitewash with their colorless ways.[64]

When Andersen returned to Weimar in late June 1854, he met many of Liszt's young Murls, and he longed to be admitted into their inner circle. In effect, Liszt had become their patron: all of them received free music instruction, and many were given housing at Altenburg as well. Liszt was also a strong proponent of the Murls' creative efforts, doing everything in his power to help further their careers. By this time, of course, Wagner's music was seen as a touchstone for creative energy. In its broadest sense, membership in the Society of Murls meant adherence to the aesthetic ideals of what Liszt called *Zukunftsmusik*, the music of the future. Seeking to prove himself worthy of Liszt's new cause, Andersen declared his allegiance to Wagner's music on 29 May during a visit to Altenburg. As he later explained in his diary: 'I was applauded because when Wagner's overture to *Tannhäuser* was booed in Leipzig, I alone applauded.'[65]

Nonetheless, Andersen was never taken seriously by this group of young artists. During his four days in Weimar, he spent most of his time with Beaulieu and Carl Alexander. Although Danish-German politics were still a bone of contention, the Grand Duke and his wife did everything they could to make

Andersen feel welcome. On the morning of Andersen's departure, Carl Alexander asked him to submit a story to the *Weimarisches Jahrbuch*, a newly founded publication that he assured Andersen was 'outside of politics and religion.'[66] Interpreting this as a sign of continued support, Andersen thanked his patron and left Weimar with a renewed sense belonging.

Andersen's place in Weimar's artistic future, however, was anything but secure. Shortly after Andersen's departure in 1854, Liszt concluded that his irreverent Society of Murls needed more administrative strength. With the hope of carrying his fight against the Philistines across Germany, he established the Neu-Weimar-Verein ('New Weimar Association'). This was a more formal organization than the Society of Murls, and it was not limited to musical issues. Visual artists, poets, musicians, and dramatists were invited to join, and the primary goal of the association was to form a united front in Weimar against conservative tastes everywhere. According to the business papers of the Verein, the first meeting was held on 20 November 1854. Twenty-one local members attended the first meeting; six out-of-town members were listed in absentia. Liszt was elected president and Hoffmann von Fallersleben vice-president. Notably absent from the membership list were Andersen, Carl Alexander, and Beaulieu. The reason for their exclusion was quite simple: their circle represented Weimar's past, not its future. As Liszt often explained, a fight against conservative tastes meant a fight against the conventions of the past. He elaborated on this idea in 1860:

> If, when I had settled here [in Weimar] in '48, I had wanted to ally myself with the *posthumous* party in music, to share in its hypocrisy, to embrace its prejudices, etc., nothing would have been easier for me because of my previous ties with the chief bigwigs of that school. I should certainly have won more consideration and courtesy from the outside world. The same newspapers that have taken it upon themselves to heap on me a mass of stupidities and insults would have outdone each other in praising and feting me to the hilt, without me having to go to much trouble.... But such was not to be my fate; my conviction was too sincere, my faith in the present and future of art too fervent and firm, for me to be able to put up with the empty formulae of the objurgations of our pseudo-classicists, who do their utmost to proclaim that art is being ruined.... [67]

After his visit to Weimar in 1854, Andersen returned to Copenhagen and did not contact Carl Alexander again until December. Perhaps he was waiting until he could fulfill the Grand Duke's commission for a new story. As he explained in a letter dated 23 December:

> I have only written a few small works, and one of these, a small picture, could be appropriate, I think, for the Weimar journal, the appearance of which your royal highness spoke to me about and within which you also should be able to grant me a place. Here is the picture. If it appeals [to you], I would be pleased to publish it. Soon another will follow.[68]

It is not known which story Andersen included with this letter. Carl Alexander replied warmly on 31 December 1854:

> You are correct in calling it a picture. Similarly I call it a very successful one. It is true and simple, hence beautiful. The form is pleasing, because it presents the soul in a very enjoyable manner. In addition, it is excellent due to a charming specialty of your talent: your fairy tale character [Märchenhaftigkeit]. I will see how I can incorporate the 'picture' into the *Weimarisches Jahrbuch*.[69]

But Andersen's submission never appeared in the journal. Although Carl Alexander had been the one to solicit the submission, he had little editorial control of the journal. Since the foundation of the Neu-Weimar-Verein in November, control had been placed in the hands of Liszt, who appointed as editors two of his most loyal allies in Weimar, Hoffmann von Fallersleben and Oskar Schade. Maintaining the mandate of the Verein, Fallersleben and Schade rejected Andersen's tale, which no doubt appeared to them to be an unwelcome link to Weimar's earlier, philistine days.

Although Andersen was dismayed by this rejection, it did not alter his resolve to maintain a working relationship with the city's new artistic elite. In September 1855 Andersen arrived in Weimar for an eleven-day visit, the primary purpose of which was to deliver his opera libretto, *The Raven*, to Liszt and Beaulieu. On 6 September he recorded his first meeting with Liszt of the visit:

> Liszt came, and *The Raven* was discussed. I showed him many of the most beautiful sections. He flipped through the pages and said it was worthy, and it was decided that it would be produced. We then talked about *Little Kirsten*. He looked at it, found it to be fresher and now preferred it instead. A translation was needed: I offered to supply one with the help of Beaulieu. We began everything right away, on the same evening.[70]

Andersen and Beaulieu worked on the translation for four days straight, completing it on 9 September. Liszt was apparently happy with their work. After reading the new libretto, now entitled *Klein Karin*, he 'sincerely promised to take care of the music and the work's performance.'[71] *Klein Karin*, with music by J.P.E. Hartmann, received its première in Weimar on 17 January 1856, and records show that reception of the opera was lukewarm. (Liszt himself was not present: he was in Vienna for a centennial celebration of Mozart's birth.) A critic for *Signale* printed a laconic 'Sie gefiel' (It pleased).[72] In a letter to Hartmann shortly after the première, Andersen gave a more detailed description: 'I can tell you that in Weimar all the music folk were quite pleased with the work, but the complaint has been made that the city was too small-minded to digest properly an artwork that was so new, so fresh in nature, without pepper and excessive salt.'[73] Liszt wrote some kind words to Hartmann after the première, and Andersen mentioned this on 17 May 1856 in a letter to Carl Alexander:

> I am very happy that Hartmann's beautiful music to *Klein Karin* has been performed for the first time in Weimar. Liszt wrote a warm and quite pleasing letter about this tone poem [Tondichtung], which will now also be performed in Mannheim: the score has been ordered. Since this music becomes more and more pleasurable each time one hears it, I really hope that it will gradually pave the way. The folk character of the melody, which Hartmann showed so superbly, gives the whole work its meaning.[74]

In the same letter, Andersen made it clear to Carl Alexander that his ties to Denmark – and his recognition there – were growing stronger. In his response, Carl Alexander praised the poet's touching description of artistic life in Copenhagen, explaining that Weimar had also begun to take on a national character. He then invited Andersen to revisit Weimar, to witness the city's thriving artistic culture. Andersen arrived in June 1856 for a brief, five-day visit. This time, however, instead of staying with Beaulieu or Carl Alexander, he checked into the Erbprinz Hotel. As Andersen explains in his diary, he was nervous about seeing the Grand Duke again, especially since their correspondence had fallen off over the last year. Much to his relief, however, the Grand Duke welcomed him with open arms: 'The Grand Duke hugged me and kissed me on both cheeks. Tears came to my eyes. It occurred to me that I, the poor shoemaker's and washerwoman's son, was being kissed by the Czar of Russia's nephew.'[75]

Andersen's diary entries from this visit reflect the city's new division into two distinct artistic factions: one connected to the aristocracy and concerned primarily with preserving the literary tradition of Weimar's 'golden age;' and one embracing Liszt's 'new Weimar,' focused primarily on the 'music of the future.' During Andersen's brief stay, he socialized almost exclusively with the 'old' faction, whose contempt for Liszt and the changes that he had wrought was no secret. On 26 June, after spending an evening at Ettersberg with the royal family and friends, Andersen recorded the main topic of discussion: '[Franz von] Schober talked about Liszt, saying that he was no blessing for Weimar or the duke; talked about the princess, who has now been wiped out in Russia, without rank, without property.'[76] On the last day of his visit, 27 June 1856, Andersen decided that he should call on Liszt at least once before departing. But when he went to Altenburg, he was told that Liszt was out taking a walk. Instead of waiting for the composer's return, Andersen made his way back into town and spent the afternoon gossiping with Beaulieu's wife:

> Talked with Frau Beaulieu about [Liszt]. The relationship with the Princess Wittgenstein is a scandal. She has not been able to renew her Russian passport and has been cast out of Russia. The daughter, who apparently is now under the protection of the Dowager Grand Duchess, has everything, and so the mother must now live off [her]. Consequently she refuses to leave her [mother], and this is why the engagement with Talleyrand was broken off. The Dowager Grand Duchess gave [Marie] a room at the castle with Duchess Fritsch and said that she could visit her mother as often as she like, but the mother is not allowed, in her

current status, to socialize at court. 'Where my mother cannot come, then neither shall I!' said the young girl, and when lightning struck the old castle where Duchess Frisch lived, [Marie] ran to her mother and remained there. That was nice of the daughter. Liszt says: 'I do indeed want to marry the princess – she wants that as well – but we are not allowed to do so. What should I do then? I cannot leave her alone, now that she has nothing! If it becomes too oppressive for us, we'll travel to India. I can easily support a wife there with my playing.' Now when Johanna Wagner was recently in Weimar, Liszt was in ecstasy. The princess grew jealous and said horrible things – that she wanted to hang herself. She used the Princess Marie, sending her to kneel down before Liszt and say: 'Don't make my mother so unhappy! Don't leave her!' Poor little princess. As they say, she is growing up among musicians.[77]

The opening line of Andersen's diary entry from 27 June, his final day in Weimar, shows how happy he was to be making his escape from the city: 'What news this day brings – Departure!'[78] Unlike his earlier visits to Weimar in the 1840s, when he had lamented leaving the city he called his 'second home,' his visit in 1856 was characterized by bad weather, bothersome stomach aches, and a recognition that he was no longer an esteemed guest at court. Indeed, Andersen's correspondence with the Grand Duke over the next year reveals that his final visit to Weimar, in September 1857, was made under duress. Carl Alexander had scheduled a centennial celebration of his grandfather's birth for the first week of September, and he wanted Andersen to participate. Andersen first responded to the invitation on 9 August, while visiting friends in Dresden. Since he knew that the Grand Duke 'would always feel friendly' toward him, he explained that he had no time for a visit:

> The Royal Theater begins its season on the first of September, and I have business that I definitely must be there for! To come to Weimar every year – I was there last year and the years before – could easily cause one to grow tired of me. Hence it is much better to be needed and not to become too intrusive.[79]

As might be expected, an insulted Carl Alexander sent back an angry missive on 16 August 1857, demanding Andersen's presence at the festivities:

> You wrote to me on the ninth of this month that 'you know: I will always feel friendly towards you.' How is it – if I may ask – that you know this so well? And who told you that it will always remain that way? Life is grounded on reciprocity; that is on [giving] reciprocal access into [each other's] character. Whoever does *not* do this for the other one loses the relationship to him. This seems to have been your intention. When you corresponded with me regularly, you knew that it was important to me, because otherwise I would not have answered you. But now you write no more. You know your presence is dear to me, and yet you do not come. You know my wish is to see you at the September festival in Weimar, and you send me excuses in place of notification of your arrival. And now, in addition, you assure me that I will always feel friendly towards you. I will *not* always feel friendly, I tell you, if you continue to treat me like this, and if you do not come to Weimar the second, third, fourth, fifth, and sixth of September. This

festival is of greater importance than the *annual, recurring* opening of your Copenhagen theater; and your business with it, believe me, can be put off for six days. Therefore I await you in Weimar, for God's sake. Otherwise I will declare war against you.[80]

Andersen quickly acquiesced to the Grand Duke's 'invitation,' and he made it clear in his response that the final day of the festivities, scheduled for 5 September, would be especially important to him:

In *Mit Livs Eventyr* I remarked that the fifth of September is a meaning-ful day for me. Every year I celebrate it in tranquility. On the fifth of September I came to Copenhagen for the first time, a poor child. That was when my fight and struggle began. On the fifth of September, coincidentally, I first crossed the Alps into Italy, and there through [my novel] *The Improvisatore*, I founded my international reputation as a poet. On the twenty-fifth anniversary of my arrival in Copenhagen, I celebrated the occasion at the table of my beloved King Christian VIII. If I may say so, the king stood by me then as a friend, sympathetic and good, [and] spoke of [my] achievements and enduring reputation. Now I shall also spend my tranquil celebration once with you, my dear, noble Grand Duke, with you, whom I revere more than you can imagine. It will be a new pleasure for me – a time to remember.[81]

Andersen arrived in Weimar on the evening of 2 September 1857, just in time for the festivities that were scheduled to begin the following day. The first event took place in the royal vault. At six o'clock in the morning, the court and all invited guests assembled around the tomb of the old grand duke, where they decorated it with flowers and said a prayer. At nine o'clock a thanksgiving service was held in the Herder church, followed by a festive procession to the Fürstenplatz, where Carl Alexander laid the foundation stone for a statue to honor his grandfather. A eulogy was offered and the ceremony concluded with a perfor-mance of 'Weimars Volkslied,' a new anthem composed by Liszt for the royal family. An evening of entertainment in the Court Theater, featuring works by Goethe and Schiller, brought the day's festivities to an end.

The next day, 4 September, was the highlight of the festival. Early in the afternoon, a statue dedicated to the poet Wieland was unveiled, followed by a second performance of Liszt's new anthem. Shortly thereafter, guests were invited to a square outside the theater. Here a crowd of onlookers gathered while members of the royal family took their places on a platform in front of two large, draped statues. After a pre-arranged signal, Carl Alexander approached the statues and cut the cords holding the veil, revealing two shining bronze figures of Weimar's greatest poets, Goethe and Schiller. According to an eye witness, the crowd burst into spontaneous cheers that one 'never heard the like of again.'[82] Andersen was also moved by the ceremony:

When the veil fell from the statues of these two masters, I saw one of those acts of fate that seem poetically intended. A white butterfly flew over the heads of Goethe and Schiller, as if not knowing upon which of them it should alight – a symbol of immortality. After a short flight about, it rose in the clear sunshine and vanished. I told this little incident to the Grand Duke, and to Goethe's widow and Schiller's son.[83]

That evening works by Goethe and Schiller were again performed in the theater.

When Andersen awoke on 5 September, he no doubt anticipated that something would be said officially about his own contributions to Weimar, for he had pointedly explained the symbolic importance the day held for him to Carl Alexander. But neither Andersen nor his work were mentioned. Instead, the day was dominated by a large concert not only conducted by Liszt but also featuring a selection of his works. At a lecture given before the concert, Liszt described the event as 'a dogmatic display of *Zukunftsmusik.*'[84]

Andersen was put off by this celebration, the implications of Liszt's speech, and the music itself. He left the theater directly after the performance, avoiding the party at Altenburg, and went back to his room, confiding to his diary: '[Liszt's music] was wild, melodious, and turbid. At times there was a crash of cymbals. When I first heard it, I thought a plate had fallen down. I went home tired. What a damned sort of music.'[85] He wrote a more detailed description the same evening in a letter home to his close friend, Henriette Hanck:

> I read [your letter] in the theater, as otherwise the music would have killed me. Everything was Liszt. I could not follow this wildness – this thoughtless composition in my view. When they played the cymbals, I thought a plate had dropped. But the audience was in raptures, and it rained wreathes! It is a strange world.[86]

Andersen left Weimar the following day, never to return again. As he later explained in his autobiography, he was unsympathetic toward the direction that Liszt's music was taking:

> Liszt composed the music for the celebration at the theater: it brought out a storm of applause and he was called out. It did not move me.... It was like wave after wave of dissonances that rise to form a harmony, but it did not move me. I felt vexed with myself that I could not respond as the others did. [I was] unpleasantly embarrassed about Liszt.... The next day he invited me to dinner. He received a company of his friends – all certainly admirers. I felt that I could not honestly fall in with the common applause. It grieved me, and I formed a hasty resolve to travel the same day from Weimar....[87]

Andersen had a ticket for a performance of *Tannhäuser* that Liszt was scheduled to conduct on 6 September, but he did not remain in town long enough to use it. Unable to bear another moment of Liszt and his fawning admirers, he bade farewell to Carl Alexander (who begged him in vain to spend a day with him at Wartburg) and took a one o'clock train to Kassel. Andersen apparently did not inform Liszt of his early departure, and he never saw the musician again.

Although Andersen's departure from Weimar in 1857 marked the end of his relations with Liszt, his association with Carl Alexander continued for several years. Perhaps in an effort to explain his sudden departure from Weimar and his consequent rejection of Liszt's *Zukunftsmusik*, Andersen wrote the fairy tale 'Pebersvendens Nathue' (The Pepperman's Nightcap), en route back to Copenhagen and mailed it to the Grand Duke shortly thereafter.[88] Carl Alexander had always advised Andersen to use his tales to express his deepest anxieties, and in this case he obviously followed that advice. Although the story has multiple levels of meaning, the basic narrative concerns a 'pepperman' (the Danish nickname for an old bachelor) named Anthony, who lives alone in a small hut in Copenhagen and sells spices. Weary from a life of hard work and heartbreak, he lies in his cold cot, crying into his woolen nightcap and thinking of happier days. In his youth, Anthony lived in Eisenach and was the son of a wealthy merchant. At that time he was in love with the mayor's daughter, a brave girl named Molly, who played at the foot of 'Venus Mountain' and was never afraid, as was Anthony, of 'Lady Halle,' who tempted 'the noble knight, Tannhäuser.'

> They said Lady Halle was beautiful, but her beauty was that of a tempting fiend. Saint Elisabeth, the patron saint of the land, the pious princess of Thuringia, whose good deeds have been immortalized in so many places through stories and legends, was more beautiful and much more graceful. Her picture hung in the church surrounded by silver lamps. It did not resemble Molly in the least.[89]

In their youth Anthony and Molly planted an apple seed, and after several months, two green leaves sprouted out.

> 'They are Molly and me,' said the boy. 'How delightful they are, and so beautiful!'
> Soon a third leaf appeared.
>   'Who does that stand for?' he thought. And then another came and another. Day after day, week after week, until the plant became a tree...[90]

Eventually, the tree produced two apples, one for Molly and one for Anthony. The future seemed secure, until fate took a turn for the worse. Molly went away to live in Weimar, while Anthony was forced to remain in Eisenach. Anthony never forgot his love for Molly (which was like that of 'Tristan and Isolde'), and he pined after her for three long years. When he finally earned enough money to travel to Weimar:

> He received a hearty welcome, a glass full of wine, pleasant company, a cozy room, and a good bed. Still, his reception was not what he had expected. He could not comprehend his own feelings or the feelings of others. But it is easy to understand! A person can be welcomed into a house or family without becoming one of them.... This is similar to what Anthony felt when Molly talked with him about the old days.

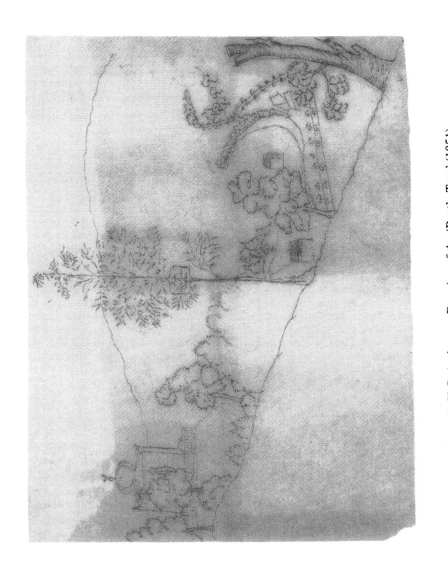

Fig. 4.4 H.C. Andersen. Drawing of the 'Poet's Tree' (1851).
(Odense: The Andersen House Museum)

'I am a straight-forward girl,' she said. I will tell you that myself. Many things have changed since we were children together; everything is different, both inwardly and outwardly.'[91]

Realizing that he was no longer the center of Molly's life, Anthony left Weimar in anger, never to return. His father went bankrupt, and Anthony was forced to move to Copenhagen and work as a lowly pepperman. Several years later, when passing through Eisenach, he noticed, much to his surprise, that the apple tree that he had planted with Molly was still flourishing and bearing fruit. Only a single branch had been broken off. It lay dead and barren on the ground. At the sight of the tree, Anthony's anger subsided, and in the years that followed he looked back fondly on his early days with Molly. At the story's end, Anthony lies on his deathbed, alone and forgotten.

Now and then he seemed to feel sensations of hunger and thirst – Yes, he felt them! But no one came to take care of him. No one wanted to come. He thought of those who had suffered from starvation, of Saint Elisabeth when she wandered the earth ... that highly esteemed lady who visited the poorest villages, bringing hope and relief to the sick. Her pious deeds filled his mind with light.... In this way, the saint resided in the thoughts of poor Anthony. She was a living figure who stood before him at the foot of his bed. He wiped his brow and looked into her kind eyes. The fragrance of roses spread through the room, mingled with the sweet smell of apples. He saw the branches of the apple tree spreading above him.

It was the tree that he and Molly had planted as little children. The fragrant leaves of the tree fell upon him and cooled his burning brow; to his parched lips they seemed like refreshing bread and wine. And as they rested on his breast, a peaceful calm stole over him.... 'I will sleep now,' he whispered to himself. 'Sleep will do me good. In the morning I will be back on my feet, strong and well. Glorious! Wonderful! The apple tree that was planted in love now appears before me in heavenly beauty.' And he slept.[92]

The next morning, Anthony was found dead in his hut, clutching the woolen nightcap. 'Where were the tears he had shed? ... They were still in the nightcap. Such tears can never be washed out, even when the nightcap is forgotten.'[93]

After Anthony's burial, the nightcap is passed around from one owner to another. No one keeps the cap for long, because each person who puts it on is tormented by painful visions. 'The old thoughts and dreams' of Anthony still remained inside. Anthony was gone, but his memories lived on.

Carl Alexander had little to say about Andersen's tale. In his letters he offered a few indifferent compliments, but did not mention the story's symbolic meaning. It is generally assumed that Andersen portrayed himself in the character of Anthony, while Molly represented the Grand Duke. Those familiar with Liszt's output during the late 1850s might suggest that the figure of Saint Elisabeth represented the composer, since he was working on a new oratorio, *The Legend of St. Elisabeth*, during Andersen's final visit to Weimar.[94] References to Wagner's *Tannhäuser* also appear in the tale. Indeed, Anthony (Andersen) is literally identified as Tannhäuser, and he makes his feelings regarding the tempting Lady Venus and blessed Saint Elisabeth clearly known.[95] But the 'Pepperman's Nightcap' is not a mere retelling of Wagner's opera; the story evokes *Tannhäuser*, but then subverts the operatic version.[96] Elements of the story have nothing to do with *Tannhäuser*. For example, the apple tree is clearly a metaphor for the artistic community that blossomed in Weimar in the 1840s. Although it was Andersen (Anthony) who had originally planted the seeds for a 'New Athens' with Carl Alexander (Molly), Liszt (Saint Elizabeth) became the protector of the tree when Andersen's connections, like the lone branch, were broken off.

Andersen never gave a formal explanation of 'The Pepperman's Nightcap,' but he alluded to the story's inherent meaning in a letter to Carl Alexander on 22 May 1858. Frustrated by the Grand Duke's refusal to comment upon the story, Andersen sent a translation of a review that had been published in Copenhagen – one that obviously pleased him:

> 'The Pepperman's Nightcap' is filled with a deep melancholy, in which the poet cautions us about the insecurity of all earthly hopes and points to renunciation as a balsam. For [renunciation] alone is what makes it possible for us to tolerate life and never to give up the idealism of youth.[97]

Until now, this explanation of 'The Pepperman's Nightcap,' as a renunciation of earthly hopes in the search for idealism, has been overlooked. Instead, scholars have interpreted this tale as little more than a story of unrequited friendship. Yet the tale has a deep, intrinsic meaning that stretches beyond the confines of personal affection. Although the relationship shared by Andersen and the Grand Duke is mirrored in the characters of Anthony and Molly, the prominent allusions to music by Wagner and Liszt imply an aesthetic message that has little to do with Andersen's personal feelings toward his patron. 'The Pepperman's Nightcap' represents the final episode in this chapter's story of the poet, the pianist, and the patron. Written as an allegory concerning the foundation and evolution of an artistic community in the nineteenth century, 'The Pepperman's Nightcap' describes Andersen's involvement with the foundation of Carl Alexander's Weimar and the city's eventual transformation under the leadership of Liszt.

Interlude 4

The Pepperman's Nightcap

by Hans Christian Andersen

There is a street in Copenhagen with a very strange name. It is called 'Hysken' street. Where the name came from, and what it means, nobody knows. It is said to be German, but that is unjust to the Germans, for it would then be called 'Hauschen,' not 'Hysken.' 'Hauschen' means a little house; and for many years it consisted of only a few small houses, which were scarcely larger than the wooden huts we see in the marketplaces at fair time. They were perhaps a little higher and had windows, but the panes were made of horn or bladder skins, since glass was then too expensive. This was a long time ago; so long ago that even our grandfathers would speak of those days as 'olden times.' Indeed, many centuries have passed since then.

The rich merchants in Bremen and Lübeck who carried on trade in Copenhagen did not reside in the town themselves, but sent their clerks, who lived in the wooden huts on Hysken street and sold beer and spices. The German beer was very good, and there were many sorts from Bremen, Prussia, and Brunswick. There was also a large quantity of spices of all types: saffron, aniseed, ginger, and especially pepper. Indeed, pepper was the primary article sold here. That is why the German clerks in Denmark were given their nickname of 'peppermen.' It had been made a condition of these clerks' employment that they should not marry, which meant that those who lived to be old had to take care of themselves. They had to attend to their own comforts. They even had to light their own fires; that is if they had any wood to burn. Many of the peppermen were elderly, lonely fellows with strange thoughts and eccentric habits. Consequently, all bachelors who reach an advanced age without marrying are called 'peppermen' in Denmark. These peppermen are often ridiculed. They are told to put on their nightcaps, draw them over their eyes, and go to sleep. Some young boys in Denmark have even written a song about them:

> Poor pepperman cut your wood,
> Such a nightcap was never seen;
> Who would think it was ever clean?
> Go to sleep, it will do you good.

So they sing about the Pepperman. This is how they make fun of the old bachelors and their nightcaps, and all because they really know nothing about them. The Pepperman's nightcap is a thing that no one should desire or ridicule. Why not? Well, we shall hear why not in this story.

In olden times Hysken Street was not paved, and pedestrians would stumble out of one hole into another, as they generally do along unfrequented roads. The street was so narrow, and the huts leaning against each other were so close together, that in the summer time a sail would be stretched across the street from one hut to another. At these times the odor of the pepper, saffron, and ginger grew incredibly strong. As a rule, there were no young men behind the counter. The clerks were almost all old men. But they did not dress the way we are accustomed to seeing old men dressed, with wigs, nightcaps, knickers, and a coat and waistcoat buttoned up to the chin. We have seen portraits of our great-grandfathers dressed in this way, but the peppermen had no money to have their portraits made, though one of them would have made a very interesting picture for us now, if taken as he had appeared standing behind his counter, or going to church on holidays. On these occasions the peppermen wore high-crowned, broad-brimmed hats; occasionally a younger clerk would stick a feather in his hat. The woolen shirt was concealed by a broad, linen collar. The tight jacket was buttoned up to the chin, and the cloak hung loosely over it. The pants were tucked into broad-tipped boots, for the clerks wore no socks. They generally stuck a table-knife and spoon in their belts, as well as a larger knife that could be used for protection. Such a weapon often proved to be very necessary.

Anthony was dressed according to this fashion on holidays and festivals, except that instead of wearing a high-crowned hat, he wore a kind of bonnet, and under it was a knitted cap, a regular nightcap, and he was accustomed to wearing it always. He had two of them – nightcaps I mean, not heads. Anthony was one of the oldest clerks, and the perfect subject for a painter. He was as thin as a rail and wrinkled around the mouth and eyes. He had long, bony fingers; bushy, grey eyebrows; and over his left eye hung a thick tuft of hair that did not make him handsome, but nonetheless made his appearance unique. People knew that he came from Bremen. It was not exactly his home, although his employer lived there. His ancestors were from Thuringia and had lived in the town of Eisenach, close by Wartburg. Old Anthony seldom spoke of this place, but he thought of it often.

The old clerks of Hysken Street rarely socialized. Each one remained in his own hut, which was closed in the evening when the street grew dark and dismal. Only a faint glimmer of light struggled through the horn panes in the little window on the roof. Inside the hut, the old clerk usually sat on his bed, singing his evening hymn in a low voice, or he would scurry around inside the hut until late at night, working on various small projects. It certainly was not a happy life. To be a foreigner in a foreign land is a bitter lot. No one notices you unless you happen to get in their way. Often, when it was dark outside and raining or snowing, the place looked quite deserted and gloomy. There were no lamps in the street except for a very small one that hung at one end of the street in front of a picture of the Virgin painted on the wall. The splashing of water against the bulwark of a neighboring castle could clearly be heard. Evenings such as this are long and dreary if one cannot find something to do. So Anthony found it. There were not always things to be packed or unpacked, and the paper bags did not have to be made often or the scales polished. So Anthony made up things to do. He mended his clothes and patched his boots, and when he finally went to bed his nightcap, which he wore out of habit, remained on his head. He only had to pull it down a little further over his forehead. Soon, however, it would be pushed up again to see if the candle was properly out. He would touch it, press the wick together, and at last pull his nightcap over his eyes again and lie down. But often he would soon begin to wonder whether every coal had been extinguished in the hearth in the shop below. If even a tiny spark had been left to burn it might start a fire and cause great damage. Upon thinking this, he would get out of bed, creep down the ladder – for it could hardly be called a flight of stairs – and check the hearth only to find that not a spark of light could be seen. He would then return to bed. But often, on the way to his bed, he would imagine that the iron bolts on the door were not properly fastened, and his thin legs would climb down the ladder again. By the time he finally crept back to bed, he would be so cold that his teeth chattered in his head. He would draw the blanket closer around him, pull his nightcap over his eyes, and try to turn his thoughts away from trade and the labors of the day and focus on past times. But this was not a pleasurable form of entertainment, since old memories raise the curtain of the past and sometimes pierce the heart with painful memories that bring tears to wakeful eyes. And so it was with Anthony. Often hot tears would fall from his eyes onto the blanket; like pearls they would roll to the floor with a tinkling sound similar to the breaking of heartstrings. Sometimes a memory would arise like a lurid flame and ignite a picture of life that had never faded from his heart. When he dried his eyes with his nightcap, the tears and the picture were temporarily crushed. But the source of the tears remained, and it welled up again in his heart. These pictures did not follow one another in the chronological order in which they had occurred. Often, the most painful pictures would appear together, and when the most joyful images appeared, they always had the darkest shadow cast over them.

The beech woods of Denmark are acknowledged by everyone to be very beautiful, but more beautiful still in the eyes of old Anthony were the beech woods in the neighborhood of Wartburg. More grand and venerable to him were the old oaks around the proud baronial castle, where the creeping plants hung over the stony crests of rock; there the perfume of the apple blossom was stronger than in Denmark. Vividly he saw, in a glittering tear that rolled down his cheek, two children at play – a boy and a girl. The boy had rosy cheeks, golden curls, and clear, blue eyes. It was himself, the son of a rich merchant also named Anthony. The little girl had brown eyes and black hair and was clever and courageous. She was the Mayor's daughter Molly. The children were playing with an apple. They shook the apple and heard the seeds rattling inside. Then they cut it in two and each took one half. They also divided the seeds and ate all but one, which the little girl proposed should be planted in the ground.

'You will see what will come out,' she said, 'something you don't expect. A whole apple tree will come out, but not right away.'

Then they got a flower pot, filled it with earth, and were soon both busy taking care of it. The boy made a hole in the earth with his finger, and the girl placed the seed in the hole, then they both covered it over with earth.

'Now you must not take it out tomorrow to see if it has taken root,' said Molly. 'No one should do that. I did so with my flowers, but only twice. I wanted to see if they were growing. I didn't know any better then, and the flowers àll died.'

Little Anthony kept the flower pot, and every morning during the long winter he looked at it, but there was nothing to be seen but black soil. At last, however, the spring came. The sun shone warm again, and two little green leaves sprouted forth in the pot.

'They are Molly and me,' said the boy. 'How wonderful they are, and so beautiful!'

'Soon a third leaf appeared.

'Who does that stand for?' he thought. And then another came and another. Day after day, week after week until the plant grew into a tree. This image appeared to old Anthony as a reflection in a single tear, which could soon be wiped away and disappear, but might come again from its source in the old man's heart.

In the neighborhood of Eisenach stretches a ridge of stony mountains, one of which has a rounded outline that rises above the rest without a tree, bush, or grass on its barren summit. It is called the 'Venus Mountain,' and the story goes that a heathen goddess named 'Lady Venus' lives there. She is also called 'Lady Halle,' as every child around Eisenach well knows. It was she who enticed into her mountain the noble knight Tannhäuser, the minstrel from the circle of singers at Wartburg.

Molly and Anthony often stood by this mountain, and one day Molly said, 'I dare you to knock and call out loudly, 'Lady Halle, Lady Halle, open the door. Tannhäuser is here!' Anthony did not dare. But Molly did, although she only called out the words 'Lady Halle, Lady Halle.' The rest she muttered under her breath, and Anthony was certain that she actually said nothing at all. Still, she looked quite bold and confident, just as she did when she was in the garden with a group of other young girls. They would all stand around Anthony and try to kiss him. But he did not like to be kissed and always pushed them away. Only Molly dared to resist him. '*I* may kiss him,' she would say proudly as she threw her arms around his neck. She was vain about her power over Anthony, for he always submitted quietly and made nothing of it. Molly was very charming and quite bold – she was a dreadful tease.

They said Lady Halle was beautiful, but her beauty was that of a tempting fiend. Saint Elizabeth, the patron saint of the land, the pious princess of Thuringia, whose good deeds have been immortalized in so many places through stories and legends, was more beautiful and much more graceful. Her picture hung in the chapel surrounded by silver lamps. It did not resemble Molly in the least.

The apple tree that the two children planted grew year after year until it became so large that it had to be transplanted into the garden. There the dew fell and the sun shone upon it warmly. It increased in strength, so much so that it was able to withstand the cold of winter. After passing through the severe winter, it seemed to produce blossoms out of joy over the final arrival of spring. In autumn it produced two apples, one for Molly and one for Anthony. It could not produce any less. After this, the tree grew very rapidly, and Molly grew with the tree. She was as fresh as an apple blossom, but Anthony did not get to behold the beauty of this flower for long. Everything suddenly changed. Molly's father left his home town, taking Molly with him. Today such a journey would only take a few hours, but at that time it took more than a day and a night to travel eastward from Eisenach to a town called Weimar on the border of Thuringia. Molly and Anthony both wept, and these tears flowed together into a single tear that had the rosy shimmer of joy. Molly told him that she loved him – loved him more than all the splendors of Weimar.

One, two, three years went by, and during the all this time Anthony received only two letters from Molly. One came by carrier; the other was brought by a traveler. The road was very long and difficult, with many twists and turns through small towns and villages. Anthony and Molly had often heard the story of Tristan and Isolde, and Anthony had thought that the story applied to him. Although it should be noted that the name Tristan, which means 'born in sorrow,' did not aptly apply to him; and he hoped he would never say of Molly what Tristan said of Isolde: 'She has forgotten me.' But in truth, Isolde had not forgotten her faithful friend Tristan; when they were both laid in their graves, one on each side of the church, the linden trees that grew next to each grave spread over the roof and bent toward one another, mingling their blossoms together. Anthony thought this a very beautiful but mournful story. Yet he never feared anything so sad would happen to him and Molly, and each time he passed the church he would whistle the tune of a song called 'The Willow Bird' composed by a minstrel named Walter. The song began: 'Under the Linden trees, out on the heath.' And one stanza in particular pleased him: 'Through the forest, and in the vale, sweetly warbles the nightingale.'

This song was often upon his lips, and he sang or whistled it on a moonlit night when he rode horseback along the deep, vacant road to Weimar. He was on his way to visit Molly. He wished to arrive unexpectedly, and so he did. He received a hearty welcome, a glass full of wine, pleasant company, a cozy room, and a good bed. Still, his reception was not what he had expected. He could not comprehend his own feelings or the feelings of others. But this is easy to understand! A person can be welcomed into a house or family without becoming one of them. We converse with those we meet just as we converse with our fellow travelers in a stagecoach. – We know nothing of them, and perhaps we are inconveniencing one another the whole time, each wishing that the other would go away. This is similar to what Anthony felt when Molly talked with him about the old days.

'I am a straightforward girl,' she said. 'I will tell you that myself. Many things have changed since we were children together; everything is different, both inwardly and outwardly. We can not control our wills or the feelings in our hearts through the rigors of custom. Anthony, I would not for the world make an enemy of you when I am far away. Believe me when I say that I hold the warmest wishes for you in my heart. But to feel for you what I now know can be felt for another man is impossible. You must try and reconcile yourself to this. Farewell, Anthony.'

Anthony also said 'Farewell.' He did not shed a single tear. He felt he was no longer Molly's friend. Hot iron and cold iron both take the skin from our lips; we feel the same sensation if we kiss either one. Anthony's kiss was now the kiss of hatred even though it had once been the kiss of love. Within twenty-four hours Anthony was back in Eisenach, and the horse that he had ridden was completely ruined.

'What does it matter?' said Anthony. 'I am ruined as well. I will destroy everything that reminds me of her, and Lady Halle or Lady Venus, the heathen woman. I will cut down the apple tree and tear it out by its roots. Never again will it blossom or bear fruit.'

But the apple tree was not cut down, for Anthony was soon struck ill by a fever. Eventually he rose up again. What caused him to do so? Life forced him to take a dose of a specific medicine – a bitter remedy that made his sick body and oppressed spirit shudder. Anthony's father lost all his property and went from being one of the richest merchants to a very poor man. Dark days and heavy trials, with poverty at the door, came rolling into the house like waves from the sea. Sorrow and suffering deprived Anthony's father of his strength, giving Anthony something else to think about besides his love sorrows and anger against Molly. He had to take his father's place, to give orders, to act with energy, to help, and finally to go out into the world and earn a living. Anthony went to Bremen, and there he learned what poverty and suffering really are. Such experiences often harden the character and soften the heart – sometimes too much.

How different the world and the people in it appeared to him now. The minstrel's songs no longer mattered. They were nothing but an echo of the past, sounds long vanished. At times he would think like this. But again and again the songs continued to sound in his soul, and his heart eventually grew gentle and pious.

'God's will is the best,' he would say. 'It is good that I was not allowed to keep my power over Molly's heart and that she did not remain true to me. How horrible I would have felt if she had deserted me now. She left me before she knew of my changed circumstances; she had no idea what lay before me. Fate was merciful to me in this way. Everything has happened for the best. She could not help it, and yet I have been so bitter and felt such hostility towards her.'

Years passed. Anthony's father died, and strangers moved into the old house. Anthony had visited it once since then. His rich employer sent him on business trips, and on one occasion he passed through Eisenach. The old Wartburg castle stood unchanged on the rock where the monk and nun were carved in stone. The great oaks formed a frame for the scene that he remembered so well from childhood. The Venus Mountain stood out grey and bare, overshadowing the valley below. It would have made him happy to call out 'Lady Halle, Lady Halle, open the mountain. I will gladly remain here in my native soil.' But that was a sinful thought, and he offered up a prayer instead to drive it away.

Then a little bird in the thicket sang out clearly, and old Anthony remembered the minstrel's song. The memories flooded back to him as he gazed through tears at his native town! The old house was still standing as it had in the past, but the garden had undergone great changes. A pathway now led across the lawn and outside the garden, and beyond the path stood the old apple tree that he had wanted to destroy. The sun still shined down upon the tree, and the refreshing dew still nourished it. It was so overloaded with fruit that the branches bent down to the earth under the weight. 'It is still flourishing,' said Anthony as he looked at it. But one of the tree's branches had been broken. Mischievous hands must have done this in passing, since the tree now stood along a public path. 'The blossoms are often plucked,' said Anthony. 'The fruit is stolen, and the branches broken without a thankful thought of their profusion or beauty. It might be said of a tree, as it has been said of some men – it was not foreseen at his birth that he would come to this. How brightly began the story of this tree. Yet what is it now? Forsaken and forgotten in a garden by a hedge in a field close to a public road. There it stands, unsheltered, plundered, and broken. It certainly has not yet withered, but as the years pass the number of its blossoms will eventually diminish, and eventually it will cease to bear fruit altogether. Then its story will be over.'

Such were Anthony's thoughts as he stood under the tree and during many long nights when he lay in his lonely room in the small, wooden hut on Hysken Street in Copenhagen – in the foreign land where his employer, the rich merchant from Bremen, had sent him on condition that he should never marry. 'Marry! Ha, ha!' he laughed bitterly to himself as he thought of it.

One year winter came early; the weather was freezing and harsh. A snowstorm outside caused everyone who could to stay at home. Thus it happened that Anthony's neighbors did not notice that his shop remained closed for two days, and that he had not ventured out during that time. These were grey, gloomy days, and in the house without glass for its windowpanes, twilight and darkness reigned in turns. During these two days, old Anthony did not leave his bed. He did not have the strength to do so. For some time now, the bitter weather had affected his limbs. There lay the old Pepperman, forsaken by all and unable to help himself. He could barely reach the water jug that he had put next to his bed, and the last drop was gone. It was not fever or sickness that laid him low, but old age. In the little corner where his bed stood, he was overshadowed by perpetual darkness. A little spider, which he could not see, cheerfully spun a web above him, so that there would be a make-shift banner flying over him when his eyes finally closed. The time passed slowly and painfully. He had no tears to shed, and no thought of Molly came to his mind. He felt as though the world now meant nothing to him, as if he were lying beyond it with no one to think of him. Now and then he seemed to feel sensations of hunger and thirst – Yes, he felt them! But no one came to take care of him. No one wanted to come. He thought of those who had suffered from starvation, of Saint Elisabeth when she wandered the earth, the saint of his home and his childhood, the noble Duchess of Thuringia, that highly esteemed lady who visited the poorest villages, bringing hope and relief to the sick. Her pious deeds filled his mind with light. He thought of her as she went about speaking words of comfort, tending to the wounds of the afflicted and feeding the hungry, despite the rage such activities incurred from her cruel husband. He remembered a story told about her, that once when she was carrying a basket full of wine and provisions, her husband, who had observed her, stepped forward and asked angrily what she was carrying in her basket. Whereupon with fear and trembling she answered: 'Roses that I have plucked from the garden.' Then he tore away the cloth that covered the basket and, much to the woman's surprise, the wine and food had turned into roses.

In this way, the saint resided in the thoughts of poor Anthony. She was a living figure who stood before him at the foot of his bed. He wiped his brow and looked into her kind eyes. The fragrance of roses spread through the room, mingled with the sweet smell of apples. He saw the branches of the apple tree spreading above him.

It was the tree that he and Molly had planted as little children. The fragrant leaves of the tree fell upon him and cooled his burning brow; to his parched lips they seemed like refreshing bread and wine. And as they rested on his breast, a peaceful calm fell over him, and he felt inclined to sleep. 'I will sleep now,' he whispered to himself. 'Sleep will do me good. In the morning I will be back on my feet, strong and well. Glorious! Wonderful! The apple tree that was planted in love now appears before me in heavenly beauty.' And he slept.

The next morning, the third day his house had been closed, the snowstorm ended. His neighbor from across the street came to check on him. There Anthony lay stretched on his bed, dead, with his old nightcap tightly clasped in his hands. The nightcap, however, was not placed on his head in his coffin. He wore a clean white one instead. Where were the tears he had shed? What had become of those wonderful pearls? They were still in the nightcap. Such tears can never be washed out, even when the nightcap is forgotten. The old thoughts and dreams of a pepperman's nightcap remain. Never wish for such a nightcap. It will make your forehead hot, cause your pulse to beat with agitation, and conjure up nightmares that seem real.

The first man who wore old Anthony's cap realized the truth in this, though it was fifty years later. The man was a mayor with a comfortable home and family. The moment he put the cap on his head, he dreamed of unrequited love, bankruptcy, and dark days. 'How this nightcap burns!' he cried as he tore it from his head. Then a pearl rolled out, and another. One by one they fell to the floor. 'What can this be? Is it paralysis, or something dazzling my eyes?' thought the mayor as the pearls glimmered. They were the tears that had been shed by poor Anthony half a century earlier.

Every man who has put the nightcap on from that day forward has had visions and horrible nightmares. His own story is changed into that of Anthony, and it eventually becomes reality. In this way, many stories have been made by others, but we will leave them to tell these tales. We have told the first one, and our last bit of advice is this: 'Don't wish for a pepperman's nightcap.'

Chapter 5

The Patriot

Politics are no affair of mine. God has imparted to me another mission.
Hans Christian Andersen

We have seen that Andersen's gradual withdrawal from Weimar in the 1850s was primarily fueled by growing political tensions between artists and patrons there and between Denmark and Germany in general. As Andersen himself so often explained in his diaries and correspondence, the political upheavals of the 1840s caused him to question his place in society, both as a writer and as a Danish citizen.[1] Consequently, the purpose of this chapter is two-fold: to discuss the reasons for Andersen's growing sense of insecurity, and to describe the influence that Denmark's political struggles had on Andersen's view of the arts and his composition of texts for several patriotic songs and musical stage works from the late 1840s to the mid 1860s.

Scholars have debated Andersen's loyalty to Denmark for nearly two centuries.[2] During his lifetime, he was often criticized for being either 'too patriotic' or a cultural traitor, and because evidence supporting both descriptions can be found in Andersen's publications and correspondence, some modern-day scholars have concluded that he was simply an opportunist when it came to issues of national devotion. But as I hope to show in the following pages, Andersen's loyalty to Denmark was consistent throughout his life. His thoughts concerning nationalism and its effect on society as he witnessed it troubled him and consequently greatly influenced his creative output during the middle decades of the century.

Andersen was a cosmopolitan at heart, and he viewed himself as both a loyal subject of Denmark's king and a citizen of Europe. How could such a dichotomy in identity exist? The answer lies in the development of Denmark's national identity over the course of the nineteenth century and Andersen's struggles and priorities as a writer.

*

There is no set formula for the creation of national identity. Political instability, the weakening of organized religion, the rise of historical consciousness, interest in cultural uniformity and/or racial purity – since World War II all of these conditions, and numerous others, have been described as essential ingredients of modern nationalism. But broad, sweeping definitions of nationalist ideologies should not be categorically applied to the cultures of centuries past or the whole of

Fig. 5.1 Caricature of Andersen (artist unknown) that appeared in *Corsaren* on 28 March 1848. (Copenhagen: The Royal Library)

Western Europe. It is dangerous to view all types of nationalism through the lens of the early-twenty-first-century experience, to apply modern ideologies to historical situations. The global communities so common today were unimaginable in Andersen's time. Instead, the development of national identities emerged on a local level and was the result of historical and cultural changes specific to circumscribed regions and/or territories. National identity did not arise in Denmark overnight, but, rather, evolved over the course of several decades; and its development in the small, provincial country was quite different from the rise of nationalism in larger, more politically powerful European countries like Germany, France, and Italy.

In general, the development of Denmark's national identity during Andersen's lifetime was the result of a shift in ideology from what I shall call political patriotism in the first half of the century to cultural nationalism in the second half of the century.[3]   Andersen was cognizant of this shift in ideology, and he commented upon it regularly in his correspondence and fictional works. But before we can fully discuss his reaction to these changes, we must first acquaint ourselves with the historical incidents that fostered them.

During the first half of the nineteenth century, the concept of patriotism was strongly linked to Jaucourt's definition of *patrie* as it appeared in Diderot's *Encyclopédie*. As Jaucourt explained, *patrie* (often translated in English as 'country,' 'fatherland,' or 'homeland') indicated one's birthplace and was also understood to include the society to which one belonged and the rule of law that ensured one's happiness and well-being.[4] Consequently, political patriotism was a type of national identity linked to political allegiance and geographic boundaries – a commitment to 'king and country.' This approach toward national unity was effective during the first half of the nineteenth century, when a citizen of Denmark was seen as anyone who was born on Danish soil (this included present-day Denmark, Norway, sections of Northern Germany, the Faroe Islands, the North Atlantic Islands, Iceland, Greenland, some minor colonies in Guinea, and Tranquebar in India) and pledged allegiance to Denmark's monarch.

Later in the century a second ideology, cultural nationalism, came to the forefront of Danish consciousness. Cultural nationalism was firmly rooted in theories concerning language and cultural heritage that grew out of Germany. The nation, as explained by Herder, was defined in terms of its ethnic and linguistic features. This ideology was transferred into Danish thought by N.F.S. Grundtvig, a theologian, philosopher, and poet who was the first to describe Denmark's national identity along cultural and linguistic lines.[5] According to Grundtvig, the Danish nation was not defined by political and/or geographical borders. Instead, the citizens of Denmark were unified by a common language (Danish), a common land (the Danish-speaking regions of Denmark), a common history (the Vikings), and a common culture (Norse mythology, folk songs, etc.).[6]

Denmark's shift in ideology from political patriotism to cultural nationalism was a slow process spurred on by decades of hardship and political defeat. In 1807, Copenhagen was attacked by Great Britain, and Denmark's navy, a symbol of national pride, was laid to waste. The following years were plagued by war and economic hardship.   In 1813 Denmark declared bankruptcy, and in 1814 Norway seceded under the Treaty of Kiel.   In seven short years the nation was brought to its knees.   Grundtvig was shocked by these tragedies, and he reacted by producing a series of publications.   Influenced by the works of Herder, Goethe, and Walter Scott, Grundtvig sought to rejuvenate the spirit of his worn-torn compatriots through a rediscovery of their homeland's glorious past, when Vikings roamed the seas and Scandinavia was blessed with a pantheon of powerful gods and heroes.[7] For Grundtvig, the glory of Denmark was found in its history and language.   With patriotic poems, hymns, and publications such as *Udsigt over Verdens-Krøniken* (Overview of the Chronicle of the World, 1812–17), *Danne-Virke* (Denmark's Bulwark, 1816–19), *Saxo og Snorre* (Saxo and Snorre, 1818–22), *Beowulf* (1820), *Nyaars Morgen* (New Year's Morning, 1824), and *Nordens Mythologie* (Nordic Mythology, 1832), Grundtvig initiated an era of literary antiquarianism in Denmark.   He believed in the rejuvenating power of folk poetry, and his work in this field inspired a number of Danish writers and musicians.[8]

Andersen came to Copenhagen just as this rejuvenation began, and he witnessed the increased patriotic fervor that resulted from Denmark's economic recovery in the 1820s and Christian VIII's creation of the Provincial Assemblies in 1834.[9]   Christian VIII was a rather enlightened ruler, and under his reforms Denmark was divided into four regional governments: Holstein, Schleswig, Jutland, and the rest of the kingdom.   Another event that led to an increase in Danish patriotism was the founding of Selskabet for Trykkefrihedens rette Brug (The Society for the Proper Use of the Press) in 1835.   Created in an effort to guarantee freedom of the press in Denmark, the society attracted many members, including Andersen.[10]   Its goal was 'folkeoplysning' (educating the people), in this case through the printed word, and it published many political works, among them translations of Tocqueville's *Democracy in America*.

Such was the political atmosphere during the first half of Andersen's life. Danish identity was characterized by political patriotism, and there was little conflict between the nation's various cultural groups.   But this situation began to change in the 1840s, when escalating conflicts between the Danish- and German-speaking regions challenged accepted ideals of Danish identity. Although most of Denmark supported Christian VIII's establishment of the Provincial Assemblies, the German-speaking duchies of Schleswig and Holstein were displeased; the reforms placed them in separate assemblies and consequently weakened their political and economic unity.   Within a relatively short amount of time, seeds of discontent were sown among Denmark's German-speaking citizens, and political patriotism began to give way to cultural nationalism, a trend closely tied to language and perceived ethnicity.

The political unrest initiated in Schleswig and Holstein by the creation of the Provincial Assemblies came to a head in 1848.   Christian VIII died in January and was succeeded by his son, Frederik VII, who, although loved by his subjects, had a somewhat capricious temperament and only limited political sense.   He had barely settled on the throne when the revolution in Paris engendered a chain of liberal revolts in Germany that sparked similar political upheaval in Denmark's German-speaking duchies. In March, Schleswig and Holstein united and demanded a separate constitution for a Schleswig-Holstein state. When Frederik VII refused, the duchies formed a provisional government and called upon the German states to aid their cause. Soon German and Prussian volunteers strengthened the Schleswig-Holstein forces. What began as a struggle within Denmark's borders soon escalated into a battle with its neighbors. As Andersen later noted, 'The year 1848 rolled up its curtain – a remarkable, volcanic year, when the heavy waves of time also washed over our country with the blood of war.'[11]

With the onset of the Schleswig-Holstein War, Denmark's Danish-speaking citizens rallied around their king in a great upsurge of national sentiment, and Andersen was among them. With their national identity threatened – an identity largely associated with political patriotism – many Danes looked to the teachings of Grundtvig for guidance and, consequently, found a new identity in Denmark's language and culture. Grundtvig took an active role in the Schleswig-Holstein controversy and soon became an advocate for the pro-Danish forces. On 14 March 1848, he expressed his views concerning Schleswig and Holstein in a lecture that was later published under the title *Frihed og Orden* (Freedom and Order). Here he defined Denmark's borders along cultural lines: 'The Danish land only reaches as far as Danish is spoken and basically not further than to the point where the people will continue to speak Danish.'[12] Grundtvig's goal was to revive a strong faith in Denmark's culture through literature and the arts. His dedication to the Danish language took on something of a missionary character, and under his urging many of Denmark's writers and musicians were promoted as living examples of the nation's worth.[13]

When the war began, Andersen was among the poets praised as Danish treasures, and he embraced this identity wholeheartedly. Secure in his belief that Denmark was justified in its claim on the German-speaking duchies, he published a number of patriotic poems during the early months of the war that described Denmark as an historic nation united by its king and encouraged its people to fight bravely for the cause. On 31 March, his 'Slagsang for de Danske' (Battle song for the Danes) appeared in *Fædrelandet*:

For Denmark!
This is a very serious time,
But all our suffering is for God's will,
We therefore take the rightful path
For Denmark!

Upon the country's coat-of-arms have always stood
Three lions symbolizing courage,
[And] Nine hearts, which are honorable blood
For Denmark!

For Danmark!
Det er en stor alvorlig Tid,
Men fast til Gud staaer al vor Lid,

Vi stride jo den gode Strid
For Danmark!

I Landets Vaaben altid stod
Tre Løver, de betyde Mod,
Ni Hjerter, det er ærligt Blod
For Danmark! [14]

'Battlesong for the Danes' contains no talk of cultural divisions, no description of a specific Danish ethnicity. The Danes are simply described as an honorable people, united under the symbols of the monarch's coat-of-arms.

Advocates for the German side, however, did not see it this way. Reports of Denmark's cruelty to its German-speaking citizens proliferated across the continent. Andersen was distressed by what he viewed as inaccurate descriptions of the war, and his correspondence during this period reveals a concerted effort on his part to correct the stories coming out of Germany. For example, in a letter to a friend in Germany, Caroline von Eisendecher, dated October 1848, Andersen wrote:

> You mentioned the Schleswig-Holstein prisoners of war, that the manner in which they are handled by us is revolting and contentious for our time. It pleases me to be able to recommend you look at a German newspaper, the *Leipziger illustrierte Zeitung*, the last issue in July. Therein you will hear from a German a true report concerning the prisoners' treatment. I implore you to read it. Promise me that. I'm counting on you to do it! The prisoner ships are sheltered with a view of the sound. The steamships pass close by on a daily basis, there is life and variety. I couldn't wish for a prettier place to live myself. The prisoners have daily recreation, they can go for walks along the harbor, yes even swimming. They are also free to go into town and to recreation spots. But they have abused their freedom. For example, a few have begun to sing 'Schleswig-Holstein' in public, and this is indeed, to say the least, not very clever. For the sake of maintaining peace and order, this cannot be permitted at the moment. Yet most German newspapers give such untrue reports about Denmark, present most things in such a false and bad light, that each honorable German who actually witnessed the truth would be furious over [these reports]. Germany has shown me such kindness; there are so many people there that I remain bound to out of gratefulness and affection. Thus, I suffer in my heart over this war – suffer as a Dane to see the mass of lies that are told about us. I am sure that Germany will soon see this itself, for the truth will be victorious! [15]

As this letter reveals, Andersen firmly believed that Denmark's fight to retain the German-speaking duchies of Schleswig and Holstein was justified, and in an effort to present his point of view to readers outside the Schleswig-Holstein conflict, he wrote a letter to William Jerdan, editor of the English *Literary Gazette*, on 13 April 1848. As this letter reveals, Andersen was concerned about how the rest of Europe might look upon Denmark's battle with the German states. Serving as a spokesman for his country's cause, he wrote to Jerdan with the hope that his report might be embraced by the press. Several days later his letter appeared in print:

Dear Friend,

A few weeks only have elapsed since I wrote to you, and in the history of time lay a range of events, as if years had passed. Politics has never been my business; poets have another mission; but now, when convulsions are shaking the countries, so that it is impossible to stand upon the ground without feeling it to the very ends of the fingers, we must speak of it. You know how momentous it is in Denmark; we have war! But a war carried on by the entire animated Danish people, – a war where noble-born and peasant, inspired by a righteous cause, place themselves voluntarily in the ranks of battle; and enthusiasm and patriotism fill and elevate the whole Danish nation. The false light in which the leaders of the Schleswig-Holstein party have for many years, through German newspapers, brought us before the honest German people;... all this has excited the Danes,... Young counts and barons place themselves as subalterns in the ranks of the soldiers.... Among the volunteers is also the son of the Governor of Norway, – a young man who belongs to one of the first families. He was here on a visit last winter, and, carried away by our honest cause, he wished to share in the combat, but as a foreigner could not be admitted. He then immediately bought a Danish house, presented himself as a Danish citizen, put on a soldier's jacket and marched off as a subaltern in one of the regiments ... and like him Danish men of all classes have done the same; the gentleman and the student, the rich and the poor, all go together, singing and rejoicing as to a festival! Our King himself has gone to the army's headquarters. He is Danish and honest-minded for his righteous cause.... In our time the storm of change passes through all lands, but there is One above all who changes not – it is the just God. He is for Denmark, which only demands its rights; and they will and must be acknowledged, for truth is the conquering power for all people and all nations.

'May every nationality obtain its rights, and all that is truly good have its progress!' This is and ought to be Europe's watchword, and with this I look consolingly forward. The Germans are an honest, truth-loving people; they will come to see more clearly the true state of affairs here, and their enmity will be transformed into esteem and friendship. May that hour soon arrive! And may God let the light of his countenance shine on all lands.[16]

This letter, with its defense of Denmark's military action and final appeal for peace, amply illustrates Andersen's patriotic state of mind at the time and his growing dismay over what he viewed as the German states' misguided aggression. His sympathy for those who shared his point of view was clearly expressed on 21 April, when he published a second patriotic poem in *Fædrelandet*, this one entitled 'Den Frivillige' (The Volunteer):

I cannot remain, I have no peace,
I must go with the others to the encampment!
Our cause is just, and we dare to trust that God
Is with us; he will grant us the victory.

For centuries Denmark was powerful and great,
But then it was plucked and plucked.
Now it no longer achieves what it once achieved,
For so long now Denmark has sighed.

They can overrun our little land,
But cannot shake [our] courage or will.
For now we all strike, every one of us;
Our shield is as clean as a lily.

For what you must experience and endure,
In camp, on guard, and in sleet,
Brings tears to many an eye,
God help you! – You will endure!

Jeg kan ikke blive, jeg har ingen Ro,
Jeg maa med de Andre til Leiren!
Vor Sag er retfærdig, og Gud tør vi troe
Er med os, han giver os Seiren.

Aarhundreder Danmark var mægtigt og stort,
Men saa blev det plukket og plukket.
Nu skal de ei gjøre, hvad før de har gjort,
For længe har Danmark nu sukket.

De kan overvælde vort lille Land,
Men rokke ei Mod eller Villie.
Thi nu slaae vi Alle til yderste Mand,
Vort Skjold er saa reent som en Lilie.

For hvad Du maa prøve og døie,
I Kamp, paa Vagt og i Slud,
Staae Taarer i mangt et Øie,
Gud signe Dig! – Du holder ud! [17]

'The Volunteer' is more intimate in tone than Andersen's earlier patriotic poems. Reflecting the restless thoughts of an anonymous soldier, it offers an emotionally charged mix of anxious enthusiasm, melancholy for the past, and hope for the future. Verse one begins with a longing for justice and an affirmation of Denmark's destiny. A contemplation of Denmark's recent decline from glory is the topic of verse two, while verse three considers the possibility of Denmark's defeat. As the fourth verse of the song explains, military defeat will not destroy the soldier's faith, for he knows that his countrymen and God are always with him. [18] Undoubtedly it was this intimate, expressive quality that made the poem so popular among Danish readers. Shortly after its initial publication, 'The Volunteer' was set to a well-known tune by F.L.Æ. Kunzen and distributed in numerous songbooks.

Fig. 5.2 H.C. Andersen. Drawing of Danish soldiers (undated). (Odense: The Andersen House Museum)

As a song, 'The Volunteer' took on another layer of meaning. Because the Kunzen tune had originally been written in 1796 for a royal birthday celebration, it symbolized the monarchy in the minds of many Danes. Thus, the intimate emotions of a lone soldier took on an even greater patriotic meaning when combined with Kunzen's well-known 'royal' melody. In this new form, 'The Volunteer' was warmly embraced by student societies and political leaders, and its central character soon came to be seen as a role model for the nation's young men. During the early months of the war, volunteer soldiers like the one in Andersen's poem filled the ranks of Denmark's military. Generally untrained and ill-equipped for battle, Danish soldiers found a sympathetic voice, a sign of hope in 'The Volunteer.' Far from being a battle cry or call to arms, the song came to serve as a poignant reflection of the Danish population's apprehensions and struggles.

Andersen strongly supported Denmark's efforts in the war, but he nonetheless found it hard to believe that Germany, the home of so many friends and patrons, had become Denmark's enemy. The German-speaking lands had served as the foundation of Andersen's international career, and his readership there was larger and more welcoming than the one he faced at home. In Weimar specifically, he had found a second home and an enthusiastic patron and friend. Only two months earlier, Carl Alexander had awarded him the Order of the White Falcon, an honor he had coveted for several years and which he described as 'a visible tie that connects me with the home that Goethe, Schiller, and the great writers of German literature call theirs.'[19] As Andersen explained in his autobiography several years later, the eruption of the Schleswig-Holstein war clearly troubled him:

> I felt more than ever before how firmly I had grown to my native soil and how Danish my heart was. I could have taken my place in the soldiers' ranks, and I would have gladly given my life as an offering for victory and peace. But at the same time, it clearly occurred to me how much good I had enjoyed in Germany, the great acknowledgement my talent had received there, and the many individuals there I loved and to whom I was grateful. I suffered infinitely! And sometimes, when I came across an agitated individual who, in anger or bitterness, sought to destroy my feelings, then it was often more than I could bear![20]

Andersen's horror over the conflict between Denmark and Germany increased as the war progressed. On 11 May Andersen traveled to Glorup, where he was close to the front line (fig. 5.2). He remained there for six weeks, and judging from the entries in his diary, he took every opportunity during this period to talk with soldiers and learn of their plight. On 13 May he wrote:

> [I] heard a great deal about the battle: the men shot in the chest or head had lain as if they were asleep. Those shot in the abdomen had almost been unrecognizable because their faces were so convulsively distorted with pain. One had lain literally biting the dust with his teeth, his hands clutching at the turf.[21]

Andersen saw Denmark's soldiers as the underdogs in the war – the unjustly oppressed. But even more distressing to him was the destruction of his homeland

and the cruelty suffered by innocent townspeople at the hands of the Prussians. On 24 May Andersen expressed these sentiments in a letter to his editor in England, Richard Bentley:

> These are heavy, unhappy days; a great injustice is being done to little Denmark. You know that the Prussians penetrated the country itself, have occupied Jutland and are daily requisitioning foodstuff, wine, and tobacco; [they] are sending out troops to take away whole herds of horses, cloth from factories – in short they are oppressing in the hardest way possible this poor country and are arresting the civil servants if they are unwilling to give them what they demand. And just these last few days they have levied – and that is really the limit – a forced contribution of four million rixdollars, payable before 28 May, as otherwise it is their intention to use the power and the terror of war! Jutland is unable to pay this sum, not even half of it is available; so the Prussians intend to plunder and set towns on fire. That such things can happen in our times, that such things can happen in civilized nations, that is to me as if I were dreaming a bad dream.... Denmark is a small country, she is being overpowered, she is suffering the greatest injustice, she is bleeding to death.[22]

Andersen's experiences at the front line changed his attitudes about the war. No political issue was worth the suffering he witnessed in Glorup, and he feared the cry to battle would soon prove a death knell to the arts. Upon witnessing the power and ferocity of the Prussian troops, Andersen realized how diminutive Denmark had become in the realm of European nations. And in an effort to revitalize his homeland's interest in the wealth it held among its many artists, writers, and musicians, he composed a one-act vaudeville for the Royal Theater called *Kunstens Dannevirke* (Bulwark of the Arts).

Bulwark of the Arts was commissioned as part of a week-long celebration marking the centennial of Denmark's Royal Theater. Andersen was asked to write a dramatic prelude that could be presented each evening before various featured performances. Taking the commission as an opportunity to express his attitudes about the war, Andersen used his vaudeville to praise the bravery of Denmark's soldiers and glorify the treasures found in the nation's poetry, art, and music. As Andersen later explained:

> My plan for the prelude ... was based entirely on contemporary concerns. I knew what feelings the people had when they came to the theater, and how little attraction it had for them, since their thoughts were with the soldiers in the war. Therefore, I decided to let my poem begin where their thoughts were [on the battlefield] and then have it carry them back to the Danish stage. My conviction told me that [Denmark's] strength no longer lay in the sword, but in intellectual ability.[23]

Bulwark of the Arts is set at an unnamed military checkpoint similar to the one Andersen visited in Glorup. The characters include two volunteer soldiers, who have traded in their careers as poet and sculptor to fight for the glory of Denmark, and three Valkyries. Although the resolution of both soldiers is unwavering, their interest is not so much in Denmark's victories on the battlefield as in the riches of its poetry, specifically the dramatic works of Ludvig Holberg, Denmark's greatest eighteenth-century dramatist.[24] As the sculptor and poet explain throughout the course of the drama, their homeland's strongest attribute will never be overpowered, for it abides in the heart and mind of each Danish citizen. Holberg's ingenious characters, both the comedic and serious, live in the memories of each Dane, and as such they contribute to the great 'bulwark' that protects the Danish populace from the challenges and struggles of life.

Upon first reading *Bulwark of the Arts*, one might ask: Why are only sculpture and poetry represented? What about painting and, more specifically, music? A consideration of the work as a whole, as it was performed at the Royal Theater in 1850, reveals that both of these art forms actually were represented, albeit in a more subtle manner than poetry and sculpture were. Great attention was given to the scenery and costumes used for *Bulwark of the Arts* – so much so that the appearance of the stage on opening night resembled one of the many realistic Danish landscapes and city scenes by C.W. Eckersberg and Christen Købke, artists of Denmark's 'golden age.'[25] Music also played a dominant role in the production, through the presentation of both purely instrumental numbers and numerous popular songs. Andersen used music as a means of communicating the emotional content of *Bulwark of the Arts*. Devoid of specific meaning when presented alone, music stood as the most apolitical of all the arts. And when combined with poetry, as it was in the vaudeville's many songs, music imbued the specific message of Andersen's text with a psychological/emotional dimension impossible to express through words alone. Responding to the aesthetic theories promoted by figures such as Schelling and Hegel, Andersen appears to have looked to music as a metaphor for the poetic. Reflecting the eternal essence of the ideal as well as the ephemeral quality of the experienced present, music symbolized both the poetic spirit and the immediacy of the senses. Through music, Andersen was able to show audiences that their current encounters with war, though no doubt horrifying, were only the result of a temporary political struggle. Denmark's spirit, as expressed in music, was eternal. With its bulwark of the arts standing firm, the glory of the nation would never be extinguished.

This sentiment is strengthened toward the end of the vaudeville when the sculptor departs – his regiment has been called into battle – and the poet falls to sleep. As he dreams of Denmark's glory, three Valkyries appear on winged horses. They scour the battlefield in search of courageous souls to carry back to Odin. Upon finding the poet, they sing to him of the glory of Denmark's artists, especially the work of Johannes Ewald, 'who sang about the Danes' road to power and might, and showed us with the beacon's flash our ancient times.'[26] Their appearance is ominous yet propitious, for it signals both mortal death and immortal glory for many of Denmark's soldiers. 'Denmark's magnificence will never wane,' sings one of the Valkyries. 'The people will come to understand what God has granted them. This will hold them together, even in times as difficult as these.'[27]

When the poet finally awakens, he finds that his courage has been strengthened by the images in his dreams. Singing to the melody 'Danmark deiligst Vang og Vænge,' he concludes by asking Denmark to celebrate the glory of its arts. 'Light the festive candles in all Danish hearts, just as the dream [of Glory] has been lighted in mine. The honorable and the beautiful will stand strong forever in Denmark's Kingdom. And the arts will bear us branches, fresh, green – Immortal!'[28] The significance of this final song was great, for while the text encouraged audiences to remember the wealth found in their nation's artists, the music aroused a specific patriotic sentiment. When *Bulwark of the Arts* premièred in 1848, the melody to 'Danmark deiligst Vang og Vænge' was already well-known as the accompaniment of two patriotic songs published in 1839, one by Andersen and the other by Grundtvig.[29]

Bulwark of the Arts was warmly received by the public, but as Andersen later explained in his autobiography, Denmark's critics were less generous:

At the première it was received with great applause[30] ... the public was transported. Then came the newspapers: one of them blamed me for making the work into a disgusting prattling about the glories of Denmark, saying that we ought to let others praise us and not do it ourselves.... Another newspaper described the work in such a manner that I could not tell if it had been written in a spirit of folly or malice.[31]

Andersen regretted that the work was performed every evening of the festival. At the third performance 'the reception was now rather tepid' and by the fourth performance it had already 'become an old story.' Critics began attributing various unintended messages to the vaudeville, and 'the audience no longer applauded.'[32] The number of negative reviews increased as the series of performances progressed. Andersen was criticized for being too patriotic, too assured of Denmark's victory and the superior status of its artists. He was accused of using the nation's stage as a propaganda tool. Some even claimed that he used the occasion for self-promotion. In *Bulwark of the Arts*, the poet, especially the 'poet of plays,' is deemed the most virtuous Danish soul since his power lies not just in his use of words, but his ability 'to reach an entire audience all at once.'[33] Although Andersen never actually named himself in *Bulwark of the Arts*, audiences could not help but see the character of the poet as yet another example of Andersen's many self-portraits. This interpretation was strengthened by the vaudeville's music; two-thirds of the melodies used in *Bulwark of the Arts* came from operas with libretti by Andersen, and the final melody, 'Danmark deiligst Vang og Vænge,' was associated with one of his earliest patriotic songs.

The war inspired in Andersen an interest in Norse mythology, specifically the power of the Valkyries and the splendor of Valhalla. While visiting Stockholm in 1849, Andersen conceived of a plot for 'a little ballet-opera' called *Valkyrien* (The Valkyrie) that he thought would be well suited for Copenhagen's Royal Theater. While talking with the Danish diplomat Carl Steen Andersen Bille, Andersen realized Denmark's pivotal importance to both the history and geography of

Scandinavia. As Bille saw it, Denmark was 'the bridge' between Germany and the rest of Scandinavia, and as such it was duty-bound to stop battling against its neighbors. On 26 May, Andersen spent the day with Bille and later recorded the gist of their conversation in his diary.

> Bille said: the Danes are always stubborn when they are right. They forget that they are a small [land], forget to recognize their true gifts; thus they stuck with Napoleon, didn't want to join with the other powers, and had to give up Norway. They went to battle against Sweden until they lost all of Norway. Denmark then reconciled it a bit and now has become friends with Sweden, has sided with it in sympathy. Now it hates Germany and maintains its right, despite the fact that circumstances might require that it again surrender a portion of its [territory] – but there will come a time when [Denmark] will understand its place as a bridge between Germany and the North, when it will be in good standing with both its neighbors and will even benefit from this.[34]

Just as Denmark served as the geographical bridge between Germany and Scandinavia, Norse mythology served as the unifying cultural force. The age of the Vikings as portrayed in the mythic tales of Thor and Odin were claimed by both Germany and Scandinavia as the roots of their modern culture. Thus it comes as no surprise that within a day of his discussion with Bille, Andersen began work on a ballet-opera featuring a consciously apolitical storyline that was designed to show off the musical talents of a specific German composer, Franz Gläser.[35] On 27 May Andersen noted in his diary that he 'wrote a ballet program and a letter to [August] Bournonville.'[36] The following day he 'completed the first scene of *The Valkyrie*.'[37] He must have finished the rest of the draft later that evening, since his diary indicates that on 29 May he 'sent a letter to Henriette Wulff, wherein he included a letter and opera plan for Bournonville.'[38] The letter read as follows:

> Dear Friend,
>   Last night I arrived here, and I am rushing to send you a sketch for the little ballet-opera as it has materialized during my travels. I hope that I have captured my idea correctly, and I ask you if it is possible to send me in the next post your judgment of it – what you have noticed, what you would remove or perhaps what you would add. Give Gläser a copy of it; he has asked for it specifically, since he wanted to think about the plot. You indicated that you think Ms. Heiberg could be the Valkyrie – that she is a good speaker; but after thinking about it, I believe that it remains most advisable not to include Ms. Heiberg at all. What is more, allowing the lead character to speak will disrupt the proper musical unity, and one thing that is quite certain is that Ms. Heiberg would not like to take on such a role. Indeed, she is very weak and must be spared; we do not have many pearls like her. I recommend that the Valkyrie remain a large singing role that can be given to [Leocadie] Bergnehr or Miss Lehmann. – Over the next few nights I will revise the whole and then, as soon as I get a letter from you, make the changes you wish to see done according to the given plan, and then I will send you and Gläser the whole thing right away.[39]

Set in the age of the Vikings, the dramatic scenery and amorous plot of *The Valkyrie* would have offered Gläser the opportunity to compose a score filled with the same rich, expressive power that he had become known for a decade earlier in Berlin with his score to *Des Adlers Horst*. As one can see in the following excerpt, the sketch Andersen submitted to Bournonville was more about the struggles of love than the battles between nations:

The Valkyrie:
A Ballet-Opera in two acts by Bournonville,
Music by Gläser, Text by H.C. Andersen

Act I: A large, spacious beamed hall, fireplace in the middle of the floor, background open, one can see the sea. Poor Embla sits with her maidens, each by her loom. They sing a song about their work, Embla [sings] about marriage and the bridegroom. They dance and play. The bridegroom, Thoralf, 'Vanquisher of Kings,' comes from the Viking ship with treasures and captives. Transition song. Dance (for example, character dance by the captives). In the mean time, between the opening in the beams above is seen Thoralf's Valkyrie. She sings that the hero wastes away in his lover's arms, that the beamed hall is confining, that he is not Embla's, but hers, and then she disappears. The wedding is prepared, and a youth appears – it is the Valkyrie herself – she reports that a sea king [Viking] has landed at Holmgang and prepares for battle. Thoralf arms himself. Departure. The Valkyrie sings: 'He is mine!'

Act II: Valhalla. Transition song between Thor and Freja about war and love; then [they] describe Thoralf and Embla and the Holmgang battle. One hears from the earth below rumbling and war-like song. The Valkyries float up with fallen heroes. Finally, the Valkyrie arrives with Thoralf, who is greeted by Thor and Freja. She reminds him of Embla. His thoughts turn toward earth. One hears singing; it is coming from his graveside where the stone is being set. Embla's cries of sorrow reach all the way to Valhalla; louder and louder the Valkyrie sings her song and along with this the line-dance and battle begin. Thoralf takes part and is handed the horn by the Valkyrie.[40]

Nothing came of Andersen's plan for *The Valkyrie*.[41] Nonetheless, his enthusiasm for its topic tells us much about his creative interests during the war. In both *The Valkyrie* and *Bulwark of the Arts*, Andersen's focus on Denmark's culture and language and his use of figures from Norse mythology reveal a subtle reaction to the cultural nationalism that was sweeping through Denmark under the leadership of Grundtvig. Indeed, Andersen's use of the melody 'Danmark deiligst Vang og Vænge' at the end of *Bulwark of the Arts* was not just a reference to his own work, but a reference to Grundtvig as well, since he also published words to the tune in 1839. But if Andersen toyed with the idea of following the lead of the nationalists in 1848 and 1849, he quickly abandoned such thoughts when their isolationist attitude toward the rest of Europe intensified. As the war progressed, Andersen struggled to come to terms with his identity as both a loyal Dane and a citizen of the world. By 1850, he appears to have found a happy medium, a compromise clearly expressed in the text of one of his most famous poems, 'I Danmark er jeg født' (In Denmark I was Born).

'In Denmark I was Born' was published in *Fædrelandet* on 30 March 1850 under the title 'Danmark, mit Fædreland!' (Denmark, my Fatherland). As Hans Kuhn explains, this poem is a declaration of love for the fatherland, not a call to arms. It does not express a collective sentiment, but, rather, the spontaneous confession of an individual. The text was quickly set to music by Henrik Rung and was performed shortly thereafter by the Skandinaviske Selskab, a men's choir, to raise money for a monument commemorating the Battle of Fredericia, the decisive turning point in the war.[42] To this day, 'In Denmark I was Born' is considered the most intimate, patriotic song of the Danish repertory.

> In Denmark I was born. That's where my home is,
> There I have roots, from there my world extends.
> You, Danish language, you are my Mother's voice,
> With you my heartbeats like sweet music blend.
> You fresh Danish shore,
> Where ancient gravesites
> Stand between apple orchards, hop and mallow,
> It's you I love – Denmark, my native land!
>
> Oh, where does summer strew her bed all over
> With lovelier flowers than here, by the open shore?
> Where shines the full moon on field of clover
> So beautifully as in the beech tree's native land?
> You fresh Danish shore,
> Where Dannebrog waves,
> God gave it to us – God, grant the best Victory!
> It's you I love – Denmark, my native land!
>
> Once all the Nordic lands were in your power
> And England too – now you are called weak,
> A little land – And yet, all across the world
> Is heard the Danes' song and strike of the chisel.
> You fresh Danish shore,
> The ploughman finds the golden horns;
> May God grant you a future, as he has given you memorials!
> It's you I love – Denmark, my native land!
>
> You, land where I was born, and where my home is,
> Where I have roots, from where my world extends,
> Where language is my Mother's soft voice,
> And like a sweet music, it draws my heart near!
> You fresh Danish shore
> With the nests of wild swans,
> On green islands, my heart's earthly home,
> It's you I love – Denmark, my native land!

I Danmark er jeg født, der har jeg hjemme,
Der har jeg Rod, derfra min Verden gaaer.
Du danske Sprog, du er min Moders Stemme,
Saa sødt velsignet Du mit Hjerte naaer.
Du danske, friske Strand,
Hvor oldtids Kæmpegrave
Staae mellem Æblegaard og Humlehave,
Dig elsker jeg! – Danmark, mit Fædreland!

Hvor reder sommeren vel blomstersengen
Meer rigt end her, ned til den aabne Strand?
Hvor staaer Fuldmaanen over Kløverengen
Saa dejlig, som i Bøgens Fædreland?
Du danske, friske Strand,
Hvor Dannebrogen vaier, –
Gud gav os den – Gud, giv den bedste Seier! –
Dig elsker jeg! – Danmark, mit Fædreland!

Engang Du Herre var i hele Norden,
Bød over England – nu Du kaldes svag,
Et lille Land, – og dog saa vidt om Jorden
End høres Danskens Sang og Meiselslag;
Du danske, friske Strand, –
Plovjernet Guldhorn finder. –
Gud, giv Dig Fremtid, som han gav Dig Minder!
Dig elsker jeg! – Danmark, mit Fædreland!

Du Land, hvor jeg blev født, hvor jeg har hjemme,
Hvor jeg har Rod, hvorfra min Verden gaaer,
Hvor Sproget er min Moders bløde Stemme,
Og som en sød Musik mit Hjerte naaer!
Du danske, friske Strand
Med vilde Svaners Rede,
I grønne Øer, mit Hjertes Hjem hernede,
Dig elsker jeg! – Danmark, mit Fædreland! [43]

The patriotism of 'In Denmark I was Born' is not abstract or markedly political.
Looking at the poem, three themes stand out: the speaker's love of Denmark's
landscape, the glory of its past, and the treasures found in its art. Compared to the
poetry of Grundtvig, the historical/nationalistic elements in Andersen's poem play
a subordinate role. The location described in the first stanza is not Copenhagen, or
even the whole of Denmark; rather, it is the 'green islands' Andersen knew as a
boy. The beech trees, flowery meadows, and open shores so familiar from
Andersen's fairy tales set a personalized, intimate scene for the entire poem.
Denmark's history and national strength play no real role in the poem. The only
appearance of an historic event is the allusion to Denmark's strength in Viking
times (under Canute the Great, who reigned from 1014 to 1035), and it quickly
becomes apparent that even this allusion is included for no other reason than to

serve as a foil to the description in verse three of Denmark's weakened political power in the nineteenth century. The glory of Denmark's cultural past is also declared in verse three. 'The plowman' who 'finds the goldhorns' (Plovjernet Guldhorner finder) is a reference to the golden horns of Gallehus, whose disappearance in 1802 caused a national crisis in Denmark. When the horns were stolen and melted down, a great cultural artifact was lost. This reference, echoed by the 'memorials' (Minder) of the following line, evokes the passing of an historical golden age. But Andersen does not bemoan his nation's current circumstances; he does not call for retribution or renewed military glory. Instead, he turns to Denmark's artists, 'The Dane's song and the strike of the chisel' (Danskens Sang og Meiselslag), clear allusions to the characters first seen in *Bulwark of the Arts*, to serve as Denmark's glory in contemporary times.[44]

The wild swans' nest mentioned in verse four is an element not found in other patriotic songs of the time, and its inclusion adds a fairy tale touch to the poem that symbolizes Andersen's connection to both Denmark and the rest of Europe. For readers in Copenhagen, the reference to swans recalled the plot of Andersen's fairy tale, 'De vilde Svaner' (The Wild Swans), first published in 1838. Wild swans are migratory birds, and they symbolized cosmopolitan travelers, like Andersen and Thorvaldsen, whose trips abroad in no way diminished their loyalty to Denmark. After the publication of 'In Denmark I was Born,' H.C. Ørsted wrote to Andersen, complaining that with the phrase 'Sang og Hammerslag' only the fine arts were represented. Ørsted suggested that the sciences also should be counted among Denmark's treasures.[45] Andersen took Ørsted's suggestion to heart. Two years later, in 1852, he published an allegorical sketch called 'Svanereden' in *Berlingske Tidene* wherein he described Denmark as a swan's nest from which flocks and individuals had taken off at various times. In the present, 'three golden swans' could still be observed living in the nest of Denmark: one touching the strings of a golden harp (Oehlenschläger), another releasing beautiful figures in marble (Thorvaldsen), and the third 'spinning the thread of thought' (Ørsted).[46]

*

Andersen's view of the arts as his homeland's fortune influenced his decision to take part in the growing trend toward popular theater that took root in Denmark during the Schleswig-Holstein War. On 26 December 1848, the Casino, Copenhagen's first authorized public theater, opened under the direction of Hans Wilhelm Lange, a friend of Andersen's from the theater in Odense. Housed in Amaliegade near Kongens Nytorv where the Royal Theater is located, the Casino brought popular theater to the general public at an affordable cost and, in so doing, became a unifying cultural force for the war-weary citizens of Copenhagen.

Lange was limited, however, in the types of performances he could produce at the Casino. Popular comedy, ballad opera, vaudeville, farce and pantomime were the only genres permitted according to the theater's license. Serious theatrical genres – specifically tragedy and opera – were only licensed for performance at the Royal Theater. Consequently, when the Casino first opened, many of Copenhagen's prominent playwrights ridiculed the theater's cultural mission and the social status of its patrons – as Henrik Hertz acerbically pointed out in 1849, the Casino was not a venue for the elite, but rather 'a theater for the people, peasants, burghers, and coachmen.'[47] Andersen did not share in such class prejudice. He embraced the Casino's mission immediately, and Lange gave him complete creative freedom – quite a contrast to the unresponsive, dismissive treatment Andersen had endured for so many years at the Royal Theater. Andersen's enthusiasm reached beyond his activities as unofficial house dramatist and librettist. Within a few months he was working as the Casino's literary consultant and serving on its board of directors. Andersen wrote libretti for a number of one-act vaudevilles and fairy-tale operas during the war years, and his success at the Casino soon attracted other established writers and composers to its stage.

Generally speaking, the majority of Andersen's works for the Casino were inspired by a popular form of theater known as *Zauberspiel* (also known as *Zauberoper* or *Zauberposse*), which was refined in Austria by the dramatist Ferdinand Raimund.[48] The *Zauberspiel* was essentially a singspiel featuring an array of magical elements, spectacular stage effects, and a mixture of borrowed arias and ballads. The plots were primarily inspired by the world of fairy tales, a trait that Andersen found fascinating, and they often featured a mixture of the supernatural with everyday, contemporary life. Andersen first encountered the *Zauberspiel* in Vienna. He was particularly enthusiastic about Karl Meisl's *Das Gespenst auf der Bastei*, which he saw at the Theater an der Wien on 2 July 1834. 'The whole light, fantastical humor delighted me,' he wrote in his diary.[49] In 1838, Andersen tried to secure a production at the Royal Theater for a similar work by Raimund, entitled *Der Verschwender*, but with no success.[50] It was only with the opening of the Casino that Andersen's aspirations of bringing *Zauberspiel* to Copenhagen were finally realized.

In Andersen's mind, the *Zauberspiel* offered a two-fold advantage for Casino audiences in the 1840s. First, as a genre defined primarily by fantasy and farce, it served as an escape from the troubling political issues associated with the Schleswig-Holstein War. Second, with its complex arrangement of popular musical numbers from works by Danish, German, Italian, and French composers, it served as a means of reinforcing the cosmopolitan, pan-European culture that Denmark had previously embraced and that Andersen had come to identify with during his many travels abroad. At the Casino, Andersen quickly succeeded in capturing the spirit and flavor of the Viennese *Zauberspiel*. Renaming the genre 'Eventyr-Comedie' (Fairy-tale Comedy),[51] he believed that the success of such works was only a matter of time since, as he explained, 'the talent the world acknowledges in me as an author of fairy tales must eventually bear some fruit in this direction as well.'[52] Like the 'poets of plays' described in *Bulwark of the Arts*, Andersen capitalized on the opportunity to 'reach an entire audience all at once.' On 3 October 1849 his first fairy-tale comedy, *Meer end Perler og Guld* (More than Pearls and Gold), premièred at the Casino and soon proved to be a resounding success.

Based on Raimund's *Der Diamant des Geisterkönigs* and the story of Prince Zeyn Alasnam and the Genie from *The Arabian Nights*, *More than Pearls and Gold* uses a mixture of topical details and fantastical spectacle to tell the story of a young man who is promised a statue made of diamonds if he can find a girl who has never told a lie. This fanciful plot lent itself well to numerous comedic scenes, and as in the *Zauberspiel* of Raimund, music played an important role. Throughout the course of the play, the audience was treated to a variety of musical numbers that brought to life scenes both real and imagined. H.C. Lumbye's popular waltz orchestra, by this point a famous feature of Tivoli Gardens, opened the performance with a well-known overture, most commonly one of the many vaudeville overtures composed by Ludwig Zinck. Andersen selected the melodies used for the various musical numbers, and his selection says much about his taste in music at the time. As we saw in chapters 1 and 2, the melodies Andersen selected for his vaudevilles of the 1830s and early 1840s often came from works that had recently been performed at the Royal Theater; thus they reflected the public's taste as much as Andersen's own. But such was not the case with his selection of music for *More than Pearls and Gold*. When putting together the music for this work, Andersen's first priority was to select melodies that effectively reflected the mood of his new text and/or deepened the meaning of his text through references to the melodies' original lyrics.[53] For example, the melody of the popular French song 'Le roi d'Yvetot,' written by Pierre Jean de Béranges in 1813, served as the basis for one of the instrumental numbers in Andersen's production. The audience at the Casino would have surely known the text, which tells of a jolly little king who would rather eat and drink than fight wars or expand his kingdom.[54]

Of the thirty-six musical numbers in *More than Pearls and Gold*, thirty are vocal works and six are for instruments only. Twenty-two of the selections come from operas and singspiels from across Europe: two are Danish, seven are French, six are Italian, and two are German. The rest of the music represents popular romances, folk songs, and dance tunes. Locating the exact sources Andersen used when assembling his music is difficult. His diaries and letters indicate numerous sources: the Royal Theater, performances of Italian opera at the Court Theater, performances at Tivoli and the Casino, the Vauxhall Festivals put on by Georg Carstensen, not to mention the numerous theaters he visited during his many treks across Europe. By the time Andersen began writing for the Casino, his previous encounters with music of all types had made him a virtual repository of European popular song. Thus it should come as no surprise that his selection of melodies for *More than Pearls and Gold* came from a assortment of disparate sources, including: Donizetti's *Elixer of Love*, *Lucia di Lammermoor*, *La fille du régiment*, and *Lucrezia Borgia*; Bellini's *Norma* and *La Sonnambula*; Weber's *Oberon*; Meyerbeer's *Robert le Diable*; Auber's *La Muette de Portici*; Isouard's *Jeannot et Collin*; F. Hérold's *Marie*; Hartmann's *Liden Kirsten* and *Ravnen*; Kuhlau's *Elverhøi*; Henrik Rung's incidental music to *Svend Dyrings Huus*; Louis-Jacques Milon's ballet *Le carnival de Venise* with music by Rodolphe Kreutzer; Carl von Holteis' song 'Die Wiener in Berlin;' the American tune 'Mary Blane;' the

Neapolitan folk song 'Te voglio bene;' various Danish folk songs; dance tunes by Joseph Lanner, Johann Strauss Senior, and H.C. Lumbye; and instrumental numbers composed by Niels W. Gade and Carl Malmquist.[55]

This potpourri of musical numbers served Andersen well in his attempt to bring to life a number of disparate scenes derived equally from fantasy and everyday life, including: Denmark's newly formed parliament, a balloon ride over the Danish countryside, and 'Monkeyland,' a satirical version of a bourgeois salon where Copenhagen's elite gathered to see and be seen. Copenhagen's public clamored to see performance after performance of *More than Pearls and Gold*, and critics praised Andersen's effective use of music. The production enjoyed a long succession of sold-out performances in the 2,500-seat Casino, with over one hundred performances staged during Andersen's lifetime. The success of Andersen's first *Zauberspiel* encouraged him to produce a second one, *Ole Lukøje* (Ole Shuteye), a few months later.

Inspired by one of Andersen's own fairy tale characters, Ole Shuteye (Denmark's version of 'the Sandman'), this *Zauberspiel* is peppered with numerous literary references. The basic dream structure of the work is drawn from the framework of Franz Grillparzer's *Der Traum, ein Leben*, wherein the hero dreams in such a way that his real life is influenced by what he has experienced when asleep. Thus *Ole Shuteye* is really a play within a play, an intermingling of reality and fantasy, spoken text and music. The central character in the *Zauberspiel* is a discontented chimneysweep named Christian. Wishing for a life of great wealth, he encounters, while dreaming, the ghost of a vagabond 'dressed all in white with a white cane and cigar.'[56] The ghost offers Christian three wishes, which he foolishly wastes. Like the coal-burner Peter Munk in Wilhelm Hauff's fairy tale, 'Das kalte Herz,' he offers his soul in exchange for money, and a Faustian junk-dealer named Blake replaces the beat of his heart with the ticking of a gold watch.[57] Thus the moral of *Ole Shuteye* is quite similar to that found in Raimund's *Der Bauer als Millionär* or Hauff's 'Das kalte Herz:' 'Es ist doch besser, zufrieden sein mit wenigem, als Gold und Güter haben, und ein kaltes Herz' (It is far better to be satisfied with little, than to have gold and riches and a cold heart).[58]

As one might imagine, the complex dream sequences in *Ole Shuteye* required a wealth of evocative music as well as a series of special effects. Audiences witnessed an array of surprising scene changes, lavish dance numbers, and what can only be described as supernatural transformations and a display of 'black magic' in Blake's second-hand shop, where 'furniture danced, portraits moved, and the fire iron performed pirouettes!'[59] No production records of the first performances now exist, but the mechanical effects must have been convincing, since Andersen himself reported that everything functioned 'as properly as possible' on the 'small, narrow, oppressive stage at Casino.'[60]

Reviews of *Ole Shuteye* were not as complementary as those Andersen received for *More than Pearls and Gold*, and they clearly show how disconnected and condescending the self-styled critics who disparaged the idea of a public theater such as Casino could be. M.A. Goldschmidt, for example, chastised

Andersen for basing his work on the *Zauberspiel* of Raimund, explaining that:
'many a spectator of such a folk-comedy perhaps goes home to his simple parlor
and finds it poorer than before, is even more dissatisfied with life than before going
to the theater.'[61]   In Goldschmidt's mind, the audience that frequented the Casino
was ill equipped to appreciate the spectacle of Andersen's *Zauberspiele*. Believing
that the theatrical arts should be designed to give pleasure to those well acquainted
with beauty and wealth, he feared that exposing the masses to such productions
would only lead to discontent among Copenhagen's encroaching servant class.
Unfortunately, attitudes such as these affected the success of Andersen's *Ole
Shuteye* and *Hyldemoer* (Mother Elder, premièred on 1 December 1851).
Although both were performed well over thirty times during Andersen's life,
neither attained the popularity of *More than Pearls and Gold*. As Andersen
commented later when reflecting on his activities with the *Zauberspiel* genre, 'I
came to realize that most of my countrymen didn't have a great sense for fantasy.
They didn't want to climb too high, but instead remained on the ground and
nourished themselves hungrily with wretched dramatic recipes right out of a
cookbook.'[62]

*

The first Schleswig-Holstein War ended in the fall of 1850, and in February of the
following year Denmark's victorious soldiers entered Copenhagen, an event
Andersen captured in a poem entitled 'Landsoldatens Hjemkomst' (Soldier's
Homecoming) (fig. 5.3). This poem, along with several others by Andersen ('For
Danmark,' 'Den Frivillige,' 'Soldaternes Sang til Dannebrog,' and 'Til
Landsoldaten'), was published on 18 February in a small commemorative album
entitled *Fædrelandske Vers og Sange under Krigen* (Verse and Songs of the
Fatherland during the War).[63] Happy that the war was finally over, Andersen set to
work mending the cultural ties with Germany that had been severed during the
war. One of his first steps in this endeavor was to attempt collaboration once again
with the German composer Franz Gläser. With the war over, Andersen turned his
attention to the Royal Theater. The first work he and Gläser produced together
there was an opera called *Brylluppet ved Como-Søen* (Wedding at Lake Como).[64]
Based on Alessandro Manzoni's novel *I Promessi sposi* and featuring several
dance scenes choreographed by Bournonville, the opera was well received on
opening night. In his almanac Andersen commented on the audience's applause:
'Never before heard it stronger.'[65]

A letter to Carl Alexander dated March 1849 reveals that Andersen viewed his
work with Gläser as a sign that, despite the ravages of war, Denmark and Germany
could remain united through music:

> Your royal highness knows that in the midst of war and strife, the composer
> Gläser and I have peacefully been working together at home in the garden of art.
> The work is now finished and has been brought to the stage.... Here at the Royal
> Theater it has been received enthusiastically; it has created an excitement unlike
> any that I have ever known the performance of an opera here to create. Almost

Fig. 5.3 David Monies. Episode from a Soldier's Homecoming at the Church of the Holy Spirit (1850). (Copenhagen: The National Museum at Fredriksborg)

every number received applause, and at the première the composer received a triple Hurrah, so that one could rightfully see that here in the world of art no one is asked about nationality.

Gläser is unspeakably happy; this work stands far above the others that he has created up to this point, and I think this opera will also become a box office hit in Germany. He recently asked me about the opera situation in Weimar. I think Gläser's opera would find a home there.[66]

Although Andersen's hopes for a performance of *Wedding at Lake Como* in Weimar never materialized, he and Gläser continued to collaborate on projects they hoped would facilitate a sense of goodwill between their homelands. In May 1849 they began making plans with Bournonville for the ballet-opera *The Valkyrie*, and on 12 February 1853 an opera entitled *Nøkken* (The Nix or Water Sprite) premièred at the Royal Theater.[67] Possibly inspired by the playing of Ole Bull – Andersen often claimed that Bull's playing reminded him of a water sprite – the opera featured music inspired by 'the national dance of Sweden.' Still, the production was limited to a mere seven performances. Reviewers offered little praise, an unfortunate circumstance that Ingemann tried to account for in a letter he wrote to Andersen on 25 February:

It pleased me to read the little, jovial opera text with the understanding of what was to me until now an unknown aspect of the national dance in Sweden. The melancholy figure of legends, 'the Nix,' also appealed to me right away [even] in 'the foreign' guise; but when [the plot] turned into a camouflaged and eerie version of the legend in order to appeal to the taste of the educated world, I did not like it. It was like murdering the Nix and then acting out a comedy on his grave.... Nonetheless, if the music to your 'Nix' is good, then it seems to me the piece must be entertaining. Those that disparaged the text in the newspapers have obviously hardly read it.... That the composer is a German has perhaps also mixed a bit of concealed political spite into the newspaper reviews.[68]

After *The Nix* closed, Andersen approached Gläser with yet another opera project – a pointedly political work entitled *Befrielsen* (The Liberation). But Gläser was obviously tired of swimming against the current of cultural nationalism that was sweeping across Denmark. In a letter to Andersen dated 25 October 1853 Gläser declined Andersen's offer, claiming that the subject matter, the Greeks' liberation from the Turks, did not appeal to him:

Enclosed I am sending back the opera manuscript you sent me for *The Liberation*; I thank you for sharing it with me. I find the poetry itself, as I've already told you in person, very beautiful. The arrangement of the vocal parts, however, is not conducive to an opera.... The story material doesn't appeal to me at all, especially since it moves within the region of the Greek and Turkish sphere. Every other nationality in Europe is more appealing to me.[69]

Upon receiving Gläser's negative response, Andersen did not pursue the opera project any further.

In addition to his work with Gläser, Andersen began to renew contacts with friends and patrons in Germany. A look at his correspondence shortly after the war reveals a virtual flood of letters to members of the German aristocracy, and these efforts yielded numerous rewards. In addition to being welcomed back into the fold of Weimar's cultural elite, Andersen established a strong relationship with King Maximilian of Bavaria, who eventually awarded him the Maximilian Order for Art and Science in 1859, telling him: 'your writings have a very German ring about them, and your tales are so popular in Germany.'[70]

Such interactions with German patrons so soon after the conclusion of the war did not win Andersen much support among his compatriots. The trouble reached a boiling point in 1855, when Andersen published a revised edition of his autobiography that included many warm sentiments about members of the German aristocracy who had generously supported him throughout his career. In Denmark, such comments were viewed by many as little less than cultural treason. Indeed, even friends as close as Henriette Wulff criticized Andersen for the sentiments expressed in his autobiography:

> To me it is a total denial of oneself, of one's own person, of the gifts God has graciously given us, such an incomprehensible self-humiliation that I am surprised when somebody like *you*, Andersen – if you recognize that God has given you special spiritual gifts – that *you* can consider yourself *happy* and *honored* to be placed – well, that is what it says – at the table of the King of Prussia or of some other high-ranking person – or receive a decoration, the kind worn by the greatest scoundrels, not to mention a swarm of extremely insignificant people. Do you really place a title, money, aristocratic blood, success in what is nothing but outward matters *above* genius – spirit – the gifts of the soul?[71]

Andersen offered no reply to this question; instead he continued to seek the support of royal patrons both in Denmark and abroad. A patriot who still held warm affections for his German neighbors, Andersen found no shame in embracing, once again, his cosmopolitan lifestyle now that the war was over. Members of the aristocracy, no matter what their culture or national allegiance, could still serve as worthy patrons. And as long as they embraced his Danish heritage, he would accept their support and admiration. In Andersen's mind, Denmark's artists were its finest treasure. What better way was there to glorify himself and his homeland than to spread the beauty of this treasure across all of Europe?

*

So far, this chapter has examined Andersen's creative activities during the war years and beyond in an attempt to explain his relationship to Denmark's changing national identity. But in order to get a more complete view of circumstances in Denmark during this period, it is necessary to turn for a moment to the topic of Andersen's general reception by the Danish public, a reception that is perhaps most accurately reflected in the nation's prolific production of songbooks during the middle decades of the century.

Throughout the Schleswig-Holstein War and beyond, Andersen remained a true patriot of Denmark. Dedicated to his homeland's people and king, he wrote patriotic poems venerating Denmark's artistic treasures and *Zauberspiele* promoting an apolitical, universal morality and pan-European repertoire. Yet Andersen also cautiously avoided the wave of cultural nationalism initiated by the writings of Grundtvig, and it was this avoidance that eventually led some to question his loyalty to Denmark. Although the context of the present chapter does not allow for a complete discussion of Andersen's relationship to his homeland as shown in his diaries and correspondence,[72] a look at his reception in Danish songbooks of the nineteenth century reveals much about how Andersen's continued allegiance to political patriotism eventually put him out of step with the majority of his countrymen, who were coming under the influence of cultural nationalism.

Singing was a major pastime in nineteenth-century Denmark, and as such it came to serve as an important political tool. Demand for Danish songbooks was tremendous, and as the country's national identity changed from political patriotism to cultural nationalism, the content and structure of Danish songbooks followed suit.[73] In the first half of the century, songbooks were primarily produced by commercial publishers who used music performed at the Royal Theater as the basic source for material. Beginning in the 1820s and 30s, these commercial songbooks began to adopt a patriotic tone. Based on folk tales and/or stories of Denmark's history, the poems in these songbooks generally praised the common good (i.e. Denmark's monarchy) and opposed the pursuit of individual desires. With the establishment of the Provincial Assemblies in 1834, the production of patriotic tunes increased, and revolutionary songs from various parts of Europe (i.e. the 'Marseillaise' and Ernst Moritz Arndt's 'Was ist dem Deutschen Vaterlands?') were printed side by side with texts by Grundtvig and Ingemann. At the same time, Denmark's multiple languages and cultures were seen as an asset.[74] In the 1840s an increased interest in traditional folk ballads led to the publication of numerous anthologies, including C.E.F. Weyse's *Halvtredsindtyve gamle Kæmpevise-Melodier harmonisk bearbeidede* (Seventy old Folk Song Melodies Harmonically Reworked) (1840) and Berggreen's *Folkesange og Melodier, fædrelandske og fremmede* (Folk Songs and Melodies: Native and Foreign) (1842).[75] At this point, political patriotism was still viewed as paramount to the success of national unity. All regions of Denmark, despite their language and/or cultural heritage, were unified by their allegiance to an absolute monarch, and this ideology was reflected in the nation's songbooks.[76] This paradigm changed, however, with the onset of the Schleswig-Holstein War. When Denmark's German-speaking duchies seceded and joined forces with Prussia in 1848, the groundwork was laid for a shift from political patriotism to cultural nationalism. Song texts began to take on a culturally oriented tone as politically motivated individuals and groups dominated the production and dissemination of songbooks. By the end of the 1860s, commercial publishers had practically disappeared from the market, and cultural nationalism was the overriding identity promoted in Danish songbooks.

Given this shift in the production and publication of popular songs, it is interesting to take note of Andersen's role in the history of nineteenth-century Danish song literature. As Hans Kuhn has noted, Andersen's popularity as a writer of songs was strongly affected by the changing tides of fashion and political identity. Although he was well represented in songbooks featuring music from productions at the Royal Theater in the 1830s and continued to be a popular contributor of patriotic texts to commercial songbooks of the 1840s, by the 1850s his presence in Danish songbooks had declined substantially. The newer, politically motivated collections rarely included his poems. A few children's songs and selections from some of his fairy-tale comedies for the Casino Theater continued to be published, but his patriotic poems were virtually banned from the politically motivated, Grundtvig-inspired collections fueled by the rise in cultural nationalism. In fact, the few patriotic poems that Andersen wrote during the second Schleswig-Holstein War in 1864 were never set to music, nor were they included in political songbooks, primarily because they promoted a type of national identity that was no longer in vogue and consequently drew negative reactions from the public. A case in point is the poem 'Fortrøstning' (Song of Trust), which was published in the Danish newspaper *Dagbladet* in 1864:

No mortal knows what tomorrow shall bring;
None knows or sees save God our King;
But when comes Denmark's darkest day,
Then deliverance from God will come our way.

When torn and plundered the country lay,
Niels Ebbesen's courage was her stay;
God led us in his own great way,
And Denmark saw a brighter day.[77]

O'er the white capped waves that dark winds sweep,
Our vessel rocks on the stormy deep;
But God our Lord at the rudder stands
And, wiser than man, gives his commands.

No mortal knows what tomorrow shall bring;
None knows or sees save God our King;
But when comes Denmark's darkest day,
Then deliverance from God will come our way.

Ei Nogen veed, hvad imorgen skeer;
Alene Gud Herren det veed og seer;
Men naar det for Danmark saae mørkest ud
Kom altid Frelse og Hjelp fra Gud!

Da Landet laae splittet og reent faldet hen
Opmandet det blev af Niels Ebbesen,
Gud Herren ledte vor Velfaerds Sag,
Og hele Danmark saae Atterdag.

Det er en Stormnat, høit Søen flaaer,
Vort lille Fartøi paa Dybet gaaer,
Men Gud Vorherre ved Roret staaer,
Han raader, hvad ogsaa end Mennesket sparer.

Ei Nogen veed, hvad imorgen skeer;
Alene Gud Herren det veed og seer;
Men naar det for Danmark saae mørkest ud
Kom altid Frelse og Hjelp fra Gud! [78]

'Song of Trust' drew an angry response from Denmark's public. Shortly after its publication, an anonymous reader wrote to Andersen, chastising him for his poor choice of subject matter and lack of national pride:

If Herr Professor should again feel himself disposed to give the people faith respecting the impending campaign, it might be well to choose another form for inspiring our departing brothers.... The Danish warrior who goes away, glad and proud, to fight for our righteous cause, cannot understand that there is any occasion for gloomy thoughts over the present times. [79]

Andersen recorded this negative response in his autobiography; a sign that he understood, but could not fall in with, his countrymen's nationalistic fervor over another war:

[When I wrote 'Song of Trust'] I still believed in a deliverance from God, but was sometimes filled with anxiety ... I clung to my native land. Yet I did not forget how much affection, good fellowship, and courtesy I had encountered in Germany, how many dear friends, men and women, I there had, but now a sword was drawn between us.... How heavily it all lay on my heart; it seemed to me that I could not bear it. [80]

As a patriot who still held warm affections for his German neighbors, Andersen found himself compelled to write poems that appeared to many to be adverse to the prominent wave of cultural nationalism sweeping across his homeland. A cosmopolitan man of the people, Andersen continued to honor his king but refused to imprison the arts within national borders defined by linguistic and cultural difference. Even after the defeat of Denmark in the second Schleswig-Holstein War, a defeat that caused Andersen to temporarily sever connections with some German friends, he could not bring himself to participate in the isolationist national fervor that came to dominate his homeland. To Andersen, politics was a dangerous drink that quickly poisoned the blood of the artist, and he wanted nothing to do with it. As he explained in the final edition of his autobiography published in 1865, just one year after the disastrous conclusion of the second Schleswig-Holstein War:

Political life in Denmark had ... arrived at a higher development, producing both good and bad fruits.... I felt no call thereto, and no necessity to mix myself up in such matters; for I then believed that the politics of our times were a great misfortune to many a poet. Madame Politics is like Venus: those that she lures to her castle perish.... People forget that initial ideas cannot always be carried out, and that many things contemplated from the top of the tree look different when they are seen from its roots. I will gladly bow before him who is influenced by a noble conviction, and who desires what is conducive to good, be he prince or man of the people. Politics are no affair of mine. God has imparted to me another mission: that I felt, and that I feel still.[81]

Despite Denmark's many years of political strife and isolationism, Andersen remained a cosmopolitan at heart who was intent on reaching beyond the narrow confines of his homeland for inspiration and a receptive readership. Andersen's primary mission was that of an artist, and as we shall see in the final chapter of this book, he took this mission especially seriously during the last decade of his life, when he sought to discover artistic leaders for the next generation and in so doing lay a course for the future of literature and music.

Interlude 5

Bulwark of the Arts

by Hans Christian Andersen

Characters:
A Sculptor   (Volunteer in Danish Army)
A Poet   (Volunteer in Danish Army)
Three Valkyries

Scene is at one of the less important military outposts.
There is a forest path and a view of the sea in the background.
The two volunteers, the poet and the sculptor, are armed like Danish soldiers.

Duet (to the melodies: 'Piben lyder, Trommen skralder' and 'Saa kjæmped de
   Helte af anden April'):

Sculptor:
   The tent of stars sparkles tonight,
   While all around a song begins.
   See over there, a fire burns bright;
   The kitchen, hall, and bedroom light,
   Just like the grounds, yield beauty.

Poet:
   What a show over there! Is thought every hour,
   Each forgets what he suffers daily.
   Fly forward Danish lions from the battle field;
   You are missed nine-fold by all hearts.

Sculptor:
   The drum stirs! You sense
   Life's strong pulse,
   Here are visions the thoughts hide,
   Hours the heart never forgets,
   Born under the weapon's bang.

Poet:

    I saw a grandmother standing with grandchildren,
    And the path was completely paved with flowers,
    With folded hands she prayed with the small ones
    'Our father, save the Danes!'

Sculptor:

    The heart's fresh, inner thoughts
    Rush forward like the strong seas;
    United is the will not to yield.

Both:

    United is the thought of Denmark's kingdom,
    Holy where the enthusiastic die.

Poet:

    I do not forget my host, the lead citizen;
    Unfortunately thousands think like him!
    He thinks that our age was not poetic,
    That everything beautiful is a thing of the past!
    Let the clouds cover the sun, they will go away,
    [The sun] shines eternally young with light and warmth.

Sculptor:

    Our age is full of seriousness and creative [ones],
    The great master (pointing to sky) carves [it] out of stone!

Poet:

    Never before has life stood before me
    As multi-colored and exciting as now.
    Life in the field is quite difficult; but I want,
    Nonetheless, to be a part of it.
    Oh, how beautiful it was, the dawn we sailed
    Across Svendborg Sound in delightful sunshine;
    On the coast the flag waved; the salute shot sounded;
    We were eight ships; – now come waves
    And shudders of the tugging vessels filled
    With new troops. Hurrah! sounded the cry.
    The horn blasts reciprocally gave signals;
    The drummers struck the drums; songs sounded.
    I forgot the present difficulty in all the beauty!
    Oh Beauty, you are the flower on our tree of life.

Sculptor:

    I feel it, as you, but can not find the words.

That is a life for poets and painters!
A sculptor – carves himself through!
That's what I've done, through fences and hedges.

Poet:

Yes, it always goes forward – it carries [one] away.

Sculptor:

How boring were the fires, last battle;
We only had one battery against the enemy's
Five or six; and therefore we retreated.
We had to [go] over ditches, through hedges;
Bullets whistled, and all around
Cannon balls threw up chunks of earth;
But then our machineguns arrived
With artillery, and we charged ahead.
See, it gave strength. Since then I have slept delightfully
On the open field with my weapon in hand.
I did not see the blaze of the lighted farmhouse;
I did not hear the cavalry's gunshot.
I slept blessedly.

Poet:

I cannot sleep,
Especially when there are long, quiet days
When nothing happens. But I am not bored!
I have a whole world inside my mind!

Sculptor:

And I have mine with me in my knapsack.

Poet:

Your knapsack?

Sculptor:

Yes, alive and eternal!
A treasure for Denmark. No enemy's hand
Can tear it from us.

Poet:

What do you mean?

Sculptor:

You have to ask? You, a poet. Well then!
During my stay in Italy

I visited the Herculanum, living and eternal.
Just see!
(He takes a book out of the knapsack.)
An entire generation, all of Holberg's age. –
Just as the people felt, talked, and walked,
They live here once again. Our Herculanum.

Poet:

You have your Holberg with you! I like that.
He also sculpted and chiseled statues!
However, time has transformed a few
Of the figures.

Sculptor:

No, just the drapery,
And not very much! See, only that on the people.

Poet:

Where is 'von Tyboe' then?

Sculptor:

Just wait until peacetime,
Then he will come forward again! He will still be found.
And the children of our age believe this is true.
From old Holberg, you learn to know your neighbor.
(Speaks in character, as Erasmus Montanus.)
'Think of what you do, Erasme Montane, Musarum & Apollinis pulle! Here
you have the opportunity to let it be seen that you are a true philosophus; –
Think what your Commilitones will say, when they hear such a thing; it is no
longer the Erasmus Montanus, who until now has defended his opinion to the
last drop of blood. If the uneducated general public reproaches me for my
infidelity against my sweetheart, then philosophy will, on the other hand, lift
me up to the clouds. – I must therefore stand against this temptation. I stand
against it. I overpower it. I have overpowered it completely. The earth is
round. Jacta est alea! Dixi! –'

Poet:

Splendid! Ah yes, there are enough exemplars
Of new Montanes. I know mine!
(Speaks in character, as Herman von Bremen)
'When I could not sleep tonight, I thought how the government here in
Hamburg could best be organized, so certain families, out of which people
born to mayors and councilors, could be shut out from the highest authorities'
dignity, and a complete peace could be introduced. I thought, one should
interchangeably take lords now from one vocation, now from another, then the

entire population would take part in the government, and all professions would come to flourish; for example, when the goldsmith becomes mayor, he looks after the goldsmiths' interests, a tailor after tailors' progress, a candle maker after the candle makers'; and no one could be mayor longer than a month, to ensure that one family could not flourish more than any another. If the government were organized in this way, then we would be called a truly free people.'

(In his natural voice)

That is for all people and all times!

Sculptor (as Peer in *Jakob von Tyboe.*):

Why is one who was born crooked-legged called Your Honor? Why is one called well-educated today, when he could hardly spell yesterday? Why does one write French extracts in a letter that goes between Slagelse and Ringsted? Why can one not instead think of a word for Franco? And a thousand other things, which to me are impossible to enumerate!' –

(In his natural voice.)

Oh unequaled Holberg! Oh my, how you knew your time, our time, and all times!

Poet:

(Breaks off a beech-tree branch)

Come, let me weave this fresh branch,

Into a wreath around his work. –

Sculptor:

Of all artists

The poet is the luckiest, for he

Can penetrate the people; and each [man],

Yes even the poorest, can possess him

Entirely, just as I do here.

Poet:

But is not the luckiest of all the poet

Who can speak from the stage's podium?

It is not just upon a single person, but upon the masses

That his full sunlight shines.

Sculptor:

And that is what Holberg has done.

Poet:

This year it is exactly a century since

The Danish stage was opened and Holberg,

Your Holberg, became its pride; characters

Not unworthy of him, born of blood and truth
Have followed!

Sculptor:
Oh, I see a pretty line.
The German Herr Spazier in *The Virtuoso*,
The venal goal of *The Gold Box* with Miss Trækom,[*]
She comes home from a walk in the moss.
And Trop and Klister with his good eye,
I remember them so well! I remember them all!
Nyboders people, Kaninstokslægten,[†]
As well as the entire circle from the bank,
And from 'The Debate!' – yet I say this:
My Holberg, he goes in front, he is the first;
In him I celebrate a combination of them all!

Poet:
And yet only half of it! – He [is] the bright day;
The melancholy thoughts live in the night,
And both reign.

Sculptor:
Holberg is my part.
(Melody: 'Det er et Land, dets Sted er højt I Norden').
By the ice fjord is the mountain, you know it,
That's where I'm going, see Jeppe comes from there.
In the smallest house, where tallow lamps burn,
Holberg's wit is now the peasant's property.
I hold in my hand the comedy book,
And young and old gladly gather around.
It is a celebration for them; they feel the spirit
And cheer loudly: 'He is immortal!'
Echo (answers) – 'is immortal!'

Poet:
I go to the renters' forest, to the Harz Valley,
Where memorial stones stand in the moonlight.
I see the ancient heroes ride out across the valley;
A bright shiver passes through the grove.
The bard, who burst out of death's grave,
Saw the north's strength and love showed itself.
I praise him in the bright morning light.

---

[*] From *Gulddaasen* by Oluf Christian Olufsen
[†] From *Capriciosa eller Familien i Nyboder* by Thomas Overskou.

Here the echo calls: 'He is immortal!'
Echo (answers) – 'is immortal!'

Sculptor:

    The fresh drink of life is what Holberg offers,
    As the world is and will stay, we see it;
    In the vapor of everyday life a ray breaks through,
    And we laugh heartily at the world's wickedness.

Poet:

    But the spirit's greatness, the world's best strengths –
    These the serious bard reveals to you.
    And you understand what the soul is longing after. –
    Rule the day! – Rise, Night! – Each is immortal!
Echo (answers) – 'is immortal!'

Poet:

    The festival's candles have not yet been fully lit;
    Now, the moment's need is for us to bow down;
    They [the candles] burn, however, in all Danish hearts,
    And Denmark's golden splendor is fully understood!

Sculptor:

    Well said my honorable man! – Give me your hand.
    (One hears a call to arms which is repeated)
    My regiment's call! Now I must leave.
    But I have my riches with me! I have doubled them.
    My poet is now here! (He points to knapsack)
    And here! (He points to forehead)

Poet:

    I have mine here. (He points to heart).

Sculptor:

    So then both of us are well armed;
    We are with the Danes – for all times,
    Even in times of war. Farewell. The call to arms sounds.
    (He rushes out).

Poet (listening to the sounds around him):

    It sounds beautiful here under the forest's crown,
    And [these sounds] lead one's thoughts to life at camp.
    Oh, if only I could lift up with music's full tones

Every bended heart to victory,
The true victory, beauty's true victory.
Homeland of mine, do you know the power you hold?

In science and art are found
Our strengths and the power of our greatness.
In the sagas about the great achievements in ancient times,
In Tycho Brahe's Astrology,
In the fresh branch of knowledge,
As well as in the hard marble stone,
The song about the Danes' strength and the Danes' great name
Rings out loudly from valley to valley.
Feel your inheritance, Fatherland.
Embrace it inwardly and completely!

A building, lit up like a church,
Is built of the Danish language;
It is our spirit's bulwark
With the heavenly, blessed Dannebrog!
Each is blessed by the call of the soul,
From Holberg to the youngest bard,
And so it rises as a mighty work,
The nation's mark and its rock.
God is with us; he can not let us fall;
My beloved Denmark, you are strong!
(He kneels down)
Protect us God from what we still might face.
Place your truth in what the bard sings:
That – 'no place else are the roses so red,
And no place else are the thorns so small!'
(Sits down on a stone close to the hill; soft music begins)
I rest my head against the rough slope,
But my eyes look to the stars that God has lighted.

(The music swells higher and higher, a red glow falls over the stage; three Valkyries float forward to the melody of *Balders Død*.)

All Three:
Over forest and over valley
The Valkyries travel
On storm-strengthened wings!
Every oak is a rush.
The call to battle rings on high.
Fight! Battle breeds life!
This is the message she brings.

The First:
> In the song of the bards,

The Second:
> Now,

The Third:
> In the future,

All Three:
> Your glory shall ring!
> The best you bring to
> Your fatherland.
> Over forest, over valley
> The Valkyries travel
> On storm-strengthened wings!
> (The first two disappear, the third walks up to the Poet and speaks);

[The Third]:
> To the Valkyrie, your great virtue is art.
> You stand armed, and armed she stands.
> Understand your duty and look me in the eye,
> Your poet-dream is reality itself.

> Take this spruce branch, brought from Norway,
> And braid it into your crown for Denmark's Holberg;
> A reminder of that land, where he was a child,
> His works seem to show the spruce tree's branch;
> Its needles are the tips of pillars, but always green.

> Behind Axel's force, where the church's organ rings
> Out over rising old building stones
> I stood beside a grave, the grave of the one
> Who sang about the Danes' road to power and might
> And who showed us with the beacon's flash our ancient times.
> Not in his life, not by his grave stand flowers,
> Johannes Ewald! – And the voice I heard,
> His voice, like one from the breast of youth, sounded
> In the beating of the drums and playing of the fife.
> 'A great master has completed my work,
> The gods of the north come to life, the north's heroes!'
> And I saw Hakon Jarl and Palnatoke
> And between the rune stones stood Signe,
> Fresh as a rose, love's rose;

And under the church's organ tones comes Valborg;
She gave the Bard his name, – the living one.
'I greet you my love!' she says.
In the word was a sound so strong and so great,
And the weapon in my hand shot flowers and branches,
And the future's visions rose, as you believe them:
Your fatherland is strong, and the strongest one
Is exactly he whom the most wonderful father gave.
With your bard's strong harp tones
Stands language's power for its tribes and nations!
With knowledge, through the Great Spirit's journey,
Vølund has forged us the best sword,
And Denmark's magnificence will never wane.
And the people will understand what God has given them.
That will hold them together during these difficult times,
And will shower down around them into a rebellious sea.

(Music to 'Den Gang jeg drog afsted' plays softly. Cannon shot ignites; reality has just broken into his dream)

Hear the moment! It dies, then comes the next one.
You have loved the holiest and the best.
It lives! Lives! – On to the battle dance.
Firmly keep in mind the crown of Denmark's army.

(A shot is fired, the sleeping ones jump up, the Valkyrie has disappeared, daylight shines. The melody: 'Danmark deiligst Vang og Vænge' sounds more and more loudly.)

Poet:
The Valkyrie called me!
My soul she sweetly soothed;
Light the festival's candles
In all Danish hearts,
As my dream has lighted them in mine.
The honorable and beautiful will stand strong
In Denmark's kingdom,
And the arts will carry the branches, fresh, green,
Immortal!
(The entire orchestra joins in with the conclusion of the melody and the curtain drops quickly.)

Chapter 6

The Tone-Poet

*In the very near future we might well come to see not only new authors but even
men with established reputations profiting in some degree from the ideas
expounded by Wagner and passing successfully through the breach opened by him.*
Charles Baudelaire

*I will gladly bow before him who is influenced by a noble conviction and who
desires what is conducive to good, be he prince or man of the people.*

It is quite unfortunate that I didn't learn counterpoint and become a composer.
Hans Christian Andersen

The above quotations reveal much about Andersen's artistic outlook during the
final years of his life. Disillusioned by the political upheavals of the last two
decades, he was searching for a new philosophy, a figurehead who could introduce
a fresh set of values and, in so doing, lead him toward a bright and innovative
future.

After experiencing the horrors of the two Schleswig-Holstein wars, Andersen
dreamed about various reconciliations: between Germany and Denmark, between
the idealism of his youth and the discoveries that were being made in the natural
sciences and, perhaps most importantly, between poetry and music. As Denmark
struggled to establish a new national identity founded on its cultural past, Andersen
sought a course for the future that was more cosmopolitan in scope. He viewed the
arts, specifically literature and music, as important keys to the future; they
provided a human link between science and faith and consequently served as the
only means through which humanity could reconcile its yearning for both earthly
progress and the metaphysical sublime. Andersen's cosmopolitan view of society
led him to envision the future as moving toward a global civilization, where human
rights and democracy compensated for national selfishness and the irrationality of
power. He dreamed of a new world order founded on the leadership of the best
men and women, a nobility of talent centered on the arts. These thoughts were
planted in his mind in the 1850s during his interactions with Liszt in Weimar. But
Liszt was not the only source for such ideas. Andersen's attempts to prophesy the
future role of the arts as a vehicle for a new world order were the result of his
interaction with numerous scientists, philosophers, performers, composers, and
writers during the second half of the nineteenth century. Indeed, Andersen's
travels across Europe after the revolutions of 1848 and his growing interest in the

natural sciences in the decades that followed eventually led him to embrace a view of the future that involved a fusion of literature, music, and philosophy.

Scientists such as H.C. Ørsted and cultural events like the 1867 World Exhibition in Paris contributed to Andersen's new view of the arts, as did discussions of race, religion, and theories of evolution. But as this chapter will show, it was the music and reputation of Richard Wagner that had the most profound impact on Andersen.[1] In his final years, Andersen embraced Wagner as the herald of a new age, a model for both poets and musicians. Andersen's interpretation of Wagner's music and artistic philosophy, however, evolved over a period of roughly a decade and was quite different from what we might expect. Thus, to fully understand how and why Andersen became such a devotee of Wagner's works, we must return briefly to the intervening years of the Schleswig-Holstein Wars and Andersen's activities as a writer of tales and essays.

Andersen's wish to bring about a fusion of the arts was first prominently displayed in two essays from the early 1850s, 'Poesiens Californien' (Poetry's California) and 'Om Aartusinder' (In the Next Millennium). In both works, the future of the arts plays a prominent role, albeit in markedly different ways. Whereas 'Poetry's California' sets forth a path for writers hoping to connect with audiences through the wonders of science, 'In the Next Millennium' contemplates which artists from the past and present will continue to be revered in the centuries to come.

'Poetry's California' is a short essay that Andersen appended to his travelogue *I Sverrig* (In Sweden), published in 1851. As Elias Bredsdorff has noted, *In Sweden* was no ordinary travelogue. Andersen did not arrange the chapters according to an actual itinerary, but wrote them as 'a mixture of fact and fiction, of legends, fantasy, history and personal experience.'[2] Andersen completed most of *In Sweden* during the first Schleswig-Holstein war, when his only outlet for escape was touring parts of Scandinavia that had remained unknown to him until then. With his image of a united Europe crumbling before his eyes, Andersen desperately searched for a way to pull the disparate pieces together again. When writing the chapters of *In Sweden*, Andersen resisted telling readers about the prominent figures he encountered, about his visits with royalty and the praise he received from Sweden's public.[3] Instead, he conceived of the book as a series of literary experiments, a manifesto on the art of creating itself.[4] The reason behind this change in approach was made clear in the book's final essay, 'Poetry's California.' Here Andersen presented a new path for the arts – a model of the future inspired by the wonders of natural science and the innovations of scientists and philosophers such as H.C. Ørsted.[5]

Written during the height of the gold rush in the American west, 'Poetry's California' describes California as the land of discovery, where hard work yields 'the treasures of Aladdin.' In a similar manner, science is promoted as the poet's California, where advancements in knowledge offer an uncharted mine of new inspiration. 'Our time is the time of discoveries,' writes Andersen. Instead of following the old romantic muse, who represents superstition and a glorification of the past, poets should look to the leaders of the next generation, who promote science and knowledge, calling out: 'Follow me towards life and truth.' The wonders of science reveal 'a living world full of creatures' in 'a drop of marsh water.'[6] To writers like Andersen who were obsessed with seeing the world, inventions such as the steam engine and telegraph machine introduced an age of travel and communication never before imagined:

> Thin iron ties were laid over the Earth and along these the heavily laden carriages flew on wings of steam like the flight of a swallow; mountains were compelled to open themselves to the inquiring spirit of the age; plains were obliged to raise themselves; and human thoughts were carried as in words, through metal wires, to distant cities with the speed of lightning. 'Life! Life!' sounds through the whole of nature. 'It is our time! Poet, you possess it! Sing of it in spirit and truth!'[7]

The primary influence behind Andersen's new enthusiasm for science was a recently published work by Ørsted entitled *Aanden i Naturen* (The Spirit in Nature).[8] In the first volume of this work, Ørsted discussed his discovery of electromagnetism and presented his various experiments in chemistry and physics as an argument against the then popular concept of materialism. He continued this discussion in the second volume, presenting his scientific experiments as evidence supporting a philosophy of art and science. In an attempt to bridge the gap between the natural sciences and fine arts, Ørsted argued that man's perception of beauty was actually nothing more than an understanding of the laws of nature. Thus the discoveries made by man in the natural sciences were best understood as the 'spirit in nature' – a mystical force that would likely never be fully comprehended. These concepts led Ørsted to propose a new approach to the study of both art and science: because the world drawn by the poet, with all its freshness and daring, obeys the same laws that our spiritual eye discovers in the real world, the artist and the natural philosopher follow complementary paths, thus freeing both art and science from the misconceptions of the romantic age.

Ørsted published both volumes of *The Spirit in Nature* in 1850 and, knowing that Andersen would likely be interested in the work, sent him a copy on 5 July.[9] Andersen read the treatise almost immediately, and in a letter to Ørsted dated 3 August he declared his profound admiration:

> Thank you for your friendly disposition toward me, especially the spiritual light that you have made enter into my thoughts. I should have written you right away and thanked you for your letter and the book; but I began reading it immediately, and I felt so fulfilled by it, that I wanted to wait and write to you only after having read the entire book. You thought that [the second part] wouldn't have an influence on me like the first part; [but] I cannot separate the [two] parts from each other; it is like a rushing current; and what especially made me glad was that here I seem only to have seen my own thoughts, which previously I had not made clear to myself in such a way. It is my belief, my own conviction that lies before me in clear words.... I am pleased by your book, pleased also with myself for finding it is so easy to read. It almost seems to me to be the result of my own thoughts. Upon reading it, I am able to say: 'Yes, I too would have liked to have said that!' The truth in it has moved me and become a part of me.... Next time

we meet I will show you a little piece I wrote called 'Poetry's California.' You will observe in it the vitalizing effect your books have had upon me.[10]

Further evidence of Ørsted's influence is found in a letter Andersen wrote to Carl Alexander on 21 December of the same year:

I have entered into a new world, which one of my oldest friends, our famous H.C. Ørsted, has opened up for me. At the beginning of this year his work *The Spirit in Nature* appeared. I've mentioned this work previously. It is a piece closely related to Humboldt's *Cosmos* and yet far from it. I am forty-five years old, but I often feel in many ways as if I were twenty. I believe that, as a poet, I still have several stages to go through, and that I have reached one of those by means of Ørsted's work. This book has awakened in me a longing for science, and I have most recently read a good deal in this direction.... Ørsted has always been good to me. He has been my faithful friend for many years; but now he is even more to me – he has understood my sincere aspiration. Under this evolutionary process my last work, *In Sweden*, has been changed and changed again. When you see this work at the beginning of next year, a few sections will show you how life and the world are now reflected in me. But do not worry; I will not leave the fresh life of poetry to wander into the regions of philosophy or to write didactic poems; that is impossible. For me, the human heart is the magic lamp [Wunderlampe] of poetry to which I remain committed. And with this lamp I stand like Aladdin in the glimmering cave of Science, thus the power of nature should not look on me as its servant. No, I will call forth the spirits, who after my command must build me a new palace of poetry.[11]

Andersen was clearly on a new course, and 'Poetry's California' served as his informal manifesto. In letters to friends and colleagues written shortly after the publication of *In Sweden*, Andersen explained how the future of art required a fusion with science. 'Poetry's California' laid out the rules for a new approach to writing and showed 'how life and the world' were now 'reflected' in Andersen's work.

Andersen's fascination with what the future might bring continued throughout the decade. In 1852 he wrote 'In the Next Millennium,' an essay that, in addition to predicting which figures would still be revered in the twenty-first century, gives an uncannily accurate description of America's youthful 'Let's Go' crowd, traveling across the Atlantic in an 'air steamboat' to see the whole of Europe in a few days:

Yes! In the next millennium people will fly on the wings of steam through the air, over the ocean! The young inhabitants of America will become visitors of old Europe. They will come over to see the monuments and the great cities, which will then be in ruins, just as we in our time make pilgrimages to the tottering splendors of southern Asia. In the next millennium they will come.[12]

As Andersen describes the itinerary of these future travelers, we learn much as he predicts how the treasures of each nation will one day be envisioned. In England, 'they first step on the European shore, in the land of Shakespeare, as the educated call it – in the land of politics, the land of machines, as it is called by others.' The journey then continues 'through the tunnel under the English Channel' to France – the land of Charlemagne, Napoleon, and Molière. Here there is rejoicing for 'the names of heroes, poets, and men of science' – figures the nineteenth century does not yet know, but who will one day be born 'in Paris, the center of Europe.' In Spain the Americans learn of Columbus, Cortez, and Calderon. Italy and Greece are nothing but ruins, where 'a single crumbling wall' is all that remains of St. Peter's, and Byzantium is only a memory. Germany is described as the highlight of the journey, especially 'the region where Luther spoke, where Goethe sang, and Mozart once held the scepter of harmony. Great names shine there, in science and in art, names that are still unknown to us.' Finally, Scandinavia is described as the forefront of natural science, 'the homeland of Ørsted and Linnæus.'[13]

'In the Next Millennium' praises the innovations of great artists and scientists from the past, present, and future. It also prophesizes the downfall of Catholicism and the Greek Orthodox Church as Andersen knew them. Although science is promoted as the key to understanding, Andersen does not rule out spiritual belief altogether. Luther holds a firm position in the future of Europe, along with Goethe and Mozart, figures strongly aligned with the German idealism Andersen promoted in his youth. Still, something is missing in the tale. There is no sense of where the future will lead or which path is best for the development of the arts. Several years would pass before Andersen attempted to tackle such questions, but an event that influenced his eventual move in this direction was his one and only encounter with the composer/philosopher Richard Wagner.

Andersen first met Wagner in Switzerland on 24 August 1854. His diary entry from this date simply states: 'Visited the composer Wagner who warmly received me. I was there a good half hour and promised I would today send him Hartmann's *Funeral March for Thorvaldsen.*'[14] An account of the visit preserved in Andersen's autobiography gives greater insight into the event. Apparently Wagner felt no resentment toward Andersen or Denmark on account of the Schleswig-Holstein War. Instead, he seemed quite interested in learning more about Danish opera, and Andersen lost no time in giving him a quick history lesson on his homeland's most notable composers:

In Zürich the composer Wagner lived in exile. I knew his music, which I have mentioned previously. Liszt had warmly and vivaciously told me about the man himself. I went to his residence and found a friendly reception. Of the works of Danish composers, he was only familiar with Gade's, and he spoke of this man's importance as a musician. Then he expressed his opinion of Kuhlau's compositions for the flute, but he was not familiar with his operas. Hartmann he knew only by name. So I began to tell him about the grand repertoire of Danish operas and ballad operas, from those by Schultz, Kunzen, and Hartmann Senior to those by Weyse, Kuhlau, Hartmann Junior, and Gade. Wagner listened with great attention. 'It is as if you have related an entire fairy tale from the world of music, raised a whole curtain for me beyond the Elbe.' I told him about Sweden's [Carl Michael] Bellman, akin to Wagner in that he also wrote the lyrics to his music, but

otherwise the complete opposite of Wagner. The famous musician left me with
the fullest impression of the great, ingenious personality he is.   It was an
unforgettable, joyous hour, the likes of which I have never since experienced.[15]

Upon reading the above description, one cannot help but wonder if Wagner
actually participated in this conversation, or if he simply listened as Andersen
chattered away.   Andersen's reference to Bellman's practice of writing both the
libretto and music to his operas suggests that Wagner might have mentioned his
ideas concerning a new synthesis of the arts and his predictions about the future,
but this is only speculation.   Although Wagner had recently completed several
treatises on these topics – *Art and Revolution* (1849), *The Art-Work of the Future*
(1850), and *Opera and Drama* (1851), Andersen's diaries and correspondence give
no indication of how familiar he was with these works, or if he even knew of their
existence.   Indeed, the only hint we have that Andersen might have known about
Wagner's growing interest in Norse mythology and his efforts to reform opera
comes from a letter written by Carl Alexander on 14 February 1854, wherein he
mentions Wagner's work on *Die Niebelungen*, 'whose noteworthy and highly
poetic libretto has already created the greatest astonishment among the small circle
to which it was distributed.'[16]

Andersen had no further personal contact with Wagner after this first meeting.
If he ever wrote to Wagner, the letters no longer exist, and it appears Wagner never
received the promised copy of Hartmann's *Funeral March for Thorvaldsen*.
Perhaps Andersen's growing discontent toward Liszt and his followers in the mid-
1850s dampened his initial enthusiasm for Wagner, or perhaps he simply neglected
to follow through on his promise.   Whatever the case, Andersen appears to have
only been distracted by Wagner for a moment; the theories promoted by Ørsted
continued to influence his ideas about the nature of art and the role of the artist in
society.   In Andersen's mind, the arts clearly served as the spiritual foundation of
the future, the 'religion' of a new age.   Artists were the prophets of this new faith
in science, and through their efforts, art would eventually serve as God's
nourishment for the human soul.   In 1858, Andersen publicly proclaimed these
ideas in a speech he delivered to the newly formed Workers' Association in
Copenhagen.   After reading a few of his most recent tales, Andersen presented a
commentary on the state of poetry and its relation to religion and science:

In England's Royal Navy, through all the rigging of small and large ropes, there
runs a red thread, signifying that it belongs to the Crown. Through all men's lives
there also runs a thread, indeed an invisible thread that shows we belong to God.
  To find this thread in the small and large, in our own life and in everything
around us, the poet's art helps us.... In the earliest times the poet's art dealt mostly
with what are called Wonder Stories. The Bible itself has enclosed truth and
wisdom in what we call parables and allegories. Now, all of us know that an
allegory is not to be understood literally according to the words, but according to
the signification that lies within them, by the invisible thread that runs through
them.

We know when we hear an echo from a wall, from a rock, or the heights, it is not the wall, the rock, and the heights that speak, but a resounding from ourselves; and so we should also see ourselves in the parable and the allegory – [we should] find the meaning, the wisdom, and the happiness we can get out of them.

In this way the poet's art places itself at the side of Science and opens our eyes to the beautiful, the true, and the good.[17]

It is interesting to note that the same year Andersen delivered this speech he also set forth on a new direction in his tales. Andersen had never been more confident as a writer, and between the winter of 1858 and the spring of 1859 he wrote a volume of tales wherein he experimented radically with both form and the presentation of characters. Some of these tales showed a continued interest in predicting the future, while others experimented with the creation of dark psychological moods and atmospheres through the integration of words and sound. On 21 March 1859, Andersen wrote to Carl Alexander about two of his most inventive new tales, 'Vinden fortæller om Valdemar Daae og hans Døttre' (The Wind Tells of Valdemar Daae and His Daughters) and 'Anne Lisbeth':

They form some of my best work. One of the stories, 'The Wind Tells of Valdemar Daae and His Daughters,' is perhaps, in terms of construction, of special significance. I have tried, and I hope I have succeeded, in giving the entire narrative tone as if one hears the wind itself speaking. Another story, 'Anne Lisbeth,' I consider the best from a psychological point of view. I have endeavored to show how a small germ of good and evil is in the heart, and how it springs to life accordingly when touched by either 'a sun beam or by a wicked hand.'[18]

In 'The Wind Tells of Valdemar Daae and His Daughters,' Andersen plays with the idea of the unending march of time by letting the wind serve as narrator. Through the wind, we learn of the downfall of the aristocratic Daae, an alchemist so obsessed with discovering gold that he ignores his daughters and lets his castle crumble around him. Andersen gives the wind an almost musical quality,[19] as is heard in this account of life's ephemeral nature:

And the winter passed away; winter and summer, both passed away, and they are still passing away, even as I pass away. As the snow whirls along, and the apple blossom whirls along, and the leaves fall – away! away! away! – and men are passing away too![20]

At the end of the tale, the wind reminds us that time and progress stop for no one. Each life is but a single step in the evolution of mankind:

New times, changed times! The old high road now runs through cultivated fields; the new road winds among trim ditches, and soon the railroad will come with its train of carriages and rush over the graves which like the names of the dead are forgotten – shh-hush! passed away! passed away![21]

'Anne Lisbeth' uses dreams to suggest the haunting nature of guilt and shows how pride and respectability can be brought down by obsessions of the mind that are beyond the realm of rational control. The story tells of a young girl who rejects an ugly son in order to serve as nursemaid to a handsome, aristocratic child. When she reaches old age, however, the aristocratic child rejects her and her own son dies. Alone and haunted by guilt, Anne Lisbeth spends many nights wandering along the seashore and digging a grave for her dead child. As Wullschlager so aptly describes, Anne Lisbeth is 'suspended between hallucination and reality.' With this tale Andersen 'delves into the workings of the unconscious mind in ways which anticipated Freud and writers of the early twentieth century.' Indeed, 'Anne Lisbeth herself is less a character than a consciousness floating across the story.'[22]

Leaving behind the folk models of his youth and the grand classical archetypes of his middle years (as seen in 'The Ugly Duckling' and 'The Nightingale'), Andersen reinvented the fairy tale in 1858, turning it into a modern, self-referential, experimental genre. His reinvention of the tale might be seen as a parallel to some of the refashioning that was going on at the same time in European instrumental music – particularly program music. Although we saw in chapter 4 that Andersen did not embrace Liszt's *Zukunftsmusik* when he first encountered it in 1857, we cannot help but think that the experience nonetheless affected him, especially given his many accounts of it in his letters, diaries, and literary works from the time. Just as extra-musical elements played a major role in defining the structural plan of Liszt's tone poems, Andersen's 'extra-narrative' use of the wind – or his interest in Anne Lisbeth's psychological state – had much to do with the creation of structure in his newest tales. In stories such as these, Andersen anticipated many of the elements that would later be attached to early modernism, namely the expression of meaning through style, form, and poetic image; fluidity of character and an awareness of the irrational workings of the unconscious mind; and a diminished importance of plot.

As Andersen grew older and a second war with Germany loomed upon the horizon, he became pessimistic about the future and civilized values. Although he was attempting to map out a path for the future, doing so only increased his anxieties about the value of art and its destined role in society. Andersen's later tales, with their sense of fragmentation and psychological confusion, served as a personal response to the uncertainties surrounding art and culture during the second half of the nineteenth century. The age of idealism was over, and as the specter of the next age appeared, new 'scientific' approaches to the field of aesthetics, such as French positivism and various theories of evolution, began to influence Andersen's point of view.[23]

Andersen's reactions to these new schools of thought are clearly reflected in a tale called 'Det ny Aarhundredes Musa' (The Muse of the New Century), published in 1861. The tale begins with a simple set of questions: 'When and how will the muse of the new century ... reveal herself? What does she look like? What is the theme of her song? Whose heartstrings will she touch? To what heights will she lift her century?'[24] As Andersen sets out to answer these questions, he realizes that 'in a busy day like ours, when poetry is almost superfluous' such questions might seem pointless. Nonetheless, he presses on, realizing that 'many "immortal" productions of today's poets will, in the future, perhaps only exist as charcoal tracings on a prison wall, seen and read by a few curiosity seekers.' Andersen describes the various types of poetry that are popular in his age: patriotic songs that 'serve in the ranks,' noble works and cheap entertainment. 'There is a demand for whatever is supplied,' he claims. But determining the 'poetry of the future,' along with 'the poetry of music,' is something else entirely. It is 'like reckoning with the Don Quixotiana.' To speak of it is science fiction, 'like talking about a discovery voyage to Uranus.'[25]

But Andersen is not deterred. He ridicules the positivists in France whom he believes incorrectly employ science to explain aesthetics, describing 'resonant outpourings of feeling and thought' as nothing more than 'the offspring of nervous vibrations.' 'Enthusiasm, joy, and pain ... are simply vibrations of the nerves, and each of us is a string instrument.'[26]

But if this is true, then 'who touches the strings?' asks Andersen. 'Who causes them to vibrate into sound?' Ørsted's 'unseen heavenly spirit' is the answer, a spirit who echoes in each of us his emotions and feelings. It is through this spirit that many string instruments – i.e. humanity – join together in 'melting harmonies or clashing dissonances.' 'So it was, and so it shall be, in mankind's forward march toward the consciousness of freedom.'[27]

Andersen claims that although we might not recognize her, the muse of the new century is already with us, 'amid the roar of today's machinery.' She is a child of the common man and the aristocracy, who 'has in her the blood and soul of both.' She is surrounded by the scientific wonders of the present: 'the occult riddles of nature,' 'the diver's bell,' 'the map of the heavens,' and the wonders of 'photography.' Yet her nursemaid sings to her of 'Eivind Skalde-spiller and Firdasi, of the minnesingers, and what Heine sang from his soul as a boy.' She knows the *Edda*, frightful fairy tales, and the *Thousand and One Nights*. The muse of the new century is only a child, but as Schopenhauer might say, she 'is governed by will,' and her progress is certain, if not fully known.[28]

Andersen describes the new muse's education through a depiction of the artwork in her nursery:

> Greek tragedy and Roman comedy are carved there in marble. The folk songs of the nations cover the walls like withered vines;... The mighty tones and thoughts of Beethoven, Mozart, Gluck, and the other great masters surround her with eternal chords. On her bookshelves many are laid to rest who in their day were immortal ... and there is still room for many others, whose names we hear clicking from the telegraph of immortality.[29]

'The muse is cosmopolitan,' claims Andersen, 'for she has combined Holberg with Molière, Plautus and Aristophanes.' She is also apolitical. When the 'skillful politician' asks: 'What does she stand for?' Andersen replies: 'Better to ask what she does not stand for!'

She will not appear as a ghost of bygone times! She will not fashion her dramas from discarded architecture with its dazzling colors of lyric drapery! ... She will not shatter normal human speech into fragments, so that it can be cobbled together for an artificial music box with tones from troubadour tournaments. Nor will she separate aristocratic verse and plain plebeian prose – twins are they in voice and power! Nor will she carve from the saga blocks of Iceland the ancient gods, for they are dead; no sympathy or fellowship awaits them in our day! Nor will she command her generation to occupy their thoughts with the fabric of a French novel; nor will she dull them with the chloroform of everyday history! She will bring the elixir of life; her song, whether in prose or verse, will be brief, clear, and rich. The nations' heartbeats are but letters in the endless alphabet of mankind's growth; she grasps each letter with equal lovingness and arranges all of them into words that she weaves together with rhythms into the hymn of her age.[30]

But as magnificent as the coming of the muse of the new century will be, all progress comes at a price. In the final lines of the tale, Andersen welcomes the new muse, making it clear to the reader that as she blossoms into maturity, the artists of the present suffer a painful death:

Greetings, you muse of poetry's coming age! Let our salutation be heard in a manner similar to the worm's hymn of thanksgiving – the worm that is cut to pieces beneath the plow, while a new spring is dawning and the plowman draws his furrow among us worms, crushing us, so that your blessing may be bestowed upon the coming generation. Greetings, you muse of the new century![31]

'The Muse of the New Century,' for all its questions and predictions, does little in terms of offering a path toward the future. Largely philosophical in nature, the tale rejects many of the trends that had become fashionable during Andersen's day – lyric opera, the use of dialect, the retelling of myths and sagas, French novels, and popular histories. The act of contemplation is placed in the foreground of the tale, leaving little room for guidance concerning the actual creation of art and its role in society. These were issues that Andersen would later tackle in a tale called 'Sneglen og Rosenhækken' (The Snail and the Rosebush.) Realizing that pessimistic musings were of as little use to the future as mindless productivity, he pitted the two extremes against one another in search of a happy compromise.

'The Snail and the Rosebush' follows the lives of a beautiful rosebush who spends her days producing flowers and a snail who sits beneath her branches thinking. As they grow old, the snail says:

You are an old rosebush. You should hurry up and die. You've given all you can to the world, whether it was of much importance is a question that I have not had time to ponder. But this much is clear, you have not done the least for your inner development, or you would have produced something else. Do you have anything to say in your defense?[32]

When the rosebush replies that she has never really thought about it, the snail continues: 'No, you have never taken the trouble to think at all. Have you ever asked yourself why you bloomed? Or how your blooming comes about – why in that one way alone and no other?' The rosebush replies: 'I bloom in gladness because I cannot do otherwise.' To this the snail says that the rosebush has had an easy life – everything has been given to her. 'But still more was given to you,' she replies. 'Yours is one of those deep-thinking natures, one of those highly gifted minds that astonish the world.' The snail responds that he has no intention of astonishing the world. 'The world is nothing to me. What have I to do with the world? I have enough to do with myself, and in myself.' And so they continue, arguing until the end of their days.[33]

'The Snail and the Rosebush' has often been interpreted as representing Andersen's view of the intellectual life versus the creative one, with the snail serving as an embodiment of Kierkegaard and the rosebush representing Andersen himself. An equally compelling interpretation, however, has been offered by Wullschlager. She sees the story as 'a shrewd comment on the narrow-minded impetuosity of youth versus the tolerance and generosity towards the wider world that comes with middle age.'[34] This interpretation has much to do with what Andersen described as his inspiration for the story. While traveling with Jonas Collin (the son of Andersen's friend and patron, Edvard Collin) through Italy in 1861, Andersen got into an argument with his young companion over the individual's obligation to society. Andersen was attempting to show the value in hard work and productivity, while Jonas claimed that his aristocratic cousin, Viggo Drewsen, ranked far above any well-known poet, even though '[he] was concerned with his own development and did not concern himself with other people.' Ten days later, Andersen presented Jonas with the tale inspired by their argument. It was not well received: 'Jonas found [in it] great malice against Viggo Drewsen, who – even if he were never to show any results to the world, [and] even if he were to lie naked in the street like Lazarus – would nonetheless rank as an *excellent* human being.'[35]

In 'The Snail and the Rosebush' we learn that while the philosopher deliberately ponders the world for himself, the artist instinctively creates artwork for others. Thus the tale can be interpreted as a reflection of the negative qualities found in both approaches toward life. If only the snail (philosopher) would try to please someone other than himself, and if only the rosebush (artist) would think a bit more about what she creates and why, the arts might evolve. What the world needs is a figure who embodies the best of both the snail and the rosebush – a philosophical artist. But as Andersen pessimistically implies at the end of the tale, such an artist will likely never come. The snail and the rosebush eventually die, but those that follow simply continue along a similar course. Thus Andersen explains that there is no need to reread the story: 'It will only be the same again.'[36]

Andersen's call for a more philosophical artist in the early 1860s was followed by what can only be seen as a logical rejection of virtuosic instrumental music several years later. Although opportunities to see virtuosic soloists in Copenhagen diminished during the second Schleswig-Holstein war, Andersen's diaries reveal that even when such occasions arose, he often avoided the performances or, when attendance was compulsory, was little impressed by them. A case in point is his reaction to a series of concerts given by Ole Bull in Copenhagen in 1866.

Andersen came across his old acquaintance in January of that year, and although he was cordial, his respect for the violinist had clearly diminished. After hearing a concert on 16 January, Andersen wrote in his diary: 'Went to Casino to hear Ole Bull and got through the first one and a half pieces. There was a full house.... Ole's playing didn't excite me; he is himself an old man, easily moved like Lord Chamberlain Levetzau. I left before it was over.'[37] He elaborated on these comments the next day after hearing Bull play at the Royal Theater: '[Ole Bull] has become grey haired and has Lord Chamberlain Levetzau's posture (it seemed that he could have buttoned the pants for a king). I was bored. I can't take violin playing – if once I was moved by Ole Bull, it must have been my imagination, or now I've lost my sensibility. Hartmann said that [the performance] was flawed artistically.'[38] For Andersen, virtuosic performances devoid of philosophical meaning were a relic of an earlier age. The future demanded more than the sensual pleasures created by technical games. Science, philosophy, and a sense of cosmopolitanism needed to be reflected in the arts, and Andersen soon found all of these during trips to Paris in the spring (15 April–9 May) and early fall (7–22 September) of 1867.

The excitement Andersen felt upon his arrival in Paris is described in a tale he wrote shortly thereafter called 'Dryaden' (The Dryad):

> Engine after engine, train after train, rushed forth from the town, whistling and screaming all hours of the day. In the evening, towards midnight, at daybreak, and all through the day came the trains. Out of each one, and into each one, streamed people from the country of every king. A new wonder of the world had summoned them to Paris.[39]

The 'new wonder' was the World Exhibition of 1867, a spectacle Andersen visited on numerous occasions. To Andersen, the World Exhibition served as a symbol of the future.[40] Here the best of each nation stood united; art, industry, science, and culture had been brought together for the whole world to see.

> 'A splendid blossom of art and industry,' said one, 'has unfolded itself in the Champs de Mars; a gigantic sunflower, from whose petals one can learn geography and statistics and can become as wise as a lord mayor, and raise oneself to the level of art and poetry, and study the greatness and power of the various lands.'
> 'A fairy tale flower,' said another, 'a many-colored lotus plant, which spreads out its green leaves like a velvet carpet over the sand. The beginning of spring has brought it forth, the summer will see it in all its splendor, the autumn winds will sweep it away, so that not a leaf, not a fragment of its root shall remain.'[41]

When Andersen first visited the World Exhibition, he was accompanied by a young Danish journalist named Robert Watt (1837–94). Watt was a rather rakish fellow who worked as a foreign correspondent for the Danish arts magazine *Figaro*. He was a great fan of Andersen, and was determined to show the 'old man' the best that Paris had to offer. According to Andersen, this often included some of the city's less-dignified locales. For example, on April 17 Andersen wrote in his diary: '[Watt] told me many wild, sensuous stories. My insight into Parisian life was greatly increased.'[42] And on 5 May, the telling of such stories put Andersen in search of more erotic activities:

> After dinner I walked about in unfulfilled desire then went suddenly up to a shop which traded in human beings. One was painted with powder, the other plain looking, a third quite a lady. I spoke with her, paid twelve francs, and left without having sinned in action, but probably in thought. She asked me to come again, said that I seemed to be very innocent for a gentleman. I felt so light and happy when I emerged from this house. Many would call me a spineless fellow, am I this here? In the evening I wandered about on the boulevard and saw painted ladies sitting in the coffee shops, playing cards, drinking beer and chartreuse.[43]

Watt introduced Andersen to a number of his journalist friends in Paris, and together the group socialized in cafés and music halls, frequented brothels, attended performances of Gounod's *Faust* and Offenbach's *Granduchesa di Gerolstein* and *La Vie parisienne*, and visited the various 'nations' on display at the World Exhibition. They enjoyed each other's company immensely, so much so that many of the French journalists traveled to Copenhagen for a couple of weeks in August before Andersen and Watt returned to Paris in September.

Given Watt's fascination for the erotic and his predilection for Paris's bawdier locales, one cannot help but wonder if he introduced Andersen to the works of Baudelaire, in particular the collection of erotic poetry *Les Fleurs du Mal* (1857). The fourth poem in *Les Fleurs du Mal* is a piece called 'Correspondences,' which also appeared in 1861 as part of an article entitled 'Richard Wagner and *Tannhäuser* in Paris.'[44]

Baudelaire died on 31 August 1867; thus it is not unreasonable to assume that his work as a poet and critic would have been a major topic of conversation when Andersen and Watt arrived in Paris on 7 September. Although 'Richard Wagner and *Tannhäuser* in Paris' was Baudelaire's sole piece of music criticism, it nonetheless had a great impact on Parisian culture in the 1860s and is today generally considered the first prominent example of French *wagnérisme*. The history of French music criticism on Wagner is extremely complex, and there is not time in the present study to discuss the topic in any comprehensive manner. That being said, the movement in French aesthetics commonly referred to as *wagnérisme* was a reaction against positivism and is perhaps best understood as the Wagnerian influence that grew out of an essentially literary infatuation with the composer's ideas and the synaesthetic effect created by his operas *Tannhäuser* and *Lohengrin*. Whereas music critics such as F.J. Fétis criticized Wagner for the limitations they found in his philosophical works, literary figures such as Baudelaire found an artistic escape in Wagner's music and philosophical ideas – a new state of consciousness that was often compared to dream states and drug-induced stupors.

Baudelaire's writings, both poetic and critical, stressed the role of the imagination in Wagner's works, the importance of fantasy and freedom to the creative process. For a poet, this meant a highly wrought and deliberate use of language: 'Handling a language with skill is to practice a kind of evocative witchcraft,'[45] said Baudelaire. This sentiment could also have been applied to Andersen, who had already displayed a similar approach toward writing in his tales of 1858 and 1859. Baudelaire's 'witchcraft' was an attempt to reveal hidden correspondences between words, colors, and sounds, an approach he elaborated on in the sonnet 'Correspondences:'

> Nature is a temple, where the living
> Columns sometimes breathe confusing speech;
> Man walks within these groves of symbols, each
> Of which regards him as a kindred thing.
>
> As the long echoes, shadowy, profound,
> Heard from afar, blend in a unity,
> Vast as the night, as sunlight's clarity,
> So perfumes, colors, sounds may correspond.[46]

The binding together of art, nature, poetry and imagination in 'Correspondences' echoed many of the sentiments found in Ørsted's *The Spirit in Nature* and Andersen's 'Poetry's California.' Also appealing to Andersen would have been Baudelaire's final assessment of Wagner's impact on the future, despite the success or failure of his work in contemporary theaters:

> Recently, I heard someone say that if Wagner scored a brilliant success with his opera, that would be a purely individual accident, and that his method would have no subsequent influence on the destiny and development of lyric drama. I feel entitled by my study of the past, in other words of the eternal, to say just the opposite, namely that a total failure in no way destroys the possibility of new experiments in the same direction; and in the very near future we might well come to see not only new authors but even men with established reputations profiting in some degree from the ideas expounded by Wagner and passing successfully through the breach opened by him. Where in history have we ever read of a noble cause being lost in one throw?[47]

In Baudelaire's mind, Wagner was not striving for instant gratification. Instead he was laying the groundwork for a new artistic path in literature, a path that the future would embrace as a true and noble cause.

There is no concrete evidence showing that Andersen actually read *Fleurs du Mal* or 'Richard Wagner and *Tannhäuser* in Paris.' Nonetheless, the influence of *wagnérisme* on Andersen's work in the 1870s, especially the Wagner-inspired novel *Lykke Peer* (Lucky Peer), is more than mere coincidence.[48] Upon returning home form Paris in May 1867, Andersen noted in his diary a renewed interest in Wagner's work, specifically the opera *Tannhäuser*,[49] and by 1868 he was looking forward to the premières of Wagner's complete operas at the Royal Theater.

Wagner was quickly becoming Andersen's artistic ideal, a cosmopolitan poet/composer who, like Andersen himself, reached beyond the confines of tradition and national borders in an effort to create a new standard for the artwork of the future. Curiously, just as Andersen's interest in Wagner began to grow, his abhorrence for the composer's nemesis, Johannes Brahms, was quickly coming to a head.

The major cultural event in Copenhagen in 1868 was a series of three concerts in March given by Brahms and the singer Julius Stockhausen. Although Andersen awaited the arrival of these musicians with great expectation – he had heard of their talents from the Schumanns and had read about their success in the *Neue Zeitschrift für Musik* – his diary entries reveal how disappointed he was by their visit.[50] Andersen attended the musicians' first concert on 17 March and later that evening recorded his opinion of it. He applauded Stockhausen's singing, 'it was perfect, here was everything that a singer could give; here was the ideal of a concert singer. I don't know how broad a range his voice has, how high or deep, but oh how fresh with youth it filled me, it tore through me in such a way that no critique could be made other than to say: it was perfect.' About Brahms's playing, he had little to say: 'too dry and one-sided.'[51]

During their first week in Copenhagen, Brahms and Stockhausen visited Andersen almost every day, and with each visit Andersen's tolerance for Brahms weakened. Most upsetting to Andersen was Brahms' arrogant behavior and his obvious disdain for Danish culture. A native of Hamburg, a city that bordered the German-speaking provinces that seceded from Denmark in 1864, Brahms had felt the effects of the Schleswig-Holstein conflict his entire life, and he did not hesitate in telling the Danes his opinion of the matter. In Brahms' mind, Denmark had no cultural claim to the German-speaking duchies, and their final separation from the monarchy after the second Schleswig-Holstein war had been a just and inevitable solution. Brahms repeatedly ridiculed the Danish language and referred to Denmark's artistic culture as provincial at best. He even had the audacity to claim while visiting the Thorvaldsen Museum in Copenhagen that, given the artist's international status, a fine museum such as his did not belong in Denmark and would be better suited in a German city like Berlin. As one might imagine, Brahms's public voicing of such sentiments did not win him many supporters in Denmark. Disdain for Brahms quickly spread across the country, complete with satirical poems and indignant editorials. In fact, Brahms was practically run out of town after infuriating a group of Copenhagen's elite at a party hosted by Niels W. Gade. After lavishly extolling the virtues of Bismarck to a crowd of shocked dignitaries, Brahms's final concert was cancelled without comment, and the musician left town under cover of night.[52]

Andersen's own patience with Brahms apparently reached its breaking point as early as 23 March, when he, Brahms, and Stockhausen were invited to have lunch at the home of Lauritz Eckhardt, an actor at the Royal Theater. In his diary, Andersen reports that although Eckhardt recited a German toast for Stockhausen and Brahms and then offered a second toast for Andersen, the occasion was not one of warm camaraderie. 'Scharff and I spoke with each other childishly; he was a Mephistopheles against Brahms, calling him a 'Schleswig-Holsteiner.' Eckhardt asked me to read a couple of my fairy tales in German, but I didn't feel like it. So I refused.'[53] Andersen then proceeded to give away his tickets to the Brahms concert scheduled for that evening and made a point of avoiding any further contact with the musician during his stay in Copenhagen.[54]

It is interesting to note that shortly after Brahms's music was virtually banned from Denmark's concert halls following the debacle of his first and only visit, plans were being made at the Royal Theater for the Danish première of Wagner's *Lohengrin*. Whereas Brahms was viewed as a German nationalist – a true 'Schleswig-Holsteiner' by Denmark's public – Wagner was seen in quite a different light. The composer's long exile from Germany and his lengthy stays in Paris and Switzerland caused many in Copenhagen, most especially Andersen, to view him as something of a cosmopolitan – a man of the world. Wagner also had a supporter in Gade, who, as director of Copenhagen's Musikforeningen, made every effort to bring the composer's music to Danish audiences.[55]

Since World War II, the image of Wagner as a German nationalist has dominated our perceptions of him, but looking at Wagner's early reception in Denmark (a reception founded primarily on one opera, *Lohengrin*), we realize that in Andersen's day, a very different image of Wagner permeated parts of Europe. In the realm of music history, Wagner has been associated with aggressive German nationalism. But this was not the Wagner that Andersen and many of his contemporaries knew. Andersen never witnessed performances of *The Ring* or *Parsifal*, and he had no contact with the 'nationalist' Wagner who later built a Mecca of German culture in the small town of Bayreuth. The Wagner Andersen knew was the composer of *Tannhäuser* and *Lohengrin*; the Wagner who had not yet shown the influence of Schopenhauer; the Wagner who in *Opera and Drama* argued against the 'nationalist trend,' which he viewed as inimical to 'the great human lot' (das Allgemeinschaftliche).[56] In the terminology of Wagner's early philosophical writings, 'national' and 'conventional' formed a group that he compared unfavorably to 'natural' and 'original.'[57] In Andersen's mind, Wagner was the first to realize in literature and music 'the spirit in nature' proposed by Ørsted in 1850. Wagner was the artist of the future, and as such he served as a source of inspiration for Andersen and many others of his generation.

There are no specific references in Andersen's diaries and letters to Wagner's philosophical works, but references to various conversations Andersen had in the late 1860s reveal that he was cognizant of debates that had been fueled by some of Wagner's more controversial essays, specifically 'Das Judentum in der Musik.' Originally published in two installments of the *Neue Zeitshrift für Musik* in September 1850 under the pen name 'K. Freigedenk,' 'Das Judenthum in der Musik' initially did not attract much attention;[58] and if Andersen actually read the article, he obviously never associated it with Wagner. But such was not the case in 1869, when the article was republished as an individual pamphlet, this time with Wagner's name upon it.[59] When 'Das Judenthum in der Musik' appeared in print the second time something of a firestorm ensued in the press.[60] Wagner had interwoven his theory of the artwork of the future with offensive threads of anti-

Semitism. Meyerbeer was the primary target of Wagner's attack, but the music of other composers also came under fire. Wagner assailed Jews as being the cause of society's ills. He also claimed that they were incapable of creating true cultural works. In an attack on Mendelssohn specifically, he stated that despite the composer's wealth, privilege, and musical skill, he was culturally inferior and did not possess the ability 'to call forth in us the deep, heart-searching effect which we expect from Art.'[61] Wagner ascribed to the belief that Jews were avaricious, constantly striving to rule the world. 'As the world is presently constituted,' he wrote, 'the Jew is truly already more than emancipated: he rules and will rule, so long as money remains the power before which all our actions and responsibilities are subjugated. That the historical adversity of the Jews and the rapacious rawness of Christian-German potentates have put this power in the hands of Israel's sons needs no argument of ours to prove.'[62] Wagner concluded his essay by proclaiming the impossibility of changing the Jew and making him a productive member of society. In his eyes, the only solution to the 'Jewish question' was the total exclusion of Jews from society. Thus, the final line of his essay made a recommendation to the Jews: 'But know this, that only one thing can redeem you from the burden of your curse: the redemption of Ahasuerus – annihilation.'[63]

Such condemnation of the Jews would have greatly upset Andersen during the final decade of his life, if for no other reason than because his closest friends and patrons at the time, the Melchiors and Henriques, were prominent members of Copenhagen's Jewish elite[64] (figs. 6.1 & 6.2). Andersen spent a great deal of time with these families during the late 1860s and 1870s, and his diaries from this period indicate that many discussions concerning the Jews' place in society and the attributes of various Jewish composers arose when he was in their company. For example, on 26 February 1868 Andersen recorded a conversation he had with M. A. Goldschmidt at the home of Anna Rosenkilde, an actress at the Royal Theater. At this point, Andersen appears to have given little thought to a composer like Offenbach's Jewish heritage:

> Goldschmidt annoyed me. I began to speak about the composer Offenbach, whom I don't hold in high regard, and Goldschmidt said that he had just written about Offenbach's importance, [an essay] that will only be published after his (Goldschmidt's) death; it draws on the Talmud, and will be read in one thousand years; [He said] I didn't know Judaism and couldn't see Offenbach's merit. I answered that he no doubt could write a brilliant essay about Offenbach and his music, but it would never convince me or anyone else that Offenbach, as he put it, was the most important of Jewish composers, since Mendelssohn, Meyerbeer, Halévy, etc. stood much higher. Offenbach took subjects that remind one of the bad French humorous practice of setting a famous man on paper with a colossal head and a little body; he also creates distorted pictures of antiquity's heroes and historical figures.[65]

But Andersen's awareness of the 'Jewish question' and his sensitivity toward growing anti-Semitism in Copenhagen soon became more pronounced. In early October 1868 an offensive article concerning the negative characteristics of Jews

Fig. 6.1 Israel B. Melchior. Photograph of Andersen reading aloud for the Melchior Family (1867). (Odense: The Andersen House Museum)

Fig. 6.2 Group photo of H.C. Andersen and members of the Henriques and Melchior Families (1868). (Odense: The Andersen House Museum)

appeared in *Dagens Nyheder*, a daily paper that was then under the editorial control of Andersen's young friend Robert Watt. According to Andersen's diary, the issue was first brought to his attention on 10 October 1868: 'Watt was in a bad mood because he had received a letter from Moritz Melchior saying that he was canceling his subscription to *Dagens Nyheder* on account of the contempt for the Jews that was printed therein.'[66] When Andersen visited the Melchiors at their summer home the following day, he saw that they were still noticeably upset by the article: 'I went to Rolighed where Melchior calmly spoke about the situation. His wife, however, was vehement in a way that I have never seen her before.'[67] On October 12, after dining again with the Melchiors, Andersen recorded the main topic of conversation: 'Moses Melchior was especially angry about the article concerning the Jews in Watt's newspaper, and he thinks that everyone should boycott the paper. At the very least all Jews should cancel their subscriptions.'[68] Apparently the issue was still unresolved on 14 October: 'Visit from Watt who was sorry about the article. He told me who wrote it. I said that [the article] was untrue and offensive to the Jews. I spoke with Bille at the theater about it. He said that Jews and poets were an irritable breed, like a flayed eel.'[69]

As Andersen became more aware of the Jews' plight, he made a point of seeking out the monuments of Jewish composers he especially admired. For example, in May 1868 he visited the Jewish cemetery in Paris for no other reason than to see 'Halévy's grave and monument.'[70] And in December 1869 he went to Nice to pay homage to Meyerbeer: 'I climbed up to the cliff terrace, went all the way up to the great, round tower. Here Meyerbeer reportedly began composing his *African Queen*.'[71] Andersen always held a special place in his heart for Mendelssohn, as is clearly shown in the descriptions of his encounters with the composer preserved in the various editions of Andersen's autobiography. But undoubtedly the clearest example of Andersen's changed attitude toward the Jews is found in his late literary works. Although Andersen had made use of negative Jewish stereotypes in some of his earlier novels and travelogues – most notably in *Only a Fiddler* and *A Poet's Bazaar* – his growing respect for friends like the Melchiors and Henriques led to his abandonment of such practices in the 1870s. In fact, it was at the Melchior summer home that Andersen completed his sixth and final novel, *Lykke Peer* (Lucky Peer) – an artistic novel that contemplates the 'music of the future' and quotes the Talmud in an effort to explain the cultural significance and eventual fate of composers such as Beethoven, Mendelssohn and Wagner.

In many ways, *Lucky Peer* is a reinterpretation of the basic storyline in Andersen's début novel, *The Improvisatore*; and a comparison of the two reveals just how much Andersen's aesthetic outlook had changed over the thirty-seven years that separate the two works. Like Antonio, Peer represents Andersen's artistic ideal. The son of a poor warehouseman, Peer socially outdistances a wealthy boy named Felix by becoming an innovative composer of operas inspired by the works of Wagner.

Andersen began writing *Lucky Peer* the evening before the Danish première of *Lohengrin*, and the influence that this opera had on his writing of the novel is undeniable. Andersen saw *Lohengrin* on opening night, noting in his diary that it was 'magnificently done and very well received.'[72] *Lohengrin* was scheduled for a total of nine performances that season, and Andersen had purchased tickets for every one. His reaction to the music in 1870 was quite different from his first encounter with it in Weimar almost 20 years earlier: 'For me it was quite enjoyable, and I did not feel fatigued as I did abroad.'[73]

Lucky Peer can be viewed as an example of music historiography, above all a meditation on the relationship that had developed over the course of the nineteenth century between visions of the future and a respect for the past.[74] Although Wagner's operas are presented as the model for a new age, the immortal spirit of Mozart's string quartets and Beethoven's symphonies are revered as well.

Peer's talents are first revealed through dance and then through song. He is employed at the Royal Theater as a young boy, and there he is exposed to the music of foreign composers for the first time. At private gatherings with theater personnel he is moved by the instrumental works of Beethoven, Mozart, and Haydn.

> Once a week, there was quartet music. Ears, soul, and thought were filled with the grand musical poems of Beethoven and Mozart.... It was as if a kiss of fire traveled down [Peer's] spine and shot through all his nerves. His eyes filled with tears. Every musical evening here [in the salon] was a festive evening for him that made a deeper impression upon him than any opera in the theater, where ... imperfections are revealed. Sometimes the words do not come out right.... Sometimes the effect is weakened by faults in dramatic expression.... Lack of truthfulness in stage settings and costumes are also observed. But all this was absent from the quartet. The musical poems rose in all their grandeur ... here he was in the world of music which its masters had created.[75]

On another evening Peer hears Beethoven's *Pastoral* Symphony, the description of which is obviously inspired by Ørsted's *The Spirit in Nature*:

> It was the andante movement, 'the scene by the brook,' which stirred and excited our young friend with a particularly strange power. It carried him into the living, fresh woods. The lark and the nightingale rejoiced; the cuckoo sang there as well. What beauty of nature! What a wellspring of refreshment it contained! From this hour he knew within himself that it was the pictorial music, in which nature was reflected and the emotions of human hearts were set forth, that struck deepest in his soul. Beethoven and Haydn became his favorite composers.[76]

As one discovers upon reading *Lucky Peer*, the significance of the hero's name is multi-faceted. He is 'lucky' for many reasons, some of which, no doubt, turn out to be quite surprising to the reader. In the novel, Peer encounters the passing of time as well as his own relationship to a larger sense of history. In fact, the description of his music education serves as a rough narrative of the evolution of French opera in the nineteenth century. The first role Peer's singing master asks him to learn is that of John Brown in Boieldieu's opéra-comique *La Dame blanche*:

> He quickly learned the words and music, and from Walter Scott's novel, which had furnished the material for the opera, he obtained a clear, complete picture of the young spirited officer who visits his native hills and comes to his ancestral palace without knowing it. An old song awakens recollections of childhood. Luck is with him, and he wins a castle and a wife.[77]

The singing master then leads him to Ambroise Thomas' *Hamlet* and Gounod's *Faust*.

> [Peer] much preferred regular opera to singspiel. It was contrary to his sound, natural music sense to go from singing to speaking and then back to singing again. 'It is,' he said, 'as if one were going from marble steps onto wooden steps, sometimes even onto mere chicken roosts, and then back onto marble. The whole poem should live and breathe in its passage through tones.'[78]

Eventually Peer discovers the music of Wagner and, against the wishes of his teacher, sings the lead in *Lohengrin*, which sets him on a new artistic path.

> The music of the future, as the new movement in opera is called, and for which Wagner in particular is a banner-bearer, had a defender and admirer in our young friend. He found here characters so clearly drawn, passages so full of thought, and the entire action characterized by forward movement, without any pause or frequent repetition of melodies.[79]

But the old singing master is not persuaded: 'I bow to the ingenuity that lies in this new musical movement,' he states, 'but I do not dance with you before that golden calf.'[80] He would prefer to hear Peer sing Don Ottavio's aria 'Tears, cease your flowing' from Mozart's *Don Giovanni*. 'It is like a beautiful lake in the woods, by whose shore one rests and enjoys the music that streams through it!'[81]

It should be noted that in addition to being a strong promoter of music's glorious past, Peer's singing master is a Jew. Andersen took great care in developing this character. After witnessing the effect that anti-Semitism had on friends like the Melchiors and the Henriques, Andersen made every effort to learn as much as he could about the Talmud and Judaism in an effort to present the character of the singing master in a respectful manner.[82] We first learn of the singing master's religion in chapter eleven, when Peer and his teacher are having a conversation about the benefits of being generous:

> One evening [the singing master] read aloud from the newspaper about the beneficence of two men, which then led him to speak about good deeds and their reward.
> 'When one does not think about it, it is sure to come. The rewards for good deeds are like the dates spoken of in the Talmud: they ripen late and only then are they sweet.'

'Talmud?' asked Peer. 'What sort of book is that?'

'A book, from which more than one seed of thought has been implanted in Christianity,' was the answer.

'Who wrote the book?'

'Wise men in ancient times – wise men from various nations and religions. Here wisdom is preserved in a few words, as in Solomon's Proverbs. What kernels of truth! One reads here that men from all over the world, for many centuries, have remained the same. "Your friend has a friend, and your friend's friend has a friend; be discreet in what you say!" is found here. It is a piece of wisdom for all times. "No one can jump over his own shadow!" is here also, and "Wear shoes when you tread on thorns!" You ought to read this book. You will find in it the proof of culture more clearly than you will find in the layers of soil. For me as a Jew, moreover, it is an inheritance from my forefathers.'

'Jew?' said Peer. 'Are you a Jew?'

'Didn't you know that? How strange that we have never spoken about it before today!'

[Peer's] mother and grandmother didn't know anything about it either. They had never thought about it, but had always known that the singing master was an honorable, wonderful man.[83]

This excerpt tells us much about Andersen's image of the Jewish singing master and in doing so serves as a refutation of Wagner's 'Das Judentum in der Music.' To begin, one cannot tell by any physical attributes or specific Semitic characteristics that the singing master is any different from Peer and his Christian relatives. The singing master's religion is also of little consequence to Peer, who believes that music is the new universal religion; through music men of all backgrounds can come together in celebration. As Peer explains during a conversation with Felix's mother, the opera house and theater have become the new pulpits of the Lord, and 'most people listen more there than in church.'[84] And as the singing master himself explains, both Judaism and Christianity have a long literary tradition rooted in the Talmud and Old Testament. Most importantly, Andersen tries to show through the virtuous character of the singing master, that a good citizen should be judged by his actions and benevolent nature, not according to his race or choice of religion. In *Lucky Peer* Andersen goes to great lengths to show that the singing master's Judaism is as culturally valid and respectable as his love of Mozart's opera.

When Peer finally makes his début in *Lohengrin*, his talent is celebrated with great acclaim. Yet he is still unsatisfied. Inspired by Wagner's ability to write both libretto and score, Peer decides to write an opera himself and struggles to find the right subject. After many months of searching, the title of his new opera finally comes to him – *Aladdin*.

In the years that follow, Peer rejects the lure of female companionship and dedicates every moment to the creation of his opera. He hopes to surpass Wagner, for in addition to writing the libretto and music to *Aladdin*, he eventually plans to sing the lead role at the première:

To write the text and music for an opera, and be the interpreter of his own work on stage, was a great and happy aim. Our young friend had a talent in common with Wagner in that he could construct the dramatic poem himself. But did he, like Wagner, have the fullness of musical emotion to create musical work of any significance?

Courage and doubt alternated in him. He could not dismiss this persistent thought.... With understanding and delight he read and reread the beautiful Oriental story [of Aladdin]. Soon it took dramatic form; scene after scene grew into words and music, and the more it grew, the richer the musical thoughts became. At the close of the work it was as if a font of tones had been pierced for the first time, and all the abundant fresh water streamed forth. He then re-composed his work, this time in a more powerful form; many months passed before the opera *Aladdin* finally emerged.[85]

When *Aladdin* is performed in public, the audience is mesmerized by the beauty and subtlety of Peer's music:

A few chords sounded from the orchestra, and the curtain rose. The strains of music, as in Gluck's *Armide* and Mozart's *Magic Flute*, arrested the attention of everyone as the scene was revealed, the scene in which Aladdin stood in a wonderful garden. Soft, subdued music sounded from flowers and stones, from streams and deep caverns, various melodies blending into one great harmony. An air of spirits was heard in the chorus. It was now far off, now near, swelling in might and then dying away. Arising from this harmony was the song of Aladdin.... The resonant, sympathetic voice, the intense music of the heart subdued all listeners and seized them with such rapture that it could not rise higher when he reached for the lamp of fortune that was embraced by the song of spirits.[86]

With this description, Andersen replicated the dream states and drug-induced stupors described by French writers such as Baudelaire in reaction to Wagner's music.[87] This implementation of a dream-inspired mood effectively sets the stage for the novel's final scene, a shocking twist in plot that troubled many readers. After singing the lead role in *Aladdin*, Peer returns to the stage and greets the audience:

Bouquets rained down from all sides; a carpet of living flowers was spread out before his feet.

What a moment of life for the young artist – the highest, the greatest! A mightier one could never again be granted him, he felt. A wreath of laurel touched his breast and fell down in front of him.... A fire rushed through him; his heart swelled as never before; he bowed, took the wreath, pressed it against his heart, and at the same time fell backward. Fainted? Dead? What was it? The curtain fell.

'Dead!' resounded through the house. Dead in the moment of his triumph – like Sophocles at the Olympic Games, like Thorvaldsen in the theater during Beethoven's symphony. An artery in his heart had burst, and like a flash of lightning, his days here were ended; ended without pain, ended in an earthly triumph, in the fulfillment of his mission on earth. Lucky Peer! More fortunate than millions![88]

As Andersen might have expected, reviewers did not like *Lucky Peer*. But this did not discourage him, as is evident in a letter he wrote to Vilhem Boye on 1 December 1870:

> Thank you for your letter! I hope to receive yet another one when you have read *Lucky Peer*. ... Many have thanked me for this work; only the newspapers keep silent, except *Fædrelandet*. Therein a young man, Winkel-Horn, presented his opinion, which is not mine at all. He contends that it is completely wrong that Peer dies, that it is a chance misfortune. Yet I believe it is his highest measure of good fortune, and I wanted to say exactly that. The reviewer was otherwise polite, just as one says the Russians are when they want to flog their priest: they kiss him first on the hand, then they hammer away, and thereafter give him once again a hand kiss.[89]

Many of Andersen's friends also objected to elements of the novel, primarily its promotion of Wagner's music. For example, in a letter written to Henriette Collin on 12 August 1870, Andersen said:

> I read *Lucky Peer* for Mrs. Heiberg, and it seemed to have especially interested her; she only found that I was too complimentary therein of Wagner's music. The first part of the story, as you know, is the most amusing. The rest is, in contrast, the most poetic. My description of an opera that I have Peer compose is especially pleasing, and the most unusual. It is quite unfortunate that I didn't learn counterpoint and become a composer.[90]

Andersen already knew that many readers in Copenhagen would disagree with his assessment of Wagner's music. Although the première of Wagner's *Lohengrin* had been awaited with great expectation, enthusiasm for the composer began to wane once the Danish public actually heard the opera. Andersen's diary reveals the frustration he felt when confronted with his friends' indifference toward Wagner's music. For example, on 2 May 1870 he wrote: 'Heard the first two acts of *Lohengrin* at the theater. Mr. Brosbøll said he did not understand a bit of it. Mrs. Heiberg also dislikes Wagner's music.'[91] And on 9 May:

> Phister assured me that I could not understand the music since he couldn't, and he was born with a highly developed musical sense. I replied that the music interested me. It excites me and I follow along. He assured me that only trained musicians like Mr. Gerlach could appreciate it; without knowledge of counterpoint I could not get any pleasure from it. All this he said with confidence and haughtiness.[92]

Clear evidence of Copenhagen's negative reception of Wagner is found in the sudden schedule changes made at the Royal Theater shortly after the opera's première. As interest in *Lohengrin* began to wane, the theater cancelled some of its performances. For example, on 6 May Andersen noted in his diary: 'Tonight the performance of *Lohengrin* is being replaced by *Liden Kirsten.*'[93] Gounod's *Faust* took its place on 14 May.[94] Andersen obviously felt that many of his friends and colleagues dismissed Wagner's music too hastily.

As he had with his writing of 'The Nightingale,' Andersen used *Lucky Peer* to chastise Danish readers for their misguided musical tastes. He wanted audiences to understand not only the mastery of Wagner's operas, but also the undeniable importance of these works to contemporary European culture. In his novel, Andersen used the musical development of young Peer as a means of highlighting the generation gap that he noticed developing among Danish audiences. Thus, in the characters of Peer and the singing master, the reader not only recognizes a contrast between Christian and Jew, modern and traditional, but also the impetuosity of youth versus the reliable foundation offered by maturity and tradition. Peer and the singing master stand as the ideals of music's future. While Peer pushes forward, striving eternally for the inventive and new, the singing master preserves the treasures of the past, ensuring that their beauty is passed on to the next generation.

Many of Andersen's friends and colleagues reacted strongly to the ideas about music presented in *Lucky Peer*. Although they recognized that Peer and the singing master were not to be interpreted as exact copies of Wagner and Mendelssohn, they nonetheless understood that some parallels should be made. Influenced by the music of Wagner, Peer stood as the antithesis of his wealthy friend Felix, just as the Jewish singing master was meant to be interpreted as the musical opposite of Wagner. Constructing his cast of characters in this manner enabled Andersen both to praise the music of Wagner and separate himself from the composer's distasteful anti-Semitism. And with the death of Peer at the end, Andersen left it to the reader to decide if works like *Aladdin* would be included in the repertoire of the future.

Lucky Peer received a mixed reception from Andersen's contemporaries; and of all his friends and colleagues, Jenny Lind had the most to say about the novel. Except for a single letter written the year before, Lind had been out of touch with Andersen for nearly twenty years when she wrote to him on 11 December 1872.[95] Having read the book with great care, she felt it her duty as a musician to write to Andersen and offer her opinion of it. Obviously troubled by the death of Peer, she took fourteen pages to tell Andersen about her views on art – which were based on a strong religious conviction – and her continued sadness over the untimely death of Felix Mendelssohn. Lind clearly understood Andersen's ideas about the future of music, but she did not agree with him. She chastised Andersen for killing the novel's hero, explaining that she would never wish for such an end, even though she had witnessed the passing of her own fame many years previously.

Despite the criticism of Andersen's contemporaries, I cannot help but see Peer's death as one of Andersen's most profound statements on the transitory nature of music. Opera, more than any other musical genre, is a product of popular taste. And as such, its assurance in the halls of immortality is questionable. Thus the best death for an opera composer, according to Andersen, is an early one.

Lucky Peer is 'lucky' because he dies at the peak of his career and is thus spared the torment of watching tastes change. Peer will never know the biting critique of an opera critic, and he will never have to witness the eventual neglect of his greatest achievement – a Wagner-inspired opera called *Aladdin*.

That Andersen was contemplating the longevity of his reputation is made evident in many of his diary entries from 1870. As Andersen grew older and witnessed changes in taste and fashion, he began to envy Peer's early but glorious exit. Fame had been Andersen's great reward, and in his final years he was haunted by the idea that his reputation would fade once he was dead. After attending the centennial celebration of Thorvaldsen's birth on 19 November 1870, Andersen wrote in his diary:

> I need not hide on these pages (which will never be published but stem instead from my daily thoughts) that I once felt I had so much in common with Thorvaldsen – our lowly birth and our struggle, our great world recognition. To be sure, I am as well known in the world now as he. Although our countrymen don't see it, it is certainly true. But I think his name will live longer than mine. Indeed, I do believe my name is now better known around the world than his, but mine will be forgotten and his will live. Is this vanity? Will I ever know?[96]

Five days later he wrote: 'I'll be quickly forgotten and flung to the winds by the next generation – "It's over! It's all over! And that's how it is with all stories!"'[97]

In Andersen's final years, the inevitability of death grew more prominent in his thoughts, and his faith in the immortality of his own work continued to wane. Thus it should come as no surprise that in January 1875, eight months before his death, Andersen set to work updating his libretto for the opera *Festival at Kenilworth*. As Andersen explained in a letter to Countess Frijs-Frijsenborg on 27 January, if the opera were to have any hope of surviving after his death, it had to be updated according to modern tastes:

> I have again taken up Weyse's singspiel *Festival at Kenilworth* (I wrote the text in 1831); the dialogue is too long and diffuse for our time. I am now also shortening and revising the recitatives, which the young composer Liebmann[98] will set to music, and then we'll have a through-composed opera that can again be produced on stage. It makes me happy to have a work in preparation like this.[99]

Another project Andersen worked on in 1875 was a large screen of pictures, which he hoped would serve as a visual record of his life. Reitzel gave him engravings and English illustrated magazines, and the court photographer Hansen sent photographs of eminent Danes. Others sent issues of Danish magazines like *Illustreret Tidende*. Andersen divided his screen into eight panels, and these tell us much about how he viewed his own life. The first two panels were devoted to Denmark, then one for Sweden, Germany, Great Britain, France, the Orient and Childhood. Each panel showed pictures of historic buildings and famous people, surrounded by images from his fairy tales and everyday life. Andersen included cut-outs of himself, of his contemporaries (e.g. Jenny Lind, Kierkegaard, Niels W.

Gade), and of his favorite historical and literary figures (e.g. Napoleon, Walter Scott, Dickens, Goethe). Revealing the cultural landscape of his life, the screen was installed in the bedroom of his apartment and in many ways served as Andersen's final autobiographical statement. That being said, it is interesting to note that the panels for Denmark, France, and especially Germany are crowded with portraits of the composers and performers who occupied his interest throughout the century, from Mozart, Beethoven, Gluck and Mendelssohn to Liszt, Thalberg, Meyerbeer and Wagner.

When Andersen died in 1875, *Lucky Peer* was embraced as his last great opus – his ultimate statement on the role of music in society. Combining the ideas of figures as diverse as Ørsted, Baudelaire, and Wagner with his own quest for immortality, he offered younger generations a view of the future that embraced both innovation and tradition. Indeed, the future of the arts would be a careful balance of old and new. As the plot of *Lucky Peer* subtly explained, figures such as Mozart and Beethoven would no doubt live forever, but each age would also have its own temporary Wagner, Andersen, or Peer.

Fig. 6.3 Woodcut of H.C. Andersen's burial (artist unknown) that appeared in *Illustreret Tidende* on 8 November 1875. (Copenhagen: The Royal Library)

Coda

The Death of a Romantic

Andersen's final years were plagued with illness, and his diaries reveal a series of dramatic fluctuations between hope for the future and utter despair. Thus, it is telling that in the work he presented as his final fairy tale, 'Tante Tandepine' (Auntie Toothache), he gives an account of a failed poet's sufferings and eventual slip into obscurity.

Written in 1872, 'Auntie Toothache' stands as a testament to Andersen's ultimate abandonment of German idealism. Returning to the Hoffmannesque model of a story preserved only in fragments, he explains to the reader that the tale was salvaged from a grocer's wastepaper basket and is actually an autobiographical sketch by a young student. Upon reading the tale, we learn that thanks to the moral support of his Auntie Mille, who constantly offers him sweets (a metaphor for an adoring public who fails to comprehend his works), the student is on his way to becoming a renowned poet. But then the sweets begin to cause a painful side effect. Auntie Toothache appears in a surreal dream sequence and tortures the student with her own style of excruciating music:

> 'A splendid set of teeth,' she said, 'just like an organ to play upon! We shall have a grand concert, with Jew's harps, kettledrums, trumpets, piccolo-flute, and a trombone in the wisdom tooth! Grand poet, grand music!'
>
> Then she commenced to play ... each finger was an instrument of torture; the thumb and the forefinger were pincers and wrench; the middle finger ended in a pointed awl; the ring finger was a drill; and the little finger squirted gnat poison. 'I am going to teach you meter!' she said. 'A great poet must have a great toothache, a little poet a little toothache!'[1]

Upon hearing this, the student begs to be a little poet, or better yet, not a poet at all. He makes a pact with Auntie Toothache: in exchange for a life free from suffering, he promises never to write another line of verse. Thus the student chooses mortal comfort and eventual death over a life made immortal through art. To be a true artist, one must suffer greatly.

When the student awakes, Auntie Mille is at his side. She tempts him with sweets but to no avail. He refuses to write a single line, and it is at this point that the tale abruptly ends. As Andersen explains:

My young friend, the grocer's assistant, could not find the missing sheets. They had gone out into the world as papers wrapped around the salted herring, the butter, and the green soap. They had fulfilled their destiny! ...Now Auntie is dead. The student is dead – he whose sparks of genius went into the wastepaper basket. This is the end of the story – the story of Auntie Toothache....[2]

... and the story of Hans Christian Andersen and music.

Notes

INTRODUCTION

1. For a recent study on the alteration of Andersen's fairy tales in Disney films see: Regina Bendix, 'Seashell Bra and Happy End. Disney's Transformations of "The Little Mermaid,"' *Fabula. Zeitschrift für Erzählforschung* 34 (1993): 280–90.

2. Jackie Wullschlager, *Hans Christian Andersen: The Life of a Storyteller* (London: Allen Lane, 2000); Jens Andersen, *Andersen: En Biografi* (Copenhagen: Gyldendal, 2003).

3. *New York Times*, 10 June 2001.

4. Over the last decade a number of studies concerning Andersen's interest in the visual arts have appeared: Johan de Mylius, *'Hr. Digter Andersen.' Liv, Digtning, Meninger* (Copenhagen: Gads Forlag, 1995), 347–57; Hans Chr. Andersen, 'The Author at the Museum,' *Hans Christian Andersen: A Poet in Time*. Johan de Mylius, Aage Jørgensen, and Viggo Hjørnager Pedersen, eds. (Odense, DK: Odense University Press, 1999): 205–34; Inge Lise Rassmussen, 'Hans Christian Andersen Watching Art,' *Hans Christian Andersen: A Poet in Time*, 301–10; Heinz Barüske, *Hans Christian Andersen in Berlin* (Berlin: Hendrik Bäßler Verlag, 1999). See also *H.C. Andersen som Billedkunstner*, the catalogue for an exhibition presented at Fyens Kunstmuseum in Denmark in 1996.

5. The most noted studies concerning Andersen's possible homosexual relations have been written by Jens Andersen, *Andersen: En Biografi*; Jackie Wullschlager, *Hans Christian Andersen: The Life of a Storyteller*; Allison Prince, *Hans Christian Andersen. The Fan Dancer* (London: Allison and Busby, 1998); and Heinrich Detering: *Das offene Geheimnis: Zur literarischen Produktivität eines Tabus von Winckelmann bis zu Thomas Mann* (Göttingen: Wallstein, 1994) and *Intellectual Amphibia: Homoerotic Camouflage in Hans Christian Andersen's Works* (Odense: H.C. Andersen-Centret, 1991). Lise Præstgaard Andersen, 'The Feminine Element – And a Little About the Masculine Element in H.C. Andersen's Fairy Tales' in *Hans Christian Andersen: A Poet in Time*, 501–14, discusses the 'feminine' elements in Andersen's work while Jack Zipes, *When Dreams Came True: Classical Fairy Tales and Their Tradition* (New York: Routledge, 1999) presents Andersen as a socially and sexually dominated figure. Hilding Ringblom, 'Om H.C. Andersens påståede homosexualitet,' *Anderseniana* (1997): 41–58 also addresses Andersen's alleged homosexuality. The effect such studies have had on recent general descriptions of Andersen are reflected in the Andersen entry in the *Oxford Companion to Fairy Tales*, Jack Zipes, ed. (Oxford: Oxford University Press, 2000) and Diana and Jeffrey Frank, 'The Real Hans Christian Andersen,' *The New Yorker* (8 January 2001): 78–84.

6. For a general overview of Andersen's connection to the music of his age see Johan de Mylius, 'Hans Christian Andersen and the Music World,' *Hans Christian Andersen: Danish Writer and Citizen of the World*, ed. Sven Hakon Rossel (Amsterdam: Rodopi, 1996): 176–208; and Gustav Hetsch, *H. C. Andersen og Musiken* (Copenhagen: H. Hagerups Forlag, 1930) and 'Hans Christian Andersen's Interest in Music,' *The Musical Quarterly* 16 (1930): 322–29.

7. Leon Botstein, 'Between Aesthetics and History,' *19ᵗʰ-Century Music* 13 (1989): 168.

8. Recent books exploring the depiction of nineteenth-century musical culture in British fiction include: Nicky Losseff and Sophie Fuller, eds. The Idea of Music in Victorian Fiction (Aldershot: Ashgate, 2003); Delia Da Sousa Correa, George Eliot, Music and Victorian Culture (Basingstoke: Palgrave, 2002); Alisa Clapp-Intyre, Angelic Airs, Subversive Songs: Music as Social Discourse in the Victorian Novel (Athens, OH: Ohio University Press, 2002); Emma Sutton, Aubrey Beardsley and British Wagnerism in the 1890s (Oxford: Oxford University Press, 2002); John Hughes, 'Ecstatic Sound': Music and Individuality in the Work of Thomas Hardy (Aldershot: Ashgate, 2001); Phyllis Weliver, Women Musicians in Victorian Fiction, 1860–1900: Representations of Music, Science and Gender in the Leisured Home (Aldershot: Ashgate, 2000); and Beryl Gray, George Eliot and Music (London: Macmillan, 1989).

9. H. Topsøe-Jensen, *Omkring Levnedsbogen: En Studie over H.C. Andersen som Selvbiograf 1820–1845* (Copenhagen: Gyldendal, 1943).

10. *Gesammelte Werke*, 1–2. Leipzig: Carl B. Lorck, 1847.

11. Trans. Mary Howitt, London: Longman and Co., 1847; Boston: J. Monroe, 1847.

12. H.C. Andersen, *Mit Livs Eventyr* (Copenhagen: C.A. Reitzels Forlag), 1855.

13. H.C. Andersen, *The Story of my Life*, trans. Horace Scudder (New York: Hurd and Houghton), 1871.

14. *H.C. Andersens Dagbøger 1825–75*, Kåre Olsen and H. Topsøe-Jensen, eds. (Copenhagen: Det danske Sprog- og Litteraturselskab/G.E.C. Gad, 1971–76) vol. 8, 365–66.

15. Pages of the diaries are occasionally missing. Andersen did not number the pages, and at his death they consisted of a pile of loose sheets. A critical, though unannotated, complete edition did not appear until 1971 (*H.C. Andersens Dagbøger 1825–75*, 1–12. Kåre Olsen and H. Topsøe-Jensen, eds. Copenhagen: Det danske Sprog- og Litteratursel-skab/G.E.C. Gad, 1971–76). Although a single volume collection of excerpts was translated into English (*The Diaries of Hans Christian Andersen*, selected and editied by Patricia Conroy and Sven H. Rossel) the 12-volume complete edition is still only available in Danish.

16. From 1862 until 1872, these almanacs give little more than a list of Andersen's correspondences. This is likely due to the fact that Andersen began to expand his diary entries greatly during these years. Like the diaries, the only complete edition of Andersen's almanacs is accessible in Danish only (*H.C. Andersen Almanakker 1833–1873*. Helga Vang Lauridsen and Kirsten Weber, eds. Copenhagen: Det danske Sprog- og Literatur-selskab/G.E.C. Gad, 1990).

17. Bille and Bøgh, *Breve fra Hans Christian Andersen*, vol. 2, 94 (Letter to B.S. Ingemann, 20 November 1843).

18. Erik Haugaard, 'Portrait of a Poet: Hans Christian Andersen and his Fairytales,' (Washington, D.C.: Library of Congress, 1973), 16–17.

19. Ibid., 4.

CHAPTER 1: THE NIGHTINGALE

1. H.C. Andersen, *Levnedsbogen 1805–1831* (Copenhagen: Det Schønbergske Forlag, 1988), 42. *Hermann von Unna* was a singspiel by Abbé Georg Joseph Vogler based on the novel by Benedikte Naubert.

2. Sven Hakon Rossel, 'Hans Christian Andersen: The Great European Writer,' in *Hans Christian Andersen: Danish Writer and Citizen of the World*, ed. Sven Hakon Rossel (Amsterdam: Rodopi, 1966), 6–7.

3. In later years, Andersen kept in touch with his teacher there, sending greetings to Carstens on his golden wedding anniversary. For information on Andersen's interaction with Denmark's Jewish communities see: Erik Dal, 'Jødiske elementer i H.C. Andersen's skrifter,' in *Andersen og Verden,* ed. Johan de Mylius, Aage Jørgensen, and Viggo Hjørnager Pedersen (Odense: Odense Universitetsforlag, 1993), 444–452; and Bruce Kirmmsee, 'Hans Christian Andersen og Jødepigen, En historisk undersøgelse af noget 'underligt,'' *Rambam, Tidskrift for jødisk kultur og forskning* 31 (1992): 59–66.

4. H.C. Andersen, *Mit Livs Eventyr* (1859), ed. H. Topsøe-Jensen (Copenhagen: Gyldendals Bogklub, 1975), vol. 1, 43–44.

5. Andersen, *Levnedsbogen,* 39–40.

6. As Frederick J. Marker explains in *Hans Christian Andersen and the Romantic Theater* (Toronto: University of Toronto Press, 1971), 15, these two theater works represented genres that would prove influential to Andersen's early years as a dramatist for the Royal Theater, namely the Viennese *Zauberposse* and the singspiel derived from a popular play or novel.

7. For the date of these performances in 1812 see Topsøe-Jensen, *Omkring Levnedsbogen,* 108.

8. Letter to Jonas Collin, 27 March 1825 in *H. C. Andersens Brevveksling med Jonas Collin den Ældre og andre Medlemmer af det Collinske Hus.* H. Topsøe-Jensen, Kaj Bom, and Knud Bøgh, eds. (Copenhagen: Ejnar Munksgaard, 1945–48), vol 1, 21.

9. Andersen, *Mit Livs Eventyr,* vol.1, 38.

10. Facsimiles and a study of Andersen's entries are found in: Hans Brix, *Det første Skridt* (Copenhagen: Carit Andersens Forlag, 1943).

11. Original manuscript found in Copenhagen: The Royal Library, Collin Manuscript Collection.

12. Andersen, *Mit Livs Eventyr,* vol.1, 51.

13. According to Marker, 16: 'This adaptation of the Cinderella story was flavored with humorous and sentimental elements characteristic of this type of opéra-comique; hence the evil stepmother was made a comic stepfather, and an Italian Renaissance setting, a wizard named Alidor, and an exciting disguise intrigue were added.'

14. Andersen, *Levnedsbogen,* 44.

15. Andersen, *Mit Livs Eventyr,* vol. 1, 47.

16. Ibid., 52.

17. Kirsten Grau Nielsen, 'Fru Ottilies dagbog. Den unge Comediantspiller,' *Anderseniana* (1990): 14.

18. Andersen, *Mit Livs Eventyr,* vol. 1, 54.

19. For a complete description of the pogrom in Copenhagen see I. Davidsen, *Jödefejden i Danmark 1819* (Copenhagen, 1869).

20. This quote comes from Andersen's third novel, *Only a Fiddler* (Book 2, chapter 8), wherein he recreates the pogrom he had witnessed in Copenhagen in 1819. See *H.C. Andersens Samlede Skrifter* 2nd edition (Copenhagen: C.A Reitzels Forlag, 1879), vol. 4, 199.

21. Andersen, *Levnedsbogen,* 54.

22. Ibid.

23. Ibid., 54–55. The musical number that Andersen attempted to perform is from a high point in the operetta, when Anine (Cinderella) sings a charming French song about a peasant girl named Colinette who struggles to survive at court. Between each stanza, Anine dances to a rhythm she plays on a tambourine. In the Odense production of this operetta that Andersen took part in, this scene occurred shortly after his single spoken line.

24. Ibid., 55.

25. For a detailed description of the atmosphere at Bakkehuset see Wullschlager, 47–48.

26. Andersen, *Levnedsbogen*, 55–56.

27. Ibid., 58.

28. In the opera, Indian savages prevent Virginie from embarking for Europe and assassinate the captain of the ship who has come to take her to France. Paul and Virginie are then happily reunited.

29. Andersen, *Levnedsbogen*, 58.

30. Ibid., 60.

31. Ibid., 61.

32. Andersen, *Mit Livs Eventyr*, vol. 1, 60. It should be noted that Andersen used the feminine forms of the Italian terms for 'thief' and 'foreigner' when describing the Danish audience's reaction to Siboni – such a switch in gender would have only added insult to injury at the time.

33. For a description of Siboni's years in Copenhagen see J.P. Keld, 'Rids af Giuseppe Sibonis virksomhed i årene 1819–1839: i anledning af 200-året for hans fødsel,' *Dansk Aarbog for Musikforskning* xi (1980): 57–78. Information concerning Siboni's full career is found in G. Schepelern, *Giuseppe Siboni* (Copenhagen, 1989). In the early 1820s, Danish audiences only knew the work of Rossini. *Tancredi* was first performed at the Royal Theater in 1820, and *Il Barbiere di Siviglia* followed two years later. Both operas were sung in Danish by local performers, and one can only imagine that much of what we might call 'the Italian spirit' in these works was lost in translation, especially since little attention was given to virtuosic improvisation.

34. Andersen, *Levnedsbogen*, 65.

35. J.M. Thiele, *Af min Livs Aarbøger 1795–1826* (Copenhagen, 1873), 204.

36. Andersen, *Mit Livs Eventyr*, vol. 1, 65, and *Levnedsbogen*, 66–67.

37. Copenhagen: The Royal Library, Collin Manuscript Collection.

38. For example, in the story 'Auntie' and the novel *Lucky Peer*, Andersen recaptured the atmosphere of the Royal Theater's Ballet school as it must have been in the early 1820s. A number of articles have appeared in recent years concerning Andersen's years with the theater, most notably: Povl Ingerslev-Jensen, 'Statist Andersen: Bidrag til en teaterdagbog 1818–1822,' *Anderseniana* (1971): 137–87 and Tove Barfoed Møller, 'Christian Andersen og Det Kongelige Theater 1819–22. Ny- og nærlæsninger af documenter, breve, levnedsbeskrivelser og andet materiale der belyser hans forhold til teatret i denne periode,' *Anderseniana* (1991): 23–54.

39. *Røverborgen*, like all Kuhlau's operas, was a singspiel with spoken dialogue. The libretto was written by the well-known Danish poet Adam Oehlenschläger. The première took place at the Royal Theater on 26 May 1814, and the work not only meant a breakthrough for the composer, but it was also understood as a renewal of the traditional Danish opera repertoire. Its enormous success was undiminished for a long time, and the opera was performed nearly every year of Kuhlau's lifetime. With its ninety-one performances up to 1879, it was second only to *Elverhøj*, Kuhlau's most often performed dramatic work.

40. Premièred at the Royal Theater in 1809.

41. On 8 October 1820 Claus Schall conducted the première of *Der Freischütz* Overture at the Royal Theater in Copenhagen. As John Warrack explains in the second edition of his book *Carl Maria von Weber* (Cambridge: Cambridge University Press, 1976), 244, fn. 2: 'Max Maria evidently knew nothing of this, for he describes a subsequent Dresden performance as the première.' For further documentation of Weber's visit to Copenhagen see: Erik Abrahamsen, 'Carl Maria von Weber in Copenhagen,' *The Chesterian* (June 1926). For descriptions of some of these operas and a general overview of the Royal Theater at this time see: Gorm Busk, 'Friedrich Kuhlau's operas and theatre music

and their performances at the Royal Theatre in Copenhagen (1814–1830): A mirror of European music drama and a glimpse of the Danish opera tradition,' *Musik og Forskning* 21 (1996): 93–127.

42. Premièred in Paris at the Comédie-Italienne on 14 January 1789. The libretto was written by Benoît-Joseph Marsollier des Vivetières. Marsollier's plot forms part of a common strain of sentimental 'humanity' operas that proved to be popular in Denmark during the first half of the nineteenth century.

43. Andersen, *Mit Livs Eventyr*, vol. 1, 66. In *Levnedsbogen*, 78, Andersen tells the same story and identifies the singer who ridiculed him as Johan Daniel Bauer.

44. Vincenzo Galeotti, an Italian choreographer, was renowned internationally for his pantomime ballets. He served as the head of the Royal Theater's Ballet School from 1775 to 1816 and staged over fifty ballets there. Today he is generally considered to have created the Danish ballet's illustrious tradition that August Bournonville so successfully cultivated.

45. This topic was first presented as an opéra-comique called *Nina, ou La folle par amour*, with text by Marsollier des Vivetières and music by Nicolas-Marie Dalayrac (1786, Paris).

46. Andersen, *Levnedsbogen*, 78.

47. The ballet premièred on 12 April 1821.

48. Andersen, *Mit Livs Eventyr*, vol. 1, 67.

49. H.C. Andersen, *Fodreise fra Holmens Canal til Østpynten af Amager i Aarene 1828 og 1829* (Copenhagen, 1940), 43.

50. Andersen was in good company; the other demons included the dancers Fredstrup, Lundgreen, Villeneuve, Poulsen, Hamberg, Aagaard, and Scharff. See Jan Neiiendam, 'H.C. Andersen og Hofteatret,' *Anderseniana* 2 II:4 (1954): 3.

51. August Bournonville saw Andersen's performance and made special note of it twenty-four years later in *My Theater Life*, trans. Patricia N. McAndrew (London, 1974), 443.

52. H.C. Andersen's theatrical diary, Copenhagen: The Royal Library, Collin Manuscript Collection.

53. Andersen, *Levnedsbogen*, 79.

54. Ibid., 77.

55. This piece was made famous a century later by Carl Nielsen's opera of the same name.

56. *Johanne Montfaucon. Tragedy i 5 Akter. Oversat med adskillige Forandringer og forøget med Chor ved N. T. Bruun* (Copenahgen, 1802).

57. Andersen, *Mit Livs Eventyr*, vol. 1, 73. As Marker, *Hans Christian Andersen and the Romantic Theater*, 31, explains: 'Although only a single scene of this play, published in A.P. Liunges' magazine *Harpen* (xxxvii, 1822), survives, the melodramatic dialogue in the robbers' den gives ample evidence of the drama's exaggerated *sturm und drang* tendencies.'

58. Andersen, *Levnedsbogen*, 90.

59. Andersen, *Mit Livs Eventyr*, vol. 1, 76–77.

60. The most thorough descriptions, published in English, of Andersen's school years can are found in Wullschlager, 55–76; and Elias Bredsdorf, 47–68.

61. Andersen, *Levnedsbogen*, 160–61.

62. Andersen, *Mit Livs Eventyr*, vol. 1, 100.

63. Ibid., 101. Andersen described this work as 'a humorous, peculiar book – a sort of fanciful arabesque that nonetheless fully revealed my complete personality and point of view at that time.'

64. Kristi Planck Johnson, 'Hans Christian Andersen's Educational Roots Through his Own Eyes,' *Hans Christian Andersen: A Poet in Time*, 163–72.

65. *H.C. Andersens Samlede Skrifter*, (Copenhagen: Rietzels Forlag, 1877), vol. 6, 163.

66. As Wullschlager, 84, aptly explains in her description of *A Walking Tour*, '... world literature is also represented as a defeated army of tired and worn-out volumes marching to Amager, followed by ambulances, stretchers and hearses, with Amager a mock Pantheon or poetic recycling ground, delivering fresh cabbage heads, or transitory works of literature, for consumption in the capital.'

67. Andersen, *Mit Livs Eventyr*, vol. 1, 101.

68. All musical improvisations contain a point of departure as the obligatory basis of performance. Eighteenth-century method books explained this aspect of musical improvisation as part of the standard training for any musician. For example, in C.P.E. Bach's *Essay on the True Art of Keyboard Playing*, first published in 1753, we are told: "the key to successful improvisations ... is a solid knowledge of progressions and consistency of harmonic rhythm." Improvisations could also be constructed around a given theme or melody. In the late eighteenth and early nineteenth centuries, improvisations generally fell into two categories: free improvisations that combined fragments of one or more pre-composed melodies – these works were generally given titles such as fantasy, capriccio, or impromptu; and improvised embellishments within a larger, pre-composed work – such as an improvised cadenza within a concerto.

69. This definition itself is one of the 451 'fragments' published by Schlegel.

70. E.T.A. Hoffmann's *Fantasy Pieces in Callot's Manner: Pages from the Diary of a Traveling Romantic*, trans. Joseph M. Hayse (Schenectady, NY: Union College Press, 1996), 12–13.

71. Ibid., 16.

72. Ibid., 262–64.

73. When the first installment of *Fantasy Pieces* was published in 1815, Hoffmann insisted his name be kept off the title page because 'it should become known to the world only through a successful musical composition.' See Joseph M. Hayse, 'Introduction' to E.T.A. Hoffmann's *Fantasy Pieces in Callot's Manner: Pages from the Diary of a Traveling Romantic*, xi.

74. *H.C. Andersens Samlede Skrifter*, vol. 6, 177.

75. Ibid., 178.

76. Michael, Bønnesen, 'Den Kongelige Opera,' *Det Kongelige Theater: Historie og repertoire* (Copenhagen: Kongelige Theater, 1995–96): 46–57.

77. With the help of his wife, Nissen wrote the first authoritative Mozart biography (published posthumously in 1828). For studies concerning Mozart reception in Denmark see: P. Branscombe, *W.A. Mozart: Die Zauberflöte* (Cambridge: Cambridge University Press, 1991); Inger Sørensen, 'Et Mozartportræt in Danmark: Løsning på en gåde,' *Magasin fra Det Kongelige Bibliotek* 7, no. 4 (March 1993): 55–63; Carsten E. Hatting, 'Bemærkninger til Mozarts biografi,' *Musik og Forskning* 11 (1985–86): 5–41, *Mozart og Danmark* (Copenhagen: Engstrøms & Sødrings Musikbibliotek, 1991), and 'Mozart und Dänemark,' *Mozart-Jahrbuch* (1991): 371–79.

78. J.L. Heiberg, *Maanedskrift for Litteratur* 1 (1829): 169–72.

79. Wullschlager, 84. He had also gained a level of notoriety for his successful courtship with the Royal Theater's new up-and-coming star, seventeen-year-old Johanne Louise Pätges.

80. Heiberg's version of the vaudeville differed from the French model produced by Eduard Scribe. Although both used melodies borrowed from popular songs, Scribe regarded the songs of little importance, while Heiberg considered them meaningful 'decorations on the dialogue.' Consequently, the vaudeville style established in Denmark by Heiberg featured extensive musical numbers. For a more detailed description of the vaudeville in Denmark see Marker, *Hans Christian Andersen and the Romantic Theater*, 32–41.

81. H. C. Andersen, *Digte* (Copenhagen, 1830). The volume bears the date 1830, as was the practice at the time for volumes appearing in December of the previous year.

82. *H.C. Andersen Samlede digte*, Johan de Mylius, ed. (Copenhagen: Aschehoug, 2000), 83.

83. Andersen probably first read the play in a Danish translation published by his former teacher, Meisling: *Dramatiske Eventyr af Carlo Gozzi*.

84. Søren Sørensen, 'En dansk Guldalder-opera: Den musikalske karakteristik i Hartmanns *Liden Kirsten*,' *Guldalderstudier. Festskrift til Gustav Albeck den 5. juni 1966*, Henning Høirup, Aage Jørgensen og Peter Skautrup, eds. (Aarhus, DK: Universitetsforlaget): 219–33; Ulrik Skouenborg, 'E.T.A. Hoffmann's Idee der romantischen Oper unf J.P.E. Hartmann's dänische Oper *Ravnen* (H.C. Andersen nach Gozzi's *Corvo*),' *Carlo Gozzi: Letteratura e musica Roma* (Rome: Bulzoni, 1997): 229–42; Inger Sørensen, 'H.C. Andersen og J.P.E. Hartmann: Et livslangt venskab,' *Anderseniana* (1997): 5–40, and *J.P.E. Hartmann og hans kreds 1780–1900*, 3 vols. (Copenhagen: Museum Tusculanum, 1999).

85. Molbech's complete report, dated 22 August 1830, is presented in Gustav Hetsch, *H.C. Andersen og Musikken* (Copenhagen: H. Hagerups Forlag, 1930), 15–16.

86. Ibid., 16–17.

87. Ibid., 17 (dated 24 August 1830). In other words, if the music is good, the opera will be a success despite the questionable quality of the text. In nineteenth-century Denmark, operas were clearly about the music, not the libretto.

88. In his preface to the published libretto, Andersen wrote: 'I have tried to include the entire novel in this brief theater evening and have used everything I thought could be used.' For a study of Walter Scott operas see: Jerome Mitchell, *The Walter Scott Operas. An Analysis of the Operas Based on the Works of Sir Walter Scott* (Alabama: The University of Alabama Press, 1977) where Andersen's *Bruden fra Lammermoor* is discussed on pages 127–36. Articles focusing primarily on Andersen's Walter Scott libretti include: Tove Barfoed Møller, 'H.C. Andersens Scott-libretti i samtids- og nutidsbelysning.' *Anderseniana* (1996): 11–24 and Erik Sønderholm, 'Hans Christian Andersen als Opernlibrettist. Eine kritische Untersuchung.' *Anderseniana* (1996): 25–48.

89. Hetsch, 18–19 (2 March 1831).

90. Ibid., 19 (4 March 1831).

91. *Bruden fra Lammermoor* was first performed 5 May; *Ravnen* appeared in print on 26 October and was premièred at the Royal Theater three days later 'on the occasion of the Birthday of Her Gracious Majesty, the Queen, and Her Royal Highness, the Crown Princess.'

92. The production of *Ravnen* was most notable for its lavish scenery and costumes and rich musical score. Although reviews in 1832 criticized Andersen's treatment of the *commedia dell'arte* figures, the publication of selections from the opera in 1840 led to a six-page review in the *Neue Zeitschrift für Musik* written by Robert Schumann that generously praised both the music and text.

93. *Kenilworth* was one of Scott's most frequently adapted novels. Before Andersen's text appeared, no fewer than twelve stage versions had been produced in England, and in 1825 Scribe and Auber produced an opéra-comique in Paris entitled *Le Château de Kenilworth*. For a discussion of Andersen's setting see Mitchell, 222–29.

94. Perhaps the weakest element of the production of *Bruden fra Lammermoor* was the fact that the lead character, Lucie, sang no solo arias. As Marker, *H.C. Andersen and the Romantic Theater*, 42–43, explains: Andersen had designed the leading role for Anna Wexschall, a well-established actress who, unfortunately, did not possess a strong singing voice. As a result, he was forced to avoid arias in Lucie's part and maintain many of the

most dramatic scenes, such as Edgar's entrance at the wedding, with dialogue alone. A reviewer for *Den danske Bi* (18 November 1832) was particularly critical of this flaw in the production.

95. Hetsch, 22–23.

96. Ibid., 23.

97. Ibid., 32.

98. C. St. A. Bille and Nicolaj Bøgh, *Breve fra H.C. Andersen* (Copenhagen: Aschehoug, 2000), vol. 1, 89.

99. Hetsch, 33–34.

100. Ibid., 35.

CHAPTER 2: THE IMPROVISOR

1. Bille and Bøgh, *Breve fra H.C. Andersen*, 98–100 (Henriette Wulff, 16 February 1833).

2. Ibid., 59–60 (Letter to B. S. Ingemann, 31 December 1830).

3. Ibid., 62–63 (Letter to C.H. Lorenzen, 18 February 1831).

4. For information concerning Heine's influence in Denmark see Sven H. Rossel, 'Heinrich Heine I Danmark – med særlig henblik på Buch der Lieder,' *Der nahe Norden. Otto Oberholzer zum 65. Geburtstag. Eine Festschrift.* (Frankfurt am Main: Peter Lang, 1985), 99–110.

5. For a general study of Andersen's documentation of his travels see: Kirsten Maegaard, 'Hans Christian Andersen's travel album,' *Fontes artis musicæ* 42, no. 1 (January–March 1995): 82–84; for his travels in Italy specifically see: Hans Edvard Nørregård-Nielsen, *Jeg saae det Land: H.C. Andersens rejseskitser fra Italien* (Copenhagen: Gyldendal, 1990).

6. *H.C. Andersen's Dagbøger*, ed. Helga Vang Lauridsen (Copenhagen: Det Danske Sprog- og Litteraturselskab, 1971) vol. 1, 129.

7. The performance of this work as *The Last Judgement*, at the Norwich Festival of 1830, laid the foundations of Spohr's reputation in England as one of the greatest composers of the age. Among his other notable compositions in these years were the first two of his four double string quartets, the splendid String Quintet in B minor, several string quartets and concertos, and the Third Symphony.

8. Due to political disturbances in 1830, the opera theater in Kassel had been closed for two years. When Andersen arrived, Spohr was in the process of re-establishing the city's opera season and was eager to find fresh talent.

9. Andersen, *Dagbøger*, vol. 1, 129.

10. Andersen must have made a strong impression on Spohr, for the composer worked hard at getting Andersen and Hartmann's opera *Ravnen* performed in Kassel, and it was even scheduled to be performed on the Duke's birthday.

11. Ibid.

12. Ibid.

13. Andersen, *Mit Livs Eventyr*, vol. 1, 130.

14. 'Canon zu 6 Stimmen,' now in Copenhagen: Royal Library, Andersen collection, Andersen Album I. A facsimile of this piece is found in *H.C. Andersen Album 1–V*, ed. Kåre Olsen, Helga Vang Lauridsen, and Kirsten Weber, (Copenahgen: Lademann, 1980), facsimile vol., 31.

15. Andersen, *Dagbøger*, vol. 1, 129.

16. Ibid., vol. 1, 138. For a facsimile of the album leaf see *H.C. Andersen Album 1–V*, facsimile vol., 79.

17. Bille and Bøgh, *Breve fra H.C. Andersen* (Letter to Ludvig Müller, 14 May 1833).

18. Andersen, *Mit Livs Eventyr*, vol.1, 147–8.

19. For further information on Agnete and the Merman see Thomas Bredsdorff, 'Nogen skrev et sagn om 'Agnete og Havmanden,' hvem, hvornår og hvorfor?' *Fund og Forskning* 30 (1991): 67–80; Peter Meisling, *Agnetes Latter*, (Copenhagen: 1988) and 'De sympatiske Havmænd – En lille replik til Thomas Bredsdorff,' *Fund og Forskning* 30 (1991): 81–86; Iørn Piø, *Nye veje til Folkevisen II: DgFT 38*, Agnete og havmanden (Stockholm, 1970). Also, Søren Kierkegaard analyzed this ballad in his philosophical work Fear and Trembling.

20. Hetsch, 55.

21. Andersen, *Mit Livs Eventyr*, vol. 1, 135.

22. Andersen, *Dagbøger*, vol. 1, 144.

23. Andersen, *Mit Livs Eventyr*, vol. 1, 135–6.

24. In the novel *Only a Fiddler* Andersen recalls a production of *Robert le Diable* that he saw in Paris in June 1833: 'The moon shines into the gloomy hall where crumbling grave monuments stand. At the stroke of midnight the candles in the ancient brass chandeliers suddenly begin to glow, the tombs open, and the dead nuns rise up. By the hundreds they raise themselves from the graveyard and hover; they seem not to touch the ground.... Suddenly the shrouds fall, they all stand, fully naked, and a bacchanal begins.' In a letter to Ludvig Müller dated 29 June 1833 Andersen included a similar description, adding 'It could drive one mad!' (Bille and Bøgh, *Breve fra H.C. Andersen*, 108).

25. Andersen, *Dagbøger*, vol. 1, 147.

26. Andersen, *Mit Livs Eventyr*, vol. 1, 133.

27. Andersen, *Dagbøger*, vol. 1, 146–47.

28. Ibid., 148–9 (17 May 1833).

29. Bille and Bøgh, *Breve fra H.C. Andersen*, 107. Andersen's later account in *Mit Livs Eventyr*, vol. 1, 136, gives a markedly different version of the encounter: 'One day I entered Europe Litteraire, a kind of Parisian "Atheneum" that Paul Duport had told me about. A little Jewish man came toward me. "I hear you are a Dane," he said, "I am a German: Danes and Germans are brothers, therefore I offer you my hand!" I asked for his name, and he said: "Heinrich Heine!" – the poet whom I ... admired so much, and who had so entirely expressed my own thoughts and feelings in his songs. There was no man I could have wished more to see and meet with than he, and so I told him.'

30. John Daverio, 'Heinrich Heine,' *New Grove Dictionary of Music and Musicians*, ed. Stanley Sadie (London: Macmillan, 2002).

31. Cf. George F. Peters, *The Poet as Provocateur: Heinrich Heine and his Critics* (Rochester, NY: Camden House, 2000), 23.

32. Andersen, *Mit Livs Eventyr*, vol. 1, 137.

33. Bille and Bøgh, *Breve fra H.C. Andersen*, 112–14.

34. Andersen, *Mit Livs Eventyr*, vol. 1, 137.

35. Victor Hugo, *Les rayons et les ombres* (1840). Although Hugo is better known to the English-speaking world as a novelist, it was as a poet that he broke new ground, and wherein he passed on much of his philosophy about the arts. Hugo believed that the poet's purpose should be two-fold: to echo universal sentiment by revealing his own feelings, uniting the voices of mankind, nature and history; and to guide the reader: 'faire flamboyer l'avenir' – to lead the way. In his epic, *La Légende des Siècles* (1859) he attempted to depict, by reference to historical events, humanity's struggle to emerge from obscurity into enlightenment.

36. Andersen, *Mit Livs Eventyr*, vol. 1, 137.

37. Hetsch, 55.

38. Andersen, *Dagbøger*, vol.1, 181 (19 September 1833).

39. Ibid., 185 (21 September 1833).

40. Ibid., 192–193 (30 September 1833).

41. Ibid., 287 (25 January 1834).

42. Ibid., 192–93 (30 September 1833).

43. Ibid., 208–209 (9 October 1833).

44. Ibid., 210 (10 October 1833).

45. Ibid., 218 (21 October 1833).

46. Ibid., 225 (30 October 1833).

47. Ibid., 227 (5 November 1833).

48. Ibid., 263–264 (29 December 1833).

49. Ibid., 349 (11 March 1834).

50. Ibid., 196 (2 October 1833).

51. Ibid., 253 (16 December 1833). For a comprehensive overview of Heiberg's criticism see Niels Birger Wamberg., *H.C. Andersen og Heiberg: Åndsfrænder og Åndsfjender*, (Copenhagen: Politikens Forlag, 1971), 70–82.

52. As Wullschlager, 137, explains, *The Improvisatore* was the first of many fictional autobiographies that Andersen would write over the next forty years. 'The protagonist, Antonio, is a poor Roman boy from the slums with no father, an indulgent mother and an eccentric, terrifying uncle Peppo. Antonio is a promising singer with a special gift for improvisation, and his talent attracts the interest of the eminent Borghese family, who become his patrons. He is educated at a Jesuit college run by the tyrannical Habbas Dahdah, and eventually, after much suffering and loneliness ... he achieves his social success and romantic happiness in Naples.'

53. Andersen, *Dagbøger*, vol. 1, 215–16 (17 October 1833).

54. Ibid., 247–48 (8 December 1833).

55. Bille and Bøgh, *Breve fra H.C. Andersen*, 168–74 (Letter to Signe Lassøe begun 18 March 1834 and completed 8 April).

56. Andersen, *Dagbøger*, vol. 1, 416–34. He even began reading Dante's *La Divina Commedia*, but appears to have only gotten through the first two parts. For a study of *Corinne* and its image of the improvisatore tradition see the introduction in: Madame de Staël, *Corinne, or Italy*, trans. Sylvia Raphael, (Oxford: Oxford University Press, 1998).

57. *H.C. Andersen og Henriette Wulff. En Brevveksling*, vol. 1, 177–78 (Letter to Henriette Wulff dated 15 May 1834).

58. Steven Paul Scher, 'Theory in Literature, Analysis in Music: What Next?,' *Yearbook of Comparative and General Literature* 32 (1983): 51.

59. Andersen, *Dagbøger*, vol. 1, 418.

60. Bille and Bøgh, *Breve fra H.C. Andersen*, 175–80 (Letter to Ludvig Müller, 16 May 1834).

61. Ibid., 182–186 (Letter to Henriette Wulff, 17 June 1834).

62. Ibid., 199–203 (Letter to Henriette Wulff, 26 September 1834).

63. Ibid., 228–30 (20 April 1835).

64. Wullschlager, 139.

65. Anonymous (F.C. Olsen), 'Anmeldelse af H.C. Andersen: Improvisatoren og O.T.,' *Maanedsskrift for Litteratur*, 18 (1837): 61–87.

66. Andersen, *Mit Livs Eventyr*, vol. 1, 193.

67. H.C. Andersen, *Improvisatoren* (Copenhagen, 1835). The edition I am quoting from was edited by Mogens Brøndsted (Copenhagen: Det danske Sprog- og Litteratursel-skab, 1991), 99.

68. H.C. Andersen, 'Italiensk Musik, Sang og Theatervæsen,' *Søndagsblad* (8 February 1835): 91–94 and (15 February 1835): 104–12.

69. Ibid., 93.

70. Ibid., 110–11.

71. Bille and Bøgh, *Breve fra H.C. Andersen*, 239–41 (Letter from H.C. Andersen to Thomas Overskou dated 8 January 1836). Andersen was so disgusted with the outcome of *Festival at Kenilworth* that he claimed he would never write another opera libretto – a vow he, fortunately, broke several years later. In Andersen's mind it had become clear that a librettist in Denmark was nothing more than a slave to the will of the composer, and he wanted nothing more to do with it.

72. For a fuller description of the work's reception, see Marker, 44.

73. For a further discussion of the origins of the Copenhagen Davidsbund see Celenza, *The Early Works of Niels W. Gade*, 13–17.

74. Dagmar Gade, *Niels W. Gade: Optegnelser og Breve* (Copenhagen: Gyldendalske Boghandels Forlag, 1892), 16–17.

75. Felix Gade, unpublished biography of Niels W. Gade, chapter 3, Copenhagen: The Royal Library, Gade Collection.

76. Robert Schumann, *Neue Zeitschrift für Musik* 2 (2 January 1835): 3.

77. In *The Improvisatore* Antonio succeeds in a similar challenge, winning his freedom from a band of robbers after performing an improvisation for them.

78. H.C. Andersen, *Vandring gjennem Opera-Galleriet* in *H.C. Andersens Samlede Skrifter* (Copenhagen: H.C. Reitzel, 1878),vol. 10, 85.

79. Ibid., 89.

80. Ibid., 96.

81. Andersen, *Mit Livs Eventyr*, vol. 1, 295.

82. Bille and Bøgh, *Breve fra H.C. Andersen*, 475–78 (Letter to B.S. Ingemann, 20 November 1843).

83. Clara Schumann commented on Copenhagen's obsession with Italian opera when she visited the city in 1842. In a letter to her husband dated 28 March she wrote: 'Yesterday I lost faith in the taste of the people in Copenhagen. Let me tell you, they should send that Italian opera to the bottom of the deepest sea, so that it won't ever come to the surface again.... I didn't hear a single note that wasn't off key; I am not exaggerating. And then one of the most prominent ladies comes here today and tries to persuade me for an hour that the opera is divine; when she saw that I wasn't convinced she said, "My dear, don't be so one-sided; let your feelings be your guide, too, not only your head." The best thing here is to keep your mouth shut.' And on 2 April she commented on an upcoming concert: 'I am not looking forward to it since all the Italians are invited and I will be hearing a lot of bad music. They are crazy about the Italians here.' *The Complete Correspondence of Clara and Robert Schumann*, ed. Eva Weissweiler (New York: Peter Lang, 2002), vol.1, 313 and 320.

84. Throughout the nineteenth century, performers at the Royal Theater in Copenhagen were expected to supply their own costumes for theatrical performances. This was especially true of touring artists making special appearances. For a more detailed description of theater practices during Andersen's lifetime see Marker, *Hans Christian Andersen and the Romantic Theater*.

85. Bille and Bøgh, *Breve fra H.C. Andersen*, 475–78.

86. H.C Andersen, 'Nattergalen,' in *H.C. Andersens Samlede Skrifter* (Copenhagen: H.C. Reitzel, 1878) vol. 13, 224–34.

87. Ibid., 232–33.

88. Helga Vang Lauridsen and Kirsten Weber, eds., *H.C. Andersens almanakker 1833–75* (Copenhagen: Det danske Sprog- og Litteraturselskab/G.E.C. Gad, 1990), 109–10.

89. This was a message that Andersen had expressed earlier, although not with regard to music specifically, in 'The Emperor's New Clothes.'

90. This is a reference to the three-act comedy *Grev Létorières Proces* by librettist Jean-François-Alfred Bayard and Guillaume Dumanoir that was performed at the Royal Theater on 1 and 8 July 1842.

91. Wilhelm Holst played the role of the Merman in the première of *Agnete and the Merman*.

92. The original letter is housed in Copenhagen: Royal Library, Ny kgl. Saml. 1716 4°.

93. For a thorough study of the ballad in early nineteenth-century Denmark see: Niels Martin Jensen, *Den danske romance 1800–1850 og dens musikalske forudsætninger* (Copenhagen: Gyldendal, 1964).

94. For a further discussion of folk tune influence see Celenza, *The Early Works of Niels W. Gade*, 115–17.

95. Andersen, *Dagbøger*, vol. 1, 61–62.

96. 20 April and 2 May 1843.

97. Johan Ludvig Heiberg, *Intelligensblade*, no. 30 (1843).

98. *H.C. Andersens brevveksling med Edvard og Henriette Collin*, C. Behrend and H. Topsøe-Jensen, eds. (Copenhagen: Levin & Munkagaards Forlag, 1933), vol. 1, 339–40.

CHAPTER 3: THE VIRTUOSO

1. H. Topsøe-Jensen, *H.C. Andersen og Henriette Wulff: En Brevveksling* (Copenhagen, 1959–60), vol. 1, 223.

2. *H.C. Andersens Brevveksling med Henriette Hanck 1830–46*, Svend Larsen, ed. *Anderseniana* (1941–46): vol. 10, 165.

3. *H.C. Andersen Album 1–V*, vol. 1, 445 (12 September 1835).

4. H.C. Andersen, *O.T.* in *Romaner og Rejseskildringer* (Copenhagen: Gyldendal, 1943), vol. 2, 133.

5. Bille and Bøgh, *Breve fra H.C. Andersen*, 249–252.

6. F.W.J. Schelling, *Philosophy of Art* (Minneapolis: Minnesota University Press, 1988).

7. For a more detailed discussion of the influence in Copenhagen of foreign musical periodicals, especially Schumann's *Neue Zeitshrift für Musik*, see Celenza, *The Early Works of Niels W. Gade*, 11–14.

8. Andersen, *Mit Livs Eventyr*, vol. 1, 203.

9. H.C. Andersen, *Kun en Spillemand* in *Romaner og Rejsekildringer* III (Copenhagen: Gyldendal, 1944), 284–85.

10. Andersen, *Mit Livs Eventyr*, vol. 1, 203.

11. Bille and Bøgh, *Breve fra H.C. Andersen*, 274–76 (11 February 1837).

12. *H.C. Andersens Brevveksling med Henriette Hanck 1830–46*, *Anderseniana* (1941–46): 195.

13. Andersen, *Mit Livs Eventyr*, vol. 1, 204.

14. For a translation of the complete text see: Søren Kierkegaard, *Early Polemical Writings*, Julia Watkin, trans. (Princeton: Princeton University Press, 1990), 12–23.

15. Andersen, *Mit Livs Eventyr*, vol. 1, 284.

16. Bille and Bøgh, *Breve til H. C. Andersen* (Copenhagen: C.A. Reitzels Forlag, 1877). 285. As Kofoed, 234, explains, with this passage Ingemann presented Andersen with the basic metaphor for his most famous tale, 'The Ugly Duckling' (Den grimme Ælling).

17. Andersen obviously held no grudge against Kierkegaard for his critical remarks; in 1848 he sent him a new volume of his tales with the inscription: 'Dear Mr. Kierkegaard, *Either* [i.e. whether] you like my little ones *Or* you do not like them, they arrive without *Fear and Trembling*, and that in itself is something. Sincerely, the Author.' This is an obvious pun using the title of two books published by Kierkegaard in 1843 – books that

Andersen had no doubt read. See Jens S. Bork 'Andersen – Kierkegaard: To boggaver.' *Anderseniana* (1994): 51–54.

18. Bille and Bøgh, *Breve Fra H.C. Andersen*, 316–19.

19. Ibid., 336–38.

20. Ibid.

21. Ibid.

22. Ibid.

23. Ibid., 339–40.

24. Ibid.

25. Ibid., 340–42.

26. This was the first of many biographical articles and poems he would write about virtuoso musicians for Danish publications.

27. See *H.C. Andersen Album I–V*, facsimile vol., 127 and 136. Andersen wrote a poem about Rieffel that appeared in *Portefeuillon* on 10 November 1839.

28. Here Andersen is referring to the E.T.A. Hoffmann character.

29. Andersen, *Dagbøger*, vol. 2, 46–47.

30. Ibid., 62.

31. Hetsch, 96.

32. Andersen, *En Digters Bazar* in *Romaner og Rejseskildringer*, vol. 4, 352–53.

33. Andersen, *Dagbøger*, vol. 2, 249 (11 June 1841). This reference is to the J. Strauss, Senior (1804--49).

34. Andersen, *En Digters Bazar* in *Romaner og Rejseskildringer*, vol. 4, 352

35. Bille and Bøgh, *Breve fra H.C. Andersen*, 373–76.

36. Andersen, *Mit Livs Eventyr*, vol. 1, 232.

37. *H.C. Andersens Dagbøger*, vol. 2, 51–52 (11 November 1840).

38. Bille and Bøgh, *Breve fra H.C. Andersen*, 414–15 (28 November 1840).

39. Edvard Collin, *H.C. Andersen og det Collinske Huus* (Copenhagen, 1862), 117.

40. *H.C. Andersens Dagbøger*, vol. 2, 264.

41. Andersen, *En Digters Bazar*, 359.

42. *H.C. Andersen Samlede Digte*, 410.

43. For a general introduction to Andersen's activities as a journalist see: Erik Svendsen, 'Hans Christian Andersen – An Untimely Journalist.' *Hans Christian Andersen: A Poet in Time*, 485–500.

44. Susan Bernstein, *Virtuosity of the Nineteenth Century: Performing Music and Language in Heine, Liszt, and Baudelaire* (Stanford: Stanford University Press, 1998), 58.

45. Heinrich Heine, *Sämtliche Schriften*, ed. Klaus Briegleb (Munich: Carl Hansler Verlag, 1971), vol. 3, 353. Translation in Bernstein, 62.

46. Andersen, *En Digters Bazar*, 10–13. Lawrence Kramer, *Musical Meaning, Toward a Critical History* (Berkeley: University of California Press, 2002), 68–69, 86–89, describes Andersen's narrative of Liszt's performance as an 'ideal type' and includes a fascinating discussion of its place in the 'virtuoso public sphere.' Similarly, Bernstein, 110, addresses Andersen's awareness of the 'uniqueness and specificity of [Liszt's] bodily presence.'

47. Bille and Bøgh, *Breve fra H.C. Andersen*, 443–45.

48. Johan de Mylius, 'Hans Christian Andersen and the Music World,' in *Hans Christian Andersen: Danish Writer and Citizen of the World* (Amsterdam: Rodopi, 1996), 196.

49. Andersen, *En Digters Bazar*, 360–61.

50. Mylius, 'Hans Christian Andersen and the Music World,' 197.

51. Weissweiler, vol. 3, 298.

52. Ibid., 301.

53. Ibid., 315.

54. Ibid., 320. Letter from Clara to Robert dated 2 April 1842.

55. In her letters to Robert, Clara commented on 7 and 11 April that Andersen was 'deeply in love' with her, an assumption that was supported in a letter written by her companion Marie Garlichs on 20 April (Weissweiler, 330, 337, 350). Clara also informed Robert of his fame in Copenhagen. On 22 March she wrote: 'You have no idea how people here regret that they can't meet you. Everyone keeps asking about you; everyone knows your journal, and even if they don't know your compositions, they know your name.' (Weissweiler, 298).

56. Schumann is correct about the translation. Chamisso's German translation is close to the original, but not exact. Consequently, I am including Andersen's original poem and a literal English translation. Med dæmpede hvirvler trommerne gå/ – Ak, skal vi da aldrig til stedet nå/ at han kan få ro i sin kiste?/ – Jeg tror mit hjerte vil briste!/ Jeg havde i verden en eneste ven,/ Ham er det, man bringer til døden hen,/ Med klingende spil gennem gaden,/ Og jeg er med i paraden!/ For sidste gang skuer han nu Guds sol,/ – der sidder han alt på dødens stol;/ de binder ham fast til pælen,/ –forbarm dig Gud over sjælen!/ På engang sigter de alle ni,/ De otte skyder jo rent forbi;/ De rysted' på hånden af smerte,/ – kun jeg traf midt i hans hjerte!

With muffled whirls the drums go by/ – Oh, will we never get to the place/ where he can find peace in his coffin?/ – I believe my heart will break!/ I have in this world a single friend,/ It is he who is being led to death,/ With sonorous playing down the street,/ And I am part of the parade!/ For the last time he now sees God's sun,/ – there he sits, everything on death's chair;/ They bind him tightly to the pole,/ – May God take pity on the soul!/ All at once all nine took aim,/ The eight, however, completely missed;/ Their hands shook with grief,/ – only I hit directly in his heart!

57. Bille and Bøgh, *Breve til H. C. Andersen*, 550–51.

58. Andersen, *Dagbøger*, vol. 2, 416–17.

59. Ibid., 417.

60. Bille and Bøgh, *Breve til H.C. Andersen*, 551–52.

61. At this point Gade was living in Leipzig permanently and serving as Felix Mendelssohn's assistant conductor of the Gewandhaus orchestra.

62. Ibid., 552–53.

63. Andersen, *De to Baronesser* in *H.C. Andersens Samlede Skrifter* (Copenhagen: C.A. Reitzel, 1877), vol. 5, 31.

64. Ibid., 32–33.

65. Ibid., 37.

CHAPTER 4: THE POET, THE PIANIST, AND THE PATRON

1. These contemporary accounts were written by figures such as George Eliot, Joachim Raff, and Richard Wagner, to name just a few. See Alan Walker, *Franz Liszt: The Weimar Years 1848–1861* (Ithaca: Cornell University Press, 1989); George Eliot, *Essays*, ed. Thomas Pinney (New York, 1963), 83–95; James Deaville, 'A 'Daily Diary of the Weimar Dream:' Joachim Raff's unpublished letters to Doris Genast,' *Liszt and His World* (Stuyvesant, NY: Pendragon, 1998), 181–216; Charles Suttoni, 'Liszt and Wagner's Tannhäuser,' *New Light on Liszt and His Music: Essays in Honor of Alan Walker's 65th birthday* (Stuyvesant, NY: Pendragon, 1997), 17–51.

2. Andersen, *Dagbøger*, vol. 2, 399–400 (26 June 1844).

3. For a general study of life at court during this period see: Angelika Pöthe, *Schloss Ettersburg: Weimars Geselligkeit und kulturelles Leben im 19. Jahrhundert* (Weimar, 1995).

4. Andersen, *Dagbøger*, vol. 2, 401.

5. Ibid., 402. Andersen preserved these leaves, along with other tokens of his visit to Weimar, in his scrapbook, and referred to them and the linden tree branch in his correspondence.

6. Ivy York Möller-Christensen and Ernst Möller-Cristensen, *Mein edler theurer Großherzog! Briefwechsel zwischen Hans Christian Andersen and Carl Alexander von Sachsen-Weimar-Eisenach* (Göttingen: Wallstein Verlag, 1998), 7, and Ivy Möller-Christensen, 'My Dearly Beloved Grand Duke ...' *Hans Christian Andersen: A Poet in Time*, 177–188.

7. Letter dated 26 September 1844. Originally titled *Mulatten* (The Mulatto), this play was inspired by a story of Fanny Reybaud called *Les Épaves* (1838). Set in Africa, the theme of the play is a common one for Andersen: the life of an outcast. The truly significant feature of the work is Andersen's bold portrayal of the reckless, sensual passion of one of the principle female characters. This combined with Andersen's vivid descriptions of exotic locales no doubt drew Carl Alexander's attention to the piece.

8. Möller-Christensen, *Briefwechsel*, 10.

9. Ibid., 17–18.

10. H. C. Andersen, 'The Bell,' *H.C. Andersens Samlede Skrifter*, 2nd edition (Copenhagen: C.A Reitzels Forlag, 1879), vol. 13, 304.

11. Ibid., 305.

12. Andersen, *Dagbøger*, vol. 3, 45–46.

13. Ibid., 53 (29 January 1846).

14. Ibid., (30 January 1846).

15. Collin, *H.C. Andersen og det Collinske Hus*, 226.

16. Joan Bulman, *Jenny Lind: A Biography* (London: J. Barrie, 1956), 118 (February 1846).

17. Andersen visited Weimar in 1846 (16 August–3 September) and 1847 (7–12 September).

18. La Mara (Ida Maria Lipsius), *Briefwechsel zwischen Franz Liszt und Carl Alexander, Grossherzog von Sachsen* (Leipzig: Breitkopf & Härtel, 1909), 13.

19. In December 1847 he dedicated the epic poem *Ahasverus* to his new patron. *Ahasverus* tells the legend of the wandering Jew, who travels through time and across nations sharing tales about the life of Christ and the transgressions of man. Andersen had discussed the poem with Carl Alexander during his visit in 1846, and perhaps he hoped the tale would send a subtle message to his persistent patron. Carl Alexander was unrelenting in his efforts to attach Andersen to Weimar permanently, but the poet, like the character of Ahasverus, felt compelled to continue his nomadic lifestyle.

20. Andersen, *Dagbøger*, vol. 3, 175. (1 September 1846).

21. Ibid., 43. (10 January 1846).

22. Möller-Christensen, *Briefwechsel*, 48.

23. Ibid., 50. As with the concert in Hamburg, Andersen gave a more vivid impression of the concert in his diary on 8 March 1846: 'At half past twelve, I went to Liszt's third concert – one string snapped after the other. It was hot, and there was a draft. Once again, I heard his fantasy about Robert [Meyerbeer's *Robert le Diable*]. He is a stormy spirit who plays with notes – a juggler of notes. I am amazed but not overwhelmed. *H.C. Andersens Dagbøger*, vol. 3, 73.

24. Möller-Christensen, *Briefwechsel*, 111 (13 January 1848).

25. Ibid., 113 (25 January 1848).

26. Ibid., 116.

27. Ibid.

28. Ibid., 131.

29. Ibid., 142.

30. Ibid., 165.

31. Andersen's ideas concerning the relationship between art and politics is revealed in a play he wrote called *Kunstens Dannevirke* (The Bulwark of the Arts). The title is a reference to the ancient rampart in Schleswig built to protect Denmark against the Germans, and it suggests a mobilization of the arts against the enemy.

32. Möller-Christensen, *Briefwechsel*, 123 (2 August 1848).

33. Richard Wagner, *My Life* (New York: Dodd, Mead & Co., 1911), vol. 1, 449.

34. Möller-Christensen, *Briefwechsel*, 139 (18 August 1849).

35. Ibid., 155–6.

36. Shortly after the war, Andersen tried to convince the German composer Franz Gläser to collaborate with him on an opera entitled *Befrielsen* (The Liberation).

37. Möller-Christensen, *Briefwechsel*, 156.

38. Originally titled *Hyldemoer*, this one-act fantasy play premièred in Denmark on 1 December 1851. During Andersen's lifetime, the play enjoyed a total of 60 performances, but, contrary to Carl Alexander's interest in the work, it was never performed in Weimar.

39. Möller-Christensen, *Briefwechsel*, 169. Carl Alexander's confirmation of Beaulieu's friendship with Andersen is likely in response to a disagreement Andersen had with the baron just a few months earlier. Afraid political sentiments against Danes might be unfavorable in Weimar after the war, Andersen wrote to Beaulieu in June 1851 and asked if it were safe for him to visit. Offended by the question, Beaulieu wrote back and said that if Andersen were so Danish that he could only see the side of Denmark in the war, then as a Dane it would be better if he did not come to Weimar. However, if this were not the case, then he would no doubt be welcomed, as always, as 'the dear, brave poet ... with whom one does not speak about politics.' Andersen responded to Beaulieu shortly thereafter and promised never to discuss politics again: 'Time will clear up everything, and I know that the Germans and the Danes will be best friends.... Truth and Beauty will build the bridge between us.' (See Möller-Christensen, *Briefwechsel*, 314–15).

40. '[The Altenburg] was a treasure trove of items that Liszt had collected on his tours – including Beethoven's Broadwood piano, the priceless death mask of Beethoven, a writing desk that had belonged to Haydn, and jewels and medallions received from half the crowned heads of Europe.... The main reception room on the grand floor was dominated by Liszt's Erard concert grand, while the walls were lined with his music library. A linking room contained all Liszt's souvenirs from his *Glanzzeit* – oriental rugs, mother-of-pearl tables, Turkish pipes, Russian jade, and a silver breakfast service. Pictures of the great composer adorned the walls, as well as two life-size portraits of Liszt and the well-known canvas by Ary Scheffer called *The Three Magi*, whose central figure bears the unmistakable imprint of the musician's features. On the second floor was the music room proper. It contained two Viennese grands, a spinet that had once belonged to Mozart, and a huge instrument called a 'piano organ' ... The library had been placed in an adjoining room, and on its shelves rested many of the books he had acquired in his Paris days, by Hugo, Lamartine, Sainte-Beuve, Lamennais and others. Also stored there was his unique collection of autographed scores by Chopin, Schumann, Beethoven, Wagner, Mozart, and dozens of composers he had met on his tours across Europe.' (Cf. Walker, 77–78).

41. Andersen, *Dagbøger*, vol. 4, 83.

42. Beaulieu was not the only one displeased by Liszt's growing dominance in Weimar. On 20 May Andersen recorded a conversation he had with Eckermann: 'He told me about Liszt who lives here together with Princess Wittgenstein, and it is an open secret; he [Liszt] does great harm to the theater, refuses to perform Mozart, who is a thing of the past he says; instead he performs Wagner and other composers of that effect.' (Andersen, *Dagbøger*, vol. 4, 79).

43. Andersen, *Dagbøger*, vol. 4, 81.

44. Ibid., 87.

45. Ibid., 88.

46. Ibid., 91 (8 June 1852).

47. H.C. Andersen, 'Skyggen,' in *H.C. Andersens Samlede Skrifter*, vol. 13, 365–66.

48. Andersen, *Dagbøger*, vol. 4, 84–85. (29 May 1852).

49. Ibid., 86.

50. A facsimile of the Schiller autograph given to Andersen by Liszt is found in *H.C. Andersen Album*, facsimile volume, 66.

51. Ibid., 87.

52. Andersen later took a strong interest in Wagner's literary talents. In a letter dated 14 February 1854, Carl Alexander discussed the merits of Wagner's libretto for *Die Niebelungen*. (See Möller-Christensen, *Briefwechsel*, 192).

53. Andersen, *Dagbøger*, vol. 4, 85.

54. Ibid., 89. George Henry Lewes and George Eliot had a similar reaction during a visit to Weimar in October 1854. Lewes wrote: 'we came to the conclusion that [Wagner's music] was not for us.' (Cf. Walker, 251).

55. Andersen, *Dagbøger*, vol. 4, 91.

56. La Mara (Marie Lipsius), ed., *Briefe hervorragender Zeitgenossen an Franz Liszt* (Leipzig: Breitkopf & Härtel, 1895–1904), vol. 3, 20.

57. Möller-Christensen, *Briefwechsel*, 182.

58. Walker, 163 (16 February 1853).

59. Ibid., 164 (17 February 1853).

60. La Mara, *Briefe hervorragender Zeitgenossen an Franz Liszt*, vol. 4, 160.

61. The sculptor Karl Steinhäuser.

62. For a complete description of the Goethe Foundation (*Goethestiftung*) see Walker, 126–29; and Detlef Altenburg, 'Franz Liszt and the Legacy of the Classical Era,' *19th-Century Music* 18, no. 1 (1994): 46–63.

63. Möller-Christensen, *Briefwechsel*, 190.

64. Walker, 228.

65. Andersen, *Dagbøger*, vol. 4, 155 (29 June 1854).

66. Ibid., 156.

67. La Mara (Ida Maria Lipsius), ed., *Franz Liszt's Briefe* (Leipzig: Breitkopf & Härtel, 1893–1905), vol. 3, 136. Translation by Walker, 339–40.

68. Möller-Christensen, *Briefwechsel*, 195.

69. Ibid., 196.

70. Andersen, *Dagbøger*, vol. 4, 187.

71. Ibid., 188. Andersen also noted that an article about the upcoming performance appeared in Weimar's Sunday paper.

72. Hetsch, 64.

73. Angul Hammerich, *J.P.E. Hartmann: biografiske essays* (Copenhagen: G.E.C. Gad, 1916), 65.

74. Möller-Christensen, *Briefwechsel*, 201.

75. Andersen, *Dagbøger*, vol. 4, 213 (23 June 1856).

76. Ibid., 215.
77. Ibid., 215–16. (27 June 1856).
78. Ibid., 215.
79. Möller-Christensen, *Briefwechsel*, 208.
80. Ibid., 209.
81. Ibid., 210.
82. Adelheid von Schorn, *Das nachklassische Weimar* (Weimar: G. Kiepenheuer, 1912), vol. 2, 71.
83. Andersen, *Mit Livs Eventyr*, 426. A similar description is found in Andersen's diary: *H.C. Andersens Dagbøger*, vol. 4, 286 (4 September 1857).
84. La Mara, *Briefe hervorragender Zeitgenossen an Franz Liszt*, vol. 3, 97.
85. Ibid., vol. 4, 287 (5 September 1857). In a letter to Liszt dated 27 August 1857, Joseph Joachim expressed a similar reaction to Liszt's music: 'Your music is entirely antagonistic to me; it contradicts everything with which the spirits of our great ones have nourished my mind from my earliest youth. If it were thinkable that I could ever be deprived of ... all that I feel music to be, your strains would not fill one corner of the vast waste of nothingness.' (Cf. Walker, 347).
86. *Hans Christian Andersen's Correspondence with the late Grand Duke of Saxe-Weimar, Charles Dickens, etc., etc.*, ed. Frederick Crawford (London: Dean, 1891), 368 (6 September 1857).
87. Andersen, *Mit Livs Eventyr*, vol. 2, 200.
88. According to Andersen's diary, he wrote the entire story on 14 October while staying in the manor house of Basnæs. (Cf. Möller-Christensen, vol. 4, 295).
89. H.C. Andersen, 'Pebersvendens Nathue,' in *H.C. Andersens Samlede Skrifter*, vol. 14, 151.
90. Ibid., 150.
91. Ibid., 153.
92. Ibid., 156–57.
93. Ibid., 157.
94. In 1854 the Austrian painter Moritz von Schwind completed a series of frescoes based on the life of St. Elisabeth of Thuringia in the halls of Wartburg Castle. Inspired by the saint's life story and connection to Weimar, Liszt began work on a dramatic choral-orchestral work. In 1855 he commissioned Otto Roquette to supply a libretto, the first parts of which he received in 1856 and began to set in 1857. Derek Watson, *Liszt* (New York: Schirmer, 1989), 105.
95. The reference to the 'fragrance of roses' at the end of the tale, can likewise be connected to the Pope's 'flowering staff' in *Tannhäuser*, which symbolizes the hero's spiritual salvation.
96. Andersen was not the only writer to do this, as is shown in Emma Sutton's *Aubrey Beardsley and British Wagnerism in the 1890s*. Although Sutton's study focuses on literature after Andersen, it nonetheless presents a fascinating look at how Wagner's operas were simultaneously referenced and subverted in fiction.
97. Möller-Christensen, *Briefwechsel*, 225 (22 May 1858).

CHAPTER 5: THE PATRIOT

1. For discussions of Andersen's relationship to Germany in the 1840s see: Johan de Mylius, 'Der deutsche Andersen: Zur Begründung des biographischen Andersen-Bildes in Deutschland,' *Dänisch-deutsche Doppelgänger: Transnationale und bikulturelle Literatur zwischen Barock und Moderne*. Heinrich Detering, Anne-Bitt Gerecke, and Johan de Mylius, eds. (Göttingen: Wallstein Verlag, 2001): 157–73 and 'Hans Christian Andersen –

on the Wave of Liberalism.' *Hans Christian Andersen: A Poet in Time*, 109–24; Heinrich Detering, "Dänemark und Deutschland einander gegenüber:' Kosmopolitismus, Bikulturalität und Patriotismus bei H.C. Andersen,' *Dänische-deutsche Doppelgänger: Transnationale und bikulturelle Literatur zwischen Barock und Moderne*, 174–95.

2. An overview of this debate is presented in Ole A. Hedegaard, *H.C. Andersen 1848–50 og 1864* (Copenhagen: Bent Carlsens Forlag, 1980).

3. Carl Dahlhaus, *Between Romanticism and Modernism: Four Studies in the Music of the Later Nineteenth Century*, trans. Mary Whittal (Berkeley: University of California Press, 1980), 82–83, gives a general description of this shift in ideology: 'Nationalism underwent a profound alteration in the nineteenth century. In the first half of the century the 'nationalist' was also, perhaps paradoxically, a 'cosmopolitan' a 'citizen of the world.' But after 1849 nationalism adopted a haughtily exclusive or even aggressive stance, and although it was the oppressors who initiated this unhappy change and were the primary offenders under it, the attitude of the oppressed was equally affected by it.'

4. Rousseau, on the other hand, believed that *patrie* referred to one's native land, irrespective of its political regime. In short, the terms *patrie* and 'nation' often converged in the writings of Rousseau. For a more detailed description of the history of the term *patrie* see Joseph Llobera, *The God of Modernity: The Development of Nationalism in Western Europe* (Berg: Oxford and Providence, 1994), 151–54.

5. For an in-depth study of Grundtvig see A.M. Allchin, *N.F.S. Grundtvig: An Introduction to his Life and Work* (Aarhus: Aarhus University Press, 1997).

6. Grundtvig's ideas concerning Danish nationalism are discussed in Uffe Østergård, 'Peasants and Danes: The Danish National Identity and Public Culture,' *Becoming National: A Reader*, ed. Geoff Eley and Ronald Grigor Suny (Oxford: Oxford University Press, 1996): 179–202.

7. Lorenz Rerup, 'N.F.S. Grundtvig's Position in Danish Nationalism,' *Heritage and Prophecy: Grundtvig and the English-Speaking World*, ed. A.M. Allchin, D. Jasper, J.H. Schjørring, and K. Stevenson (Norwich: The Canterbury Press, 1994), 241–42.

8. Hans Kuhn, *Defining a Nation in Song: Danish patriotic songs in songbooks of the period 1832–1870* (Copenhagen: C.A. Reitzels Forlag AS, 1990), 10.

9. The king declared his intention to establish the four assemblies in 1831. The legal framework was approved in 1834, and in 1835 the Provincial Assemblies were put into practice.

10. The society had almost two thousand members by the end of 1835 and five thousand at its peak in 1840.

11. Andersen, *Mit Livs Eventyr*, vol. 2, 67.

12. 'Tale i den Slesvigske Hjelpforening 14/3. 1848,' *Danskeren* I (1848): 84–96; G. Christensen and Hal Koch, eds., *N.F.S. Grundtvig, Værker i Udvalg*, (Copenhagen, 1842), vol. 5, 260–61.

13. For an in-depth study of Grundtvig's participation in Danish politics see Vagn Wåhlin, 'Denmark, Slesvig-Holstein and Grundtvig in the 19th Century,' in *Heritage and Prophecy: Grundtvig and the English-Speaking World*, ed. by A.M. Allchin, D. Jasper, J.H. Schjørring, and K. Stevenson (Norwich: The Canterbury Press, 1994), 243–70. For a detailed study of the evolution of Andersen's relationship to Grundtvig's ideology see Hilding Ringblom, *H.C. Andersen og trådene til Grundtvig*, (Odense: H.C. Andersen-Centret, 1986).

14. H.C. Andersen, *Kjendte og glemte Digte (1823–1867)* (Copenhagen: C. A. Reitzels Forlag, 1867), 288–89.

15. Bille and Bøgh, *Breve fra H.C. Andersen*, 552.

16. H.C. Andersen, *The Story of My Life*, trans. Horace Scudder (London and New York, 1975), 334–36.

17. Andersen, *Kjendte og glemte Digte*, 289–90.

18. Kuhn, 239.

19. Bille and Bøgh, *Breve fra H.C. Andersen*, 539–40 (8 February 1848).

20. Andersen, *Mit Livs Eventyr*, vol. 2, 71–72.

21. *H.C. Andersens Dagbøger*, vol. 3, 279 (13 May 1848).

22. Bille and Bøgh, *Breve fra H.C. Andersen*, 544–45.

23. Andersen, *Mit Livs Eventyr*, vol. 2, 79.

24. Ludvig Holberg was the first Danish playwright to be featured at the Royal Theater in Copenhagen. He is perhaps best known for his lively character studies. For example, his play *Den Vaegelsindede* (The Weathervane) features a woman who ceaselessly changes her mind, and *Jean de France* presents a bourgeois youngster from Copenhagen who, after only a few weeks in Paris, acquires the most absurd French manners in appearance and speech. *Jeppe paa Bjerget* (Jeppe of the Hill) is about a habitually drunk Sjælland peasant who reveals himself to be a tyrant when he is led to believe he is a wealthy baron. *Jacob von Tyboe eller Den stortalende Soldat* (Jacob von Tyboe or The Grandiloquent Soldier) mocks the military while *Erasmus Montanus* caricatures a debate-crazy intellectual who misinterprets the aims and objectives of scholarship. *Den Stundesløse* (The Fusser) pokes fun at a person who achieves nothing despite his foolish bustling around, and Don Ranudo de Colibrados depicts a Spanish Grandee who stubbornly maintains an aristocratic bearing despite the fact that his dire financial straits make it impossible to maintain such high living standards.

25. Bente Scavenius, *The Golden Age in Denmark: Art and Culture 1800–1850*. Trans. Barbara Haveland (Copenhagen: Gyldendal, 1994).

26. Andersen, *Kunstens Dannevirke* in *H.C. Andersens Samlede Skrifter*, vol. 10, 309. By the late 1840s, Ewald was seen as one of the first poets in Denmark to revive an interest in Norse mythology, and with the growing interest in Danish culture and language, his works were enjoying a successful revival both in print and on the stage.

27. Ibid.

28. Ibid., 310.

29. As Kuhn, 88–89, explains, the melody was mistaken as belonging to 'an old, oral ballad tradition' until A.P. Berggreen identified P.E. Rasmussen (1776–1870) as the composer in 1840. In its 'march-like procession through the whole scale and its build-up to the third above the octave' before returning to the tonic, 'it owes more to the theater marches and drinking songs of the eighteenth century than to folksong.' In Andersen's text to the tune, 'an allegorical history of the absolute monarchy' (Enevælden), ending with Frederik VI is presented, and Denmark's bulwark is described as the foundation upon which the 'spirit of the future's church' (Nutids Aandens Kirke) will be built.

30. After the première on 18 December Andersen noted in his diary that there were 'almost three rounds of thunderous applause.' (*H.C. Andersens Dagbøger*, vol. 3, 292).

31. Andersen *Mit Livs Eventyr*, vol. 2, 79.

32. Ibid.

33. Andersen, *Kunstens Dannevirke*, 304.

34. Andersen, *Dagbøger*, vol. 3, 304.

35. It should be noted that Andersen always translated Gläser's name into the Danish spelling 'Glæser' in his correspondence and diaries. For the sake of clarity, however, I have used the standard German spelling throughout.

36. *H.C. Andersens Dagbøger*, vol. 3, 305.

37. Ibid., 307.

38. Ibid.
39. Bille and Bøgh, *Breve fra H.C. Andersen*, 560–61.
40. Ibid., 561.
41. Although Andersen's plan for *The Valkyrie* was never realized, Bournonville produced a ballet called *The Valkyrie* in 1860 that followed an outline remarkably similar to the plot written by Andersen in 1848. Despite this similarity, however, Bournonville did not mention Andersen when he spoke about the production of the ballet in his autobiography, *Mit Teaterliv* (My Theater Life) published in 1865. For a detailed chronology of Bournonville's 1861 production and a description of the primary sources see Knud Arne Jürgensen, *The Bournonville Tradition: The First Fifty Years 1829–1879*, vol II, (London: Cecil Court, 1997), 260–66.
42. Kuhn, 211–13.
43. Andersen, *Kjendte og glemte Digte*, 255–56.
44. The poet and sculptor in this poem and *Bulwark of the Arts* can also be interpreted as clear allusions to Andersen and Thorvaldsen.
45. According to Kuhn, 213: '[Ørsted] himself composed a further stanza to make up for the shortcoming.'
46. Cf. Kuhn, 213.
47. Hertz included this statement in a controversial comedy he wrote for the Royal Theater in 1849 called *Hundrede Aar*. According to Marker, 54, Heiberg also ridiculed the Casino's mission.
48. Perhaps the most famous *Zauberoper* is Mozart's *Magic Flute*. For more information on the origins of *Zauberoper* and its history in the nineteenth century see: P. Branscombe, *W.A. Mozart: Die Zauberflöte* (Cambridge: Camridge University Press, 1991); O. Rommel, *Die Alt-Wiener Volkskomödie*, (Vienna: A Schroll, 1952); G. Weisstein, 'Geschichte der Zauberpossen,' in *Spemanns Goldenes Buch des Theaters* (Berlin: W. Spemann, 1902). For more information on Raimund see: L.V. Harding, *The Dramatic Art of Ferdinand Raimund and Johann Nestroy: a Critical Study* (The Hague: Mouton, 1974); Dorothy James, *Raimund and Vienna: A Critical Study of Raimund's Plays in their Viennese Setting* (Cambridge, Cambridge University Press, 1970); A. Orel, 'Raimund und die Musik,'in *Raimund-Almanak 1936* (Innsbruck, 1936). As Marker, 55, notes: Andersen's interest in the *Zauberspiel* stayed with him for most of his life; he 'later recommended [Raimund's plays] for careful study to the young director Henrik Ibsen during his visit to Copenhagen in 1852.' For further discussion of Andersen's recommendation to Ibsen see Robert Niiendam, *Gennem mange Aar* (Copenhagen, 1950), 99.
49. Andersen, *Dagbøger*, vol. 1, 477.
50. Andersen's translation of this work was published for the first time in 2003, see Ejnar Stig Askgaard, '*En Ødeland*, Eventyr-Comedie I tre Acter bearbeidet efter Raimunds *Der Verschwender*,' *Anderseniana* (2003): 21–141. The music in *En Ødeland* is discussed by Karsten Eskildsen in 'Musikken I *En Ødeland*,' *Anderseniana* (2003): 142–45.
51. As Tove Barfoed Møller, *Theaterdigteren H.C. Andersen og Meer end Perler og Guld:' En dramaturgisk-musikalsk undersøgelse* (Odense, Odense Universitetsforlag, 1995), 374, has noted, on the title page to the original manuscript for *More than Pearls and Gold*, Andersen crossed out the first literal translation of *Zauberspiel* (Tryllespil) and wrote 'Fairy-tale Comedy' (Eventyr-Comedie).
52. Andersen, *Mit Livs Eventyr*, vol. 2, 112.
53. Møller, *Theaterdigteren H.C. Andersen og Meer end Perler og Guld*, 279.
54. Ibid., 285.

55. For an extensive discussion of Andersen's use of these selections in *More than Pearls and Gold* see Møller, *Theaterdigteren H.C. Andersen og Meer end Perler og Guld*, 227–72.

56. As Marker, 58, explains: 'The genealogy of the figure in white is not difficult to discern: the very same character haunted the Bastei, the favourite promenade in old Vienna in [Karl] Meisl's *Das Gespenst auf der Bastei.*'

57. A detailed study of the literary influences found in Andersen's *Zauberspiel* is found in H. Topsøe-Jensen, *H.C. Andersen og andre Studier* (Odense, 1966), 153–72.

58. *Wilhelm Hauffs sämtliche Werke in sechs Bänden* (Stuttgart: Cottasche Bibliothek, n.d.), Cf. Marker, 59.

59. Marker, 59.

60. Andersen, *Mit Livs Eventyr*, vol. 2, 112.

61. Review by M.A. Goldschmidt in *Nord og Syd* 1 (1849): 411.

62. Andersen, *Mit Livs Eventyr*, vol. 2, 144.

63. These poems were first edited and printed as a whole in *H.C. Andersen: Samlede Digte* (Copenhagen: Aschehoug, 2000), 437–449.

64. Andersen originally submitted the libretto for this work in 1836 under the title *Renzos Bryllup* (Renzo's Wedding). Believing that it was his 'first theater piece displaying familiarity with the stage,' (letter to J. Collin on 15 June 1836) he was greatly disappointed when the libretto was rejected. In 1848 Andersen revised the text, and it was accepted by the Royal Theater, who offered the German conductor of the Theater orchestra, Gläser, the opportunity to compose the score.

65. Lauridsen and Weber, *H.C. Andersens Almanakker*, 201. *Wedding at Lake Como* was performed at the Royal Theater twelve times between 1849 and 1852.

66. Möller-Christensen, *Briefwechsel*, 136.

67. Andersen first submitted a libretto for *Nøkken* in 1845, but the Royal Theater had some doubts about the piece. Henrik Rung was originally going to write the music, but he pulled out. In 1846 Niels W. Gade agreed to collaborate with Andersen, but this arrangement also fell through.

68. Bille and Bøgh, *Breve til H.C. Andersen*, 330–31.

69. Cf. Hetsch, 77.

70. Bille and Bøgh, *Breve til H.C. Andersen*, 11–12 (8 November 1859).

71. Cf. Elias Bredsdorff, *Hans Christian Andersen: The Story of his Life and Work* (New York: Farrar, Straus and Giroux, 1975): 234.

72. A thorough overview of Andersen's comments in his letters and diaries concerning the Schleswig-Holstein wars is found in Ole A. Hedegaard, *H.C. Andersen 1848–50 og 1864* (Copenhagen: Bent Carlsens Forlag, 1980).

73. For an excellent study of Danish songbooks in the nineteenth century see Kuhn, *Defining a Nation in Song: Danish patriotic songs in songbooks of the period 1832–1870*.

74. Kuhn, 12–13.

75. Niels Martin Jensen, 'Niels W. Gade og den nationale tone,' in *Dansk Identitetshistorie III, Folkets Danmark 1848–1940*, ed. Ole Feldbæk (Copenhagen: C.A. Reitzel, 1992), 218. Berggreen's anthology was typical for the period. As the title suggests, traditional folk ballads from Denmark were included along with songs from foreign lands, namely Norway, Sweden, Scotland, France, and Germany. Berggreen's *Folkesange og Melodier* eventually expanded into an eleven-volume series, and in the nineteenth century it was considered the most authoritative Danish source of European folk song.

76. Kuhn, 8–9.

77. Here Andersen is making a play on words. The word 'Atterdag' means 'a brighter day,' but it also is a reference to the glorious medieval king, Valdemar Atterdag.

78. Andersen, *Kjendte og glemte Digte*, 294–95.
79. Andersen, *Mit Livs Eventyr*, vol. 2, 275.
80. Andersen, *Kjendte og glemte Digte*, 274–75.
81. Andersen, *Mit Livs Eventyr*, vol. 1, 255.

CHAPTER 6: THE TONE-POET

1. For a general introduction to Andersen's relationship with Wagner see Ea Dal, 'Dansk Wagner-tilløb,' *Hvad fatter gjør ... Boghistoriske, litterære og musikalske essays tilegnet Erik Dal*, Henrik Glahn, ed. (Herning, DK: Poul Kristensen, 1982): 130–42.
2. Elias Bredsdorff, 226.
3. Ibid., 227. For an intriguing look at the role of travel writing during the nineteenth-century see Ina Ferris, 'Mobile Words: Romantic travel Writing and Print Anxiety,' *Modern Language Quarterly* 60/4 (December 1999): 451–68.
4. Ljudmila Braude, 'Hans Christian Andersen's Writer's Manifesto in *In Sweden* – Andersen and Science,' *Hans Christian Andersen: A Poet in Time*, 235–40.
5. For a basic introduction to the life and works of Ørsted see: Ole Bang, *Store Hans Christian: H.C. Ørsted 1777–1851* (Copenhagen: Rhodos, 1986).
6. In addition to being a reference to Ørsted's *The Spirit in Nature*, this is a reference to an Andersen fairytale inspired by Ørsted called 'Vanddraaben' (The Drop of Water).
7. H.C. Andersen, *I Sverrig* in *H.C. Andersens Romaner og Rejseskildringer*, vol. 7, 120.
8. Hans Christian Ørsted, *Aanden i Naturen* (Copenhagen: A. F. Høft, 1850).
9. As we saw in chapter 4, Andersen and Carl Alexander often discussed Ørsted's theories in their correspondence, and Andersen's tale *The Bell* owed much to Ørsted's ideas concerning aesthetics of beauty and acoustics.
10. Bille and Bøgh, *Breve fra H.C. Andersen*, 582–83.
11. Möller-Christensen, *Briefwechsel*, 159.
12. H.C. Andersen, 'Om Aartusinder,' in *H.C. Andersen Samlede Skrifter*, vol. 14, 41–42.
13. Ibid., 42–43.
14. Andersen, *Dagbøger*, vol. 4, 183.
15. Andersen, *Mit Livs Eventyr*, vol. 2, 190.
16. Möller-Christensen, *Briefwechsel*, 192.
17. Translation based on that in Wullschlager, 357–8. The final line of this excerpt – 'In this way the poet's art places itself at the side of Science and opens our eyes to the beautiful, the true, and the good' – is a direct quotation from Ørsted's *The Spirit in Nature*.
18. Möller-Christensen, *Briefwechsel*, 231.
19. Another story from 1859, 'En Historie fra Klitterne' (Story of the Sand Dunes), also has a musical quality to it, as if the ebb and flow of the storm serve to recount the narrative. Perhaps it was this quality that led Andersen to dedicate the tale to the composer J.P.E. Hartmann.
20. H.C. Andersen, 'Vinden fortæller om Valdemar Daae og hans Døtre,' *H.C. Andersens Samlede Skrifter*, vol. 14, 227.
21. Ibid., 233.
22. Wullschlager, 360.
23. Ibid., 361. For a discussion of music as inspiration for Andersen's style in his later tales see Johan de Mylius, 'Andersens anden revolution,' *Litteraturbilleder: Æstetiske udflugter i litteraturen fra Søren Kierkegaard til Karen Blixen*. Johan de Mylius, ed. (Odense: Odense Universitetsforlag, 1988), 37–60.

24. H.C. Andersen, 'Det ny Aarhundredes Musa' *H.C. Andersens Samlede Skrifter*, vol. 14, 360.

25. Ibid.

26. Ibid.

27. Ibid., 361.

28. Ibid., 361–62.

29. Ibid., 362.

30. Ibid., 364.

31. Ibid., 365.

32. Ibid., vol. 15, 17.

33. Ibid., 17–18.

34. Wullschlager, 372.

35. Bredsdorff, 243.

36. *H.C. Andersens Samlede Skrifter*, vol. 15, 18.

37. Andersen, *Dagbøger*, vol. 7, 10 (16 January 1866).

38. Ibid., 11 (17 January 1866).

39. H.C. Andersen, 'Dryaden,' *H.C. Andersens Samlede Skrifter*, vol 15, 162. In November 1868 Andersen wrote to his American publisher Scudder: 'I consider ['The Dryad'] as one of my best ... a tale from the Exhibition in Paris in 1867 – I fancy that I have given in that tale a lively sketch of the exhibition and have tried to prove that our present time, the time of engines, as many call it, is as poetical and as rich as any age.' (Cf. Wullschlager, 402).

40. A detailed description of the 1867 World Exhibition and its effect on Parisian music life is found in Siegfried Kracauer, *Jacques Offenbach and the Paris of His Time* (New York: Zone Books, 2002), 307–19.

41. *H.C.Andersenes Samlede Skrifter*, vol. 15, 159.

42. Andersen, *Dagbøger*, vol. 7, 267. Watt told similar stories on 21 April (vol. 7, 270).

43. Ibid., 280–81.

44. 'Richard Wagner and *Tannhäuser* in Paris' was first published in *Revue europénne* on 1 April 1861. It also appeared posthumously in *L'art romantique* (1869).

45. Charles Baudelaire, 'Théophil Gautier,' in *Selected Writings on Art and Artists*, trans. P.E. Charvet (Hammondsworth, 1972), 274.

46. Charles Baudelaire, 'Correspondences' in *The Flowers of Evil*, trans. James McGowan (Oxford: Oxford University Press, 1993), 19.

47. Charles Baudelaire, 'Richard Wagner and *Tannhäuser* in Paris,' in *Selected Writings on Art and Artists*, trans. P.E. Charvet (Harmondsworth 1972), 356–57.

48. Andersen's interest in nineteenth-century French literature is reflected in the large collection of French literature he collected throughtout his lifetime. For information on Andersen's library, especially French works, see Estrid and Erik Dal, *Fra H.C. Andersens boghylde: hans bogsamling belyst gennem breve, kataloger og bevarede bøger* (Copenhagen: Rosenkilde og Bagger, 1961), 44–46.

49. Andersen, *Dagbøger*, vol. 7, 289. During a short stay in Le Locle on 17 May, Andersen enjoyed a private chamber performance of Wagner's *Tannhäuser* Overture.

50. On 21 March Andersen wrote in his diary: 'I went to Stockhausen's concert (second); today I visited with him and Brahms, they do not please me as much as I had expected.' Andersen, *Dagbøger*, vol. 8, 39.

51. Ibid., 37 (17 March 1868).

52. Florence May, *Life of Brahms* (London: William Reeves, 1905), vol. 2, 405–06; Jan Swafford, *Johannes Brahms: A Biography* (New York:Vintage Books, 1999), 318–19;

Johannes Brahms Briefwechsel (Berlin: Deutsche Brahms-Gesellschaft, 1907–1922), XVIII, 48–49n.

53. Andersen, *Dagbøger*, vol. 8, 39–40.

54. Ibid. 43.

55. Gade first introduced Danish audiences to the music of Wagner in 1857, and Andersen was there for the event. On 30 October 1857 Andersen wrote in his diary: 'A few days ago at a concert the general public heard the *Tannhäuser* Overture for the first time. It was well received, as was Liszt's *Les Preludes*. In time *Tannhäuser* will surely be performed here in its entirety. For me, this opera is still the most interesting of Wagner's compositions.' Gerhard Schepelern, *Wagners operaer i Danmark: Et dansk Wagner-Lexikon* (Valby, DK: Amadeus, 1988).

56. Richard Wagner, *Gesammelte Schriften und Dichtungen*, ed. W. Golther (Berlin and Leipzig, n.d.), vol. 3, 259.

57. Dahlhaus, 83.

58. The only notable objection in 1850 came from eleven professors at the Leipzig Conservatory who wrote a letter of protest to the journal's editor, Alfred Brendel. The general dismissal of the article was facilitated by the disclaimer attached to the title as a footnote: 'However faulty her outward conformation, we have always considered it a pre-eminence of Germany's, a result of her great learning, that at least in the scientific sphere she possesses intellectual freedom. This freedom we now lay claim to and rely on, in printing the above essay, desirous that our readers may accept it in this sense. Whether one shares the views expressed therein, or not, the author's breadth of grasp (*Genialität der Anschauung*) will be disputed by no one.'

59. Richard Wagner, *Das Judenthum in der Musik.* (Leipzig: J. J. Weber, 1869).

60. Some of the most famous responses include: Joseph Engel, 'Richard Wagner, das Judenthum in der Musik: eine Abwehr;' E. M. Oettinger, 'Offenes Billetdoux an Richard Wagner,' Dresden, 1869; and A. Truhart, 'Offener Brief an Richard Wagner,' St. Petersburg, 1869.

61. Richard Wagner, *Judaism in Music and Other Essays*, (Lincoln: University of Nebraska, 1995), 93–94

62. Ibid., 81.

63. Ibid., 100. Also see Marc A. Weiner, *Richard Wagner and the anti-Semitic Imagination* (Nebraska: University of Nebraska Press, 1995) for a consideration of how Wagner's theoretical racism can be reconciled with his music.

64. For an in-depth study of Andersen's relationship to the Melchior family see: Elith Reumert, *H.C. Andersen og det Melchiorske Hjem* (Copenhagen: H. Hagerups Forlag, 1924).

65. Andersen, *Dagbøger*, vol. 8, 27–28 (26 February 1868). Andersen's distaste for Offenbach's music is further documented in two of his tales: 'Pieter, Peter and Peer' and 'Ugedagende' (The Days of the Week). In the first tale, Peter, a young composer, is described in what was clearly intended to be a caricature of Offenbach: 'Peter must have lain in a buttercup. He looked buttery around the corners of his mouth, and his skin was so yellow that one would think that if his cheek were cut, butter would ooze out. He should have been a butter dealer, and could have been his own signboard. But on the inside he was a trash collector with a rattle. He was the musician of the Pietersen family – "musical enough for all of them" the neighbors said. "He composed seventeen new polkas in one week, and then put them all together and made an opera out of them, with a trumpet and a rattle accompaniment. Ugh! How delightful it was!" In 'The Days of the Week,' Monday looks to Offenbach's music as an accompaniment to licentious behavior: 'Monday, a young fellow ... very fond of pleasures ... left his workshop whenever he heard the music of the

parade guard. "I must go and listen to Offenbach's music. It doesn't go to my head or my heart; it tickles my leg muscles. I must dance, have a few drinks, get a black eye, sleep it off, and then the next day go to work.'"

66. Andersen, *Dagbøger*, vol. 8, 134.

67. Ibid.

68. Ibid.

69. Ibid.

70. Ibid.

71. Ibid., 303 (1 December 1869).

72. Ibid., 362.

73. Ibid., 363.

74. Another nineteenth-century author who used the idea of music historiography in the writing of novels was George Eliot. For an in-depth study of Eliot's references to music in *Daniel Deronda* see Ruth A. Solie, '"Tadpole Pleasures:" *Daniel Deronda* as Music Historiography,' *Yearbook of Comparative and General Literature* 45/46 (1997/1998): 87–104.

75. H.C. Andersen, *Lykke Peer* (Borgen: Danske Sprog- og Litteraturselskab, 2000), 57.

76. Ibid.

77. Ibid., 63.

78. Ibid., 75.

79. Ibid.

80. Ibid., 76.

81. Ibid.

82. Andersen apparently read a Danish translation of the *Talmud*, and on 15 May 1870 he recorded in his diary that he had read Goldschmidt's study on 'Jewish Sagas.' Andersen, *Dagbøger*, vol. 8, 368. For more information on Andersen's interest in Judaism see: W. Glyn Jones, 'Andersen and Those of Other Faiths,' *Hans Christian Andersen: A Poet in Time*, 259–70.

83. Andersen, *Lykke Peer*, 59–60.

84. Ibid., 72.

85. Ibid., 86.

86. Ibid., 89–90.

87. For a more in-depth look at the reception of Wagner in Paris by writers such as Baudelaire see: Katharine Ellis, *Music Criticism in Nineteenth-century France: 'La Revue et Gazette musicale de Paris,'* 1834–80 (Cambridge: Cambridge University Press, 1995); Joycelynne Lonck, *Baudelaire et la Musique* (Paris: A.G. Nizet, 1975); and Margaret Miner, *Resonant Gaps between Baudelaire & Wagner* (Athens, GA: The University of Georgia Press, 1995).

88. Andersen, *Lykke Peer*, 90. For a discussion of this unusual ending see: Frank Hugus, 'The Ironic Inevitability of Death: Hans Christian Andersen's *Lykke-Peer*,' *Hans Christian Andersen: A Poet in Time*, 527–40.

89. Bille and Bøgh, *Breve fra H.C. Andersen*, 848.

90. Ibid., 847.

91. Andersen, *Dagbøger*, vol. 8, 363.

92. Ibid., 364–65.

93. Ibid., 364.

94. Ibid., 367.

95. Bille and Bøgh, *Breve til H.C. Andersen*, 392–95.

96. Andersen, *Dagbøger*, vol. 8, 433–44 (19 November 1870).

97. Ibid., 437 (24 November 1870). The final line is a quote from Andersen's fairytale 'Grantræet' (The Fir Tree).

98. Axel Liebmann (1849–76).

99. Bille and Bøgh, *Breve fra H.C. Andersen*, 917.

CODA: THE DEATH OF A ROMANTIC

1. H.C. Andersen, 'Tante Tandpine,' *H.C. Andersens Samlede Skrifter*, vol. 15, 294.

2. Ibid., 296.

Bibliography

Allchin, A.M. *N.F.S. Grundtvig: An Introduction to his Life and Work.* Aarhus: Aarhus University Press, 1997.

Altenburg, Detlef. 'Franz Liszt and the Legacy of the Classical Era,' *19th-Century Music* 18, no. 1 (1994): 46–63.

Andersen, Hans Christian. *Digte.* Copenhagen, 1830.

— *Fodreise fra Holmens Canal til Østpyntenten af Amager i Aarene 1828 og 1829.* Borgen: Det Danske Sprog- og Literaturselskab, 1986.

— *Gesammelte Werke.* Leipzig: Carl B. Lorck, 1847.

— *H.C. Andersen Album 1–V,* Kåre Olsen, Helga Vang Lauridsen, and KirstenWeber, eds. 3 vols. Copenhagen: Lademann, 1980.

— *H.C. Andersen Almanakker 1833–1873.* Helga Vang Lauridsen and Kirsten Weber, eds. Copenhagen: Det danske Sprog- og Literaturselskab/G.E.C. Gad, 1990.

— *H.C. Andersen Samlede Digte.* Johan de Mylius, ed. Copenhagen: Aschehoug, 2000.

— *H.C. Andersens Brevveksling med Edvard og Henriette Collin.* C. Behrend and H. Topsøe-Jensen, eds. 5 vols. Copenhagen: Levin & Munkagaards Forlag, 1933–37.

— *H. C. Andersens Brevveksling med Jonas Collin den Ældre og andre Medlemmer af det Collinske Hus.* H. Topsøe-Jensen, Kaj Bom, and Knud Bøgh, eds. 3 vols. Copenhagen: Ejnar Munksgaard, 1945–48.

— *H.C. Andersens Dagbøger 1825–75,* Kåre Olsen and H. Topsøe-Jensen, eds. 12 vols. Copenhagen: Det danske Sprog- og Litteraturselskab/G.E.C. Gad, 1971–76.

— *H.C. Andersens Samlede Skrifter.* 15 vols. 2nd edition. Copenhagen: C.A Reitzels Forlag, 1879.

— *Improvisatoren.* Mogens Brøndsted, ed. Copenhagen: Det danske Sprog- og Litteraturselskab, 1991.

— 'Italiensk Musik, Sang og Theatervæsen,' *Søndagsblad* (8 February 1835): 91–94 and (15 February 1835): 104–12.

— *Kjendte og glemte Digte (1823–1867).* Copenhagen: C. A. Reitzels Forlag, 1867.

— *H.C. Andersens Levnedsbog 1805–1831.* H. Topsøe-Jensen, ed. Copenhagen: Det Schønbergske Forlag, 1988.

— *Lykke Peer.* Borgen: Det Danske Sprog- og Litteraturselskab, 2000.

— *Mit Livs Eventyr.* Copenhagen: C.A. Reitzels Forlag, 1855.

— *Mit Livs Eventyr* (1859), ed. H. Topsøe-Jensen, 2 vols. Copenhagen: Gyldendals Bogklub, 1975.

— *Romaner og Rejseskildringer.* 7 vols. Copenhagen: Gyldendal, 1943.

— *The Story of My Life.* Trans. Horace Scudder. New York: Hurd and Houghton, 1871.

— *The True Story of My Life.* Trans. Mary Howitt. London: Longman and Co., 1847 and Boston: J. Monroe, 1847.

Andersen, Hans Chr. 'The Author at the Museum.' *Hans Christian Andersen: A Poet in Time.* Johan de Mylius, Aage Jørgensen, and Viggo Hjørnager Pedersen, eds. Odense, DK: Odense University Press, 1999, 205–34.

Andersen, Jens. *Andersen: En Biografi.* Copenhagen: Gyldendal, 2003.

Andersen, Lise Præstgaard. 'The Feminine Element – And a Little about the Masculine Element in H.C. Andersen's Fairy Tales.' *Hans Christian Andersen: A Poet in Time.* Johan de Mylius, Aage Jørgensen, and Viggo Hjørnager Pedersen, eds. Odense, DK: Odense University Press, 1999, 501–14.

Askgaard, Ejnar Stig. '*En Ødeland,* Eventyr-Comedie i tre Acter bearbeidet efter Raimunds *Der Verschwender.*' *Anderseniana* (2003): 21–141.

Bang, Ole. *Store Hans Christian: H.C. Ørsted 1777–1851.* Copenhagen: Rhodos, 1986.

Barlby, Finn. 'The Euphoria of the Text – on the Market, on Man, and on Melody, i.e. Poetry.' *Hans Christian Andersen: A Poet in Time.* Johan de Mylius, Aage Jørgensen, and Viggo Hjørnager Pedersen, eds. Odense, DK: Odense University Press, 1999, 515–26.

Barüske, Heinz. *Hans Christian Andersen in Berlin.* Berlin: Hendrik Bäßler Verlag, 1999.

Baudelaire, Charles. *The Flowers of Evil.* Trans. James McGowan. Oxford: Oxford University Press, 1993.

— 'Richard Wagner and *Tannhäuser* in Paris,' in *Selected Writings on Art and Artists.* Trans. P.E. Charvet. Harmondsworth, 1972.

— 'Théophil Gautier,' in *Selected Writings on Art and Artists.* Trans. P.E. Charvet. Hammondsworth, 1972.

Bendix, Regina. 'Seashell Bra and Happy End. Disney's Transformations of "The Little Mermaid."' *Fabula. Zeitschrift für Erzählforschung* 34 (1993): 280–90.

Bernstein, Susan. *Virtuosity of the Nineteenth Century: Performing Music and Language in Heine, Liszt, and Baudelaire.* Stanford: Stanford University Press, 1998.

Bille, C. St. A. and Nicolaj Bøgh. *Breve fra H.C. Andersen.* Copenhagen: Aschehoug, 2000.

— *Breve til Hans Christian Andersen.* Copenhagen: C.A. Reitzels Forlag, 1877.

Boetticher, Wolfgang, ed. *Briefe und Gedichte aus dem Album Robert und Clara Schumanns.* Leipzig: VEB Deutscher Verlag für Musik, 1979.

Bønnesen, Michael. 'Den Kongelige Opera.' *Det Kongelige Theater: Historie og repertoire.* Copenhagen: Kongelige Theater, 1995–96, 46–57.

Bork, Jens S. 'Andersen – Kierkegaard. To boggaver.' *Anderseniana* (1994): 51–54.

Botstein, Leon. 'Between Aesthetics and History,' *19th-Century Music* 13 (1989): 168.

Bournonville, August. *My Theater Life.* Trans. Patricia N. McAndrew. London, 1974.

Brahms, Johannes. *Johannes Brahms Briefwechsel.* Berlin: Deutsche Brahms-Gesellschaft, 1907–22.

Branscombe, P. *W.A. Mozart: Die Zauberflöte.* Cambridge: Cambridge University Press, 1991.

Braude, Ljudmila. 'Hans Christian Andersen's Writer's Manifesto in *In Sweden* – Andersen and Science.' *Hans Christian Andersen: A Poet in Time.* Johan de Mylius, Aage Jørgensen, and Viggo Hjørnager Pedersen, eds. Odense, DK: Odense University Press, 1999. 235–40.

Bredsdorff, Elias. *Hans Christian Andersen: The Story of his Life and Work.* New York: Farrar, Straus and Giroux, 1975.

Bredsorff, Thomas. 'Nogen skrev et sagn om 'Agnete og Havmanden,' hvem, hvornår og hvorfor?' *Fund og Forskning* 30 (1991): 67–80.

Brix, Hans. *Det første Skridt.* Copenhagen: Carit Andersens Forlag, 1943.

— *H.C. Andersen og hans Eventyr.* Copenhagen: Det Schubotheske Forlag, 1907.

Brøndsted, Mogens. 'Folkevisens litterære efterliv.' *Traditioner er mange ting: Festskrift til Iørn Piø på halvfjerdsårsdagen den 24. august 1997.* Copenhagen: Foreningen Danmarks Folkeminder, 1997, 117–21.

Brust, Beth Wagner. *The Amazing Paper Cuttings of Hans Christian Andersen*. Boston: Houghton Mifflin Company, 1994.

Bulman, Joan. *Jenny Lind: A Biography*. London: J. Barrie, 1956.

Busk, Gorm. 'Friedrich Kuhlau's operas and theatre music and their performances at the Royal Theatre in Copenhagen (1814–1830): A mirror of European music drama and a glimpse of the Danish opera tradition.' *Musik og Forskning* 21 (1996): 93–127.

Celenza, Anna Harwell. *The Early Works of Niels W. Gade: In Search of the Poetic*. Aldershot: Ashgate, 2001.

— 'The Nightingale Revealed: Hans Christian Andersen as Music Critic,' *Historični seminar* 3 (1998–2000): 77–96.

— 'The Poet, the Pianist, and the Patron: Hans Christian Andersen and Franz Liszt in Carl Alexander's Weimar,' *Nineteenth-Century Music* XXVI/2 (2002): 130–54.

Clapp-Intyre, Alisa. *Angelic Airs, Subversive Songs: Music as Social Discourse in the Victorian Novel*. Athens, OH: Ohio University Press, 2002.

Collin, Edvard. *H.C. Andersen og det Collinske Huus*. Copenhagen, 1882.

Conroy, Patricia and Sven H. Rossel, eds. *The Diaries of Hans Christian Andersen*. Seattle: University of Washington Press, 1990.

Correa, Delia Da Sousa. *George Eliot, Music and Victorian Culture*. Basingstoke: Palgrave, 2002.

Crawford, Frederick, ed. *Hans Christian Andersen's Correspondence with the late Grand Duke of Saxe-Weimar, Charles Dickens, etc., etc*. London: Dean, 1891.

Dahlhaus, Carl. *Between Romanticism and Modernism: Four Studies in the Music of the Later Nineteenth Century*. Trans. Mary Whittal. Berkeley: University of California Press, 1980.

Dal, Ea. 'Dansk Wagner-tilløb.' *Hvad fatter giør ... Boghistoriske, litterære og musikalske essays tilegnet Erik Dal*. Henrik Glahn, ed. Herning, DK: Poul Kristensen, 1982, 130–42.

Dal, Erik. 'Jødiske elementer I H.C. Andersens skrifter,' in *Andersen og Verden*. Johan de Mylius, Aage Jørgensen, and Viggo Hjørnager Pedersen, eds. Odense: Odense Universitetsforlag, 1993), 444–52.

— and Estrid Dal, *Fra H.C. Andersens boghylde: hans bogsamling belyst gennem breve, kataloger og bevarede bøger*. Copenhagen: Rosenkilde og Bagger, 1961.

Daverio, John. 'Heinrich Heine,' *New Grove Dictionary of Music and Musicians*. Stanley Sadie, ed. London: Macmillan, 2002.

Deaville, James. 'A 'Daily Diary of the Weimar Dream:' Joachim Raff's unpublished letters to Doris Genast,' *Liszt and His World*. Stuyvesant, NY: Pendragon, 1998.

Detering, Heinrich. ''Dänemark und Deutschland einander gegenüber:' Kosmopolitismus, Bikulturalität und Patriotismus bei H.C. Andersen.' *Dänisch-deutsche Doppelgänger: Transnationale und bikulturelle Literatur zwischen Barock und Moderne*. Heinrich Detering, Anne-Bitt Gerecke, and Johan de Mylius, eds. Göttingen: Wallstein Verlag, 2001, 174–95.

— *Das offene Geheimnis: Zur literarischen Produktivität eine Tabus von Winckelmann bis zu Thomas Mann*. Göttingen: Wallstein, 1994.

— *Intellectual Amphibia: Homoerotic Camouflage in Hans Christian Andersen's Works*. Odense: H.C. Andersen-Centret, 1991.

Eliot, George. *Essays*. Thomas Pinney, ed. New York, 1963.

Ellis, Katharine. *Music Criticism in Nineteenth-century France: 'La Revue et Gazette musicale de Paris,' 1834–80*. Cambridge: Cambridge University Press, 1995.

Eskildsen, Karsten. 'Musikken I *En Ødeland*.' *Anderseniana* (2003): 142–45.

Ferris, Ina. 'Mobile Words: Romantic Travel Writing and Print Anxiety.' *Modern Language Quarterly* 60/4 (December 1999): 451–68.

Frank, Diana and Jeffrey Frank. 'The Real Hans Christian Andersen.' *The New Yorker* (8 January 2001): 78–84.

Gade, Dagmar. *Niels W. Gade: Optegnelser og Breve*. Copenhagen: Gyldendalske Boghandels Forlag, 1892.

Gade, Felix. Unpublished biography of Niels W. Gade. Copenhagen: The Royal Library, Gade Collection.

Gray, Beryl. *George Eliot and Music*. London: Macmillan, 1989.

Grønbech, Bo. *Hans Christian Andersen*. Boston: Twayne Publishers, 1980.

Hammerich, Angul. *J.P.E. Hartmann: biografiske essays*. Copenhagen: G.E.C. Gad, 1916.

Harding, L.V. *The Dramatic Art of Ferdinand Raimund and Johann Nestroy: a Critical Study*. The Hague: Mouton, 1974.

Hatting, Carsten E. 'Bemærkninger til Mozarts biografi.' *Musik og Forskning* 11 (1985–86): 5–41.

— *Mozart og Danmark*. Copenhagen: Engstrøms & Sødrings Musikbibliotek, 1991.

— 'Mozart und Dänemark.' *Mozart-Jahrbuch* (1991): 371–79.

Haugaard, Erik. 'Portrait of a Poet: Hans Christian Andersen and his Fairytales.' Washington, D.C.: Library of Congress, 1973.

Hedegaard, Ole A. *H.C. Andersen 1848–50 og 1864*. Copenhagen: Bent Carlsens Forlag, 1980.

Heine, Heinrich. *Sämtliche Schriften*, 6 vols. Klaus Briegleb, ed. Munich: Carl Hansler Verlag, 1971.

Hetsch, Gustav. *H. C. Andersen og Musiken*. Copenhagen: H. Hagerups Forlag, 1930.

— 'Hans Christian Andersen's Interest in Music.' *The Musical Quarterly* 16 (1930): 322–29.

Hoffmann, E.T.A. *Fantasy Pieces in Callot's Manner: Pages from the Diary of a Traveling Romantic*. Translated by Joseph M. Hayse. Schenectady, NY: Union College Press, 1996.

Hughes, John. *'Ecstatic Sound': Music and Individuality in the Work of Thomas Hardy*. Aldershot: Ashgate, 2001.

Hugus, Frank. 'The Ironic Inevitability of Death: Hans Christian Andersen's *Lykke –Peer*.' *Hans Christian Andersen: A Poet in Time*. Johan de Mylius, Aage Jørgensen, and Viggo Hjørnager Pedersen, eds. Odense, DK: Odense University Press, 1999, 527–40.

Ingerslev-Jensen, Povl. 'Statist Andersen: Bidrag til en teaterdagbog 1818–1822.' *Anderseniana* (1971): 137–87.

James, Dorothy. *Raimund and Vienna: A Critical Study of Raimund's Plays in their Viennese Setting*. Cambridge: Cambridge University Press, 1970.

Jensen, Niels Martin. *Den danske romance 1800–1850 og dens musikalske forudsætninger*. Copenhagen: Gyldendal, 1964.

— 'Niels W. Gade og den nationale tone,' in *Dansk Identitetshistorie III, Folkets Danmark 1848–1940*. Ole Feldbæk, ed. Copenhagen: C.A. Reitzel, 1992.

Johnson, Kristi Planck. 'Hans Christian Andersen's Educational Roots Through his Own Eyes.' *Hans Christian Andersen: A Poet in Time*. Johan de Mylius, Aage Jørgensen, and Viggo Hjørnager Pedersen, eds. Odense, DK: Odense University Press, 1999, 163–72.

Jones, Eric. 'The Language H.C. Andersen Used in His Early Fairy Tales. Projected Aspects of Culture, Drama, Imaginative Pictures.' *Hans Christian Andersen: A Poet in Time*. Johan de Mylius, Aage Jørgensen, and Viggo Hjørnager Pedersen, eds. Odense, DK: Odense University Press, 1999, 359–64.

Jones, W. Glyn. 'Andersen and Those of Other Faiths.' *Hans Christian Andersen: A Poet in Time.* Johan de Mylius, Aage Jørgensen, and Viggo Hjørnager Pedersen, eds. Odense, DK: Odense University Press, 1999, 259–70.

Jurgensen, Knud Arne. *The Bournonville Tradition: The First Fifty Years 1829–1879.* Volume II. London: Cecil Court, 1997.

Keld, J.P. 'Rids af Giuseppe Sibonis virksomhed i årene 1819–1839: i anledning af 200-året for hans fødsel,' *Dansk Aarbog for Musikforskning* xi (1980): 57–78.

Kierkegaard, Søren. *Early Polemical Writings.* Trans. Julia Watkin. Princeton: Princeton University Press, 1990.

Kirmmsee, Bruce. 'Hans Christian Andersen og Jødepigen, En historisk undersøgelse af noget "underligt,"' *Rambam, Tidskrift for jødisk kultur og forskning* 31 (1992): 59–66.

Kracauer, Siegfried. *Jacques Offenbach and the Paris of His Time.* Trans. Gwenda David and Eric Mosbacher. New York: Zone Books, 2002.

Kramer, Lawrence. *Music as Cultural Practice, 1800–1900.* Berkeley: University of California Press, 1990.

— *Musical Meaning, Toward a Critical History.* Berkeley: University of California Press, 2002.

Kuhn, Hans. *Defining a Nation in Song: Danish patriotic songs in songbooks of the period 1832–1870.* Copenhagen: C.A. Reitzels Forlag AS, 1990.

La Mara (Ida Maria Lipsius), ed. *Briefwechsel zwischen Franz Liszt und Carl Alexander, Grossherzog von Sachsen.* Leipzig: Breitkopf & Härtel, 1909.

— ed., *Franz Liszt's Briefe.* Vols. Leipzig: Breitkopf & Härtel, 1893–1905.

Larsen, Svend, ed. *H.C. Andersen's Brevveksling med Henriette Hanck 1830–46, Anderseniana* (1941–46).

Llobera, Joseph. *The God of Modernity: The Development of Nationalism in Western Europe.* Berg: Oxford and Providence, 1994.

Lonck, Joycelynne. *Baudelaire et la Musique.* Paris: A.G. Nizet, 1975.

Losseff, Nicky and Sophie Fuller, eds. *The Idea of Music in Victorian Fiction.* Aldershot: Ashgate, 2003

Maegaard, Kirsten. 'Hans Christian Andersen's travel album.' *Fontes artis musicæ* 42, no. 1 (January–March 1995): 82–84.

Marker, Frederick J. *Hans Christian Andersen and the Romantic Theater.* Toronto: University of Toronto Press, 1971.

Meisling, Peter. *Agnetes Latter.* Copenhagen: 1988.

— 'De sympatiske Havmænd – En lille replik til Thomas Bredsdorff.' *Fund og Forskning* 30 (1991): 81–86.

Miner, Margaret. *Resonant Gaps between Baudelaire & Wagner.* Athens, GA: The University of Georgia Press, 1995.

Mitchell, Jerome. *The Walter Scott Operas. An Analysis of the Operas Based on the Works of Sir Walter Scott.* Alabama: The University of Alabama Press, 1977.

Møller, Tove Barfoed. 'Christian Andersen og Det Kongelige Theater 1819–22. Ny- og nærlæsninger af documenter, breve, levnedsbeskrivelser og andet materiale der belyser hans forhold til teatret i denne periode.' *Anderseniana* (1991): 23–54.

— 'H.C. Andersens Scott-libretti i samtids- og nutidsbelysning.' *Anderseniana* (1996): 11–24.

— *Theaterdigteren H.C. Andersen og 'Meer end Perler og Guld:'* En *dramaturgisk-musikalsk undersøgelse.* Odense, Odense Universitetsforlag, 1995.

Möller-Christensen, Ivy. *Den gyldne trekant: H.C. Andersens gennembrud i Tyskland 1831–50.* Odense, 1992.

— 'My Dearly Beloved Grand Duke ...' *Hans Christian Andersen: A Poet in Time.* Johan de Mylius, Aage Jørgensen, and Viggo Hjørnager Pedersen, eds. Odense, DK: Odense University Press, 1999, 177–188.

Möller-Christensen, Ivy York and Ernst Möller-Christensen. *Mein edler theurer Großherzog! Briefwechsel zwischen Hans Christian Andersen und Carl Alexander von Sachsen-Weimar-Eisenach.* Göttingen: Wallstein Verlag, 1998.

Mylius, Johan de. 'Andersens anden revolution,' *Litteraturbilleder: Æstetiske udflugter I litteraturen fra Søren Kierkegaard til Karen Blixen.* Johan de Mylius, ed. Odense: Odense Universitetsforlag, 1988, 37–60.

— 'Der deutsche Andersen: Zur Begründung des biographischen Andersen-Bildes in Deutschland.' *Dänische-deutsche Doppelgänger: Transnationale und bikulturelle Literatur zwischen Barock und Moderne.* Heinrich Detering, Anne-Bitt Gerecke, and Johan de Mylius, eds. Göttingen: Wallstein Verlag, 2001, 157–73.

— 'Hans Christian Andersen and the Music World,' *Hans Christian Andersen: Danish Writer and Citizen of the World.* Sven Hakon Rossel, ed. Amsterdam: Rodopi, 1996. 176–208.

— 'Hans Christian Andersen – on the Wave of Liberalism.' *Hans Christian Andersen: A Poet in Time.* Johan de Mylius, Aage Jørgensen, and Viggo Hjørnager Pedersen, eds. Odense, DK: Odense University Press, 1999, 109–24.

— *'Hr. Digter Andersen.' Liv, Digtning, Meninger.* Copenhagen: Gads Forlag, 1995.

Neiiendam, Jan. 'H.C. Andersen og Hofteatret.' *Anderseniana* II: 4 (1954): 3.

Neiiendam, Robert. *Gennem mange Aar.* Copenhagen, 1950.

Nielsen, Kirsten Grau. 'Fru Ottilies dagbog. Den unge Comediantspiller,' *Anderseniana* (1990): 5–14.

Nørregård-Nielsen, Hans Edvard. *Jeg saae det Land: H.C. Andersens rejseskitser fra Italien.* Copenhagen: Gyldendal, 1990.

Olsen, F.C. (Anonymous), 'Anmeldelse af H.C. Andersen: *Improvisatoren* og *O.T.*' *Maanedsskrift for Litteratur* 18 (1837): 61–87.

Orel, A. 'Raimund und die Musik.' *Raimund-Almanak 1936.* Innsbruck, 1936.

Ørsted, Hans Christian. *Aanden i Naturen.* Copenhagen: A. F. Høft, 1850.

Østergård, Uffe. 'Peasants and Danes: The Danish National Identity and Public Culture,' *Becoming National: A Reader.* Geoff Eley and Ronald Grigor Suny, eds. Oxford: Oxford University Press, 1996, 179–202.

Peters, George F. *The Poet as Provocateur: Heinrich Heine and his Critics.* Rochester, NY: Camden House, 2000.

Piø, Iørn. *Nye veje til Folkevisen II: DgFT 38,* Agnete og Havmanden. Stockholm, 1970.

Pöthe, Angelika. *Schloss Ettersburg: Weimars Geselligkeit und kulturelles Leben im 19. Jahrhundert.* Weimar, 1995.

Prince, Allison. *Hans Christian Andersen. The Fan Dancer.* London: Allison and Busby, 1998.

Rasmussen, Inge Lise. 'Hans Christian Andersen Watching Art.' *Hans Christian Andersen: A Poet in Time.* Johan de Mylius, Aage Jørgensen, and Viggo Hjørnager Pedersen, eds. Odense, DK: Odense University Press, 1999, 301–10.

Rerup, Lorenz. 'N.F.S. Grundtvig's Position in Danish Nationalism.' *Heritage and Prophecy: Grundtvig and the English-Speaking World.* A.M. Allchin, D. Jasper, J.H. Schjørring, and K. Stevenson, eds. Norwich: The Canterbury Press, 1994.

Reumert, Elith. *H.C. Andersen og det Melchiorske Hjem.* Copenhagen: H. Hagerups Forlag, 1924.

Ringblom, Hilding. *H.C. Andersen og trådene til Grundtvig.* Odense: H.C. Andersen-Centret, 1986.

— 'Om H.C. Andersens påståede homosexualitet.' *Anderseniana* (1997): 41–58.

Rommel, O. *Die Alt-Wiener Volkskomödie.* Vienna: A. Schroll, 1952.

Rossel, Sven Hakon. 'Hans Christian Andersen: The Great European Writer.' *Hans Christian Andersen: Danish Writer and Citizen of the World.* Sven Hakon Rossel, ed. Amsterdam: Rodopi, 1966.

— 'Heinrich Heine i Danmark – med særlig henblik på Buch der Lieder.' *Der nahe Norden. Otto Oberholzer zum 65. Geburtstag. Eine Festschrift.* Frankfurt am Main: Peter Lang, 1985.

Scavenius, Bente. *The Golden Age in Denmark: Art and Culture 1800–1850.* Trans. Barbara Haveland. Copenhagen: Gyldendal, 1994.

Schelling, Friedrich Wilhelm Joseph von. *Philosophy of Art.* Minneapolis: Minnesota University Press, 1988.

Schepelern, Gerhard. *Giuseppe Siboni.* Copenhagen, 1989.

— *Wagners operaer i Danmark: Et dansk Wagner-Lexikon.* Valby, DK: Amadeus, 1988.

Scher, Steven Paul. 'Theory in Literature, Analysis in Music: What Next?' *Yearbook of Comparative and General Literature* 32 (1983): 51.

Schorn, Adelheid von. *Das nachklassische Weimar.* 2 vols. Weimar: G. Kiepenheuer, 1912.

Skouenborg, Ulrik. 'E.T.A. Hoffmann's Idee der romantischen Oper und J.P.E. Hartmann's dänische Oper *Ravnen* (H.C. Andersen nach Gozzi's *Corvo*).' *Carlo Gozzi: Letteratura e musica Roma.* Rome: Bulzoni, 1997, 229–42.

Solie, Ruth A. '"Tadpole Pleasures:" *Daniel Deronda* as Music Historiography.' *Yearbook of Comparative and General Literature* 45/46 (1997/1998): 87–104.

Sønderholm, Erik. 'Hans Christian Andersen als Opernlibrettist. Eine kritische Untersuchung.' *Anderseniana* (1996): 25–48.

Sørensen, Inger. 'H.C. Andersen og J.P.E. Hartmann: Et livslangt venskab.' *Anderseniana* (1997): 5–40.

— *J.P.E. Hartmann og hans kreds 1780–1900.* 3 vols. Copenhagen: Museum Tusculanum, 1999.

— 'Et Mozartportræt in Danmark: Løsning på en gåde.' *Magasin fra Det Kongelige Bibliotek* 7, no. 4 (March 1993): 55–63.

Sørensen, Søren. 'En dansk Guldalder-opera: Den musikalske karakteristik i Hartmanns *Liden Kirsten*.' *Guldalderstudier. Festskrift til Gustav Albeck den 5. juni 1966.* Henning Høirup, Aage Jørgensen og Peter Skautrup, eds. Aarhus, DK: Universitetsforlaget, 219–33.

Spencer, Hanna. *Heinrich Heine.* Boston: Twayne Publishers, 1982.

Spink, Reginald. *Hans Christian Andersen and his World.* New York: G.P. Putnam's Sons, 1972.

Staël, Madame de. *Corinne, or Italy.* Trans. Sylvia Raphael. Oxford: Oxford University Press, 1998.

Stirling, Monica. *The Wild Swan: The Life and Times of Hans Christian Andersen.* London: Collins, 1965.

Sutton, Emma. *Aubrey Beardsley and British Wagnerism in the 1890s.* Oxford: Oxford University Press, 2002.

Suttoni, Charles. 'Liszt and Wagner's Tannhäuser,' *New Light on Liszt and His Music: Essays in honor of Alan Walker's 65th birthday.* Stuyvesant, NY: Pendragon, 1997.

Svendsen, Erik. 'Hans Christian Andersen – An Untimely Journalist.' *Hans Christian Andersen: A Poet in Time.* Johan de Mylius, Aage Jørgensen, and Viggo Hjørnager Pedersen, eds. Odense, DK: Odense University Press, 1999, 485–500.

Thiele, J.M. *Af mit Livs Aarbøger 1795–1826.* Copenhagen, 1873.

Topsøe-Jensen, Helge., ed. *H.C. Andersen og Henriette Wulff: En Brevveksling*. 3 vols. Copenhagen, 1959–60.

— *H.C. Andersens Brevveksling med Edvard og Henriette Collin*. 6 vols. Copenhagen, 1933–37.

— *H.C. Andersen og andre Studier*. Odense, 1966.

— *Omkring Levnedsbogen: En Studie over H.C. Andersen som Selvbiograf 1820–1845*. Copenhagen: Gyldendal, 1943.

Wagner, Richard. *My Life*. New York: Dodd, Mead & Co., 1911.

— *Gesammelte Schriften und Dichtungen*. W. Golther, ed. Berlin and Leipzig, n.d.

— *Judaism in Music and Other Essays*. Lincoln: University of Nebraska, 1995.

— *Das Judenthum in der Musik*. Leipzig: J. J. Weber, 1869.

Walker, Alan. *Franz Liszt: The Weimar Years 1848–1861*. Ithaca: Cornell University Press, 1989.

Wamberg, Niels Birger. *H.C. Andersen og Heiberg: Åndsfrænder og Åndsfjender*. Copenhagen: Politikens Forlag, 1971.

Warrack, John. *Carl Maria von Weber*. Cambridge: Cambridge University Press, 1976.

Watson, Derek. *Liszt*. New York: Schirmer, 1989.

Weiner, Marc A. *Richard Wagner and the anti-Semitic Imagination*. Nebraska: University of Nebraska Press, 1995.

Weisstein, G. 'Geschichte der Zauberpossen.' *Spemanns Goldenes Buch des Theaters*. Berlin: W. Spehmann, 1902.

Weissweiler, Eva, ed. *The Complete Correspondence of Clara and Robert Schumann*. 3 vols. New York: Peter Lang, 2002.

Weliver, Phyllis. *Women Musicians in Victorian Fiction, 1860–1900: Representations of Music, Science and Gender in the Leisured Home*. Aldershot: Ashgate, 2000.

Wullschlager, Jackie. *Hans Christian Andersen: The Life of a Storyteller*. London: Allen Lane, 2000.

Zipes, Jack, ed. *The Oxford Companion to Fairy Tales*. Oxford: Oxford University Press, 2000.

— *When Dreams Came True: Classical Fairy Tales and Their Tradition*. New York: Routledge, 1999.

Index